Made to Write

Made to Write

Lisa-Marie Calderone-Stewart, Ed.D.

ISBN 978-0-557-28609-6

To My Beloved Families...

To My House of Peace Family:

Linda Barnes... Gerri Sheets-Howard...
Shirley & Randy Bordeaux... Perry & Myrtle Williams...

Dominique McGee... Choua Pang...
Beth Peterman... Pang Vang...

Colleen Crane... Jim Van Hoven... Jessie Zvara...

Ralph Stewart... Vanessa Baldwin... Phil Gardner...
Father Al... Father Perry... Brother Mark...
Father Matthew

To My Tomorrow's Present Family:

Sean Lansing... Peter Holbrook...
The Leadership Center at Cardinal Stritch University...

Erica Weber... Marie Britt-Sharpe... Joan Feiereisen

To My Immediate Family:

Michael & Megan... Ralph & Cassie...
Evan... Isaac... Kaleb... Stewarts

Joe & Heidi... Steven & Marie...
David & Rosemary...
Bernadette... Elizabeth... Barbara... Calderones

To My Editing Family:

Dan Mulhall... Jeanne Fehlauer

To My Friends-Like-Family:

Michael Dundon... Ed Kunzman... Michael Pavia...
Kathy Vassas Gallagher... Sara Kamlay...

Jacquie Gozdowiak... Ann Erbe...
Brenda Rodriguez... David Shields...

Nancy & Chuck Cooney... Shawnee Daniels Sykes...
Kathie Amidei... Lisa Metz...

Oliver Johnson... Bob Pavlik... Lawton Merritt...

Jack & Pat Mertz... Dave & Jean Berreckman...

Judy Steers... Bob Stamschror... Ben Walker

In Memory Of:

Joseph Calderone...

Constance Croce Calderone...

Carl Croce...

Philip Calderone...

Bob Massa...

David Chang...

Bishop Ken Untener

"It helps now and then to step back
and take the long view.

The Kingdom is not only beyond our efforts,
it is beyond our vision.

We accomplish in our lifetime only a tiny fraction

of the magnificent enterprise that is God's work.

Nothing we do is complete,

which is another way of saying that the kingdom
always lies beyond us.

No statement says all that could be said.

No prayer fully expresses our faith.

No confession brings perfection.

No pastoral visit brings wholeness.

No program accomplishes the Church's mission.

No set of goals and objectives includes everything.

This is what we are about:
We plant seeds that one day will grow.

We water seeds already planted,
knowing that they hold future promise.

We lay foundations that will need further development.

We provide yeast that produces effects beyond
our capabilities.

We cannot do everything, and there is a sense of
liberation in realizing that.

This enables us to do something,
and to do it very well.

It may be incomplete, but it is a beginning,
a step along the way,

an opportunity for God's grace to enter
and do the rest.

We may never see the end results,
but that is the difference between
the Master Builder and the worker.

We are workers, not Master Builders;
ministers, not Messiahs.

We are prophets of a future not our own."

-- Bishop Ken Untener, 1937-2004

To the readers...

This book is mostly a work of fiction. Much of it is based on real life, but much of it is pure imagination.

There is no actual "House of Hope and Joy" or "Clean Teens" program. However, the dedication and wisdom of the staff of "House of Hope and Joy" is demonstrated by the staff of House of Peace in Milwaukee, Wisconsin.

The House of Peace Teen Leaders did write "This I Believe" essays. They do run an annual program called "Pebbles of Peace outweighing Boulders of Violence."

The "Lil Johnnie" Literacy Program is also real. Details for purchasing "Lil Johnnie" student workbooks can be found on the Tomorrow's Present website.

The Calderone siblings did write the song called "Joseph's Noel."
It has been sung at several Christmas Eve Masses.

All proceeds from *Made to Write* will be donated to The Legacy Fund for Tomorrow's Present.
Additional donations are always a blessing.

The Legacy Fund is "A lasting tribute to the work of Dr. Lisa-Marie Calderone-Stewart."

Tomorrow's Present was started as the youth leadership ministry of the Archdiocese of Milwaukee and Saint Francis Seminary, with a grant from the Lilly Foundation in 1998.

Tomorrow's Present moved to the House of Peace in 2005.

Tomorrow's Present became a collaborative ministry between House of Peace and The Leadership Center of Cardinal Stritch University in 2008.

In 2009, The Leadership Center of Cardinal Stritch University began the Legacy Fund for Tomorrow's Present, to continue the educational methods of Transformational Ministry, based on the research of Dr. Calderone-Stewart.

The Mission of Tomorrow's Present is
To empower youth and adults to transform their communities through learning, reflection, leadership and service.

Information, pictures, testimonies and related links can be found at our website:

www.tomorrowspresent.org

Chapter 1

Dear Sister Agnes,

I want this to be clear from the start:

I am being forced to write -- made to write -- required to write -- about my life against my will.

I do this under protest. I find it unfair, humiliating and an unwelcomed intrusion into my privacy.

You have no right to demand this. I am furious that this a mandatory component of the application process.

I have disclosed everything of importance, provided a detailed curriculum vitae, and wrote an outline of my family history. I consider these items to be more than enough documentation.

Why then is more being required of me?

With every sentence I form, I resent this requirement.

I had a happy childhood. I attended St. Dominic Grade School and St. Bernadette High School. I attended Loyola University.

I am a widow. I stay in close touch with all of my family members and friends.

I am 51 years old. I have good friends and a rich prayer life.

God is calling me to the next chapter of my life. I am not a child. I realize what a change this is. I am ready, I am qualified, and I do not see any reason for this unnecessary delay.

What else do you seek? If you want more information than I've provided, please ask me specific questions. I keep no diary, and I do not journal. I have never felt compelled to do either.

I have submitted the essentials you need to make your decision on my application.

Nell Massa

Chapter 2

Memo

Sylvia,

Keep an eye on this new vocation, *Nell Massa*.

I have heard troubling stories about her.

I'm not sure she is ready to join the *Friends of Clare and Francis*.

I'm not sure she is what we are looking for...

See if you can gain her confidence.

Do not mention my name or this request.

She and I didn't start off well together. She is very resistant to spiritual direction, which isn't unusual. But there's something about her... I'm not sure what.

I know everyone thinks she would be a great candidate for the order.

I'm just not ready to match everyone's excitement about her.

Keep me posted.

Agnes.

Chapter 3

"Say more about your family."

Dear Sister Agnes,

I wasn't surprised that you asked me a specific question, but I didn't expect something as vague as this: "Say more about your family."

Once again, I remind you that I am writing in protest.

Here's the "more" you continue to unfairly require.

I have three brothers, two older, one younger.

My two older brothers are Phil and Charlie. Phil's an eye doctor and Charlie's a scientist. They are both musicians, and they both have children.

My younger brother is Ben. He's a professor. He teaches the classics: Latin, Greek and mythology.

We had fun growing up.

My two older brothers protected me, and my youngest brother was my playmate growing up.

My dad was an ear, nose and throat doctor. He died way too young. He was funny, smart, and spiritual.

My mom worked in my dad's office. She's my biggest fan. She thinks everything I do is wonderful.

Actually, so do my brothers.

We keep in touch, we see each other frequently, we gather for most major holidays, and I'm very close to everyone in my family.

All three of my brothers married terrific women -- they are my sisters. Their children are my great joy.

I hope this satisfies your need to learn more about my "life experiences."

I look forward to receiving my acceptance letter in the near future.

Nell Massa

Chapter 4

"Say more about your brothers."

Dear Sister Agnes,

This is unbelievable.

Once again, I remind you that I am <u>writing under protest</u>.

"Say more about your brothers."

Everyone in the family was a science major or minor except for me. Phil was biology, Charlie was chemistry, Ben was psychology/classics (double major). Even my mom was a chemistry major.

I was an English major.

My two older brothers are both musicians. They both play organ and piano at church. Charlie even directs the choir.

I can't sing; I can't read music (even though I took piano lessons). I'm not musical at all. But neither is Ben. The only thing we play is the radio...

I probably ruined any musical potential in Ben because I sang to him when he was little. I was five when he was born, and he instantly captivated me. Once my mom brought him home, I don't think I ever left his side. They had to drag me to school when I found out I couldn't bring Ben.

I told him stories I made up, I sang to him, I played games with him, I just adored him. He was my life. I remember my older brothers playing with the other boys on the block, but there weren't any girls in the neighborhood, so I played with Ben. And I loved it.

I taught him how to read and write his name. I taught him how to cut and paste. We colored pictures together. Everything I learned at school, I came home and taught Ben. My mother sometimes says she doesn't remember much about Ben's childhood... because Nellie seemed to take care of his every need.

My brothers are all brilliant. My whole family is brilliant. I always tell people that my oldest brother discovered a cure for an obscure eye disease and is a hero in the medical world. My next oldest brother discovered some amazing compound that enables something or other to happen so that certain medicines can do something spectacular and save lives. It's so complicated, I can't even describe what it is. My youngest brother speaks several languages and can bring to life stories that are older than God.

I diagram sentences.

They all played baseball and basketball growing up, and all ran track. I can hardly play catch, and I can't jog half a block. But I do like to swim.

My dad taught me to swim, and my mom taught me to cook, knit and sew. She also taught me how to fold paper and cut out snowflakes so they have six points.

I hope this satisfies your need to learn more about my "family life," especially my brothers.

I look forward to receiving my acceptance letter in the near future.

Nell Massa

Chapter 5

"My Amazing brothers"

Dear Sister Agnes,

I am running out of patience with this unfair requirement.

Once again, I remind you that I am writing <u>in protest</u>.

It's not enough that you subject me to this ridiculous writing assignment every week and your hour-long "spiritual direction" sessions.

Now you ask me to write about my brothers using the adjectives "My Amazing Phil" and "My Amazing Charlie" and "My Amazing Ben" in order to bring out the unexpressed emotion you say is still buried inside me.

My Amazing brothers are all brilliant. My whole Amazing family is brilliant. My Amazing oldest brother Phil discovered a cure for an eye disease. My Amazing brother Charlie invented medicines that do amazing things. My Amazing younger brother Ben speaks several Amazing languages.

My two older Amazing brothers write Amazing music and my Amazing brother Ben tells amazing stories. They are all Amazing.

I look forward to receiving my acceptance letter in the near future.

Nell Massa

Chapter 6

"My Ridiculous brothers"

Dear Sister Agnes,

I'm disappointed that you are still not satisfied, that you now require me to explore my negative emotions by writing about "My Ridiculous Brothers."

My Ridiculous brothers are all brilliant. My whole Ridiculous family is brilliant. My Ridiculous oldest brother Phil is a Ridiculous hero. My next oldest Ridiculous brother Charlie saves ridiculous lives. My Ridiculous younger brother Ben tells Ridiculous stories older than God.

I am quite certain St. Francis and St. Clare would find this Ridiculous.

I look forward to receiving my acceptance letter in the near future.

Nell Massa

Chapter 7

Dear Sylvia,

Thanks so much for seeing me, especially since you were only in town for a short while.

Thank you for letting me be completely honest about Sister Agnes and how I detest these absurd writing assignments. "My Amazing Brothers" and "My Ridiculous Brothers" just about put me over the top.

I felt much more comfortable talking with you. I guess I understand why I need to go through his process. I wish you lived closer so you could be my spiritual director.

I appreciate your suggestion regarding my writing assignments. Instead of just reacting to Sister Agnes and her assigned topics, I will start journaling on my own. When I feel comfortable that a particular journal entry is an appropriate response to her request, I will submit that to her. That way I can take the best insights from my own reflections and present them to Agnes, minus the protest. If I work out all my feelings in a safe environment, then I won't feel so trapped and defensive in providing documentation for the order.

Have a great retreat. I hope to see you the next time you come this way.

Blessings and prayers for your ministry...

Nellie

Chapter 8

Dear Kelvin,

Hi. This seems a bit silly...

I am writing you because I am being forced to write about my feelings for my spiritual director, Sister Agnes.

Sister Sylvia, another member of the same order, suggested I write separately and just save the most significant parts of my writing for Sister Agnes.

You know I don't keep a journal or a diary... so I thought I'd just write you these notes... these letters. It thought it would be easier to tell you these things than to tell Sister Agnes.

Hopefully, after I tell you, I can write more naturally and do a better job with the official documentation I must submit to the order.

So... my next assignment from Sister Agnes is "Say more about your childhood friends."

You know I need to write about Adam...

I met Adam in kindergarten at St. Dominic Grade School; His family went to our church. We always played and talked together. Our families got to know each other.

Adam was absolutely my best friend growing up. We didn't live too far away, and we spent lots of time at each other's houses, doing homework, watching TV, and babysitting our younger siblings. Adam liked Ben, and so did Gemma, Adam's younger sister.

My mom kept a scrapbook for me when I was a little. It's full of pictures of my brothers, my cousins, and Adam. When I started middle school, I began to keep my own scrapbook. So my life is filled with pictures of Adam. Adam as a child, a playmate, my best friend from school. Adam and me hanging out during those lazy middle school summers when you were just too young for a job, but really too old for a babysitter, so all we did was ride bikes to each other's houses, swim at the local pool, go to movies, shoot baskets (he would shoot, I would pretty much run after the ball), watch TV, chase down the ice cream truck, babysit for each other's families, and talk about everything and nothing.

I adored Adam.

When we were in 7th grade, Adam wanted to try out for the Glee Club. He wanted me to try out with him. You know I could never sing, but Adam thought if I picked a simple song, I could get by. I tried, but the choir director could hear my off-key voice. We auditioned two at a time. The girl I auditioned with was a good singer, so I thought she could carry me. Mr. Borken looked at her and said, "You are an alto. Come to practice tomorrow after school." He looked at me and said, "Thank you for your audition. If you want, you can try out again next year."

Adam and I were so disappointed when I didn't make the Glee Club. We really wanted to do it together. So the next day, I just showed up for practice with everyone else. Mr. Borken saw me and asked, "What did I say when you auditioned yesterday?" I said, "You said, *'You are an alto.'* He looked confused, but he said, "OK. Go stand over there."

I was the tallest girl, and Adam was the tallest boy, so we ended up standing together at the top of the risers. I knew I would sing off-key if I sang out loud, so for two years, I never sang a note. I just mouthed the words. I was the best lip-synch performer you could imagine.

Then when we got into high school, Adam wanted to be in Glee Club again. I thought I'd never get into a high school program... I imagined the auditions would be a lot harder. But St. Bernadette's had a great policy -- you didn't have to audition for Glee Club if you had been in a grade school Glee Club! So all I had to do was tell them I was in St. Dom's Glee Club, and I was in!

I don't know anyone else who lip-synched their way through six years of music programming, but I did!

And why did I do it? I wanted to do what Adam did. I wanted to be with Adam.

One time, our basement flooded. My dad was out of town. Adam came over every day for a week to help us clean things out. It was so smelly and gross, but having Adam there made it OK. I felt less alone. My mom appreciated it, too.

We did other chores together, too. We didn't mind. We raked the leaves at my house, and then at his house. Doing twice the work with Adam was better than doing half the work without him! Lots of times, Ben came along, too. And sometimes Gemma.

We did Halloween costumes together. Once Adam and I were two trees, and we hung a hammock between us. Ben came along as the guy with the book and the lemonade. We tried to get him to sit in the hammock, but he was too heavy, or we weren't strong enough to hold him up. Gemma was a squirrel.

One Halloween, Adam and I went as goalposts, and Ben was a football player. Gemma went as cheerleader.

It's all in my scrapbooks: Adam and me in Glee Club. Adam and me in the school plays. Adam and me at the Proms. Adam and me at everything. Going to basketball games, struggling through math class together, getting A's in English and Religion together, and planning our joint graduation party together.

At some point, we started to talk about the "You of Us" and the "Me of Us" because we wanted to emphasize the importance of our unity. As in, "Does the You of Us want to see a movie tonight, go to the mall, or watch TV?" or "I believe the Me of Us disagrees with the You of Us on this matter."

I don't think I ever really "fell" in love with Adam... I think we just grew into love... we were always in love... I thought God created us to be together ... we were meant for each other. He seemed to complete me. He made my life wonderful and marvelous.

OK

I have to stop now. I can't take any more of this writing...

Chapter 9

Dear Kelvin,

It's snowing outside.

Once I spent the night at Adam's house because of a sudden snowstorm.

I stayed in Gemma's room. My parents didn't mind -- no one wanted to drive in the blizzard.

We baked cookies and made hot chocolate and stayed up late, watching the snowflakes fall... I showed everyone in the family how to fold paper and cut out snowflakes so they had six points like real snowflakes.

I remembered thinking that night, Adam and I would be married, and we'd make hot chocolate and bake cookies and cut out paper snowflakes with our own children... and we'd tell them about the first night their Mommy and Daddy ever did that together... it could become our first family tradition.

I didn't know anyone else who had a friend like that -- someone they met in kindergarten and stayed best friends with together until they graduated from high school and went to the same college together.

We laughed at the same jokes and loved all the same TV shows.

Once I told Adam I wanted to grow up and be just like Mary Tyler More...

Adam told me that he always wanted to grow up and be Dick Van Dyke!

Adam was always my "secret weapon" in life. Anytime I felt bad about anything, I would think about Adam and feel better. If someone made fun of me for any reason, I would tell myself, "Adam loves me, so who cares if you don't?" If I got a bad grade on a test, I would think, "Adam thinks I'm smart, so who cares about one crummy test?" If I got a zit, I would say, "Adam thinks I'm beautiful no matter what..." and on and on. Adam made everything OK. Adam made my life beautiful and wonderful.

Still to this day, all my passwords involve Adam's birthday in some way. It's the only thing I can ever remember. That has never changed. I still remember his childhood phone number. Oh, I adored Adam! He was my whole life. All I could imagine was having children who looked like Adam, and my family merging with Adam's family, and sharing my bed with Adam...

I understood Adam. I knew what he liked, and I liked what he liked. We liked the same books and the same movies and plays. We enjoyed the same people, and we laughed at the same jokes. We were like two peas in a pod. We grew up together, and we helped shape each other's childhood, each other's view of life, and each other's dreams for the world.

I was so crazy about Adam. He was my whole life, in a way that only young people can wrap their whole lives around another person. Before you fully realize that people die and people disappoint you, and people abandon you and everyone you meet is not going to love you, and every stranger is not safe.

Then came college. We even went to the same college! We made sure we had one class together each semester.

He was a double major -- art history and psychology. I majored in English. Not because I was such a great writer -- just because it was a language I could speak and I didn't know what else to major in.

My scrapbooking continued. Classes together, student activities together. Dances, football games, basketball games, parents weekends, homecoming weekends. Our lives continued to weave themselves together.

We kept doing everything together, dreaming our dreams, loving each other with mad passion, deepest respect and that incredible "I'm so lucky to be me" gratitude for having found that absolute best person in the world.

We got engaged our senior year of college. I was certain no one ever felt these feelings before. I was certain no one ever experienced what we had.

My husband and my best friend! The most wonderful life anyone could ever imagine.

Remember that song by Queen?... I still can hear parts of it in my mind...

"Ooh, you make me live...

You're my best friend...

I've been with you such a long time...

You're my sunshine... and I want you to know that I really love you... you're my best friend..."

I was so in love with Adam.

But one week before our wedding, Adam called it off.

No warning.

No explanation.

I just fell apart.

I was completely

Devastated

OK

Enough

Wow

I just can't do this

Maybe another day

Chapter 10

Dear Kelvin,

When I was in grade school, I used to watch football with my dad. He really enjoyed pro football, so if I wanted to spend time with him on the weekends, that's what I would need to do.

Eventually, I asked him to explain football to me. He said, "OK, let's pick a team and follow it."

I pointed to the TV and said, "Who's that playing? He has your number."

He said, "That's Don Meredith. He's the quarterback of the Dallas Cowboys."

I said, "OK. Let's follow that team."

So he showed me the newspaper standings, he told me about the National and American conferences, and the different divisions. (Back then, there were the NFC and AFC, each with East, West and Central Divisions. Dallas was in the NFC East division.)

I learned how a team could be first in their division and make it to the playoffs, even if another team in another division had a better record. So we started to follow football, especially the Dallas Cowboys.

In 1971, Roger Staubach became the starting quarterback of the Dallas Cowboys, and I had become a fan.

The year before, we had a library science assignment to use a book from the resource room and do "something creative." I decided to look up some famous football players in the "Who's Who" current biography resource, and I collected the addresses of football players from a few teams.

I wrote letters to several football players that year as part of my assignment -- to Roger Staubach, of course -- and to Bob Lilly, Bob Hayes and Calvin Hill, who were also Dallas Cowboys. I wrote to a few quarterbacks from other teams, too... Bob Griese, Terry Bradshaw, Daryle Lamonica and Joe Namath.

The only football players who wrote back were Dallas Cowboys... but the one and only football player who wrote, "Dear NELLIE" was Roger Staubach. See why I would become such a fan?

The Dallas Cowboys had won the Super Bowl on Jan. 16, 1972, two days after my birthday. It was the best birthday present ever! Roger Staubach had a great game, and they won 24-3!

The following season, he sat out during most of the games because of a shoulder injury. But one Saturday in December 1972, I was watching a playoff game with my dad. The Dallas Cowboys were playing the San Francisco 49ers. The game was almost over and they were losing by two touchdowns and a field goal. I was babysitting for a family who lived around the corner, so I had to go. I ran all the way there, so I wouldn't miss the rest of the game. I arrived just in time to see a Dallas field goal.

The family I was babysitting for were also football fans (although they liked the Giants).

Imagine my surprise when Roger Staubach came off the bench! In about two minutes, he led the Cowboys to TWO touchdowns! They won, 30-28! I was jumping up and down! I was screaming my head off! The children were jumping up and down and screaming their heads off, too!

I called my dad on the phone to say, "DID YOU SEE THOSE PLAYS! DID YOU SEE THAT TWO MINUTE DRILL???

He didn't know what I was talking about! He had decided the game was over, so he switched channels to watch another game! That was the last time he ever gave up on what Roger "the Dodger" Staubach could do!

And those children I babysat? Well, they grew up. And the youngest one, Tommy, is now the biggest Dallas Cowboys fan you could imagine. He bought a house and did an entire room in blue and silver, with Dallas Cowboy decorations.

In high school, I started writing to Roger Staubach every year on his birthday -- February 5. I drew him big posters of him and his teammates, I knitted him a scarf, I embroidered him a framed picture of himself in his football uniform, I even baked him chocolate chip cookies -- back in the days when we were much more innocent. Today, no one would ever eat cookies sent by a stranger, even if she were a loyal fan...

But year after year, he would write back to me. I had a collection of his letters and pictures.

I think the best part of being a Roger Staubach fan wasn't the victories -- it was knowing that he was a famous sports celebrity with positive, admirable values. He was a good Catholic. He cared about his faith. He was close to his family. We needed role models like that in a world that too often worshipped glamour and fast living. He provided that for children and youth. I thought that was important.

And it was so much fun to watch him with my dad.

Any time I wanted to give up on something because it was difficult, my dad and mom would say something like, "Would Roger Staubach give up so easily?" I have to admit -- it was an effective tool for them to use on me... it always worked!

One year, I taught my brother Ben how to knit. For Christmas, I helped him knit tiny scarves in blue and silver yarn (the Dallas Cowboy colors) for all his friends who played with GI Joe's. We also made one for Gemma's Barbie. Years later, Tommy wrote me a Christmas card with this note, "Remember when you knit me a Dallas Cowboys scarf for my GI Joe?"

I had truly forgotten all about it until then!

Chapter 11

"Say more about your childhood friends."

Dear Sister Agnes,

Adam was my best friend growing up.

His family went to church at St. Dominic's, and our families were close.

We grew up together and celebrated birthdays and major holidays together.

Because of Adam, I joined my grade school and high school choir. We were also in plays together.

I became an English major because I enjoyed reading books and plays.

We had many friends in common from the choir and drama club at St. Bernadette's High School. We went to basketball games and proms and parties.

Adam and my brothers were all altar servers. I wasn't an altar server because girls couldn't do it back then.

One time, Adam and I made a list of all the saints on the stained-glass windows at St. Dominic's. We had a scavenger hunt with Ben and with Adam's younger sister, Gemma. When we started, the church was empty, but eventually, an older woman came in to pray the rosary. We didn't hear her come in. We weren't doing anything disrespectful; we were just walking around, telling Ben and Gemma about the different saints and trying to get them to guess their names.

But we got in trouble with Father Kenneth. He called our parents. I knew our parents wouldn't be angry with us. But they pretended to be -- just a little -- in front of Father Kenneth. When we left St. Dominic's, they took us all out for ice cream. Ben talked about it for weeks, how we got into trouble at church and got ice cream as our "punishment."

My parents taught me how to pick my battles, when to speak up, and when to just nod and smile... and then go do things your own way. I wish more people had common sense like that.

I later realized that my parents were very pleased that Adam and I were "entertaining" Gemma and Ben with stories of the saints at church. Shame on Father Kenneth for not recognizing the value of what we were doing! I wish more brothers and sisters did creative spiritual activities like that today.

I hope this finally satisfies your need for learning more about my "childhood friends." I look forward to receiving my acceptance letter in the near future.

Nell Massa

Chapter 12

Dear Sylvia,

The day of reflection you led at St. Dominic's was great. I'm glad you thought it was important to see me, even though you were in town just a short time.

Lunch with you was even more special.

Thanks for all the encouragement regarding my volunteer ministry at House of Hope and Joy.

And thank you for saying that teaching English at St. Augustine is "ministry" as well.

Your suggestion to start a private journal before submitting anything to Sr. Agnes has really helped my attitude toward all this written reflection.

I'll say it again: I wish you lived closer. I think you would be the perfect spiritual director for me. But I will stick with Sister Agnes to see how things go and where God wants me to be.

With joy and hope,

Nellie

Chapter 13

Dear Kelvin,

My next assignment from Sister Agnes is "Life after college."

Well... I don't know what to say.

Life after college was really "recovery from heartbreak over Adam." But I am not going to get into all of that with Sister Agnes! So what else can I write about?

I had been on the swim team in college, so I kept swimming for exercise at the local Y. They asked me to help out with their youth swim team, so I did that for a while too.

I didn't have much of a social life until I met Tom at a Catholic teachers' meeting. He taught theology; I taught English. He was also the campus minister.

Maybe a week or so later, I saw Tom at Mass, and he asked me out. We went to a movie. When he took me home, he didn't even walk me to my door. He just said good night with a little kiss -- in the car. I couldn't believe it! I said, "You're not going to walk me to my door?" And he said, "Not tonight." I found that very ungentlemanly, but I figured he didn't have a lot of experience dating. Or maybe he thought walking me to my door would turn into an invitation to come in and then... well, who knows what.

So I just said goodnight and went to my apartment.

I couldn't get in!

My key unlocked the lock, but the door still wouldn't open. I realized what had happened: my door had two locks. I only used one of them -- the one I had a key for! Obviously, before we left, Tom had locked the other one.

I was furious! Who asked him to do that?

He wasn't enough of a gentleman to walk me to my door, and now, because of him, I was locked out of my apartment. We didn't have cell phones back then, so there was no way to call him up and say, "Listen, buster, because of your brilliant move, I am now locked out! Next time, don't touch anything without asking! And get over here until I find a way to get back in!"

So, instead, I walked around the apartment complex, looking for a place that had a light on. I finally found one. I knocked on the door and explained what had happened. The woman there invited me in and gave me a card with a number. "What's this?" I asked.

"The night number."

I didn't know we had a superintendent who was available during the night! I was so relieved she knew this and had the number. I called the number, and they let me into my apartment.

It was after 2:00 a.m. when I finally got in. I knew Tom was already asleep, but I called him anyway. This is how the conversation went:

"Hello?"

"Hi. It's Nellie. Were you already asleep?"

"Yes, of course."

"Well, I just wanted you to know I got into my apartment safely, so you don't have to worry."

"Are you angry because I didn't walk you to your door?"

"No. Now I'm angry because you locked me out of my apartment."

"What are you talking about?"

"You turned the doorknob lock, didn't you?"

"Yes... so?"

"You were trying to be helpful?"

"I guess..."

"Well, my key doesn't open that lock. I never use that lock. Why would you turn it without even asking me?"

"I'm sorry. I assumed you saw me do it. I assumed it was something you always did."

"No, I didn't see you do it. And it's something I never do. I had to walk around in the dark, find someone with a light on, ask to use their phone, and then wait for the night superintendent to let me in."

"Wow, you have a night superintendent?"

"Yes, we do. I just discovered that tonight. And you are lucky I do, or you would be out of your bed on your way over here if I didn't."

"I am really sorry."

"That's what I wanted to hear. You can go back to sleep now, as long as you are wide awake."

"Why do you want me to be wide awake?"

"So you don't forget this little conversation or think it was a dream."

"I promise from now on, I will always walk you to your door at night."

"Thank you. That's also what I wanted to hear."

"Going to Mass tomorrow?"

"Yeah. I'll see you there."

"Good night, then."

"Bye."

I was still angry. He didn't seem contrite enough. He made assumptions, locked me out, didn't even see me safely into my apartment, and was hardly inconvenienced by the whole thing. Did he really appreciate what I had been through? Probably not...

But he did keep his promise. He always walked me to my door after that.

Funny, Tom never used to call me on the phone to ask me out. Either I would call him, or he would see me at Mass or at a teacher's meeting and would ask me then. In fact, I made a habit of always attending morning Mass on Fridays. I figured that if I saw Tom on Friday morning, then there would be a good chance he'd ask me out for that weekend. It worked every time. And the weeks I didn't get there for Mass? I ended up with no date that whole weekend. Not Friday night or Saturday night. If I saw Tom on Sunday, then perhaps we'd do something that afternoon. But never on Sunday night or weeknights. As teachers, we were more concerned with early bedtimes on school nights than our students were.

Dates with Tom usually just ended with small kisses. Nothing too passionate. Tom had spent two years in seminary, and I always thought he'd end up back in the seminary, finishing up and getting ordained. Because of that possibility, I was content not to go too far with Tom physically, since I would hate to receive communion from a priest I had once been intimate with!

"Getting intimate with a possible future priest" wasn't a problem I'd have to worry about with Tom. He was more than content with little kisses and hugs. And remember, I was the aggressive one, calling him or showing up at Mass so he would ask me out.

None of this stuff is going to matter to Sister Agnes.

So forget about it. I'll just stop here.

I don't know why I even bothered to write it down.

Chapter 14

Dear Kelvin,

I still don't know what to write about...

I need to give something to Sister Agnes about my life after college...

Maybe if I talk about something more intellectual or spiritual...

Tom and I filled our time with deep conversation! About the Bible, about Catholic social teaching, about moral dilemmas, about political candidates and their stands, about theology, about the best way to reach reluctant students, about spirituality. That was the best part of the relationship!

Tom was quite intelligent. I learned a lot and was eager to be part of his circle of friends -- all very bright, all very dedicated to either education or ministry, and very interesting. They got together Saturday mornings to discuss different articles each week. I was never invited to those meetings -- maybe because I would have been the only woman -- none of their wives or girlfriends ever seemed to go, as far as I know. But I heard a lot about their insights and ideas, and often asked for copies of the articles. I used to wonder what Adam would have said about certain issues and what his opinions would have been, but I never told Tom about Adam.

Sometimes, teachers at Tom's school would get together on Friday afternoons for a beer. I started coming along, and I often brought some teachers from my school. We started to call it our "Friday prayer meeting." With the first round, we'd clink glasses and then we'd all say, **"Thank God** the week is over!"

I did a retreat once with Tom. It was marvelous. His students clearly loved him, and I used to wonder what they thought of me hanging out with him. I wondered if they assumed I was his girlfriend. After dating Tom for almost a year, I wondered if he would go to one of their proms, as a chaperone, and if he would invite me to join him. But he never did.

When I asked him about it later, "Did you go to the prom?" he simply said that proms were "never on his list of things to do, places to go."

Tom was full of knowledge and information. Even trivia. He never got tired of talking about that kind of stuff. Whenever we played Jeopardy or Trivial Pursuit at a party, we always won because he always knew the answers. He'd always ask me first, "What do you think?" and if I was right, he'd say, "I think that's a great answer. Let's go with that."

If I was wrong, he'd say, "I think that's a great answer. But what about this other idea... does that sound possible?" And I'd always say, "Let's go with your answer," because he was never, ever wrong.

When I had no idea, I'd say so. And he'd say, "Well, I don't know for sure, but I am thinking... this." And the fact is, I'm sure he always knew for sure.

Tom was interesting like a good encyclopedia. And he changed my life forever, because after that first retreat, he asked me to consider ministry. That first retreat had students from his theology class; some were on my swim team. I was very reluctant initially. I wasn't sure how open and honest adults had to be with young people, or if they would consider me to be "cool enough." In school, I had authority because I controlled grades, hall passes, assignments and detentions. At a retreat, all I had going for me was the influence of my... influence.

How could I inspire them with just my personality, my integrity, and my pretend "aura" of being a successful adult who "has it all together" (since I knew I did NOT have it all together)? I was afraid I would fail at this... but Tom insisted I could do it. And that's how he got me interested in youth ministry.

Somehow, I discovered I had a knack for explaining church teachings at the "teen level" and I was good at designing prayer experiences that broke open Scripture passages in ways that made their deeper meaning more available to teenagers.

I started volunteering at church more often and found out they really needed a youth minister. Lots of people are afraid of teenagers (I was at first!). I already taught high school, so I wasn't afraid of teenagers. But in order to be effective, I needed to know more about all the things Tom knew all about: Scripture, church history, liturgy, theology, morality, and the rest of Catholic Tradition. And he seemed more than willing to teach me... so that's how it all started.

It's possible that our relationship was more like mentoring than romance. Perhaps he saw me as his Pygmalion-type statue, and he could create me to be something he could fall in love with.

I mean, there was *some* romance involved. We did kiss a little. Part of his charm was his "clueless inexperience." Although he far surpassed me in knowledge of all things Catholic, I was sure he had very little experience with women. (Seminarians don't date much!) So he was shy and probably less confident with developing a physical relationship to partner our intellectual one.

I liked that. I didn't have to worry about him pushing me to do too much, too soon. Since we were both such devoted Catholics, neither of us wanted to have sexual intercourse outside of marriage… so that made me feel safe.

I'm tired. I'm going to quit.

I just don't know what to say to Agnes…

I'll try more later.

Chapter 15

Dear Kelvin,

OK. I'm just going to keep writing. Maybe I'll come up with something to say about life after college...

I was at a church party when I met Matt. He was a little older than I was, and he had children in Catholic school, so he was involved with some of the school activities as well as church activities. He was divorced and obviously looking for a companion.

He had a daughter at the school where Tom taught, so Matt suspected I was dating Tom because he had seen us together at Mass and at a few other events. Tom wasn't overly affectionate, so we never did things like holding hands in public. (I missed that about Adam. He ALWAYS liked holding hands.)

Eventually, Matt and I began talking. He was attractive and funny and engaging. I could tell that other single women who knew him were a little unhappy when he was suddenly spending all this time talking with me. Every so often, one of them would come by and try to get his attention or try to get him involved with some other conversation. But Matt stuck close to me for that entire evening, even though he knew I had come to the party with Tom. I felt awkward about the whole thing.

I happened to tell Matt that my brother Ben helped me buy a medicine cabinet for my bathroom, which had a mirror, but no cabinet. I told Matt that I would be calling Ben soon so he could put it together for me. The next day, Matt showed up with his tool kit and installed it perfectly.

I was amazed. I made dinner for him as a thank-you, and he ended up staying very late, watching a movie with me on the couch.

I felt a little bad about Matt staying over so late because I was dating Tom, but I convinced myself that nothing was going to happen with Matt. Then he kissed me. It had been a long time since I felt that kind of tenderness. I realized while kissing Matt that Tom never had that kind of passion or tenderness in him when we kissed. I realized that first evening with Matt that things were never going to work out with Tom.

Meanwhile, Matt started calling me and coming over to see me a lot, especially when his former wife had his two daughters for the weekend. When I knew such a weekend was coming, I didn't go to Friday morning Mass, so I wouldn't see Tom. That way, he wouldn't ask me out for those two days.

Even though Matt was divorced and paying alimony, he was a tax attorney and always had enough money for fun. We went to movies, plays, sports events, and did all kinds of interesting things. He was a great conversationalist. And he was always telling jokes and funny stories. I laughed a lot when I was with Matt. And he thought everything I said was brilliant and funny. How could I not enjoy myself with such a guy?

But Matt never wanted to talk deeply about anything. He liked keeping things on the surface. We would go to a movie or play and I would want to discuss the characters. I wanted to find out what Matt thought of their motivation, or what the playwright was trying to do with the moral of the story, or what loose ends hadn't been tied up. It's the kind of thing Adam and I had spent hours talking about. We would even re-write the endings or create entire plot lines for sequels or prequels. I missed that type of interaction. Matt just didn't do creative dreaming.

When I was with Tom, he would talk a lot -- and deeply -- but not about anything creative or fun. Tom preferred to talk more about God and faith and spirituality -- which are very important -- but not really much about theatre or movies -- not unless the story was about a saint or a Bible character. And then it was more of a lecture about the moral lesson, or the real history vs. the fictional parts that were added to make the story more interesting to a modern and less sophisticated audience.

Matt was much more affectionate. He asked me more questions about my thoughts and feelings, but he wasn't looking for much beyond the basics.

I saw that Matt could meet some of my needs and Tom met other needs.

But I realized I wanted to find one person who did it all -- a soul mate who was funny and affectionate, smart and spiritual. Someone who could engage me in serious and deep conversation, make me feel both brilliant and beautiful, and someone who made me laugh. I realized I would need to find someone else. Someone who wasn't Tom or Matt. Someone who was more like... Adam.

It all seemed to keep coming back to Adam...

I kept asking myself, "How was I ever going to get over Adam?"

And that is exactly just what Sister Agnes is NOT going to hear about!

Chapter 16

Dear Kelvin,

Eventually, Tom announced that he would be returning to the seminary at the end of the school year. I was not surprised. But he and I continued to go out. I think he was just "making sure" that he was choosing well. He knew he had the rest of the school year to finish, so why mess up a good thing? I didn't see any reason not to go out with him. Our kisses were reduced to pecks on the cheek, which was completely OK with me. I continued to learn from him and no longer felt guilty for dating two men at the same time.

In spite of his "lack of depth," I truly liked Matt. He was hilarious. Life was never dull -- he found a way to make anything ordinary seem special, and he even found a way to make fun of everything that went wrong. Matt used to say all the time, "Comedy is just a tragedy with some perspective." So when he went camping with his kids, and the tents leaked and fell down, or the showers and toilets were out of order, or bugs or raccoons or even bears got into their food, Matt would have his daughters laughing instead of complaining. Then they would come home and tell me the stories, and we'd all laugh about it together.

Matt was a great father, too. It was obvious that he didn't know how to fix what went wrong with his first marriage. He wouldn't talk about it. It made him too sad. But he adored his two girls. He worried about them, appreciated them, was proud of them, and cooperated fully with their mother in providing whatever they needed.

His smile was infectious.

More than once, Matt stared at me, looked me up and down, drank me in with his eyes and declared with obvious admiration, "You are absolutely gorgeous." How could I not enjoy such attention? He reminded me of the way it had felt to be with Adam.

Matt was really good looking. He was twelve years older than I was, but no one would have ever guessed it.

Like me, Matt was a swimmer. He joined my YMCA so we could do laps together. He was also a member of a health club that I couldn't afford to join. He offered to pay for my membership, but that was impractical. I would never use anything at the club except for the pool, and my Y was closer to where I lived. So Matt came to my Y when he was visiting me. At the time, I was giving swimming lessons there, served as a part-time life guard and helped coach their swim team. Once in a while, he'd come to a swim meet. I think he was the one who started the team's tradition of throwing the coaches into the pool after a victory.

Matt and I always said we had similar dads. My dad was a doctor, and his dad was a dentist. Anything that ripped in my home, office or classroom was held together with "nose tape." I never had to buy masking tape for anything. My dad used to do corrective surgery for people who had problems breathing. Each operation required a brand new sealed, sterile role of adhesive tape. After the operation, there was always tape left. He would bring home rolls of nose tape each week. He was so conscious of not wasting anything.

My family and Adam's family still have nose tape in every drawer and cabinet.

With Matt, it was dental floss. His family never bought string for anything. They all loved dental floss! They would wrap packages with dental floss and bundle sleeping bags and camping equipment with it. He used to say that he'd fly kites with it, if he could find a large enough roll. When he was a kid, one of his sisters knitted a blanket with dental floss. That became our opening story whenever we were with a new couple. He'd talk about dental floss, I'd jump in with nose tape, and everyone would be laughing in no time. We'd offer to wrap their birthday presents with nose tape and dental floss. It was a great way to get invited to birthday parties. They wanted to see if we would really do it! And we did!

I didn't think I'd ever find anyone as engaging and charming as Matt. But some people just don't go deep. Matt was like that. I needed deep. I needed smart and funny -- *and deep*. I needed someone like Adam.

Every time I tried to engage Matt in some deeper conversation, he'd say, "You know I'm not that deep of a guy" or "Whatever you say. That sounds like a very intelligent opinion. You are probably right." He had no desire to discuss politics or to tell anyone how he was voting. I never knew his stand on any controversial issue. Matt would always say, "That's up to the politicians to work out." Or "That's up to the bishops to work out" or "That's up to the voters to decide." When opposing sides of a debate would come up, he'd say something like "Who am I to say?" or "Who am I to disagree with such well justified statements?"

Eventually, I guess he got tired of my wanting to dig deeper. And he got tired of being pushed into depth he couldn't or wouldn't handle.

I'm not sure how long a person can really hover at the surface. Sooner or later, something tragic will happen. Something he will not be able to make a joke of. Like the death or injury of a friend or family member. It was hard to believe that nothing serious had ever happened yet in his life. It's actually remarkable. But it will happen one of these days.

Perhaps, he'll just remain in denial and be fine. Perhaps he'll successfully choose to stay on the surface.

But if it does affect him deeply, I wonder if he will have the emotional or spiritual foundation to cope with it. He might fall apart. He might dive into a deep depression and not know how to climb out of it. I don't know. That's the danger of trying to avoid depth, I guess.

Eventually, I suppose Matt might wonder about the meaning of life. Eventually, he might discover something behind his mask of comedy. But that's not something another person can easily force him to do. I tried to go deeper with him, but he simply wasn't interested.

So we drifted apart. I let it happen, and he let it happen.

He ended up with one of the women from that original party where we first met. I remember her disappointment when Matt showered all that attention on me. I was sort of glad she ended up with him. They got married quite quickly and had children. They were both very good looking -- in a glamorous sort of way. Their children were gorgeous. Everything about their family looks great -- at least on the surface.

Looking back, I realized that neither Matt nor Tom ever gave me the feeling that Adam had. Neither of them "felt like home." Neither of them could ever become my soul mate.

And yet, during the time period that I was dating Tom, and then Matt, I wasn't unhappy. I guess my needs were partially fulfilled. But I knew I would never marry either of them, since neither man was really right for me.

Many years later, Father Tom celebrated the wedding Mass of Matt's oldest daughter. I found that to be secretly ironic.

Chapter 17

"Say more about life after college."

Sister Agnes:

I became an English teacher after college.

I met a theology teacher who decided to enter the seminary and become a priest. I went to one of his retreats and worked with students from our parish.

He encouraged me to become a youth minister and gave me some books and notes I found very useful.

I will always appreciate his faith in my ability to reach young people and get them more interested in their faith. That's what led me to youth ministry and, eventually, to House of Hope and Joy.

This seminarian introduced me to a group of friends who were intellectual, spiritual, and committed to ministry. They used to meet Saturday mornings after Mass to discuss current articles and relevant books they had read. It was very stimulating and helpful for a teacher making the move from English teacher to religion teacher.

They sometimes held Friday night prayer meetings. I was often invited and always honored to attend.

It seemed that we had the most interesting conversations during Advent and Lent. The Scripture readings were so rich during those seasons of preparation.

I will always be grateful for the friendships of that time period of my life. They were very formational for me. They kept steering me toward my vocation of ministry and helped me understand what God wanted for my life.

I remained a high school teacher for quite a while but soon realized that ministry was really my strongest vocation. That is what led to my current ministry and desire to enter the Friends of Clare and Francis.

I hope this finally satisfies your need for learning more about my "life experiences."

I look forward to receiving my acceptance letter in the near future.

Nellie Massa

Chapter 18

Dear Kelvin,

I guess I want to try to say something else about Tom and Matt.

Even though it made me angry at first, I think I understand why Sister Agnes made me write about "My amazing brothers" and "My ridiculous brothers."

I see how she wanted me to have more passion in my reflections...

Not that it's any of her business, but I guess I haven't really done that with my relationships, and maybe it's not a bad exercise, as long as I realize it's just that -- an exercise, a tool to assist me with deeper reflection.

I'm going to try it with Tom and Matt. I'm going to use "My Darling Matt" and "My Darling Tom."

I did love my Darling Matt and the way he made me feel physically. It was nice to feel sexy again and to laugh a lot and to have fun. I missed all that fun. I missed the way Adam and I used to laugh over things when no one else would even realize the humor of the situation!

And I did love my Darling Tom, for all the wisdom and spirituality he brought to my life. I had deep conversations -- and thought about things I wish I could have shared with Adam. And after all, Tom really changed my life by introducing me to theology and youth ministry. That part is true.

But neither "My ridiculous Tom" nor "My ridiculous Matt" could ever be my true soul mate. If I had to pick negative nicknames for them... maybe I'd say ... "Surface Matt" and "Know-So-Much Tom."

Surface Matt frustrated me because I couldn't ask him deep questions or hear any true opinions from him. I realized we couldn't have a deep relationship if I really only knew him on the surface. It just wasn't enough. It didn't fill my soul.

And Know-So-Much Tom sometimes intimidated me. He wasn't really a "Know it all" Tom, because Know-it-all types will pretend to know everything and brag when they do know something. They will also fake it when they are bluffing. And Tom was never like that. He never faked it, and he never bragged. He was really quite humble, actually, and would never want anyone to think of him as a know-it-all. If he didn't know an answer, he'd be the first to tell you, and then he'd look it up and report back, and then thank **YOU** for thinking up such a challenging question and teaching him something in return!

That is NOT the characteristic of a know-it-all.

OK, I'm not very good at this yet. I'm trying to go negative, but really can't come up with much anger in me... or much frustration. I guess maybe it was too long ago... Or maybe they were really great guys. Just not soul mates for me... and that's OK.

But I guess it's important to keep trying that "negative" thing... maybe some day it will teach me something about my emotional self.

Chapter 19

Dear Kelvin,

It's time I talk about Timothy.

I know Agnes is going to ask about him, so I may as well start thinking things through.

Shortly after my Tom & Matt phase, I met Timothy through my oldest brother. He came to the house when we had one of those rare weekends together during Christmas break and were watching the NFL playoff games. He was amazed that I enjoyed football -- I guess girls are not supposed to like football. He was quite amused to hear my stories about Roger Staubach... even more amused when he found out that I had written to him every year on his birthday.

But football had always been a big part of our family. It never occurred to me that girls weren't supposed to like it.

When we were kids, any time a quarterback threw an interception my dad would say, "Whenever a quarterback throws the football, three things can happen and two of them are bad."

And I was supposed to say, "If it's caught, it's a completion. That's good. If it's not caught, it's incomplete, and that's bad. And if someone from the other team catches it, it's an interception, and that's really bad!" This was how he would teach me about football.

As I got older, I wanted to say, "But what if his teammate catches it and then drops it? Or catches it and then fumbles? Those are bad, too!" But I never got into all of that. He liked his three-two scenario teaching, and it made for a fun exchange. He liked that I always knew the answer.

Eventually, my dad would just say, "Whenever a quarterback throws the football..." and I would respond, "Three things can happen, and two of them are bad." We didn't have to elaborate; he didn't require me to name and define the three things... we both knew what the three things were.

Then when I became much older, he would just say, "Three things" and I'd reply, "Two bad!" And then we'd laugh.

So that became a family thing. A quarterback would throw an interception, and one of my older brothers would say, "Three things" and Ben and I and the other brother would say, "Two bad!"

It was especially funny when other people were visiting. They'd wonder: What's "Three things too bad?" And then we would get to tell the whole story...

Once in a while, there would be a really exciting game, and we'd want the quarterback to throw an interception, because we wanted the other team to get the ball... and we'd be chanting it like a prayer... "Three things two bad, three things two bad, three things two bad..."

Once I was at a college game with Adam, and all my brothers, and his sister, and our parents, and some other friends, and we took up part of two rows. Ben was at the other end of a long line of people. It was too loud for us to do our "Three things two bad" routine, so Ben and I looked at each other. He held up three fingers, and then I held up two fingers. Adam and Ben and I laughed so hard, we completely missed the next play.

Anyway, that's how I met Timothy: Football and "Three things two bad." He was a friend of my brother's, and he liked football. Eventually, I guess he liked me. I wasn't seeing Tom or Matt anymore, so when he called and asked me out, I thought, "Why not?"

I learned from my experiences with Tom and Matt that I needed smart and funny in the same person. It didn't work for me to go to Matt to get the funny and to Tom to get the smart. At least not for very long. And Timothy seemed to be both funny and smart. So he passed my first test. And my brothers liked him, so I guess he passed my second test.

I didn't have any other tests at that time… so I agreed to go out with Timothy.

It seemed almost everyone was in graduate school at the same time… I had one brother in med school, and another brother studying biochemistry. Timothy was in optometry school.

There was endless teasing because Phil was going to become a REAL eye doctor (ophthalmologist) and Timothy was only going to be a "pretend" eye doctor (optometrist -- not an MD), but I was happy because I could at least spell both words. At that time, Ben was still in college, learning Greek and Latin.

But we somehow found time to watch football every so often.

Timothy had played in high school and college bands, and so he had a lot in common with my two older brothers.

He never was really comfortable with the whole Roger Staubach thing. He actually talked me into giving away my scrapbook of Roger articles and pictures and letters. I gave it to Tommy.

We went out for a few years, and eventually I guess it just felt as if we could be married and live together fine and do well together. He asked me to marry him. My family liked him, he was smart and funny, we seemed to get along, and so it seemed to be the next step in my life.

I guess I learned the next thing the hard way... and I think I may have read it in some women's magazine...

"For a successful marriage....

The question to ask isn't, 'Can I live with him?'

The question to ask is, 'Can I live without him?'"

Chapter 20

Dear Kelvin,

This has nothing to do with anything, really, except it sure was a big deal when it happened. And it kind of explains some more of the Roger Staubach situation...

When I was in college, I took a poetry class and learned about a type of poem called "Sestina." The whole poem was based on the interplay of six words. The last word of every line had to be one of these words, and the order was determined by an established pattern. One of the students wrote a sestina about the Boston Red Sox, and he was so proud of that poem that he challenged the rest of us to write another "sports sestina."

So I wrote one about Roger Staubach. I wrote a "modern" sestina, meaning I had some freedom regarding the actual words -- I was able to use not only those six words, but versions of these words as well. And the length of the lines didn't have to be uniform.

It's a complicated poem to write, but even more complicated to explain! So I won't say any more. I'll just show you. Here is that actual poem I wrote:

Roger Staubach of the Dallas Cowboys

(A Sestina)

It all started one Saturday when my father was watching
football.
I asked him the **score**
And he started to talk about a **number**
Of things I had never heard of before. So I sat **down**

At his **feet**
And he began explaining things about football and **Roger**.

Let me tell you a little about **Roger**.
He is really the king of **football**.
Whether the team needs 50 yards or just a few **feet**
To **score**,
You can bet Roger will settle **down**
And play some solid football. I can name a **number**

Of times when **Number**
12 (That's **Roger**)
Has converted third **downs**
Into touchdowns. Whether he passes the **football**
Or runs with it, he's there to **score**.
Next time he scrambles, just watch his **feet**.

His dodging is incredible and his **feats**
Are just too many to **number**.
You know, some people say he "doesn't know the **score**,"
Or "He's a square," but to **Roger**,
(And this is what I like about him), Life is more than **football**.
And it's more than changing third **downs**

Into touch**downs**.
It's the sound of little **feet**
At home -- not the feet of **football**
Players, but of his children -- five in **number** --
That forms the all-star team **Roger**
Holds closest to his heart. Sure he likes to **score**

Touchdowns, but **scoring**
And winning isn't everything. When you get right **down**
To it, **Roger**

Is first a husband and father, then a quarterback.
Although his **feats**
As **Number**
12 on the **football**

Field are many in **number**, far away from the **scores**
Of **football** fans, Happiness to **Roger**
Is winding **down** at home with his family at his **feet**.

I was asked to read that poem at a college poetry reading. It was a big honor for me!

At the time my brother Phil was already dating Margaret, whom he eventually married. All of us were at college together for three of my four years there.

Margaret's father's friend was in advertising. He was working with a few commercials for Anderson Little, a clothing company... commercials starring Roger Staubach! They would be filming one of the commercials not too far from where we lived, and her dad arranged for me to meet Roger Staubach at this commercial filming!

It was the most exciting day! I walked in with Margaret's mother, and while looking at all the bright lights and camera equipment, I practically bumped right into him!

So we got to chat for a few minutes... and I watched the filming of the first commercial. His back was to the camera, and a tailor was taking a measurement of his shoulders. Roger turned around and simply said, "At Anderson Little, you can look your best for less."

During a break, we shared a bag of French fries, and he even let me hold his Super Bowl ring!

He signed my copy of *First Down, Lifetime to Go*, a book he wrote in 1974. He actually wrote,

"To Nell
Best Wishes --
A friend,
Roger Staubach."

They took a picture of the two of us, and that photograph is something I did not give to Tommy! It is still framed, and still in my room, reminding me to go the distance, even when things seem hopeless.

Chapter 21

Dear Kelvin,

OK. More about Timothy.

It's not that we didn't talk about children. We did. He knew I loved children, he knew most of my childhood was filled with Ben's childhood, and he knew I almost became a kindergarten teacher. He knew my real desire was to quit teaching school and just be a stay-at-home mom who volunteered at the church and ran the youth group.

We talked about all that. We talked about baby names. We talked about baby stuff. We got a house with two extra rooms for babies who would grow up. We just never got around to making any babies.

After a few years, Timothy confessed that he really didn't want to have babies. He never really ever wanted them. My heart ached.

I realized early on that he was uncomfortable with children. He went along with sitting on the floor and playing with nieces and nephews. I think he even changed a diaper or two along the way. But he was clearly relieved when we left, or they left, and he could be alone with adult company again.

We were together four years. We really tried to make that marriage work. But he really didn't want children, and sooner or later, I guess he didn't want a woman who wanted children.

I just thought he would come around when he finally saw one of his own in his arms. Something about a tiny, tiny human being, completely in need, completely dependent, often creates in the hearts of fathers -- even the most reluctant fathers -- this enormous emotion, this enormous bond, this "I will kill anyone who tries to harm you in any way" sense of protection and responsibility.

But we never got the chance to do that experiment.

It's one of the classic examples of what the Catholic Church would call "Grounds for annulment." If one of the partners is not open to having children, that means the marriage bond is null and void. So it was quite easy for us to get an annulment.

The healing of my heart was not so easy.

The annulment process, even though I knew what the ultimate answer would be, was horrible. All these questions about our dating habits, our sex habits, our conversations about having children. Why did you want to date him? Why did you want to marry him? What was lacking in your relationship?

I really felt like a victim, and I really felt as if I was being blamed for the whole thing. And I changed my last name. I used to be Nellie Massa. Then I became Nellie Baker. So everyone knew me as Nellie Baker. I changed my name back to Nellie Massa, and no matter where I went, or whom I saw, the questions came. So many places I had to change my name. I had to explain my situation and endure the pathetic looks from everywhere. From every doctor and dentist, from the bank, from the store, from the mailman, from the school, and especially from everyone at my church. And from the teenagers.

Timothy Baker is still Timothy Baker. No one asks him any questions or gives him pathetic looks. No one even knows the difference. But for me, the looks, stares, and disapproval never seemed to end.

"Didn't you know he didn't want children?" Of course I didn't know! He didn't tell me!

"What kind of woman marries a man who doesn't want children?" How was I supposed to answer that?

Why didn't they ask me, "What kind of man lies to a woman about wanting children?"

But I guess the answer might be "Lots of men do that.... Lots of men don't care about babies. They lie about wanting babies so their women will marry them. And then some miracle happens, and they are delighted when they finally have babies."

But my story didn't have that ending.

Plus... there's something about a married youth minister that's comforting to parents of teenagers. She seems safer. She seems like a good woman, a normal woman. A woman the girls can talk to about their female questions. And the guys? Well, they can talk to her husband, since he always volunteers with her for special trips and retreats.

It was OK for teenagers to talk to us about sex... we were supposed to be having sex. We were *married*. That makes it OK.

Not after my divorce. I can still hardly even say the word. **Divorce**. It's so awful.

Plus, suddenly, I always had to find some other male chaperone... not an easy thing.

And forget workshops about family ministry or relationships. Who am I to know about healthy families? I was rejected! I was not good enough! Who am I to know about relationships?

I lost all my credibility in the ministry world -- over something that wasn't even my fault.

"Spare me from a talk by that divorced woman."

"Do we want a divorced woman leading our youth group?"

"What kind of good Catholic gets divorced?"

It was a nightmare. It was inescapable. It was every where.

And then... *and then*... the ultimate insult!

Timothy **got married again**... to a woman who **already had children!!!**

And not only that, **they had more children together!!!**

My heartache was tremendous.

I could no longer find solace in that one little last irrefutable fact: He didn't want children.

It was no longer true.

So what was true? That he didn't want me, with or without children? That had to be it.

When my brothers speak of Timothy, his not being a "real" doctor is the least of their complaints. They mean well, but every time they insult him, I feel insulted, too. Because if he is a fool, or a jerk, or a liar, or a messed up individual, then I am surely a worse fool, or a worse jerk or a more messed up individual to have loved him and expected to have a family with him.

And people assume the strangest things. We never had children, but he has them now. So probably, many imagine, HE was the one who wanted children and I was the one who didn't want them! They think HE was the bigger man, because he took the rap to spare me the embarrassment! Or perhaps they think that I wasn't able to give him children, so he left. Well, now, that wasn't fair to poor, barren Nellie, but surely you could understand that! A man needs to pass on his name!

You can just imagine how all this talk hurt me... and I heard it all! I heard all the whispers, and I heard all the rumors other people were starting. It really just made me want to scream! And cry!

Well, mostly cry...

And that's what I did...

I cried and cried and cried...

I always pictured having a daughter. I pictured this amazing bond between my mother and me. I always thought there was nothing in the universe like a mother watching her daughter give birth to a daughter, and then knowing that her child's child will one day give birth as well...

I never got the opportunity. I felt a bit empty about that... I still do today... a little.

You know, it's "what God made me to do as a woman." Giving birth...

I know it was drummed into me by a society that mostly valued women for making babies... I know things have changed a lot since then, and intellectually I know better, but somehow the feelings are still there. And if I think about it for too long, the tears start coming, so there must be something still in my heart, some hurt that has never gone away, some hurt that I don't think about too often, but when I do, it's still so very tender...

I'll never know what it's like to have a **baby** of my own...

And once again... all this writing and nothing of any value to give to Sister Agnes...

Enough! Good NIGHT!

Chapter 22

Dear Kelvin,

At some point, my mother told me an amazing thing. She said that when she was pregnant with me, she had a miscarriage. And yet somehow, miraculously, she was still pregnant. In other words, I had been a twin.

I often wondered about my missing twin. Was it a brother? Sometimes I think it must have been a brother, since I got along so well with boys. My first love was my baby brother Ben. My first best friend was Adam. My house was filled with brothers. I was the biggest football fan in the house. My dad and I "hung out" and talked as easily as I did with my mom.

But what if it had been a girl? What if it had been my only sister? I always wondered what it would have been like to have a sister.

And now, I feel as if I have three sisters. My three brothers all married the most competent, the most intelligent, and the most amazing women I could imagine. I could not dream of better sisters.

Phil married Margaret. She is the "Renaissance woman" of the family. She played first violin in high school, varsity basketball in high school and college, draws like Norman Rockwell and even won a beauty pageant. And get this -- *she was a physics major!* She wins almost every contest or game she enters, and she never met a crossword puzzle or math problem she couldn't solve. Her grammar is better than mine (and I teach English for a living!) and she can quote books, plays and movies like nobody's business. She plays piano as well as Phil, and often plays with their two girls, Ann and Rose.

Charlie married Elizabeth... Beth. She is the ultimate Earth Mother. She's a nurse, and she knows every official and unofficial way to heal anything. She grows her own herbs, and cooks from scratch. She has two dogs and walks them up and down the hill behind the barn behind their house. She sews and she bakes and has artsy-craftsy creativity. Most of all, she loves sharing her talents with their daughter Connie.

Ben married Mary. If you look up sweet in the encyclopedia (or wikipedia), you see Mary's picture. She would have fit in perfectly with Adam and Gemma! She is funny and smart. She thinks deeply and laughs deeply. She can watch a play or movie and talk about it as if the characters were real and jumped out into real life, just as Adam used to do with me. She never tires of learning, and she appreciates life and has the wisdom that most elders would envy. Being with Mary is always like coming home and sinking down into your favorite sofa with a cup of hot chocolate. She never got to meet my dad -- well, not while he was alive -- but more about that later.

I have the best three "sisters" I can imagine... and their children are my delight. Every time one was born, I remembered my first moments with Ben as a baby, and all that joy came rushing up out of my heart, spilled out of my eyes and poured down my cheeks.

They are all teenagers now, and I find it so funny... when I was a kid, I hung around with all the boys -- Adam and my three brothers. And now, when we all get together, we have all these girls! And they are into sports, music, reading, plays, acting, singing, performing, writing and science... just like their marvelous parents.

A funny thing about my three sisters -- they are all my age! We all turned 50 the same year! We always joke about the "bumper crop of fine women" who were born that year... and I tell my brothers that they loved me so much, they had to find someone born about the same time, influenced by the same current events...

So my family life is very full and fun.

If ever there is a two-edged sword, it is simply this: that those who love the most are those who suffer the most when tragedy strikes. And our family loves fiercely.

I still have this bottom-of-my-heart sinking feeling of being abandoned... I guess it started when Adam left me, not quite at the altar, but the week of the wedding. It was this sickening shame and the humiliation of being abandoned -- of feeling left behind -- of being "not good enough" -- of being not quite lovable enough... I don't know how to describe it...

But if I hadn't loved Adam so much, it would not have hurt me so much.

And when Timothy left me, it just threw me back into that pain of losing Adam.

I think that's the way grief works. Any time something horrible happens, all the unresolved hurt from all the heartaches in your past returns... it just wells up inside of you until it overwhelms you and the world comes crashing down.

Yes, that's really it. It's the sense of the entire world crashing down.

When my father died, it felt exactly like that. He had a sudden heart attack and was dead within an hour.

Every sad feeling of being left behind came upon me, like the beams of a dilapidated structure, still heavy but not stable enough to stand... heavy beams, knocking me down, driving me into the dirt, burying me alive, covering me up in the darkness, leaving me for dead, leaving me to wonder if anyone would ever know I was under all that rubble, wondering if anyone could ever come and rescue me and drag me out and save me. With my face pressed against the ground, struggling to breathe, I was helpless. I didn't even try. Dying there in the ruins seemed like a good enough option. It was too difficult to figure out how to crawl out. Much too difficult. I was too tired; I was too emotionally drained. I was just going to close my eyes, and let death take over.

But it never did take over. Eventually, some of those giant beams got pushed aside by something. I don't know how. I couldn't come running out, or even walking out, but maybe I lifted my head a little and took a breath on purpose. The recovery was really that slow...

It must have been like that for my whole family... as I said, we all love deeply and that's the reward -- deep suffering when we lose someone we love.

So I went through the motions, but I don't think I was ever the same. The wounds never fully healed.

I just kept going through the motions.

My brothers, my sisters and my mom needed me to go through the motions. We all needed each other to go through the motions. The teenagers at my school needed me to go through the motions. And I guess House of Hope and Joy would need me to go through the motions.

I guess it's what we do when we are grown-ups.

We

Just

Learn

How

To

Keep

Going

Through

The

Motions.

I swear I don't know how any of this is going to help me write anything for Sister Agnes.

Chapter 23

"Say more about your marriage to Timothy."

Dear Sister Agnes,

Timothy was a good man. He appeared to love me very much. But he was living a lie.

I think he wanted to love me, and perhaps he did love me.

But he didn't want to have children. He lied to me before we got married. He thought he would change his mind about children... with some time and maturity. But he couldn't bear to tell me in the beginning.

It's one of the classic examples of what the Catholic Church would call "Grounds for annulment." If one of the partners is not open to having children, that means the marriage bond is null and void. So it was quite easy for us to get an annulment.

I went to the diocese office and filled out the forms and spoke with a Tribunal counselor.

I realize a failed marriage does not give much of a positive indication that a person is capable of healthy relationships.

However, to counteract that perception, I offer the examples of many relationships you know I have with colleagues who are both men and women....

I offer the examples of my family relationships...

I offer my friendships with many of the sisters of the order of the Friends of Clare and Francis...

Because there were no children from this marriage, I have no financial burdens, and no responsibilities to stand in the way of my joining the order.

This was not an easy process for me. I needed time to work through my grief.

At this point in my life, I do feel comfortable saying that that particular chapter of my life is now passed, and I am ready to start another chapter.

I look forward to receiving my acceptance letter in the near future.

Nell Massa

Chapter 24

Dear Kelvin,

I guess I'll do that "Amazing Timothy" and "Ridiculous Timothy" thing. Maybe that will help me get deeper into my feelings.

Or better yet, I'll write about "My Darling Timothy" and "Clueless Timothy"

I guess my Darling Timothy really did try to want children. He tried so hard, he managed to succeed, but not in time for me.

My Darling Timothy really tried to enjoy nieces and nephews. He just wasn't ready for them.

Clueless Timothy just had some growing up to do first, I guess.

Clueless Timothy married me and promised to love me forever and stand by me until death did us part. Physical death, not just emotional death.

And to add insult to injury, Clueless Timothy said he thought that the worst part for me wasn't that my heart was broken -- which it was -- or that my biological clock was ticking and I was afraid that I might not ever have children -- which was true -- but the worst part for me might well be that I now had this "horrific failure on my record."

So Clueless Timothy has the audacity to break his marriage vows, take away my chance to have children, and then walk away, himself justified with a moral victory, because he gets to throw in my face his crazed notion that perhaps my worst pain was, in fact, the sin of pride -- that now I would be seen as a failure, as a victim of a failed marriage.

The worst part of this hideous, outrageous accusation is that... it might be actually true.

I did want a successful marriage. I did want children in a family that went to church together and came home for family gatherings, and I did want a husband who helped out with the youth group at church. I did want a husband who taught my children baseball and basketball and said things like "Three things two bad" at football games.

I also wanted a husband to pretend to be surprised at how delicious his children's pancakes tasted, or their cupcakes, or even pop tarts stuck in a toaster. I wanted us to go swimming together and teach them how to do flip turns. I wanted Uncle Ben to tell them about Zeus and Apollo and all those other people and gods I always get mixed up.

Was that so horrible? I wanted my mother to see her daughter giving birth to another daughter. Or even a son. I wanted my children to hang out with their cousins so that we had a stronger and stronger family. And all he gave me was a broken nothing.

It was very hard to explain this to my nieces. They were too young when it happened for them to understand that sometimes a man leaves a woman, and it's not her fault. Rose wanted to know why he left me -- and what I did wrong to make him want to leave me. Once, when I was talking to Ann about what she wanted to be when she grew up, she said she wanted to be just like me. Then she immediately corrected herself and changed her mind. "No," she said, "I don't really want to be like you. I want to stay married."

What kind of example am I to my nieces now?

They look at me and realize that their Aunt Nellie was left behind, so they don't want to be like her.

To them, what do I know about healthy relationships? I'm the one who was unloved. I'm the one who was dumped. I'm the one who was rejected.

I do understand their logic...

"We don't want to be like her. We don't want to look like her, or dress like her, or go to church like her, or live like her, because what did it get her? Nothing! She's alone now. We want to have husbands. We want to be popular. We'll never get there following Aunt Nellie's example. No, we'll do something different all together."

And actually, perhaps the teenagers in my youth group thought the same thing.

I kind of lost my "street cred."

So yes, Kelvin.

Deep down, that clueless, selfish, nasty Timothy had a point. I hate being a failure. Because of what he did, I have no credibility in anyone's eyes. No one wants to be like me, because no one wants to end up like me. Most of all, I hate being a failure in the one area I always thought I was going to be most successful!

I thought I had the most wonderful man in the universe -- my very best friend ever -- my beloved Adam -- and I expected the most wonderful marriage with the most beautiful children -- and I ended up alone and childless and pitied and ashamed.

So Timothy gets it all. He gets the wife and the children who love him, and he gets to feel smug about leaving me, because after all, my worst heartache wasn't heartache... it was pride. And everyone knows that pride is a sin.

Why did Sister Agnes have to start me doing all this awful writing?

I had no idea how horrible all this writing would make me feel. All it does is make me realize how pathetic I really am. Most certainly, I will never let her know it had any impact on me.

Chapter 25

Dear Kelvin,

I can't write about Timothy and Adam anymore.

I don't want to write about my dad anymore.

I don't really know what Agnes is going to ask me about next, so I thought I would get my thoughts down about House of Hope and Joy.

You know the place all too well -- you practically grew up there.

Ruby invited me there when we started talking at one of those teacher in-services.

HHJ is a great place. It's the warmest and most welcoming community outreach center I could imagine.

With the food pantry and the clothing boutique... and the Clean Teens... I just love being part of a place that does so many good things for the community.

I came to one of their Clean Teen reunions and met all these young adults who used to come to HHJ as Clean Teens during their high school years. They pledged to stay clean -- no drugs, no alcohol, no guns, no gangs, no crime, no profanity, no sex, no immodesty.

Their goal was to stay clean, get to college, get a career, and then come back to mentor more Clean Teens from the 'hood... to get them to college, and into good jobs and careers, and then to come back, mentor others, and to keep passing it on...

Then I met you and realized that both you and Ruby had been Clean Teens.

Back in the day, all the Clean Teens were African American, but today, the Clean Teen group has become quite diverse -- Latinos, Asians, Whites, from public schools, Catholic schools, charter schools. All with the same four goals... clean, college, career, and come back.

Sometimes things just work out in ways we could never imagine or anticipate. Call it God's will or a coincidence... But some say a coincidence is just God's way of being anonymous.

So as luck -- or grace -- would have it, my church was hiring a full-time youth minister at the same time as I was introduced to HHJ. Our church really needed one, because the number of teens in our programs had been increasing, and Timothy and I would never have been able to handle all of them as volunteers anyway. I intended to stick around and help out (every youth minister needs volunteers to assist with the ministry), but I did feel awkward about my history with Timothy. After a while, it became just too painful to be there.

House of Hope and Joy was looking for volunteers to work with the Clean Teens. They had a full-time youth worker who was leaving the ministry and moving out of state. So clever Ruby! She brought me to HHJ with an ulterior motive! Get me interested, wave some bait and see if I get hooked! Well, it worked!

I thought a change was important. I needed to break away and not do things that would remind me of Timothy, so coming to the inner city to work with all kinds of diverse youth who were trying to stay clean and focused was a great opportunity for me.

What would the teens think when they realized they were losing their really cool, really hip, good looking, rap singing, styling, snappy dressing, funny and adorable youth leader? And they were getting this white-bread girl from the suburbs?

Ruby thought it would be OK. And foolish me -- I believed her. If I didn't, I never would have tried.

Ruby came with me the first two times, and so did Luz, and so did Kim. So I guess we had several skin colors covered... African American, Latina, Hmong, and white Nellie.

Ruby told me that her children would soon be graduating out of the program and on their way to college. She wanted the program still there so they could keep coming back. Luz had two daughters who were Clean *Kids* -- younger students that come to programs run by the Clean Teens. She had been a volunteer there for a while. Kim was new. He had a cousin he wanted in the group. So we all gathered for lunch and got to know the current Clean Teens.

Kelvin, you remember the staff back then. That was when Sister Matilda ran the place. She has been kind of sick for a while. But you remember her living upstairs, and the members of the staff being the ones taking care of business. There are no sisters really doing that ministry now, but there will be if I join the order.

Sheryl , the main receptionist and cook, was like everyone's mother. I like to say she runs the place. Pretty important jobs. She sees all the Clean Teens as her very own sons and daughters, and she has known them since they were children. She has been part of HHJ since coming years ago as a guest, in need of food and clothing herself.

Sheryl introduced me and had everyone tell me a story about themselves outside of HHJ. Also a story about something they did as part of an HHJ program. They were great. Very welcoming. I think it's the food -- who can be unhappy when you are eating the best fried chicken, meat loaf, mac and cheese and green beans in the city?

So just when I crawled out from under the rubble of "failure," I had House of Hope and Joy offering me an opportunity to make a difference in a new way -- with a terrific ministry in a marvelous place with a great staff and super volunteers who already seemed to welcome me and want me to be part of their outreach. How could I say no? Ruby, Luz and Kim wouldn't let me. And neither would you.

I sometimes think about the "gray cloud" that Timothy brought -- *gray* because it was all so sad and dark, and *cloud* because there is so much foggy confusion surrounding what happened...

I wondered, "Where is the silver lining to that gray cloud?" The answer was House of Hope and Joy. If Timothy and I had stayed married and raised children, I probably would have never found HHJ, and I would have never realized how much I love working with urban youth and urban outreach. True, I might have been insanely happy with my children and my married life in the suburbs. Perhaps I might never have missed this other part of my life, so I guess I can't ever know.

Things just didn't turn out the way I had planned...

But I am so blessed that I became part of House of Hope and Joy.

I tell you -- I can hear the sound of God laughing -- I think God laughs the most when we try to make our own plans for how we want our lives to go.

Chapter 26

Dear Kelvin,

I have a new strategy.

I'm going to start surprising Agnes by voluntarily giving her reflections she didn't even ask for. That way, I get two advantages... First, she will think that I am finally coming around and writing and reflecting and sharing with her as a confidant. Second, I will get to pick the topics more often, so we can stay away from "My Amazing Whatever" and "My Ridiculous Whatever."

So I'll start with House of Hope and Joy. And also with teaching at St. Augustine.

You remember what it's like to teach reluctant readers, unmotivated writers, disinterested students...

It's really hard to get them to care about anything.

One time I was driving three girls home from a community event. Somehow they got themselves there, by bus or by parents or friends, I'm not sure. But at the end of the day, they all confessed to me that they had no way home. Perhaps they just didn't want to take unfamiliar buses in the dark. I completely understand that anxiety.

So I said I'd drive them home.

In the car, they spoke to each other in Spanish, and didn't know I could understand some of what they were saying. (Yes, I took Spanish in high school and college!)

Ana was talking about her son. Wow! I didn't know she had a son! And she was in my English class! It never came up!

Berta was saying that she needed to walk over to her brother's school, once she was dropped off at home. Her father was supposed to pick up her brother and take him for a visit, but he wasn't allowed to be with her brother unless she was there also. Isn't that an interesting family dynamic?

Lupe was asking Berta about a clinic that doesn't require health insurance. Berta told her it was on the corner of 6th and National, and that you go on Tuesdays if you don't have health insurance.

Lupe asked the other two if their families had health insurance. Ana and Berta both replied, "No."

So here we have just three girls from this community gathering -- three girls from my one English class -- and just look at the issues they have to worry about! One has a son, and all the responsibilities, self-esteem issues, and poverty risk that carries. One has a home situation that is very complicated and carries very unusual responsibilities for a brother's supervision. The third one is trying to seek out medical help for her family. All three no doubt must serve as translators for their parents every time they visit a doctor, go to the bank, have teacher conferences, and make family decisions. That is too much adult responsibility for students who are barely out of childhood.

I always wonder how my students ever have any energy left over for things such as chemistry and algebra.

Who cares about protons and electrons when a student goes home at night and takes care of her son and wonders about whether he's going to grow up and join a gang? Or when she has to worry about her mother dying because she can't afford medicine, or worry about whether her family will fall apart, and if she will need to get a job if they take her father away. Who cares about solving for "x" in a meaningless math problem? They already have enough unknowns in their lives.

So many of my students come to school because they can get meals there and because school is safer than the streets. They don't care about the classes or the learning, and they seldom do homework. They are too busy with the demands of real life to care about subjects that make no sense to learn, since they have no reasonable application for life. No one expects to live past 30, which they consider to be fairly old, and many expect to be dead by 20.

It's a challenge, for sure.

I once asked the class to think about things they wished for... I was trying to get them to imagine a better future.

Keshia (I later found out she was Ruby's niece) said, "I wish our family didn't have so many people in jail." Sitting next to her, LaQuondra said that she didn't have a dad or any uncles. All the adults in her family were women. She wished her father would come back.

I took a poll of the class. "How many think that you can make a difference in the world?" No one's hand went up. I asked, "How many of you think that the world can improve -- that the world can become a better place for you and your family?" Not a single hand. I asked, "How many of you think that if the right mayor or the right president were elected, that things could get better?" No one. Finally, I asked, "How many of you think that if YOU study hard, if YOU go to college and if YOU get a good career, YOU can make a difference, at least for your own life and your own family and your own neighborhood?" Still *not one single hand!*

Keshia admitted that she believed the world COULD get better, but that it probably WOULDN'T.

That was the closest I could ever get to even a glimmer of hope!

I asked them, "How many of you have at least one member of your family who was killed because of someone else's violence?" Every hand shot up. Then, "How many of you have at least one friend -- someone your age or close to your age -- killed by violence?" Again, every single hand.

This is the kind of world that most suburban white people don't understand and can't really imagine.

This kind of challenge every day at school is why it was such a blessing for me to end up at House of Hope and Joy. It changed my life. And it changed my outlook on ways I could bring hope and joy to the students in my English classes at St. Augustine.

Chapter 27

Dear Kelvin,

What do you believe?

It's a simple question... but requires a less-than-simple answer.

Public radio has been asking people to answer that question for years. They feature one person's essay each week, and they call it "This I Believe." It was started a long time ago, and then it was started up again more recently. The essays are terrific.

I decided to have my students write their own "This I believe" essays.

We worked on them for half a semester. Every other class day, we heard someone's rough draft and gave our comments and asked our questions. It was one of the best ideas I ever had.

When the students were reading their essays, it was as if they were reading a sacred prayer. I was very touched by some of their topics.

I decided to do the same thing with the Clean Teens from House of Hope and Joy.

At the end of the year, we had a big celebration at HHJ. Students from both groups were invited. Parents, too. Everyone's essay was printed on big poster paper, framed in bright colors, and hung around the room on all the walls. Students were randomly selected to read their complete essays.

Sheryl made us a feast. Every teenager took home a paper plate covered with foil, so they could share the food with their families.

Some parents were not able to come, but every student brought at least one adult -- an aunt, a neighbor, a church minister or leader, a teacher from school, a staff member from HHJ.

At the very end, we had each student stand up. They read one sentence from their essay, and stated their full name. That was the most powerful moment of all! There was complete silence as the adults stared, open mouthed and wide-eyed, listening to the belief statements of each young person. At the very end, when the last student spoke that simple statement and name, the words hung in the air for maybe two full seconds. Then all of the visitors stood up at once, and filled the room with wild applause. There were tears streaming -- not trickling, but streaming -- down all of our faces!

I never envisioned the effect this simple evening would have on all of us! The effect was undeniable hope and absolute joy!

Here are some of the statements that hung on the walls of House of Hope and Joy that evening:

- I believe in success, especially when everyone else expects failure from you.

- I believe that everyone should greet one another with an open hand, heart and mind. Because as Plato once said, "Be kind, for everyone you meet is fighting a hard battle."

- This I believe: I'll always be thankful for what I have or what I can do. I won't always be happy with life's situations, but I will be thankful for situations I do enjoy. God has given us all gifts and talents and how you use them is our way of showing gratitude.

- I believe we all wish for that little drama to teach us something valuable, the little fight that will spark a nationwide reaction, the little scenes that happen across the world to unite people who don't even speak the same language. I believe that a little drama is a good thing.

- This I believe: because of the faith and dedication of the Jesuit fathers, this excellent tradition of quality education has been kept since the Society of Jesus began.

- I believe in animal rights, that animals should be treated with care and respect. I'm an animal rights activist and a proud member of PETA 2's street team. I'm only 15, but now I know I can make a difference.

- I believe that as a Catholic I should do my best in following God's way.

- I believe I can always find comfort in music no matter what is going on in my life because I am able to link the words back to reality and move forward.

- This I believe: If you always use your imagination, you can get through all kinds of rough times.

- I believe that I am protected by a higher being.

- I believe that music is connected to every aspect of life.

- I believe in savoring the moment, living every day like it's your last, and enjoying life.

- I believe in letting the music set the mood. For every song, there is a meaning. The meaning of songs can differ in many ways and have a certain impact on peoples' lives. Sometimes music can be that one thing in peoples' lives that they can relate to; they can see similarities between themselves and the music they are listening to.

- I believe in a new life, a new start. I believe in miracles. Anything is possible and it can happen to anyone. I think all people should be able to believe in something.

- This I believe... that guns and other violent weapons should be taken off our streets. As African Americans, we call ourselves a unified group, acting as one, trying to push this nation forward. But we are killing each other as we strive for excellence. I believe in stopping the violence.

- I am the captain of my fate and I am ready to set sail. This is what I believe. Living a life to the fullest with no regrets.

What happened as a result of this process? I think several things...

Every student was able to move from despair to hope and from poor self-esteem to healthy confidence.

The adults felt renewed hope in the future of their youth, their neighborhood, and their world, and the teenagers felt the support, pride and even admiration of the adults.

Admiration. I want to say that again. The adults in that room **admired** the teenagers. They looked up to them for the way they wrote, for the message they gave, and for the courage they showed by doing it.

Many of those adults had never spoken a word in public, and here are these bright teenagers, standing up in a room full of adults, speaking with poise and grace about their most sacred beliefs.

And most of the students in that room had never envisioned the possibility of being **admired** by adults in the community -- especially when the adults numbered teachers, church leaders, and other neighborhood elders.

It was a turning point in the lives of all my students.

In my own life, too.

This I believe.

Chapter 28

Sister Agnes:

One of the turning points of my teaching and ministry was my idea to have all my English students write their own "This I Believe" essays

I also had the Clean Teens from the HHJ write "This I Believe" essays.

It was wonderful idea. It was challenging for many of them, because it forced them to think deliberately about what was in their deepest souls... and then find the words to express it.

At the end of the year, we held a big celebration. Every essay was hung in the room -- the four walls were covered with their words.

My English students from St. Augustine got to meet the Clean Teens from HHJ; their adult guests met each other as well. Everyone discovered new neighborhood connections.

Everyone was touched... students and adults alike.

Clearly, the students were able to go from despair to hope, from sadness to joy.

And it happened, ironically, at House of Hope and Joy.

It made a huge impact on all of us. I will never forget that night. It made things crystal clear for me. I realized beyond the shadow of a doubt that I was meant to be in this urban ministry, with this community, with the order of Friends of Clare and Francis.

I am sure you will agree that this is my vocation.

Nell Massa

Chapter 29

<u>Memo</u>

Sylvia,

I have begun to have grave concerns about Nell Massa.

She is creating quite a stir, inviting community leaders to House of Hope and Joy and asking students to write about what they believe.

I think it is clear that we are the ones who should be forming each young person's conscience and training each young mind about what they ought to believe. They should not be preaching to adults about their beliefs until we have had proper time and opportunity to form those beliefs.

Ghetto children need much more guidance than she is providing.

Instead of learning what a tragedy she narrowly avoided with this event of hers, she seems to be rather proud of her accomplishments. She is using this poor judgment to attempt to convince me that this is evidence of her calling.

It is essential that you meet with her soon to assess what kind of damage she has done and what her plans are. She is impacting both students at St. Augustine as well as the teenagers at House of Hope and Joy.

Please see this as your new priority and report back to me on your progress.

Agnes

Chapter 30

Dear Sylvia,

It was so nice of you to drop by. What a surprise!

I was delighted that you had heard about our "This I Believe" essays.

The best part was having the adults affirm the young people. I was quite impressed with most of what the young people had to say, and it was clear that the community leaders felt the same way.

I encourage you to tell other sisters about this process. It's quite easy to manage.

It is being orchestrated by the local public radio station, although it's actually a national program. Anyone can contribute an essay, and so it has the following advantages:

→ It encourages the young person to reflect about his or her life and the lessons that formed those values and priorities.

→ It creates the opportunity for a writing project that means a lot to the student; constructive criticism has more meaning because it helps the students better articulate what they are already interested in saying clearly and boldly.

→ It teaches writing skills in general; it reinforces grammar lessons, paragraph construction, and the flow of a quality essay.

→ It develops oral presentation skills, since the young people have much practice reading their essays several times, in front of the peers, and in front of the community leaders. Even if they are not chosen to read their essay in its entirety, they still stand up in front of a group and read a key sentence. (We did not "choose" the students who read their entire essays by the quality of what they wrote; we randomly chose them to avoid competition.)

→ It brings the community together, brings hope to the adult leaders, brings affirmation and hope to the young people, because adults want to listen to what they have to say. It heals old wounds, when police officers show up to listen and affirm youth; it helps some adults to see that many youth are fine upstanding citizens, and it helps youth to see that not all "cops" are purposely trying to hurt them or cause them to falter, just so they can arrest them.

These positive results are just a few of the reasons why this practice could and should be repeated in many other places. We are certain to continue doing it in our neighborhood.

Thanks so much for your interest. It feels wonderful to know that you are taking such an interest in the things I am doing! I appreciate your presence and support in my life!

Love, Nellie

Phil. 2:1-11

Chapter 31

Dear Agnes,

After our "This I Believe" project, the students asked me if I was going to write my own "This I Believe" essay. I could hardly say no. So I did. Here is my essay.

This I Believe

I believe in stalling the band. Holding off the music. Delaying the song.

On a chilly Sunday morning, in the Madonna della Strada Chapel, I learned a lesson about when to wait and when to move forward.

Mass was late starting. I could see the priest was ready. I could see the cantor and the instrumentalists were ready. I could see the acolytes were ready. What was the holdup?

A young man with Downs Syndrome was standing in the aisle. He was pacing back and forth. He was visibly worried. He kept looking at the door, looking at his watch, looking at the two empty seats -- one for him and one apparently for his friend.

Everyone seemed to be waiting with him, for him. They were also concerned. It was hard not to be. Finally, after about ten minutes of everyone shifting in their seats, watching the clock and the door, and feeling sad and helpless, the priest reluctantly waved his arm to the musicians with the "Go ahead" sign. The cantor welcomed everyone to the Liturgy and announced the song. The music began. The young man sadly took his seat.

But one second later, he jumped back up again! His friend was at the door! He waved to her in an exaggerated way. Everyone in the chapel looked at her and smiled with triumphant relief. She was obviously embarrassed as she made her way to the seat her friend had saved for her.

The music continued, the priest started up the aisle, and everyone began to sing. But not in his row. No, this young man held two song booklets under his arm. He insisted on grabbing the hand of the person behind him, and joining it with his friend's hand. She bounced her head a little and rolled her eyes a tad and her face wore an expression that said, "Sorry to make you do this, but you know how he can be...!" as she endured the clumsy hand-shaking ritual with three people behind them and three more people in front of them. Finally, when he felt she had sufficiently been welcomed, he handed her the booklet, and they both began to sing, his voice louder and more confident and more off-key than hers.

This young man taught me more about the ministry of hospitality than any priest or liturgist in any class or workshop. He understood the need to welcome people. He knew the concept. You need to greet each other before you are ready to pray. Because when others are missing, the community isn't complete. Once they arrive, they need to know they are welcomed -- loved, appreciated, cherished. It has to be expressed before we can move on to whatever else might be the purpose of our gathering.

I will never forget that lesson.

This I believe: First you say hello. First you smile. First you express your appreciation. Everything else in life comes second. Even if it means stopping the music and causing a delay.

Chapter 32

Dear Kelvin,

This is the story of how I met "Lil Johnnie" at House of Hope and Joy.

His real name is Merit Jackson, but everyone calls him "Lil Johnnie" now.

He knew Leah, the HHJ social worker.

Merit had dropped out of high school and lived on the streets. His life was the life of gangs, prostitution, drug deals and gun violence. He always managed to keep ahead of the police, until he unknowingly bought a stolen car.

For that offense -- in which he was completely innocent -- he served several years in prison. Instead of sitting there, becoming bitter and resentful, thinking up plots for revenge, he used his time very productively. He thought about all those poor decisions he had made, and wondered how he might help prevent other youth from making similar mistakes.

He wrote a novel -- called *Lil Johnnie Off The Block*. It's the story of "Lil Johnnie," a fictional character made up of a composite of his life and the lives of Merit's friends and family members.

When I met him, he was looking for ways to impact the lives of young people. He was also looking for ways to market his novel, so others might read his story and see hope in the possibilities for their own lives.

Giving young people the novel is a good first step. Having discussion groups was a good second step. But the best idea came from a conversation between Merit and Pete Roberts, a university professor and reading specialist: Why not make the story of "Lil Johnnie" into a literacy curriculum for high school students?

So that's what we set out to do.

We took a few of the subplots from his novel, and built up a few lessons around them. I tried them out at St. Augustine. They worked really well. Merit even came to a few classes; the students instantly liked him.

Let me articulate what we know is the secret to being successful with teenagers -- even urban teenagers. Even though so many people are afraid of these "tough" teenagers, it's really not hard to capture their hearts. You just have to care about them, listen to them, and be authentic. Funny how that's a difficult thing for most adults to do!

Anyway, with time, we started developing lesson plans -- complete with an original story, reflection questions, classroom activities, and creative homework assignments. We kept writing the stuff, field-testing it, and making adjustments.

What can I say about this program so far? I expected the students to like it, but I had no idea *how much* they would like it! The reluctant readers who never wanted to read a page had no problem reading the "Lil Johnnie" stories! The quiet students who hardly ever answered questions in class suddenly had opinions to express, personal stories to tell, and ideas about the issues raised by the stories. Low-achieving students who never turned in homework, and didn't work much on class work, never missed their "Lil Johnnie" homework. And the effort they put into their work far surpassed anything else they had ever done.

I was really impressed with the students' work. And impressed with Mr. Jackson's talent and creativity.

We continued to work with his ideas for the curriculum. Just as writing his novel helped him to work out issues in his life, I believe this type of reflective writing has begun to help my students work out the issues in their lives.

More about this later.

Chapter 33

Dear Kelvin,

Swimming has always been a big part of my life. If I don't swim half a mile two or three times a week, I don't feel quite right. I LOVE to swim.

Swimming can seem a little like jogging to some people. I see lots of people jogging all over the place -- dressed in short shorts and tank tops in the summer or in tights and caps in the winter. They never look very happy. They always look so exhausted. They look as if the only reason they are running forward is to prevent themselves from falling over completely. I know a few runners. They tell me they hate running. They just like how it feels afterward -- when it's all over and they know they have accomplished "something healthy."

I can't imagine doing something over and over, day after day and not enjoying it. Or worse, actually hating it! I don't feel that way about swimming at all. I only feel that way about diving in. I hate diving in or easing in. The water always seems so cold right away. It's such a shock to my whole system. I hate that part. On some days in the winter, I'll actually stare at the water, saying to myself, "Ugh. It's the last thing I want to do. Who wants to be cold and wet?" But some how, I take the plunge!

And then immediately, I regret it! Especially in the winter, I start shivering right away, and it sometimes takes a few laps before the shivering stops. I hate feeling so cold. But it doesn't last. Pretty soon, I am doing my strokes and loving it! Feeling athletic and spectacular!

I guess life is like that. There are so many things we avoid doing, things we put off because we think they won't be pleasant. And then we start, and we realize we were right. We wish we had never begun. But since we did, there's only one way to go -- straight through it. And that's what we do.

Swimming is like that. Cleaning a closet is like that. You hate to start the job. So you put if off and procrastinate, until finally, you need to get everything organized! So you start by taking everything out of the closet, and then your whole bedroom is a mess. Things look even worse than before. Especially if someone else sees it before you finish. What's that first response? "Ugh! This is even harder than I thought it would be! No wonder I didn't want to start this awful job! I'll never finish!"

But then after a while, you start throwing things out, or putting them in the "recycle" pile, or in the "Pretty good shape, so I'll bring it to House of Hope and Joy" pile, and before you know it, you are having fun and thinking, "Why did I wait so long before doing this?"

You put it off, because you know you will hate it in the beginning. But you also know that once it's over, you will be glad you did it.

Cleaning a closet, exercising, and I guess many other parts of life. Writing Christmas cards. Or thank-you cards. Spring cleaning, especially the windows. Or cleaning the refrigerator. Things like that.

Except, that's not exactly the way I feel about swimming. I'm not like those people who hate running, but feel good when it's over. I feel good while I'm swimming. In fact, I love most of it. Figure this. If I swim fifty laps, and only the first two or three are cold, that's pretty good. And in the summer, even the first two or three are pretty good.

People say to me, "It's so boring. I could never swim laps. All you see is water. All you hear is water. In fact, all you taste or smell or feel is water. There is no change of scenery. At least while I'm running, I can see people, cars, dogs, buildings, homes, action in the neighborhood. I can see how bushes grow over time, I can see how a construction project progresses. I can see the leaves turn from green to yellow to brown. When you swim you don't see anything."

All true. You really need to like water. You are completely alone when you swim, with no thoughts except your own. Even if you swim with someone, you are still alone. You only see them at the beginning and end.

Unless you swim really slowly, like some of the older folks, two in a lane, the slow side stroke, so that you can actually have a conversation while you do it. Yes, that way, you can keep company while you swim. But for most folks who do laps, we don't do it for the company. No, we just hit the water, do our strokes, do our turns, and are all alone with our thoughts.

I usually have the best thoughts, the best ideas, when I swim. Most importantly, I can have the best prayer.

I wish everyone could enjoy exercise. Whatever they do -- running, lifting weights, playing tennis, biking – if they could love it as much as I love swimming, then they would stick with it for life.

I really enjoy the YMCA where I swim. The locker room has a hot tub, and I love a fifty-minute swim and then ten minutes in the hot tub! It feels so terrific. My muscles relax, and I feel good, and I am ready to start the day. Some days I am in the pool by 6:00 AM. I realize I am done swimming before some people are even getting out of bed.

And I love watching the swimming events of the Summer Olympics! Most of all, I love all the slow-motion under-water camera shots of the back stroke flip turns.

One year, some of us at the Y were talking about the Olympics, and watching highlights on the TV in the break room. Ray came in. Ray was the swim coach and director of all the aquatic programs. He was funny and smart -- so you know those were the two things I always liked in a guy. And not only that, but he liked children. After Timothy left me, I started paying attention to that sort of thing.

Ray knew I had been a swim coach and used to give swim lessons, so from time to time, he would give me a call to see if I was interested in coming back to that summer career.

Well, we were talking about the "slo-mo" shots underwater and watching flip turns and all that, and he said that a few of the lifeguards started going to a nearby bar to watch the Olympics in the evening. He asked me to come that night. Since my only plans were to watch the Olympics anyway, I said sure.

I always found Ray to be fun and engaging, and he was so good with the kids. They loved him. I was actually surprised he was still single. I was told he had done a lot of dating, but never found the woman he wanted to settle down with.

We had a good time that night at the bar. Everyone was funny. The bar was one of those places like "Cheers" where everyone knows your name. At least they know the regulars. I obviously wasn't a "regular," but because we were a group from the YMCA showing up several nights during a two-week period, I did get the sense of what it would be like "to be a regular." And I can sort of understand why people would enjoy that type of bar atmosphere -- where everyone really does know your name and they are all glad you came!

So I showed up on my own and left on my own, so no one had any reason to think that Ray and I were an "item." I liked it that way. Even if we did start dating, I wanted our relationship to stay away from the YMCA, where people knew both of us. In case it didn't work out, I didn't want things to become awkward. I already knew the awkwardness of having to gently tell people over and over about my breakup with Timothy. Yes, marriage is bigger than other breakups, but I just didn't want anyone to know it if we started seeing each other. At least not in the beginning.

I guess we did start "seeing each other" after the Olympics. We had fun talking about it, so once the medals were won, and the athletes came back home to the USA, to their adoring fans, to the covers of *Sports Illustrated*, and to the Wheaties boxes, we kind of missed that fun. So we started going to movies every so often and watching TV at my place.

Ray's whole life seemed to be the YMCA. And the pool and the events and the budget and the equipment, and the kids. He did a great job managing it all, and I learned a lot about what goes into successful programming. For example, he worked a lot with the folks at the front reception counter. You may think that it's an easy job.

Say hello, take their cards, ask if they want towels, give them the locker key.

But when you think about it, the folks at the front counter are the first impression of every member's daily experience at the Y. It's the first part of every swim, every run, every session with weights. It's the first motivator, the first positive or negative influence.

If the greeters have enthusiasm and energy when you walk in, you feel better. You feel good to be alive. You feel optimistic. If they don't know you, don't care, and treat you as if you are a nameless nobody, then that's how you feel.

Ray trained them well. They memorize faces quickly, so they could call us by name before they saw our cards. I think, during slow times, they pulled out the cards and look at them again, to help them remember which names went with which faces.

They didn't just say, "Have a good workout." To swimmers they would say, "Have a good swim" and to joggers, "Have a good run." They didn't intrude, but they would show interest and talk with everyone about whatever was brought up.

Two women in particular were really sweet, Dorothy and Audrey. They were really special. I showed them family pictures, they would tell me about their families. I even brought them cookies for Christmas and Valentine's Day... things like that.

Ray always got every member of the staff involved in decisions regarding efforts like fund-raisers and "Health Awareness" weeks. During one membership drive, every day had a different color, and everyone on the staff would wear that color. They even had snacks of that color. Strawberries and twizzlers on red day, and bananas and lemonade on yellow day. It was such fun, it made us want to tell others to join the Y.

The color thing wasn't Ray's idea, but it came from a maintenance worker, Pedro. Someone many YMCA directors wouldn't have even listened to, let alone asked. I liked that about Ray. His sense of fairness. Everyone had a voice, even the people usually overlooked.

And his sense of humor! He told the swim team he wouldn't shave or cut his hair all season, and then if they placed at the state tournament, he would let randomly selected swimmers give him his first shave and haircut at the YMCA fun fest. They had such a blast with all of that. I guess he made that threat every year, but they didn't place every year, so I was glad to see it when it happened. Lots of clowning around and funny stuff happened. The audience ate it up. I think they brought in 20% more donations that year because of the publicity of the team's success and that hair thing. They gave him this terrible haircut, shaving half of one side of his head and half of the other side of his beard. The side that still had hair was shorter in the front and still way long in the back. They put ribbons in what was left of his beard. Ray just kept laughing and looking in the mirror, and everyone in the audience was laughing, too.

He kept his hair that way for a whole week!

So that was pretty much our relationship. We went to movies, had our favorite TV shows, and talked about the Y and House of Hope and Joy. He asked me to help him coach or start swim lessons again, and I'd tell him I was too busy. It was true. I was a teacher and already had a huge volunteer commitment at HHJ. I had done the coaching thing a while back, but how could I find the time for coaching a swim team now?

Funny think about Ray, though. I never felt really close to him. I wanted to become closer, but there didn't seem a way to do that.

I never met his family. Both his parents were still alive, but he hardly mentioned them. When I asked him questions, he would be very vague. After a while, I noticed his facts weren't always consistent. One time he told me he had two brothers, and another time he said he had one brother. When I said, "I thought you had two brothers..." he said, "Do you want me to have two brothers?"

Isn't that a strange thing to say? Why would I "want" him to have any number of brothers? I just wondered how many. He seemed defensive. "Does it matter if I have two brothers or one brother? Does it make any difference?"

I didn't know what to say, So I let it drop. But kept it in my "what's up with Ray?" mental file.

Another time, he was apparently going away for a few days, and I heard him tell someone he was going to visit his parents because it was his mother's birthday. Later, he told me he was visiting his parents for his father's birthday. I commented about how it must have been easy growing up and remembering his parents' birthdays, and he didn't seem to know what I was talking about. I said I had heard him say it was his mother's birthday and then later say it was his father's birthday. So I assumed they had birthdays close together. He seemed very annoyed and said something like, "Well you seem to be good at making assumptions."

I wondered... what was that supposed to mean?

So I pressed him. Maybe I shouldn't have. But it didn't make sense to me. Why would someone need to cover up or even lie about such things? So I asked, "Well, when are their birthdays?"

He responded with hostility. "Am I under oath? Do I need my own lawyer before I answer this question? Can anything I say be used against me later in a court of law? Yes, your honor! No, your honor! What's with all these questions?"

What was Ray trying to hide? Why would he make up stories when there was no reason to? I couldn't figure it out. I wondered, was he losing his hearing? And did he become embarrassed when he realized he hadn't understood the question, so he gave the wrong answer? Was there some other explanation? I kept thinking that he was such a nice guy, there had to be a reason for this to happen. So I kept putting up with it, wondering what to expect next.

Here's another strange thing. I never went to his home. Never. He never took me there. He wouldn't even give me his address. He refused to tell me where he lived. He kept asking why I needed to know. Doesn't that seem like a strange question? How can you be close to someone and not even know where that person lives? I had no home phone number. I always called him at work. He always called me from work. I was beginning to wonder if Ray actually lived at the Y.

Ray was just a little hard to figure out. He was inconsistent. I never really felt as if I understood where he was coming from. I think he just liked to keep me guessing. Maybe that was all it was.

In the beginning, it was unclear if he wanted to date me, or if we were just going to be friends. We'd do things together -- meet at the movies, meet for supper someplace -- but there would be no affection. That was fine with me. I was learning to always take things slowly. I was so mixed up about relationships anyway, that I did not want to jump into anything too soon.

And then the dating slowly began. We would go someplace and kiss good night. And then a few "traditions" would start. Here's an example. He watched *Seinfeld* with me every week. After a while, I didn't even invite him, he just came. But as soon as it started to feel like a pattern, he seemed to decide not to come. For no reason. He just didn't come. I'd ask him later, "How come you didn't come over to watch *Seinfeld* last night?"

"Did you ask me to come over?"

"No. But you usually do."

"Usually? What's usually?"

"Well, almost every week for a month."

"Is that so? And so now you expect it from me? Are you taking me for granted?"

"Well, I guess if you do something four times in a row, I guess I do figure that maybe you'll do it the fifth time. Isn't that logical?"

"Yes, your honor. You are correct. In fact, it is logical. You recorded these past events on the official calendar, so now you have the evidence. You are justified. I have no defense. I am illogical. Case closed."

"It's not that big a deal. It's just that I thought you liked coming over."

"Why would I want to come over? What do you have to offer? What's in it for me?

"I just thought you kind of... liked me. I thought that was enticing enough..."

"Boy, you really are funny! You are a regular comedian!"

"Fine. You don't have to come over if you don't want to!"

"No, I most certainly don't have to do anything I don't want to do!"

So I thought we broke up. Doesn't that sound like a break up? In fact, doesn't this sound like an episode on *Seinfeld*?

He never called to say, "I'm sorry I acted like a jerk." So of course we had broken up!

I certainly wasn't going to call to apologize. I couldn't imagine what I would apologize for. "I'm sorry I wondered why you stopped coming over?" or "I'm sorry I thought you liked me?"

In a way, I was almost relieved. But I caught myself thinking, "I'll miss Ray's company when I watch *Seinfeld* alone this week."

Then, to my surprise, he showed up on the regular night. With Chinese takeout. When I acted surprised, he answered, "What's so surprising? *Seinfeld*'s on tonight, isn't it?"

I started to protest, saying, "But you said..."

He cut me off. "There you go again. What am I, on the witness stand? Do you have to quote my own words to me? Am I on trial? Your honor, I object! Let's just eat, watch *Seinfeld* and have a good time. Is that too much to ask?"

I just could not figure this whole thing out. It didn't make any sense to me. How did he make me feel so ridiculous when it was clear that he was the ridiculous one?

You know, that whole, "approach/avoidance" thing? When a guy only finds you attractive during the time he is trying to win you over, and then once he's won you over, he only enjoys it for a short while. As soon as he realizes that he has you, the "thrill of the chase" is gone, and he somehow doesn't feel the same way. So he starts coming by less and less frequently, or he seems less interested. And so you figure, "OK, enough with him. That's over, and I'll move on." But then he's back again! And suddenly, he wants to win you back again, and he's sending flowers or showing up with Chinese takeout, wanting you to like him again, wanting to be affectionate all over again. It makes you crazy!

So you don't want to get involved, because you know it's just going to end badly, so you resist. But as you keep resisting, he keeps persisting. Why? Because it's the "thrill of the chase," I guess! He finally wins you over... again... and you are back in a reliable relationship.

So you think it was all worth it. You figure he just went through some weird phase or rough patch, and now he's going to be normal, and things will work out. He's learned what it takes to be in a relationship. Sigh of relief!

But it only lasts a few weeks or so, because then he gets bored again! And he says he's coming over, but he doesn't show up, and he doesn't call. And so you don't eat supper, because you don't want him to show up with a pizza after you just finished your frozen leftovers. Or you don't get started on this major project you really want to tackle because that will mess up your apartment, and you want everything to look so welcoming when he finally comes, so he can look around and say, "Yes, I miss this place. I feel so comfortable and relaxed here." So you waste the whole evening doing nothing, watching dumb TV shows you don't want to watch, just in case he still comes, and he never comes.

And you say to yourself, "I have had it with him and his inconsistency!"

And then the next time he says he's coming, you don't believe it. You start to clean your closet. You put it off long enough, and now is the day to clean it out. So what if he calls and says he's coming over. He said that twice before and didn't come and never called to apologize! Those times, you fell asleep on the couch waiting! This time, you won't believe him, and you won't care if the place is a mess. At least you'll get your closet clean, and you'll feel better about yourself.

And of course, that's when he shows up with a pizza -- and bread sticks! -- and he looks around and says, "Wow. This place is a mess!" and you just want to pull your hair out!

Why do guys do that? Is the thrill of the chase really that terrific? Are they really so shallow that they need the "approach" and "avoid" dance to relieve the boredom of their lives? Are they really so scared of a regular relationship that they don't even mind being rude and inconsiderate? Do they really have no idea what they are doing to someone?

Are these the same questions women are asking about men all over?

And why do some of us women keep going out with losers like this?

Probably because we figure at least when he shows up, it's better than being alone.

But is it? Is it really better than being alone?

Or is being alone a little like diving into the pool? It stings a little when it first happens, but after a lap or two, you wonder why you put it off so long?

And after another five laps, you love it?

Because... being alone is better than being with someone and still feeling lonely!

It took a while for me to figure that out. I thought if I felt lonely when I was with someone, imagine how lonely I'd feel if I were actually alone!

But no -- it's actually better to be alone than to feel lonely with someone else. If being with someone else makes you feel lonely, than that relationship isn't worth the time, the effort, or the energy. If being with someone makes you feel awkward, self-conscious or confused, it's better to get out of that relationship. It's not helping! It's not moving you forward in life! It's not making you a better person, and it's not making him a better person!

If you are spending all that time with someone who is not making your life better, who is not making you a better person, who is not causing you happiness, and who is making you lonely, what are you doing? You are wasting time and going backwards in life!

Why did it take me so long to figure that out?

Why does it take many women so long to figure that out?

Why do so many men continue these types of annoying and inconsiderate habits? Why do women put up with them?

And how can the women of the world teach this awareness to the clueless men of the world?

I don't know. It's not my problem.

But it does sound like an episode of *Seinfeld!*

It reminds me of jogging: Doing the same thing over and over, not enjoying it. Hating it. But feeling happy when it finally stops.

Do I sound bitter? I was... but I'm not anymore. I don't have to solve Ray's problems, figure Ray out, wonder how many brothers he has or when his parents' birthdays are or where he lives.

So I guess you could say we just drifted apart. I stopped being available when he called. I stopped wandering over to his office after swimming laps, and eventually, he stopped calling. It ended kind of like that. Gradually, so there was no actual "breakup" moment or final words. I wave hello when I happen to see him around the Y. Not very often, but every once in a while.

Once we stopped hanging out, no one even noticed! I was glad about that. One thing about breakups... they don't happen in a vacuum. Everyone ends up being part of it, having an opinion, feeling disappointed and wondering what went wrong. If people just see you as "friends," then when you finally "break up," no one is really upset. No one knows. Because if you were just "casual" friends to begin with, and you can remain "casual" friends (ever so casual) then the ripples of that breakup don't go very far... to use another water image.

I also learned that honesty and openness are important to me. It's hard to trust someone who isn't honest and open. Ray was the opposite of honest and open.

That's how "honest and open" became as important as "smart and funny and spiritual" on my list of things to look for in a serious relationship. And "loves children," as well.

Ray and I didn't have much in common beyond swimming and *Seinfeld*. That's not enough to create a relationship.

I guess that's about all there is to say about Ray.

I still swim at the Y. I still enjoy the laps and the hot tub. He still asks me to coach or teach swim lessons every so often. I just smile. Every four years, when the Summer Olympics come around, I think about going over to that bar, just to watch the swimmers in slow motion do their flip turns. But I never go.

Chapter 34

Dear Sister Agnes,

I was thinking about swimming recently and about how I sometimes hesitate before diving in because the water seems so cold at first.

I thought about how life can be like that, especially spiritual life.

I thought about having two people talk about Lent in that way. Lent is something that many people hate starting. They do not look forward to it. It's a time to clean out your spiritual closet and get rid of all that junk that's just dragging you down and creating clutter -- the stuff that makes it hard to see what's really important in life.

But people hate to start cleaning their closets, because then the whole room is a total mess. It seems worse than before, because then the mess was at least contained and hidden. Now the mess is everywhere, and you have to really deal with it and get everything organized.

Some people plunge into Lent, and some just sit on the edge and let their feet dangle.

I thought that swimming might make a good spiritual metaphor. So I wrote this poem about it.

It's about two people at work having a conversation about Ash Wednesday. Each of them has a different response to the season of Lent, which they discover as they talk...

ASHES and Ash Wednesday

Wow. Ash Wednesday already. I almost forgot.

Yup. I went to early church this morning.

It's obvious. I noticed your ashes immediately. That's what reminded me. You know, in some ways, I hate Lent. All this talk about suffering. It's so unsettling.

Well, don't take it so seriously.

Really? Says the head that bears the ashes ...

OK, so I got up early and got my ashes. I'm marked as a Christian all day. Do I also have to worry about suffering? Isn't the symbol of ashes enough?

Are you fasting?

I guess. I haven't had time yet to eat today.

Abstaining from meat?

Uh, remember? I'm a vegetarian! I do that anyway...

Oh yeah. So you kind of just go through the motions and don't really think about it?

I think about it. I wore my purple sweater today. I just don't let the whole suffering thing ruin my life.

See, that's what I mean. I'm reluctant every Lent because I always seem to re-learn painful lessons. You know, the mark of ashes in a cross. Ultimately, we're nothing but ashes. Destined to carry the cross. Yet somehow all Children of God. Doesn't that just boggle your mind a little?

Whoa. You're really taking all this *way* too seriously!

Did you get your CRS Rice Bowl?

Sure did. It's on the kitchen table.

Do you read the prayers? Look at the faces of those children? Put in coins every week?

I'll write my check on Palm Sunday -- same as last year.

And it doesn't change you?

What do you want me to do -- go to Africa?

Well, no. Well, not unless you want to. But, well, praying makes me feel so... unworthy. But feeling closer to God makes me so aware of all my blessings. It's always kind of confusing. I have to sort it all out...

OK. So what? So what's wrong with that?

Nothing's wrong with it. But then fasting and trying to live a more simple life makes me think of all the luxuries I have and don't really need. The ways I waste resources. Like water. Like food. Like clothes I buy -- just for fashion. When so many other people in this country and across the globe have so little. It's not fair. It's not just.

See -- there you go with the suffering bit. That's when I draw the line. I just ignore that part. That's what I mean -- you are taking this Lent thing way over the top.

I don't know. I do like how it changes me. It's suddenly not enough for me to put coins in the rice bowl. I feel a need to volunteer at the soup kitchen. Or go on our parish mission trip and build houses.

You actually did all that last year?

Yeah, I actually did. Spring and summer, I guess I turn into a regular social activist!

Then what happens?

I don't know. Fall comes. Things change. It gets cold. You regroup and forget. You start Christmas shopping. It's hard to keep up the momentum.

So you turn into a saint every Lent, and it only lasts a season or two. And you're feeling guilty because you're not a saint all year-round? Wow! I'm impressed that you did that stuff at all! You should be proud of yourself! What's the problem?

It's like swimming laps.

Huh?

I love to swim. But every morning, I stand at the edge of the pool, hesitating. I hate to dive in. I just hate that initial sting of cold water. It only takes a few laps to warm up, and then I'm loving it. But every morning, I still hesitate at the pool's edge.

I never do laps.

No?

Never really liked to swim. I like the water. It's pretty to look at. And I like to dangle my legs over the side of the pool on a hot sunny day. But I'm not one for laps. Too boring.

Well, it's just you and God. Lots of time to think and reflect and work things out. Good exercise for the body. Good exercise for the soul. Kind of reminds me of baptism, I guess.

Hmm. I guess I do Lent the way I do water...

Yeah?

Yeah. I'll wear the ashes, but I won't dive in. I'll dip my feet into Lent, but I won't get too involved. But you! You hesitate at the pool's edge because you know what's coming. Then you dive right in and swim a mile! I think that's how we're different.

Wow. That's quite an insight.

Yea. I guess you are making me think.

I guess it's time for me to think about getting my ashes. There must be a noon Mass downtown.

I guess it's time for me to take a deeper plunge into this whole Lent thing.

Call me if the water's too much of a shock at first. I'll talk you into it.

OK. Call me next time you plan to work at the soup kitchen. I just might come with you.

Chapter 35

Dear Kelvin,

One more Ray story. Sort of.

Well, OK. Two separate Ray stories. I just wanted to write them down. I think they might be significant.

First Ray Story:

One time, I mentioned a movie I wanted to see. It had been showing for a long while, but I just never got around to seeing it. Finally, when I checked all the theatres, it was only playing for one more day in one last location. I mentioned this to Ray. He agreed to come with me and see the movie.

He said he'd be out of town that day, but he'd be back in time for the last showing. I asked him, "Where are you going?" and his response was, "That doesn't matter. What matters is that I'll be back in time to make the movie."

I found this annoying. "Is there a reason you aren't willing to tell me where you will be?"

"That's not a valid question. Why is it so important for you to know where I am? That has nothing to do with the truth of the situation. I said I would be back in time."

I pushed the issue, because this was truly beginning to bother me. "Two people develop trust by being open and honest with each other. When you insist on withholding information from me, I feel my trust level decreasing, and that's never good for a relationship."

"Do you not trust that I will be back in time?"

"I don't think that's the issue!" I continued, "When you ask me a question, I tell you an answer. I don't say that the answer to your question is unimportant or invalid. If you are asking, then it's a valid question for you. Sometimes I think you just like being secretive."

"That's an assumption you are making, not based on any facts at all."

"It's hard to base something on facts, when the facts are withheld from me. I have no choice but to make good guesses, based on the small amount of information I'm allowed to know."

"I think you are just showing how insecure you are," he said as he walked out the door. "I'll see you tomorrow night, in time for the movie."

I was surprised at how angry this exchange made me. He was just being ridiculous. When I propose that he likes being secretive, *because he is in fact keeping his whereabouts secret from me,* then he says I'm making assumptions not based on facts.

But he's not making an assumption when he says I am insecure?

So in this relationship, we play by two different sets of rules. He is allowed to make wild assumptions that are not based on fact. Yet, I am not allowed to make assumptions that are very obviously implied by his specific behavior.

I continued to analyze this in my head. He keeps information secret for no apparent reason and finds it unreasonable for me to assume he enjoys keeping secrets. Even though someone who freely chooses to do a particular behavior often (such as "keeping secrets") is by definition a person who likes that behavior ("being secretive").

I was annoyed with him all day. He made it back in time for that movie, but he never mentioned what he did that day, or why he wouldn't tell me. I never found out. But I hardly enjoyed the movie. He never apologized; I am certain he still sees nothing wrong with the way he treated me. I was still so irritated because he wouldn't answer my simple question and then had the nerve to accuse me of being insecure.

This was another red flag that made me realize I was not in a stable relationship. It's impossible to have a stable relationship with a person who is vague, inconsistent and seems to enjoy keeping you guessing all the time. That's not how you treat someone you care about. It's disrespectful, inconsiderate and immature. On top of that, to defend that kind of behavior and then accuse the person of being "insecure" is even more irritating.

What's really strange is how I still get so angry just thinking about how he manipulated me. It happened so long ago, and yet it still makes me mad when I remember what he put me through.

I should have just told him that I was no longer interested in playing those games, but I didn't know how to say it yet. And he wouldn't have heard it. In fact, he would have used that conversation as another opportunity for more game-playing!

So I never said anything. I just slowly let the relationship end. It was less direct that way, and we never had to do the big "breakup" scene. Looking back, I do think that was best.

Second Ray Story:

Some time after we drifted apart, Ray called me. He said Pedro's daughter was getting married. Then he asked me if I would go with him to the wedding.

I didn't answer right away.

He sensed the awkwardness of the silence, and so he added, "just as friends."

I said, "OK."

I mean, why not? We could go as friends. No one would know the difference. If I didn't go with him, I'd end up sitting with him anyway, because Pedro didn't know we had been dating at one time, but then we stopped dating. Pedro would have thought he was putting two "YMCA" friends at the same table with all the other YMCA people.

So I said, "OK."

And why not? I didn't know Pedro well, but he always smiled at me, and I always smiled at him. And eventually, I asked him his name, and after that, I always called him by name and said hi. Or actually, sometimes I said *Buenos Dias*. And he asked my name, and so we greeted each other by name when we saw each other. That's something I loved about the YMCA. Everyone really wanted to get to know you, but they didn't press you. They didn't make you feel uncomfortable. They just made you feel comfortable. Cared about. Almost like family.

Once I saw Pedro and his family at their church, *Prince de Paz*. Prince of Peace. I was visiting there for a program

I was doing for youth in the city. What a beautiful family Pedro has. Three daughters all dressed up. His wife Juanita, beaming. He was so delighted to see me. He kissed me on both cheeks, and then so did Juanita! I loved that he was so delighted. I heard him explain to her (in Spanish) that I swim at the YMCA. She was delighted to see me at their church!

"Oh! You swim at the Y, where Pedro works! *Qué Bueno*! Two more kisses for you!"

How could someone be that sweet? But they were! They were both so adorable!

So how could I say no to Pedro? How could I say, "No, I will not attend your daughter's wedding"? Impossible!!!

Of course I would go!

I'll be honest. I had mixed feelings. Not only because I was going with Ray, but because I was going to a wedding at all. I hadn't been to a wedding since Timothy left me. I wasn't sure I really wanted to go and witness wedding vows. I wasn't sure how I would feel. But I didn't know how to say no.

So of course I went!

I wore a nice dress... not too showy, not too dressy, but dressy enough for a wedding. It was modest and tasteful. And I wore a shawl. I didn't want to look too sexy, and give Ray the wrong idea. But I wanted to look respectfully dressy. And I felt awkward the moment Ray picked me up at my place.

"You look nice." He said. What was he supposed to say? I think the guy always has to say that when he comes and picks up a gal for a date, even if it's not a date.

So I said, "So do you." I sort of lied. Well, he didn't look bad. But I didn't actually care. I guess he looked good to an objective person who wasn't trying to figure out why he had been such a jerk in the past. But once you act like a jerk, you never really look as cute. That's the way my brain works, anyway.

To me, lots of sex appeal is internal. The more I like you, the cuter you are. If you treat me badly, I don't find you attractive, even if you just walked off the cover of a magazine and look like a movie star.

Ray and I drove to the church, and we went to the wedding.

It really was quite an ordeal for me. I didn't realize how awful it would be. I hated to cry so much. Pedro and Juanita must have been touched that I cared so much about their daughter. But of course, you know that's not why I was crying...

I was crying for myself and for the cynical way I felt about weddings.

So much money spent on a wedding day. Why does this woman need eight bridesmaids? What do all those girls do? And why does it take eight men to bring everyone to their seats? There is only one aisle, and they all had to take turns.

It wasn't really a "Mexican" thing. I know Pedro didn't have this kind of money. Pedro was much too humble to put on this kind of show. I could see it in his eyes. I think he was half embarrassed, half amazed by the whole thing.

I think it was an American "we love excess" thing. It's a "We have to spend a fortune because this is the way we show everyone how successful we are" thing. Ray mentioned that the groom's father was very wealthy. I wondered what the groom's father did for a living. The groom's father was white, and his mother was Latina.

All those flowers, and dresses, and tux rentals, and the white carpet they roll down the aisle, and the little cute flower girls dropping rose petals all along the way, and the little cute ring bearer carrying the pillow with the fake rings pinned to it because you'd never pin the real rings to a pillow and give it to a four year old...

The big, poofy, awkward wedding dress with the long train that keeps needing readjustment.

Oh! That's why the eight girls are needed! This dress was way too much work for just the maid of honor. It took two more girls to keep moving the bride's train so it always looked picture perfect. And then it took another three girls to hold the flowers of the three girls who were fixing the train, so that whole task occupied six girls. And then it took the other two bridesmaids to hold the hands of the two little flower girls, who were quite a handful because they were three and four, and children that age can only behave well for so long before getting tired and cranky...

And the vows!

They were in Spanish first, but that didn't matter. I could still understand what was being said.

Do you take this woman, for better or worse, for richer or poorer, in sickness and in health, in good times and bad, all the days of your life? Even if you decide you don't want children? Even though you said you wanted them? Even though you know her biological clock is ticking? Even though you know that she will feel like a complete failure and be humiliated for the rest of her life if you leave her until death due you part?

And he answers, yes, I am saying I will never leave you no matter what, even though I know that many marriages end in divorce. And if I do leave you, because I never changed my name, it won't have that much of an effect on me because no one will know the difference, so no big deal, even though I know that you will have to go through hell when you change your name back because everyone will know that you are a marked, divorced woman, barren without children, abandoned for no good reason, because even though I tell you I don't want children, I will go out and find another woman who already has some, just so we can make some more, and humiliate your further and make you feel completely confused and rejected and utterly worthless.

I now pronounce you husband and wife for the time being... until he breaks his vow and leaves you.

It was all said in Spanish... and that's a very loose translation... but it's the basic idea.

By the time they repeated all of that in English, I wasn't even listening anymore...

I never thought it would hit me that hard. But it did. I could not stop the waterworks pouring from my eyeballs and nose, emptying into my mouth, falling off my chin, spilling onto the floor. They weren't those dainty tears that you can dab and hope you don't smear your mascara. (I don't wear makeup, so that's never a problem for me.) These were the pathetic, sobbing tears of someone ashamed of who she was.

Kelvin, I think it was you who told me that guilt was when you realize that you did something bad, that you made an awful mistake, and you felt horrible about *your actions.* But shame was when you realized that you yourself are bad, and that you yourself are an awful mistake, and that you feel horrible about *who you are.* Only you can't change you. So you just cry and cry and want to hide and never come back out.

So I cried and cried and wanted to hide. And that was really OK. Because it was a wedding, and everyone just looked at me and marveled at how much everyone loved each other at the YMCA. It was such a close group. Like a family.

Chapter 36

Dear Kelvin,

I guess it's time to write about Adam again.

Thinking about Pedro and Juanita and their daughter's wedding, and my reaction...

I do know that a big part of my sorrow wasn't because I was with Ray or because I hate big, poofy wedding dresses...

And it wasn't only because Timothy left me.

Timothy wasn't my first love. My real first love was Adam. I guess seeing a wedding reminded me not only of the marriage that failed, but of the marriage that never got its chance.

Remember what I said about grief? When the pain comes, it brings with it all the unresolved pain from before. Losing Timothy was like losing Adam all over again, and even a little like losing my dad all over again...

Hmm... I have tried not to think so much about Adam, but it's no use.

I got so close to marrying my soul mate... and I was completely shattered when he left me...

I don't even remember what happened right away. I think I was in shock.

At first, I didn't believe it. When our wedding day came -- that day that was supposed to have been our wedding day -- I thought he would call me. I was certain he would. I prayed that he would. I planned it all out in my head. I would forgive him completely. We would still get married eventually. I would take him back. That special day could still be an anniversary, because it would be the day we got back together again.

But at midnight, when I realized he was not calling me, I went to my box of scrapbooks. I went through every page. I cried and cried. Page after page of smiling faces... Adam's face... my face... our faces together... smile after smile of two friends growing up... two people in love..

Hours later, around 3:00 or 3:30 in the morning, I started to tear out the pages. Every page -- I tore every single page out of the binding! I ripped and tore and ripped and tore ...

I didn't tear up the pictures, mind you. I just tore the pages out of the book. I needed to keep hearing that "**R-R-R-R-RIP!**" sound and feel as if I were destroying something precious. Probably because something precious had been destroyed in me. In fact, I felt as if I were being destroyed.

I never threw out those scrapbook pages. I guess deep down, I knew I loved Adam too much for that. Eventually I just put them all back into a box. I taped it all up with nose tape and put it away.

It was all so mysterious. For years -- for our whole life -- he was my best friend. Whenever he looked into my eyes, I felt all filled up with love and admiration and gratitude and delight...

But the closer we got to the wedding, and the wedding plans, and finding the apartment, and filling it up with "our" stuff, the less comforting his gaze became when we talked about our future. I couldn't put my finger on it or figure it out. He said everything was fine. And he insisted everything was fine, until he suddenly left with no explanation.

So it's easy to see why I fell apart. I didn't want to live any more. He was my life. He was my whole life. Without him, what good was life? What *was* life? I didn't even know who I was without him! I didn't know how to live! Who was the "me of us" if there was no "us"?

I had so much sadness, so much grief, the tears just poured out of me. My shirt was soaked. I was creating a waterfall, I was out of control with weeping and sobbing. My chest hurt, and I think I became dehydrated.

I was so confused. How could this be happening? What did it all mean? I only knew that he didn't love me enough to marry me. Yet he had loved me as long as I could remember.

For days, maybe weeks, I didn't want to see anyone. I just stayed hidden. I wouldn't do anything or go any place. My heart hurt so much, I was certain I would have a heart attack and die, and that would have been just fine with me.

Better to end life that way than to continue this endless existence that had no meaning and never would have any meaning... or so I thought at the time.

I hated being the person Adam "used to love," the person Adam deemed "not good enough" for marriage.

Our families tried to remain close, and for a while, it was all very awkward. Everyone was so sad for me. And so very angry with Adam. They couldn't understand how he could hurt me that way. They couldn't understand why he would string me along and dump me, or how he could fall in love and then out of love so quickly, and for no reason.

Nothing brought me any comfort. I just felt pathetic. I was probably clinically depressed.

Apparently, Adam also got depressed after the breakup. He became a hermit. He even tried hinting that I was the one who had broken up. When those stories got back to me, I was very upset. I wrote him a letter once, but he didn't write back. I guess he just had nothing to say.

I saw him maybe a year later. He was so obviously confused and in such pain, that I couldn't stay angry. My heart melted for him. I wondered if he was suffering from some kind of mental illness.

OK I have to stop writing now... this is just too painful.

Chapter 37

Dear Kelvin,

I thought about giving this one to Agnes, but it's too controversial. She'd want me to say more. She'd probably get me to write more about my feelings. Forget that nonsense!

But I wanted to record it for you.

I did think about sending a copy to Sr. Sylvia... she might understand.

It's a made-up conversation among Eve, Mary and Phoebe.

Eve is the Eve from Adam and Eve, the first two people. Mary is the mother of Jesus. And Phoebe is a leader of the early church. We don't know much about her, but Paul mentions her name.

This past Sunday, at church, we heard the reading about Adam and Eve being made of the same bone and flesh. We also heard the gospel about Jesus wanting the children to come to him and be blessed, even though his disciples thought that the children would be a bother. In this gospel, Jesus teaches that a man and woman joined in marriage are no longer two, but one flesh. As you can imagine, this was a tough Sunday for me.

Phoebe's not really in any of the readings, but we needed a mysterious church leader whose opinions we would never know in order for her to be the voice of certain women... so I'm taking liberties with Phoebe, but that's OK. I'm not trying to publish this. it's not for a Scripture class. I'm just playing around with the ideas...

A conversation among Eve, Mary and Phoebe

Eve:

I don't know what it's like to try and find a husband these days. I was created for Adam, and we knew we were meant for each other! Quite literally!

Phoebe:

Finding a good husband is not always so easy.

Mary:

Even if you find a saint, it's not easy! And it's no picnic being a widow, either. The sadness is overwhelming.

Phoebe:

The sadness of a breakup is just as overwhelming as death. Sometimes it's worse. When a husband dies, you know it's part of life. He didn't choose it. But when your husband decides to leave you, it's not only loneliness and grief. It's also profound rejection by the person you loved and trusted more than anyone.

Mary:

Men used to divorce their wives for trivial reasons. Someone else younger and more beautiful would catch their eye. And that could mean more children, more descendents, higher status in the community. It was really kind of selfish for those men to leave the women who loved them, and who raised their children. That's why my Jesus preached against it.

Eve:

Well, a marriage should be the most intimate relationship you have. Bone of my bone, flesh of my flesh. The two becoming one. Joined by God, not ever separated by any human being.

Phoebe:

That's just not always possible. Yes, I know that's the ideal. But you can only be the best partner possible. You cannot control your husband. You can't force him to love you always and be the best partner as well. No. It takes two dedicated people to make a good marriage. But it only takes one person to ruin a marriage.

Eve:

What's your story, Phoebe? Were you ever married?

Phoebe:

I'd rather not talk about my life. That's not the point.

Eve:

What *is* the point?

Phoebe:

Building on what Mary said. Jesus understood the holiness of marriage. The unselfish and other-centered love of family. The blessing of children.

Mary:

"The kingdom of God belongs to children." That's why Jesus loved to hug them and bless them.

Phoebe:

Exactly. Our children are precious. And sometimes, there are painful forces that tear families apart and make sacramental marriage impossible. Like domestic abuse, or addictions or mental health issues. Sometimes a mother has to leave her husband, for the sake of the children. It's horrible. It's a tragedy. But sometimes it's the only healthy choice.

Mary:

And most likely, in those situations, the husband who is violent or addicted to destructive substances was really never capable of making an authentic marriage commitment in the first place.

Phoebe:

And yet very often, the single mother with children gets blamed. Society looks down on such people. Not only are they heartbroken, but they become isolated and feel ashamed for their situation.

Eve:

Hey, I'm just saying it's important to uphold marriage, and celebrate children. To have high standards and high ideas. To honor commitments and be generous instead of selfish. Marriage is the ideal. Marriage is what God intended for us.

Phoebe:

And I'm just saying it's also important to be realistic and nonjudgmental. To be understanding and accepting of people struggling because of failed marriages. To not be so quick to dismiss them as selfish or unworthy. You don't know their story.

Mary:

I think Jesus was able to do both: uphold marriage and celebrate children... **and then also** embrace those who are struggling because of failed marriages.

Phoebe:

I think the Church needs to do both as well. And so should all of God's people.

Chapter 38

Dear Kelvin,

One Mother's Day weekend, when I was in high school, Adam and I went shopping for our moms. He wanted to get cut flowers for his mom. I wanted a plant.

I bought her a cactus. Adam laughed because it was just a big chunk of green. We couldn't really be sure it was even alive. But I thought my mother would like it because she liked cactus plants.

Well, she loved it. And it just started to grow and grow. It grew to the ceiling! And every so often, it had a cactus flower, with a white bloom as big as your fist.

It actually bloomed the night my father died.

He died at age 53. Not much older than I am now.

When I was in that college poetry class, I wrote a poem about my dad. I had expected him to enjoy being a grandfather to my children. Wrong on both counts. I never gave birth to any children, and he never lived long enough to have seen them anyway.

This silly poem still hangs in my mother's bedroom. This is it:

Daddy?
He's big and he's strong
And he's smart
And he tells me football.
And I hold on his neck when he takes me swimming and I won't drown.
He makes me things
He has a real live dead man's skull -- honest!

He lets me comb out the hairies on his arms.
And I know he can make the sick people better.
And he smells real nice!

My dad?
He's a physician.
And he likes to tinker around in the basement and plan his next big project.
He made me a footstool that has a drawer in it.
I think it's my favorite thing.
He gets so tan in the summer.
And he's always eating tomatoes.
You should hear him laugh when he thinks something is really funny.

My father?
He's quite a character.
I miss him.
I miss the way his bronze-colored skin shines in the sun.
And the way he grins boyishly when he asks me if I'd like to split a tomato with him.
Then he finishes my half.
But most of all, you should see his eyes sparkle the first time he sees me after a long separation.

Grandpa?
Of course he's still coming! He'll be here soon.
And he'll fix that boo-boo on your finger so it's good as new.
I'd better go slice the tomatoes.
No, Honey, I'm not crying because I'm sad.
Sometimes mommies cry when they are very happy.

My brother Phil bought a building for his medical office. On the 15th anniversary of my father's death, we blessed that building and dedicated it to my father.

My mom told me, "Wait 'til you see that cactus plant! It is full of blooms!"

All week, every night, another bloom or two opened. What giant flowers! I was afraid the plant would fall over. For some reason, we counted the blooms. **There were fifteen.** One for every year!

That cactus finally died -- I was sad when it happened. But was glad it had brought such joy to my mother for so long... and to all of us.

I remembered having lots of dreams about my dad when he first died -- maybe once a week for a while. Then at least once a month.

In each of these dreams, I saw him, and I knew he had died, and I was aware that this was an incredible opportunity to talk with him and ask him all kinds of questions. But I was never able to get him to sit down and actually talk with me. Something always happened, and he always seemed to vanish.

One dream I remember vividly:

I saw him at a party, and I was able to get over to him before he turned a corner, or went through the door and disappeared.

He saw me and smiled and waited for me to come over to him. This rarely happened in my dreams. I said, "Let's go someplace where we can talk!" He agreed! I couldn't wait to get away from the party and spend some quality time with him! I couldn't wait to hug him again!

He said, "Did you drive here? Just follow me. I know just the place."

I said, "Why don't you come in my car?" No, he didn't want to do that.

"OK, I'll come in your car." No, he didn't want to have to drive me back to my car.

"Just follow me."

I said, "OK, but keep looking back to see that I'm still there. Make sure I don't lose you."

So we drove off. And he was driving faster and faster. We were going up the side of a mountain, and the road was narrow, and it curved suddenly, and the drop off was very steep. I was frightened, but I was unwilling to lose him. I was going so fast, I was afraid for my safety, but I kept close behind.

He was trying to make a sharp turn, but he didn't quite make it. He went flying off the side of the mountain. I watched the car fall and thought, "OH NO! I lost him again!"

And then I decided, "Oh, no I didn't! I'm going after him!" and I purposely drove right off the cliff, right after him.

I awoke abruptly as my car hit the ground and smashed. I woke up. I was breathing hard and sweating. I could hardly fall asleep the rest of the night. That dream had shaken me up so much... thinking that I was willing to drive off the cliff of a mountain in order to not lose sight of my father.

But somehow, toward the morning, I did fall asleep again for just a short time. And I found myself dreaming that I was in my car at the bottom of a mountain. I could see right through my car and could see right through my dad's car. I could see we were looking at each other.

"Are you all right?" he asked me.

"Yes, I think I am. Are you?"

He smiled and said, "I'm always all right" (meaning that he had already died, so he was a spirit now, so nothing could really hurt him).

Then I remembered I had driven off a cliff and plunged from the top of a mountain. I realized since I was seeing through my car, there was a good possibility that I was also dead.

I asked him, "Am I 'always all right' now, too?"

He said, "I don't think so. But you don't know right away."

"When do you know?" I asked him.

"When you never wake up," he said.

At the words "wake up," I woke up. And I realized I hadn't died. And I still hadn't had the chance to talk with my dad the way I wanted. But I felt certain the chance would eventually come.

Chapter 39

Dear Kelvin,

I love working with House of Hope and Joy. I love working with teenagers.

Could this be my vocation? I think it must be.

I know what we do is needed. I know what we do makes a difference. I know I work shoulder to shoulder with men and women who believe in service, dream of justice, and teach respect and fairness.

Let me just say a few things about our Clean Teen program...

They are really great young people. Many of them come from difficult backgrounds. Many of them grow up in single parent homes. Most of the single parents are mothers. Some are grandmothers. As one grandmother told me, "Please watch over my grandson. He's a good kid. I want to keep him growing up in the right way. His daddy's in jail and his mama's messed up. Where else is he gonna go? What he needs is a li'l hope and joy. I don't know anyplace that can give him that, 'cept maybe y'all. Please teach him the ways of God."

This grandmother's life must be filled with grief. She's too old to be taking care of Jaquez. But all she sees in that boy is hope for a positive future and joy for his potential. And she really believes we can make a difference. We can't "keep our teens clean" because as you know, it's their decision to keep clean. But we can give them opportunities so they find a reason to stay clean, to keep doing what it takes to avoid the things that take away their "clean" lives...

So far, so good with Jaquez. We don't seem to lose too many to the streets, but some of them give us a scare now and then.

Just last year, two different times, two different moms called me up to tell me the same story. "My son hasn't been home for two days. I don't know where he is. Did he call you? Do you know anything at all?"

No, I never know. Teenagers don't let me know when they take off like that. I just pray they stay safe and come back -- in one piece -- without a criminal record, without any bad scars, without having had an abortion, without a gun, without having lost their... hope and joy.

But I have to tell you, both times, the teenagers came back fairly soon. Neither one missed more than one of our meetings. I wonder why. But I think I might know. I asked them, but they never want to talk about it. The most they say is that everything was getting to them, so they had to get away. And they stayed at a friend's house for a while. I always wonder who these friends are and what they do, but those secrets are not revealed to me.

But here's what I think. The Clean Teen program teaches leadership skills. We train our teens to give workshops to other teens. Sometimes our audience is a group of middle school students. Sometimes it's other high school students. But I think they know that when they put on a "Clean Teen" T-shirt, and when they stand up tall, with a microphone in their hands, they are somebody. They are not a nobody. They talk and people listen. They say,

"Stand up. We are going to do an icebreaker," and the whole room stands up.

Probably on the street, nobody listens to them like that. Probably nobody cares if last week, they were on the stage, holding the microphone, getting a hundred people to listen to every word they said. Nobody cares. But at House of Hope and Joy, they can be somebody. Maybe, just maybe, that's worth it to stay clean and walk away from all the empty promises of the street. Maybe that's why they keep coming back.

Maybe.

I remember our retreat a year or two ago. We gave each teen a tiny teddy bear. The teens each received a teddy bear, and sat in a special chair, and everyone was invited to say something positive about the person in the chair. Maybe their families go way back, and so they had a lot to say. Maybe they really didn't know each other very well, so they didn't have much to say. But those who did speak said some mighty powerful things. I learned about the people in the seats from what others said about them. But I learned a lot about the people doing the talking and telling the stories, too.

This particular exercise took so long that everyone complained because they were missing out on all their free time... but they still didn't want to stop. They went on and on and many of them cried. Some of them said they were scared to go off to college, and they were the first ones in their families ever to even dream of it. Others said they were so glad they weren't seniors yet, because they didn't know what to be when they grew up. I just never realized the pain in some of these young lives.

So many teens have a relative in jail. So many teens have a friend or relative who died from violence. So many teens don't know their dads. Many live in crowded apartments they share with extended family. Some don't sleep in a bedroom; they sleep on a couch. Some don't have a closet, they keep all their clothes and things tied up in a few garbage bags.

But they show at up HHJ, and their hair combed, and their clothes ironed, and they may have bags under their eyes, but they come in smiling and ready to go to work. They want to practice their skits; they want to learn their lines: they want to find out about the next workshop or presentation they get to do. They care about wanting to make a difference in their neighborhood, and in the world, so they show up tired but ready.

Jaquez, maybe most of all. He is so happy to be with the Clean Teens, he cannot do enough. He comes early and helps set up the chairs and tables. He stays late and puts the leftover napkins and wrappers in the trash. He loves his grandma. He probably loves his daddy in jail and his "messed up" mama, too. Because they are his family, and what else can he do?

But he seems to understand that loving them doesn't mean he needs to let them bring him down. He can love them and still do his best to rise above his troubles and build a better future. He told me, "If I stay with the Clean Teens for four years, and 300 people come to our workshops every year, that's more than a thousand teenagers who watch me, and hear me, and look up to me as a role model. I have to be good! I have to stay clean! I owe it to a thousand people counting on me to walk the walk if I'm talking the talk."

See why I love this work?

Of course it's my vocation.

Frederick Buechner defines vocation this way, "When our deep gladness meets the world's deep need." In other words, this type of ministry fills my spirit. I love it. I feel as if I was made to do it, created to do it.

And, it's clearly meeting the needs of many urban young people. So what else could it be other than a vocation?

That's why I feel so peaceful about my work at House of Hope and Joy and at St. Augustine School. Most people wouldn't understand that I feel so lucky, that I get to work in the central city and work with teenagers who are choosing life, choosing God, choosing honesty, choosing service, choosing integrity. What is more wonderful than that? What other lifework could be more noble or more exciting?

Is there danger here? I suppose, but I feel safer here than people I know who fly around the world on vacations. They think they are safe, but they don't even speak the language in the country they are visiting. And if something goes wrong, they can't even communicate to get their most basic needs met. I feel much safer in this city than I would in many other places, and I feel proud that my lifework has meaning. But most of all, I feel proud of young people who care enough about each other and the future that they can build to make those life-giving choices.

So that's my source of hope... and joy... in that way, Jaquez, his grandmother and I have something in common.

So why am I telling you all of this? I don't know! You already know all of this stuff, don't you?

Chapter 40

Dear Sister Agnes:

This is based on Matthew 21:28-32.

Jesus tells the story of a man who asks his two sons to go work in the fields.

The first son says yes, but never does the work.

The second son says no, but then later goes out to do the work.

Jesus ends the story by telling the chief priests and the elders that tax collectors and prostitutes are entering the kingdom of God before they are.

Can you imagine me telling my bishop that the prostitutes and drug addicts from my neighborhood would be entering the kingdom of God before he was?

What is integrity? Isn't it always walking the walk and talking the talk?

I know that the Church in some circles is infamous for all talk and no walk.

But... what if someone is all walk and not much talk?

What if God said to two people, "Will you please serve my flock?"

What if the priest told God, "Yes, I will." But then he got bogged down with parish council woes and the capital campaign and other duties. And what if the prostitute or the drug addict told God, "No... I'm not really much of a church person..." and then went off, feeding the homeless and visiting prison inmates?

I think it's best to do both, but the walking has to be more important than the talking.

We should be afraid of talking without walking... because that is how God will judge us.

So here's my poem about fearing the "yes" I tell God, knowing that I have to follow through...

Integrity

I must confess

I fear my "Yes."

I know my "No,"

More or less.

My "Yes" is rough.

My "Yes" is tough.

Because my life

Brings other stuff.

Why can't a "Maybe"

Be enough?

But no! I know

A "Yes" means yes.

Despite the fact

It brings me stress.

But if I give a "No,"

I know

That "No" is not

The way to go.

Therefore, how can I

Address

This conflict of

My "No" and "Yes" ??

I know my "No"

Must turn to "Yes."

And that's my fear.

I must confess.

Nell Massa

Chapter 41

Dear Nellie,

You are amazing. My life has been so different since I met you. You are so beautiful. I love when you laugh. You laugh so easily! At so many things! You have this deep, full, throaty laugh... it's so sensual. I think that's why I want to keep showing you funny comic strips that remind me of us... because when you laugh, my heart sings.

You are so thoughtful. You think deep thoughts. You are always sharing insights about things I never think about, until you mention them. Then I can't stop thinking about them. You ask questions I would never think of asking. Like how my mother might have adjusted differently to moving here from Puerto Rico than my father. No one has ever asked that or talked to me about that. It now makes me think all the time about what opinions have come to me because of a man's point of view, and not just a person's point of view. It's not true that "women are different." But rather, "men and women are different from each other." Also, "men are different from each other" and so "women are different from each other." I can never assume anything again. I will never be the same again. I have become more like you, asking questions about everything I thought I always knew. See what you have done to me!

You read a Gospel story, and then you find a way to take the lesson right out of it and show it to teenagers so they can never forget it or deny it. It's so creative. It's a type of brilliance. I love it. You make me look forward to Sunday more than ever, because I know you have something unusual you already prepared for your class. You give it to me after church, and suddenly, I see the message of Jesus in a new way. I never heard a homily preached as touching as one of your poems or stories. I wish the church could hear you talk about the Gospels the way your students do. They would never want to hear a boring priest again! Maybe you can teach this style to some priests... I wish they would listen.

You are so loving. You teach in a school with poor students. No, they are good students, but they are from poor families. You will never be rich, and you are just fine with that. You are rich with love and rich with creativity and rich with energy. Your students love the way you teach, because you can bring life to anything boring. Nothing is boring for long, once it is in your hands.

And you are gorgeous. You are simply gorgeous. You do not bother with painting your face, or painting your nails. I love that! Every woman I know would not let me touch their hair, because I would mess it up. They would not let me kiss them until the night was over, because it would smudge their lips. I thought that was what a woman had to be. I never saw anyone like you -- so natural and so comfortable with who you are. No high heels. Why? "Because they hurt when I walk." No painted eyes and lips and cheeks! Why? "Because it's a waste of time, a waste of money, and it all smudges when I want to kiss you!" No shopping every weekend to find new clothes! Why? "Because the fashions change in six months, and it's impossible to try to keep up! Why not just wear the clothes I already have? They still fit! I save time and money, and can do other fun things."

I just never knew a woman like you. Most women don't think like you. Now, after meeting you, I wish all women were more practical like you, and more natural, and more comfortable, and more satisfied with how they look. I want you to meet all of my nieces and cousins and let them see how they can be happy with who they are and how they look naturally! They don't have to try to copy models from magazines.

That day we stopped at the jewelry store so I could get my watch fixed... I was astonished. You just stood there, leaning against the wall. You were absolutely bored! I never saw a woman bored in a jewelry store! You didn't feel like looking at all the gold and diamonds and glittery gems and necklaces and bracelets and rings! You were not interested at all!

I remember asking you about that. You said, "I don't really need jewelry. Why should I? Does it bring us world peace? Does it end world hunger? No...

Yes, that is so logical, but it is so unusual! I wish everyone could think that way! Nellie, you are a clever woman, a beautiful woman, a natural and comfortable woman, and a woman who keeps asking questions I never thought of. I love being with you, because you keep introducing me to a new way of thinking, a new way of seeing, a new way of loving and living.

I am a better man because I love you. You have changed my life. I couldn't be happier. Happy Birthday!

With so much love,

Carlos

Chapter 42

Dear Kelvin,

I really need to write about Carlos, don't I?

Carlos came along at a time when I had become comfortably single. A decade after Timothy, when I could almost pretend to forget I was ever married. A few years after my experience with Ray had taught me that being alone didn't mean being lonely.

Some of us went to a youth conference in Chicago. Our high school students met up with the teenagers that Carlos brought from his church. So that's how I met Carlos. The first day I laid eyes on him, I said out loud (but no one heard me), "This is a man I could fall in love with." But I really didn't want to fall in love. Love had been so harsh to me. Love had not been good to me. Love had hurt me deeply and left me for dead.

Well, not "Love" so much as "Relationships with Men."

I just decided that relationships were not for me. Too much pain. Adam leaving me almost at the altar... Timothy leaving me after the altar... it was just too much.

Guys who weren't funny, guys who weren't deep, guys who had no integrity, guys who were not honest...

I was not in the market for a guy from Chicago who had me with one smile.

So I dismissed my feelings and tried hard to concentrate on other things, like the youth at our youth conference.

I met up with Carlos at one workshop, and then there he was again, sitting right behind me in another workshop. So we brought our teenagers to the same place for supper and talked about our ministry.

He was fascinating. He showed me his newsletter. He talked about the kinds of things he did. I was very impressed. I watched the way he interacted with his youth group. He was really good with them. Shoot, he was really good with me.

But it was OK, because I would be leaving Chicago and coming back home. Carlos would just be this guy who taught me a thing or two, and then moved on.

Hmm...

Well, I guess I need to reassess how well I can size up what a person's ultimate impact on my life will be...

We did exchange addresses and phone numbers, but I didn't plan to call or write him after the conference. Not unless I was trying to remember the name of some book he recommended.

What a surprise when I got a letter from him the day after I got home.

And the day after, and the day after, and the day after that.

He wrote to me every single day!

Not long letters, although once in a while, there was a long one.

More like short "I'm thinking of you" notes.

And comic strips! We both love comic strips. And he was always sending me comic strips.

So once in a while, I sent him a comic strip.

And naturally, there were those times when we both cut out the same comic strip from the paper and sent it to each other! That always cracked me up!

Getting home to read the paper to look for comics to send to Carlos became a nightly ritual for me! I couldn't go to sleep without reading the paper. National news and political editorials? Important, but first, I needed to read the comics!

So the daily letters kept coming.

I did not write to him every day. Maybe once or twice a week. His daily thing could be a bit overwhelming. But he was way in Chicago, and so I could keep a cool head about the whole thing. I expected him to eventually stop writing so often, but he didn't.

He called every week. He said he wanted to hear my voice. He wanted to hear how the Clean Teens were doing. He wanted to know about my students at St. Augustine. I told him this and that...

Truth is, I wanted to hear more about him. What did I know about this guy who kept calling me? He was Puerto Rican, and funny and smart... and deep... and spiritual... and he liked kids... And I think he had integrity... Uh, oh.

I could see where this was going. He was starting to look like the kind of man I could fall in love with.

But he lived in Chicago. And I didn't.

And I wasn't moving.

So that was that.

Until he moved here!

Next thing I know, he's at the Guadalupe Center. Guadalupe Center sometimes did projects with us at House of Hope and Joy. So I knew the place. I wasn't even surprised he was there. It made sense.

His daily letters stopped coming when he moved here. That did *not* surprise me. It was summer, my slowest time, but the busiest time for Guadalupe Center.

I was a teacher at St. Augustine and did school programs through House of Hope and Joy. But during the summer, I was on vacation from school and I was on "planning mode" for the HHJ Clean Teen programs. We still saw the Clean Teens, but everything was more casual and less structured. Many of them had summer jobs, and their time at HHJ was spent volunteering: stocking cans and boxes on the shelves of our food pantry; and sorting, folding and hanging clothing at our clothing boutique.

But Carlos had a full youth program going at Guadalupe Center. When school was out, there were all these children and youth with no place to go and often no food to eat. During the school year, many children depended on school to give them breakfast and lunch. During the summer, those school meals were no longer available for them, so they came to Guadalupe.

Guadalupe Center had daily programming for several hundred children and over a hundred youth. The children ate breakfast and lunch and did all kinds of activities. Some academic, to keep their skills up. Some social and fun. Some sports-recreational, like basketball, swimming or those slip-and-slide things you use when it's hot and you can hose it down. Every week, there was a field trip to some museum or cultural institution.

Junior high youth were enrolled as counselors-in-training or "CITs" and they got more responsibility as they got older. The high school counselors got paid. Many of my Clean Teens worked at Guadalupe during the summer. And some students from St. Augustine as well.

Guadalupe Center was a Catholic ministry, so there was Mass once a week for everyone, and each day opened and closed with prayer. They prayed before each meal as well. Carlos fit right in to this place. It was a perfect match for him. I was happy to know so many teenagers I worked with were in good hands all summer.

I remember the first fund-raiser the year he started there. Guadalupe has a big bash every summer to raise money for their programs. It's like a giant block party, and they sell tickets and have a silent auction. They serve lots of food and have music and dancing. I went to support the ministry -- and didn't mind that I'd be seeing Carlos.

He did pay a lot of attention to me that night.

I guess I hadn't been much of a dancer. Timothy didn't like to dance, and I hadn't done much dancing since college with Adam. But Carlos made it easy. We danced and danced all night! It was really fun. I stayed late and helped the crew with clean up, and then we decided to go out to eat at 2:30 or so in the morning. We talked and talked. He drove me home, even though my car was parked at the Guadalupe parking lot. He said that would give him an excellent reason to come visit me the following day.

Because we were up so late that night, I was glad he didn't come back until 3:00 p.m. I had slept until noon. He came by, and we went out to eat again. That started our "serious" relationship. It was great being with someone who understood everything I was trying to do with young people, and who respected why I chose to work in the central city instead of a "safer" suburban school or church.

And Carlos was indeed all those other things I was looking for. Funny, smart, open and honest. And spiritual, and engaging, and delightful. We had a great time together. People started noticing that we were an "item." I started thinking, "Oh, so this is what a normal relationship is like."

Unlike Ray, I knew where Carlos lived. Unlike Ray, I was proud for people to know that we were together. Unlike Ray... well, in so many ways, Carlos was unlike Ray.

Carlos just made me happier to be alive. I was better at my job, and I was a better human being because of being with Carlos. I even started listening to Spanish tapes and reading up on Spanish vocabulary, so I was better at communicating with the parents of the Guadalupe youth. And some of the young people in my program had parents who preferred Spanish, so that was helpful all around.

Carlos supported everything I did. He was terrific! I was so impressed with the way he handled problems, the rapport he had with young people, the way he talked with children, the relationships he developed with parents. I realized I really loved being with Carlos. I loved being his "partner in ministry." I loved... falling in love with him.

He was often busy during the week, because their summer programs went all day until supper time. He really didn't need to be there all the time, because he had a very competent staff, but he felt responsible that first year, to be sure everything was running smoothly.

It really all began that first summer he moved here. Carlos swept me off my feet at the Guadalupe fund-raiser. After that, he called me every day. He went from daily notes to daily calls. And we still shared comic strips!

Every weekend we were together. We went to city festivals, and library events, marches and dinners, and every church event in town. He was great -- fun and funny, passionate and expressive, smart and dedicated. He really understood urban ministry. And he knew how to network. I should have been able to introduce him to all the local people, but it was Carlos (who recently moved here) who ended up introducing people to me!

No wonder I found my self in love again... even though I started out not wanting any part of another relationship with a man.

Isn't it funny? Sometimes your gut tells you something you don't want to believe, and you never really know what's going to happen...

Chapter 43

Dear Agnes,

I thought it would be fun to write a prayer using comic strip characters.

Almighty God,

Bless us with the faith of Linus, the joy of Snoopy, and the integrity of Charlie Brown.

Bless us with the humility of Ziggy and the insight of Calvin and Hobbes.

Bless us with the commitment of Blondie and Dagwood and the perseverance of Cathy.

Bless us with the flexibility of Frank and Ernest, and the faith of the Family Circus.

And bless us with a sense of humor so that we never stop laughing through life.

Amen.

I find that comic strips are a wonderful way to make people laugh as they take a look at themselves. What makes comic strips funny is that they remind us of ourselves and of the ones we love.

It's easier to be honest about ourselves and our relationships when we are laughing... even if we are laughing about our own flaws and shortcomings.

I have decided to start using comic strips in my classes and workshops.

There's something simple about comic strips... and about God's love for us funny human beings.

Nell Massa

Chapter 44

Memo

Sylvia,

You must say something to Nell Massa.

She is completely taken with writing these idiotic poems, thinking that this will suffice as adequate reflection. She just wrote a prayer about comic strips! Can you imagine?!

I told her that I expect deeper reflection from her than this, and she keeps promising she will provide me with something of greater significance, but her amateur poetry is most difficult to endure.

I am afraid there is going to be a public relations mess in the near future...

If she keeps building relationships with community leaders, and gaining the unfortunate confidence of people who don't know any better, but nevertheless have some political power, we may have a harder time stopping her influence. That will lead to eventual embarrassment on the part of the Friends of Clare and Francis.

I can't say I have been impressed with most of what she does.

The principal at St. Augustine keeps telling me she has difficultly sticking to the curriculum. It is uncertain if she is actually able to teach English without her untested ideas and activities that take her away from what she should be teaching.

Please try to talk to her about reality. If she is intent on joining us, and we can't find a substantial objection, we will be pressured to accept someone completely unsuitable for our order.

She seems to trust you. So either we influence her to change, or we find something concrete in her family life or personal history to demonstrate why we cannot accept her. I know we are desperate for novices, but are we this desperate? I think not. We still must strive for high standards.

God help me if I ever find myself praying with comic strips!

Agnes

Chapter 45

Dear Kelvin,

Let me write about Orlando and Maya. This is such a nice story.

Luz told me her son Orlando was getting married. She invited Carlos and me to the wedding.

But my favorite part is the story about the beginning of their relationship. They met in college, and they seemed to like each other, but they were both a little concerned about their "racial differences." Neither of them was ready to say, "My parents might not approve of my inter-racial relationship" and neither one wanted to ask the other one about parental attitudes or ethnic backgrounds and attitudes.

So for the longest time, they kept it a secret that they were seeing each other. They didn't hold hands in public, and they tried to keep it looking like a friendship.

But eventually, it seemed silly to keep avoiding all talk about their families. It's what a couple naturally does when they start getting serious about each other. They want to investigate where that person's roots are. "Who is this person I'm falling in love with?"

So, all this time, Maya assumed that Orlando was African American. This is understandable. His skin is very dark, darker than many of my African-American students. His hair is kind of kinky and curly. He definitely could "pass" for Black. I know he is Puerto Rican, because I know Luz is Puerto Rican. But maybe if I didn't know that, I would have thought the same thing. Anyway, Maya wasn't sure her parents would approve of her dating a "Black guy."

Meanwhile, Orlando thought that Maya was Asian. She has straight, black hair that she wears in bangs. She always eats Chinese food with chop sticks. And she had a big panda bear in her room. Orlando didn't know what his parents would think of his dating someone from a different continent. But it turns out that Maya is Mexican!

So, here we have two young people afraid to tell their parents they are dating someone from a different "race," and it turns out that they are Latino and Latina!

However, if you know anything about "Hispanic" cultures, you know that they are not all the same! In fact, in many cities, Puerto Ricans and Mexicans have rival gangs and great animosity towards each other. In some situations, parents would be just as upset to find a Puerto Rican and Mexican mix as to find a Black-Asian mix!

But Luz and Fernando are not like that, and neither were Maya's parents. In fact, everyone thought this was an adorable story and a real (though sad) commentary on race relations.

And certainly, in our circles, Puerto Ricans and Mexicans mix without any bitterness or resentment. Carlos, a Puerto Rican, works at Guadalupe Center where most everyone is Mexican. After all, Our Lady of Guadalupe appeared to a man named Juan Diego *in Mexico*. Juan Diego was actually Aztec. His name before being baptized Christian was Cuauhtlatohuac, meaning "He who speaks like an eagle." But Mexicans and Native Americans and Asians all share some heritage, so it's quite understandable how different races can be confused.

Anyway, since Luz volunteered at House of Hope and Joy, and her son Orlando had been one of my students at St. Augustine, and a Clean Teen, the family decided to have the wedding at the HHJ chapel.

It was simple and beautiful. The couple didn't have a dozen bridesmaids and groomsmen. They had two witnesses. No one wore matching gowns or tuxedos. Maya wore a white dress, but it did not have a train, so it didn't require a two-woman crew for upkeep and maintenance. Sheryl cooked the wedding supper at the HHJ kitchen, and we decorated our meeting room with white bows and ribbons and flowers from the garden. It was a gorgeous celebration, and it really made me think.

I found myself realizing that I had spent so much time trying to find the right person for me to love, and always looking for the specific traits of "funny, smart, and open" that I forgot to notice whether or not that person was looking for someone like me.

Carlos really *pursued* me! He met me, spent a weekend with me (at the conference), and then he wrote to me *every single day* until the day he moved here from Chicago. Then, he started calling me every day. He really looked after me. He admired me. He delighted in me. He loved me. He would do whatever he could to make me happier, and my life was better because he was part of it. This is what I needed to be paying attention to.

I was no longer afraid to get into a relationship with a man. I was brave again. I was happy again. I was sort of alive again.

I realized that by the time Carlos had come into my life, I had become a walking disaster. I had almost no self-esteem left. I felt desperate to prove to myself that I was not just a piece of trash. Yet, I was also determined never to let myself become hurt again. When I was with Ray, I didn't want anyone to know. And I was so glad that no one ever found out. I couldn't take going through another "public breakup." It didn't hurt to separate myself from Ray because, number one, he wasn't treating me well, and number two, I kept myself from getting too "emotionally involved." In other words, I really didn't love Ray. At times, I hardly even liked him! I enjoyed his company, to an extent, when he wasn't acting too weird, and he filled a space in my life, but I didn't feel anything deep for him.

And because he wasn't very open, it was easy not to get emotionally involved. Intimacy and personal sharing is what makes someone care about another person. You can't really love someone until you know his story and you understand where he comes from. Ray never let me into his story.

But Carlos was the opposite of Ray!

What else can I say about him? From the start, he treated me like a movie star! He was so attentive and sweet. We started meeting other people in the city doing urban ministry, and our work at House of Hope and Joy was getting more recognition. It was seen as a sister program to the Guadalupe Center.

I started to feel complete. What a difference it makes when someone understands you and loves you and cares about your life and ministry.

And yes, how could I help but notice that Carlos is what I had been looking for all along -- someone who was smart and funny, open and honest, and willing to work with me, shoulder to shoulder, and support me through life? What seemed most important was that Carlos seemed to have been looking for someone like me. I began to think that maybe the idea of *vocation* is broader than I originally realized.

For example, (1) the vocation to your lifework... (2) the vocation to your spirituality, the way you feel most comfortable connecting with God ... and (3) your vocation to your life partner...

I know I am called to (1) the ministry of urban youth...

I know I am comfortable with (2) the spirituality of St. Francis and St. Clare...

I am just trying to figure out (3) how God is calling me to find family...

At different points in my life, I imagined myself as a happily married, stay-at-home mom with babies, babies, and more babies; as a single woman living alone; as a member of a religious order, living in community...

Looking back, I wonder how we ever discover what God wants for us in our lives. I guess the only way is to stay open and keep in close touch with God about these things.

Chapter 46

Dear Kelvin,

As you know, it's not easy when your ministry is mostly with the poor.

At House of Hope and Joy, we meet so many struggling people. They are tired of walking; they are tired of having to go from place to place to get what they need; they are tired of having people look at them and think they are trash. They are tired of personal prejudice and systemic racism.

It's understandable if they show up at the wrong hour or on the wrong day or at the wrong place and can't get the services they need, and they feel upset. Who knows how many busses they had to travel on to get there? Especially when it's raining, or snowing, or 95 degrees outside with no wind, or 25 degrees outside with a wind chill of minus 5.

They can't handle more frustration. Sometimes they do take it out on us.

It's not our fault when the weather is so bad, or the busses are running late. We always want to help, but we can't solve all of their problems.

And we need to take certain precautions, not to be rude or condescending, but to protect ourselves and HHJ from fraud and scams.

After all, there is a certain percentage of the human population who are prone to dishonesty and greed. That percentage exists in the rich and the poor; some are opportunists who bend the law and try our patience, and some will break the law and get away with it if we aren't wise to their devious methods.

This is what the staff keeps reminding me about. It's a good thing they look after us volunteers.

Leah, our social worker, is often giving me little tips about how to handle different situations. For example, if you ever make any exception to any rule, you need to make it clear that there is a specific and clear reason, or else everyone gets to talking and then everyone starts assuming that rule no longer applies!

Merry, the assistant director, is really the acting director, since Sister Matilda hasn't been able to do much directing for quite a while. Merry pretty much supervises the place and trains the volunteers. You couldn't find a better staff to work with. Monique manages the food pantry and Kim runs the clothing boutique. I like to call him the fashion consultant. Paul keeps the place shining, but it's Sheryl who nurtures us and looks after us like a mom. I have worked in several places, but never with a staff that gets along as well as this staff, a staff that functions so efficiently and keeps things moving.

I just love the ministry here and serving the needs of the community.

However, you usually don't expect to be "serving" your friends...

One morning, Carlos called me to let me know that one of the volunteers at Guadalupe Center -- Carmen (and her husband Felipe) had a fire at their apartment. There was an empty apartment in the building, and someone had broken in. They weren't sure how the fire was started, but the entire building had smoke and water damage, and they lost everything. He said they felt *destruido* -- completely destroyed. I called HHJ before heading to school, and Leah already knew about it. Luz already had called. Her husband Fernando worked at Guadalupe and they knew Carmen and Felipe fairly well.

Felipe had two part-time jobs -- he stocked shelves at a food store and worked with a landscaping company doing lawn work, painting and snow removal. He didn't have flexible hours, health insurance, or other benefits.

Carmen and her family had shown up at Luz and Fernando's home, with their children in pajamas. Carmen was still frozen in shock the next day. The children didn't go to school, and Carmen didn't want to get out of bed.

Felipe was able to borrow some clothes from Fernando, and he went to work the very next morning. Carmen needed to follow up with the insurance company, but she was just overwhelmed. Luz called Leah at HHJ, and she and Kim got together some clothing for everyone in the family. Leah and Monique brought it over during lunch-time. Leah was able to comfort and reassure Carmen enough to get her out of bed, showered and dressed.

Monique found Carmen's two kids, Rosa and Raúl. She handed them each a new blanket and a teddy bear. Without saying a word, the two of them climbed up on the couch and hugged their bears, just looking at their mom. Leah convinced Carmen that the children needed to return to school the next day, to get some "normalcy" back into their lives. Carlos invited them all to have supper at Guadalupe every night until Carmen and

Fernando could get a new place to live. Monique put together some food for breakfast and school lunches since Luz and Fernando would be hosting four extra people at their home for a few weeks.

Through all of this, I am just amazed at the deep blessings of my life. What good people surround me! They take in families in need, they open up their own homes and lives. Their struggles become our struggles. And I didn't even know all of this was happening. I spent that day at school, teaching English. The only connection I had to Carmen was when we prayed in class. I asked my students to remember in prayer this family that had a fire and lost everything.

After school, I went to Guadalupe to see Carlos. He was talking with Fernando. Then they told me the whole story. I had dinner with them at Guadalupe that night -- Luz and Fernando, Carmen and her children. Felipe was working a late shift. Raul and Rosa were extremely quiet, looking down, poking at their food. After supper, Carlos invited everyone to watch *The Wizard of Oz*. It was the perfect idea. The children -- in fact all of us -- enjoyed the singing, sitting close on the couches, laughing. It was just what this family needed. Felipe arrived in time to see Cowardly Lion, eat leftovers and enter the fantasy of Oz, taking a needed break from his own troubles.

Everything is wrapped up in love -- people taking care of people. It's there in our work, in our ministry, in our friendships, and in our community. Life brings such pain and suffering and struggle, but when it's met with love and support, the love is such a blessing.

Guadalupe Center... House of Hope and Joy... we're all dedicated to this ministry. We're all trying to do the same thing, more or less. The volunteers, the staff -- we're all on the same page. It feels so good to be with people who have similar values, people who want to do the right thing.

I don't mean to "romanticize" the ministry of Guadalupe and HHJ. Ugly, hateful, horrendous things still happen almost weekly. Drive-by shootings, rapes, burglaries, gang violence. It's on the news, and it's right in our own back-yard. It still really gets me depressed. And naturally, it's much more profound when it happens to someone you know.

Chapter 47

Dear Kelvin,

I want to write about the drive-by shooting that killed an innocent middle school child walking home on a beautiful Wednesday afternoon. Martin Bolivar. No one seemed to know who was responsible for the killing. The first people to reach out to him were a homeless mother and her little boy, who just happened to be passing by. They were lucky to not be shot themselves.

I didn't know Martin, but he was Thelma's cousin. Thelma was one of our Clean Teens. Everyone came over to HJJ that night to talk, cry, and express their anger and outrage -- at God, at society, at this evil world. Half the staff was there, along with several of our volunteers. Thelma stayed home with her family. LaToya had talked with her. She said Thelma was so mad at God, she didn't "have any need to pray." She was turning her back on a God who could let this happen to an innocent boy like Martin.

That gave us all something extra to pray for.

LaToya wrote a poem for Thelma:

"As for me and my house, we will serve the Lord."

Lil Black dude says they don't have a house

but he and his mom

still serve the Lord.

Lil Black sista say she has a house

but won't serve a Lord who kills her cousin.

Where's my family? Where's my Lord?

Where's the House of Jesus?

Where's my cousin Martin?

Come save us now, bring us all back home.

Then we'll start that talk about serving.

I thought LaToya did an excellent job expressing Thelma's anger and her feelings about God.

The teens decided they wanted to give LaToya's message to God, to society, and to everyone who walks past House of Hope and Joy.

They wanted to write that message on the sidewalk.

Carlos had some sidewalk chalk in his car. Ruby was reluctant to have so many young people on the street, in the dark, creating a crowd, but you and Carlos thought it was important for the young people to express themselves. So out we went. The words circled around the block. LaToya, the author, dictated the words, and Franklin, her boyfriend, wrote them down. The rest of the teens followed behind, embellishing the letters, making them bigger, coloring them in, drawing designs around them. Sure enough, we were stopped by police officers several times. Eventually, they brought a few cars to protect us so no one else would worry, and the group would be kept safe.

I was surprised that Sister Sylvia dropped by while this was happening. I was glad that she could see the young people expressing themselves this way and dealing with their grief in a creative way instead of going out and causing mischief, or creating vandalism or scaring people -- the way other people might react without thinking. This gives them a method for the future, a way to express their outrage and grief that is constructive and not destructive.

What a night! The next day was cloudless, like the day before. The bright colors on the sidewalk were so striking. No one could ignore the message. It was OK to express anger to Jesus. He could take it. He understood this sort of rage.

Word spread about the Clean Teens' response. People were coming by, just to see the words, and walk their way through the prayer that came from the young people's grief. The murder had been on the news Wednesday night; but this sidewalk prayer and the Clean Teens were on the news Thursday morning. And so were that little homeless boy and his mother. They were given assistance and a place to live in the neighborhood.

We attended Martin's funeral Friday morning, a third cloudless day. The funeral procession drove out of their way, from the church to the cemetery, in order to pass by that sidewalk. They had police escorts. They drove by at five miles an hour. The entire street was blocked off, to facilitate the slow driving and reading. Those young people had made a difference. Their private prayer had brought comfort to Martin's family and to an entire city.

People started talking about what the "House of Jesus" should be doing and how to "bring everyone back home" so this violence could end. They talked about ways to bring hope back to urban youth and help them grieve so they felt safe and ready to "serve the Lord" again.

It rained over the weekend. By Monday, the sidewalk was washed clean. There was no trace of the poetry and art from the week before. Some of the Teens wanted to put it back. They didn't want Martin to be forgotten. But others argued that they couldn't spend hours re-drawing their poem every time it rained. And what would they do when it snowed? They decided to create a poster instead.

The poem was written on a giant poster board and decorated beautifully. They liked it so much, they made a second one. And a third one.

To this day, a framed copy of that poem hangs at House of Hope and Joy. One was given to Martin's mother. The other one was given to Thelma.

Chapter 48

Dear Agnes,

I know you read about Thelma and LaToya's poem the Clean Teens wrote on the sidewalk all around House of Hope and Joy.

Here is another reflection based on urban life and a scripture that is often quoted.

Nell Massa

As for me and my house, we will serve the Lord. (Joshua 24:15)

I

We have a lovely home and a lovely family.

We all believe in serving the Lord.

We worship every Sunday and give money to the church.

We bring food during "Feed the Hungry Week" and we bring clothing on "Bundle Sundays."

As for me and my house, we will serve the Lord.

II

I have two homes and two families.

My mom's home and my dad's home.

My dad remarried. His home is bigger. I have my own room there, but it doesn't feel like home.

My sister has her own room, too.

My mom is single. Most of my stuff is at our apartment.

I don't have my own room.

I sleep on the couch.

My stuff is in my little sister's closet. But that's OK.

I'm the man of the house now.

Do I serve the Lord?

I don't know.

I go to two churches.

Does that mean I serve the Lord double?

III

Got no home,

Got no family,

Got no time to serve the Lord.

Living in a shelter,

Volunteering at a soup kitchen,

Still trying to find a job.

Spend every morning the same way...

Shower, dress, serve meals, connect the folks with services.

Spend every afternoon the same way...

Pounding the pavement, taking busses, filling out job applications.

Spend every evening the same way...

Serving meals, getting folks connected with services.

Do the "services" help?

Did they help me?

I guess...

I get to eat and sleep OK...

I get to shower and stay clean...

I get leads for possible jobs...

But nothing much changes.

Got no home,

Got no family,

Got no time to serve the Lord.

Chapter 49

Dear Kelvin,

Christmastime comes every December, but not everyone is full of cheer.

The need always seems greater than we can anticipate.

Some years, the folks line up at our front door hours before we open, just so they can be assured a spot.

They know we give out "Christmas meals" with a chicken or ham or turkey, and with presents for the kids.

If they are among the first 1,000 to sign up.

I remember times when we could hardly pull into the parking lot because the crowds were blocking the entrance.

I remember once when a woman collapsed during the wait. She was standing on her feet so long, and they just gave way. They had to call an ambulance for her.

I remember once when a grown man broke down and cried because he was number 1,001, and we couldn't guarantee presents for his children and grandchildren. He had been a gentleman and held the door open for an older lady who was walking with a cane. He lost his place to her because he had shown her kindness.

He came back on "leftovers day," the day we give out whatever we have left over from the food and toy donations after our 1,000 families are served. He was first in line. He showed up at 5:00 AM, and we don't usually open until 8:00. It was 10 degrees out that day, and we were worried that people would freeze out there, so we opened the doors at 6:00 that morning. We thought we'd be there plenty early. What a surprise to find out someone had been there already for an entire hour. He didn't even complain; he was just grateful to come in and warm up.

Anyway, you know how we give out numbers. 1-200, on different colored cards. Each day is a different color. Only the first 200 can come in that morning and be processed. Even with all of our volunteers, the most we can accomplish is 200 in one morning. The rest get a card with a number and color for another day, which means after waiting in line, they will need to come back another day and wait in another line.

They all sit in chairs in every conference and meeting room we have, waiting their turns. Volunteers call out the numbers in order, and they come up to our table and take a seat. They need to give us a picture ID, a piece of current mail to verify their address, and documentation of their children and ages -- school records, birth certificates, shot records, whatever they have.

We take down their home address, phone number, and date of birth and names of all their children. We also take down the names of other adults living there.

I remember people who sat across from me, with the biggest smiles I had ever seen. I remember thinking how astonishing it was that such people could smile. I would probably be complaining and whining about the long wait and having to stand on my feet so long. But most of our guests do no such thing.

I remember the woman named "Lucky" who told me that her name had never done her any good at all.

I remember a woman living alone with ten children, with three different last names. And I knew there was a story there. Maybe there's a sister on drugs, or a husband in prison, or a family member who simply ran away, leaving the kids to be taken care of by others.

I remember lots of single women with two or three children. I remember lots of grandparents taking care of their son's or daughter's children.

I remember lots of single parents taking care of both their children and their parents.

I remember several people who finally got to the point where they could sit down and take out their documentation, only to realize that they had left home one of their children's papers. I felt their pain when I saw it on their faces.

What I don't remember at all is fights, disrespectful language or any danger.

I don't mean to imply that the poor always have perfect manners.

True, many of our guests are pleasant and grateful for the food and gifts and clothing they can get at HHJ.

But we do have some who don't say, "Thank you," or who can't bear to look you in the eye because of their shame. We have some guests who haven't learned how to treat their children, who say "Shut up" and can't think of creative ways to distract them when they get whiney and impatient.

These are God's people, all of them. They didn't grow up wanting to be poor and stand in line waiting for free food and clothing. They fell upon hard times and haven't found the resources they need to get up yet. They are just doing the best they can. And I am proud to be part of an organization that brings "hope and joy" to people who need some encouragement to keep putting one foot in front of another for one more day...

Chapter 50

Dear Sylvia,

While decorating House of Hope and Joy with holly, I couldn't help but think about the symbol of holly -- it's got a reputation for both fun and tragedy... so I wrote this reflection.

Nellie Massa

> **Deck the halls with boughs of Holly!**
>
> **Fa-la-la-la-la-la-la-la-la!**
>
> **'Tis the season to be jolly!**
>
> **Fa-la-la-la-la-la-la-la-la!**

Holly wreathes with big red bows!

A sprig of holly on everyone's top hat!

Ho, Ho, Ho! Santa loves holly! Even Frosty the Snowman loves holly!

> **Have a Holly Jolly Christmas!**
>
> **It's the best time of the year!**
>
> **I don't know if there'll be snow,**
>
> **But have a cup of cheer!**

December is not the best time of the year for everyone.

Lots of people are depressed.

Sick, forgotten, lonely... Many people dread the holidays.

It's a sad time if you don't have friends or family to celebrate with.

It's awful if you don't have money to buy your children presents or provide a holiday dinner.

The holly bears a prickle

As sharp as any thorn;

And Mary bore sweet Jesus Christ

On Christmas Day in the morn.

Holly isn't always so jolly.

It has sharp edges, like the crown of thorns.

And berries the color of blood! The berries are poison!

What's so jolly about holly?

What's so jolly about Christmastime if you are poor?

It's just another reminder for you to feel ashamed of who you are.

The holly bears a berry

As red as any blood;

And Mary bore sweet Jesus Christ

To do poor sinners good.

The red blood of drive-by shootings....

The grief of mothers who bear sweet children and watch them die...

So why should we celebrate with holly?

The holly bears a blossom

As white as a lily flower;

And Mary bore sweet Jesus Christ

To be our sweet Savior.

Our Savior experienced the sweetest love and the most wretched agony...

His death was by torture, and his friends abandoned him.

But he returned to them in a perfect, resurrected body and brought them forgiveness and salvation.

Holly seems to have it all -- the red berries, the prickly green leaves, the white blossoms...

The perfect Christmas symbol of our perfect savior...

The perfect reminder that joy and relief will follow our suffering...

The perfect reminder that we need love and support to get through our grief ...

That the world is filled with so much evil and pain...

Yet also filled with so much hope and joy...

> **The holly and the ivy**
> **When they are both full grown,**
> **Of all the trees that are in the wood,**
> **The holly bears the crown.**
> **O the rising of the sun**
> **And the running of the deer,**
> **The playing of the merry organ,**
> **Sweet singing of the choir.**

So deck your halls with boughs of holly...

Remember your blessings, despite this imperfect world...

And have a holly, jolly Christmas.

Chapter 51

Dear Kelvin,

It's not unusual for people in the suburbs to be afraid of driving into the inner city. But they want to help, so we bring boxes to their churches, and they fill our boxes up with food. Sometimes the churches also collect toys after Mass.

So Paul drives all over the suburbs to collect back the boxes. We have a big white van with the words "House of Hope and Joy" written on the side of it. That way, the congregations don't have to transport all the boxes filled with cans and bags and packaged food items.

One year, we were close to running out of Christmas toys, and we still had lots of people at our doors.

But the van was filled with boxes of food, and it was taking a while to unload it, even through several volunteers were hauling the boxes into the building.

So Ruby let Paul use her car. As soon as he left, we all realized it might have been a mistake for him to drive a car alone into the suburbs.

Sure enough, he was pulled over. You know why. Not for speeding. He wasn't. Not for any traffic violation at all. He was caught DWB -- Driving While Black. Ask any Black person who lives in the suburbs, and you will hear dozens of stories about their friends being pulled over in the neighborhood for no reason at all. They are asked, "Where are you going? Whose home are you visiting? Are they expecting you?" and all of those related questions that really mean, "You are Black. You don't belong in this rich White neighborhood. You must be up to no good. We will 'catch' you and scare you away before you get the chance to break the law."

We get so tired of the DWB stories. White suburban folks will insist that such things are exaggerated. That it's just that one police officer. That he had a bad day and was unusually suspicious. That perhaps a car of that same description had been involved in some crime. But all of those explanations are ridiculous. Every Black male I know -- of any age -- can tell you about their DWB stories. I can't think of one White male -- of any age -- who has ever been pulled over by a police officer unless he was speeding or had an expired license plate, or ran a red light, or SOMETHING.

It's just one of those realities that White people don't believe and Black people know is their daily reality. White mothers hope their sons never do anything wrong -- so they never have to deal with the police. Black mothers know their sons will have to deal with the police, even though they don't do anything wrong. It is certain that sooner or later, they will be pulled over. Black mothers just hope and pray their sons never speak impatiently or move too quickly while getting the license and registration because of what a police officer might infer. Unarmed men have been shot for responding with too much frustration or pulling their license out of their pocket or their registration out of the glove compartment too quickly...

Anyway, Paul was delayed, but only for an hour or so. He soon returned with the precious toys. And we never ran out.

I'll write that again. He was delayed "only for an hour or so."

What White person would put up with wasting an entire hour -- for no reason -- dozens of times? Maybe once every couple of months. Maybe monthly, if he has a friend who lives in the White suburbs? That's just one more advantage to being White. No one pulls you over and wastes your time for no reason. It just never happens. You are given the benefit of the doubt. Every time. You're always innocent until proven guilty. You're never stopped without a reason. Never assumed guilty.

Of course, it's not just driving. The first time I went to a mall with Ruby, in the "White section" of town, as soon as we drifted apart while looking at stuff, she got all this attention. I thought people were just being polite. She helped me realize they were watching her because they expected her to shoplift.

We tried the experiment in countless stores. The same thing happened every time. EVERY TIME. 100%. No exceptions. Especially if she entered first, without me.

But once I showed up and talked with her, and joked with her, and obviously showed signs of being "connected" with her, they would leave her alone. Why? She was with me, so she must be OK... one of the "good ones."

That benefit of the doubt, that presumed innocence, is taken away from human beings whose skin is black. Don't get me started. I know you know just what I am talking about. So why am I telling you about "White Privilege"?

I just have to get all of this on paper. Why? I don't know. I don't know anything anymore. I don't why I'm recording all of these thoughts. All of these memories. I just keep writing until I can find something to say to Sister Agnes.

Some weeks, it's hard to figure out what to say. Other weeks, it's easy.

Some weeks, I feel a need to write and write and write.

And you are always there when I want to express all of this. What a blessing.

Remember that time we were doing that workshop about the difference between racism, racial prejudice and racial stereotypes? Remember those two girls who got up to speak to the group? One Latina and one African American...

They said, "We think 'White Privilege' is great!"

And we gasped!

Then they continued. "In fact, we think everyone should have it!"

Chapter 52

Dear Kelvin,

I remember a very "strange" Christmas at home ...

As you know, we inner city school teachers don't make a lot of money, and then we spend half our salaries on school supplies that the schools can't afford to buy. So we are always trying to find ways to make ends meet and get away with spending less.

One way I always did that was with Christmas presents. I always started in the summer, so I would have time, and I would come up with some project, something I could make that wouldn't cost too much money. Every so often, I'd hit the "jackpot" and come up with something made completely from items I already had, so that I didn't actually spend any money at all!

Well, one year, I did exactly that!

I had Christmas fabric left over from an art project we did at HHJ the previous year and plenty of yarn from some needlepoint ornaments I had made the year before. I made these tiny Christmas "pillow" ornaments. I embroidered each person's name and a design on the front and used Christmas fabric on the back, and then stuffed them with leftover stuffing from I don't know what project. Each person had a unique design (for my three brothers -- a music note or a Greek letter or an eyeball) and they had little yarn loops on the top so they could be hung on the tree.

I thought they looked pretty good!

So on Christmas Day, while we exchanged gifts, why was I feeling so... inadequate?

Maybe because all my brothers and sisters (in-law) were giving me these expensive, beautiful gifts! Clothing bought at really nice stores and china bowls and mugs.

I realized that they were spending lots of money on me, and I was just giving them stuff I made from leftovers. Bits of cloth, clumps of stuffing, pieces of mismatched yarn. Cheap gifts that didn't cost me a dime. Junk that was just taking up room in my closet. And to think I had been excited about my clever way of saving money!

They were buying me fine items from stores I could never even walk into, and I was giving them... recycled garbage!

For some reason, I just felt more ashamed with every fancy present I opened...

It was Mary who first noticed my mood. I really tried to cover it up, but she saw right through me. I even saw her gesture to Beth to look my way. Eventually they brought Margaret over and all three of them approached me. "What is wrong? Please tell us."

I didn't know how to explain it, so I started to cry. "You have all spent so much money on me. You have lavished me with such beautiful and expensive gifts. I didn't have any money to spend on Christmas presents, and I made all this stuff out of leftover junk that someone else probably would have thrown away! I just feel so embarrassed..."

Soon, we were all crying...

Beth spoke up first. "I love your home-made gifts! I can't believe all the time you put into each one! It must have taken hours."

Mary continued. "I would never be able to make anything like this. I don't have the talent to come up with an original design and draw it and embroider over it. I don't even know how you thought up the idea. I was sitting here, thinking how wonderful it was to have such a talented sister."

Margaret agreed. "All I did was walk into a store and look around and say, 'I think this will fit Nellie,' and hand over my credit card. In fact, I think the girls even wrapped it for me."

Beth summarized for them all. "Don't spend another second thinking that your gifts weren't good enough. What if we did the same thing? What if we looked at all the time and talent in your gifts and sat across the room thinking that OUR gifts weren't good enough? What kind of Christmas would that be? Everyone receives great presents and yet everyone is miserable thinking they were the least generous?"

Mary hugged me. She said, "Now isn't this the silliest thing for us to all cry about?" That got us all laughing.

We would have just stood there hugging and crying much longer if my brother Charlie hadn't come over to say, "What's going on here? Some kind of love fest?"

That was the last time I ever felt bad about giving people my "recycled garbage" for Christmas!

Chapter 53

Dear Kelvin,

House of Hope and Joy is such a wonderful place.

Sister Matilda has always trusted everyone, I know. But she has been sick for so long, that I sometimes wonder if she will ever be well again. She's probably in her 80s, and now she only comes down once every week or so... yet she completely trusts the staff to do the ministry.

The staff works well together. They discuss things, listen to each other, and really do their best. Naturally, no one is perfect, and we have our disagreements from time to time, but it's those disagreements that get all our different ideas and perspectives out on the table where everyone can see them, and understand them, and benefit from them.

I have learned so much about leadership from the staff and volunteers. I have learned more about social justice and about all the issues connected to poverty. The lack of resources leading to poor education, poor health care, poor parenting skills, low self-esteem, low achievement in school, lack of hope (not to mention lack of joy), and unemployment. This just fuels stereotypes and racism. There are so many obstacles in the inner city. It's easy to get depressed thinking about it.

Yet so many good things happen at HHJ. I know that St. Francis and St. Clare never dreamed that such a place would open up in their name, or that such a ministry would be known as "Franciscan." But I am certain they look upon our efforts with hope and joy.

I went to school, same as my brothers, to get a *Jesuit* education. We have this grand Jesuit tradition in our family. My dad told all of us that we had to attend not just any college, but a Catholic college. And not just any Catholic college, but a *Jesuit* Catholic college. We knew that from an early age.

So how did I end up in this Franciscan place?

Chapter 54

Dear Sister Agnes,

When I was in high school, my dad told me he would send me to any college I wanted to attend -- as long as it was Jesuit. He was Jesuit-educated, and his brother, my Uncle Philip, was a Jesuit priest who taught at a university in the Philippines. He didn't visit us often, but when he did come home (maybe every five years or so) there were so many family parties. He was like a celebrity. When I was little, I thought they named the Philippines after him!

And so I followed family tradition. My brothers and I all went to Loyola. See what I mean? Pretty Ignatian, right?

So no one could have predicted it, no one could have seen it coming! I was definitely on the Jesuit track!

I am teaching now, yes, and volunteering at a ministry center.

But at a Jesuit school? No.

At a Jesuit retreat house? No.

It's... Franciscan!

All through my fine Jesuit upbringing, I never really noticed any latent Franciscan tendencies. St. Francis is the patron saint of animals. Yet I am allergic to dogs, cats, and probably all animals. Not that I don't love all creation; I just wish it didn't make me sneeze. I get all "Ah-choo" just thinking about it.

Plus, I look terrible in brown (just ask my mother!). Black looks much better on me. That's the Jesuit color! And purple! I love purple! I don't only wear purple during Lent, but all year round! Besides, I was the college mascot for two years! I was the "Crusader" at the football and basketball games, prancing around with that sword and shield! At one game, I even got "captured" by the Providence Friars! And they're Dominicans, for goodness sake!

"Go and sell your possessions and give to the poor, and you shall have treasure in heaven; and come, follow Me." MT 19:21

Sometimes a little Scripture can be a dangerous thing.

Take St. Francis. He did exactly what that Scripture verse says. Not only did he give away everything that he had, but he also tried to give away everything his family had.

He did NOT score family points with that one.

But many centuries later, this Franciscan practice of "begging for a living" continues to mark Franciscan men and women as communities who embrace the poor and live simple lives in solidarity with them.

And it's still not scoring family points.

Poor Pietro and Pica, the parents of Francis. They raised such a good boy. He went off to war, was captured, was ransomed and released, and then suffered an illness with a slow recovery.

If he wasn't clunked on the head during battle, then it had to be that illness which obviously affected his brain.

Give everything away and beg for a living? What for?

You wouldn't have to take people's money like a beggar if you hadn't given it away in the first place! Isn't that a waste of resources?

Well, the logic of economics is not compatible with the folly of the cross.

Even the Pope at the time (Innocent III) had his doubts about begging for a living. But Francis' humility and sincerity stirred his heart. And Clare ran away in the middle of the night, against her parents' wishes to be with Francis and his friends.

And here I am in the central city, working at St. Augustine with "high risk" students, and spending the rest of my time at House of Hope and Joy!

Let me tell you -- I am not scoring family points, either!

But, after all, it was my mom who recognized that I had some potential with teaching. She saw me babysit my younger brother Ben, always telling stories, teaching him letters and numbers, singing him songs, reading him books. She thought I should look into becoming a teacher.

Good Italian girls always listen to their mothers, right?

But she's not wild about me working in a situation where we constantly have to write grant proposals and ask local businesses for sponsorship of our youth programs.

Once we did two workshops, and we tried to make some extra money by "selling" T-shirts. They simply said "Hope and Joy." Who could be against Hope and Joy? Wouldn't everyone want such a T-shirt?

At the first workshop, we showed everyone the T-shirt and told them about our ministry. We told them we couldn't sell them the T-shirts, because we didn't have a license to sell. But we said that we could certainly be persuaded to give them away for free... and that we would really appreciate goodwill donations of $10 or more.

We "sold" four T-shirts.

In a workshop of 21 people.

Next workshop, we had a better idea. We put a T-shirt on every chair. We told them about our ministry and told them the T-shirts were a free gift from House of Hope and Joy. We also told them we'd accept donations for our ministry.

After the workshops, all these people came up to us and gave us money -- checks and cash. We had made $265. In a workshop of 26 people. We made more money than if we had sold everyone a T-shirt for $10!

So here's the lesson. We tried to sell T-shirts and we failed.

But when we gave the T-shirts away, we gained even more treasure than if we had sold them!

Pretty Franciscan, huh?

So I started to beg for a living. My soul became Franciscan.

Good-bye, Ignatius. Hello, Clare and Francis. Sorry, Uncle Phil. Sorry, Mom and Dad.

What's that I said about good Italian girls?

That's something you'll have to ask Clare about. She and Francis were two Italians who both disappointed their moms. Wait until my mom meets Pica in heaven. They'll have a lot to talk about.

Like Clare and Francis, I took this leap of faith, and here I am. A Jesuit soul in a Franciscan ministry center.

I remembered those college jokes about the difference between Franciscans and Jesuits. The Jesuits were like steak and wine. Or steak and scotch. The Franciscans were more like beer and pizza. Or beer and pot luck.

I never even drank beer until after college. But I do, now. And I eat plenty of pizza -- I work with teenagers, after all, and most of what we get is mostly due to luck, I guess.

Is it all for the greater glory of God (a Jesuit question)? You bet it is! Just come and see the precious faces of our young people. Listen to their comments. Your heartstrings will flutter! Here's what they say:

> "I have learned so much as a Clean Teen here, leadership skills and peacemaking skills that I wouldn't have gotten anywhere else but at House of Hope and Joy. It has greatly affected my life. I know we all have to give back and find ways to serve the community."

> "I have learned to communicate, to solve problems and to manage conflicts without using any form of violence. If we all do our part to bring about peace in the world, then everyone gets to live their lives in the fullest way possible."

> "This program helps us youth promote hope and joy and it brings them together in a good environment so they can stay focused on their goals -- a good education and future career."

> "I now know what I can do to help bring hope and joy into other people's lives. And I'm going to do it. We are here to serve the world. I know that we all have

potential; all we have to do is find it. I will remember this for the rest of my life."

What does my Jesuit family think? Well, my mother still worries a lot. It's one thing to start wearing brown (which I haven't done yet). It's another thing to have to beg for a living. But, hey, just make me a channel of peace, and we'll see what happens. Oh, no! Did I just quote St. Francis?

Nell Massa

Chapter 55

<u>Memo</u>

Sylvia,

Nell Massa is now making fun of religious orders -- not only the Franciscans but the Jesuits!

Enclosed is her latest "reflection."

I find no humor in this, although she will make the weak excuse, "I was just trying to be funny." That's what she told me at our last meeting.

Do you see humor in this?

I keep telling you, she will become an embarrassment to the order and a public relations nightmare!

Besides, I think she has much deeper problems. She talks about the good work she does, but she seems to use that as an excuse to avoid a deeper examination of her life, her motives and her feelings. I doubt that she would be happy with us. Her independence is extraordinary, but it also makes her a poor candidate for communal living and for following religious vows -- especially obedience!

Please meet with her again. Your influence is greatly needed.

Agnes

Chapter 56

Dear Kelvin,

More about House of Hope and Joy.

Kim got us all to buy egg rolls from his church. They hold a fund-raiser twice a year and raise $20,000. So we all ordered egg rolls. He and Monique drove over to pick them up. What delicious egg rolls! What a treat to eat them fresh, the day they were made.

Kim talked about how the Hmong organize the fund-raiser. Picture this:

Tables and tables of people -- moms and dads, grandparents, children, teens. One group is shredding cabbage, one is shredding carrots, one is shredding onions. One group is making the dough. One group is cutting the dough. One group is combining cabbage, onion, carrots and meat and mixing it in gigantic metal bowls. One group is rolling the dough and folding it over the mixture of shredded cabbage, onions, carrots and meat. One group is frying the egg rolls and laying them out on paper towels over cloth towels. One group is running around, carrying supplies from one group to another, carrying potential egg rolls in various stages of development from one phase of preparation to the next. And the final group is packaging egg rolls according to hundreds of orders, marking the boxes, and putting them in paper bags.

Kim started nudging Sheryl. "You should have a fund-raiser for House of Hope and Joy. You can cook the foods you are known for! We'll get St. Andrew Dung Lac's list of egg roll customers and email all of them, then set up an assembly line of food preparation!

Sheryl wasn't convinced this was a good idea. It was a lot of work, and although she loved to cook, she didn't want the whole thing to flop.

Well, one thing led to another, and soon, the idea of a food fund-raiser turned into "The Festival of Hope and Joy." Everyone on staff had ideas and the project just grew and grew.

Monique talked about making it a block party and providing entertainment. She suggested African dancers. Luz thought that was a great idea. She suggested the Mariachi band that always played at Guadalupe fund-raisers. I said I'd call Carlos to ask how they always got so many donations for their silent auction every summer.

Leah thought we should invite different organizations to send representatives so there could be tables of information for families. Health clinics, legal clinics, halfway houses, shelters for battered women, prison ministries, and all kinds of support services.

Merry took the idea to Sister Matilda. She hadn't been feeling too well lately, but Merry said she smiled and thought it was a delightful idea. Merry gave us the go-ahead.

You know I can't take much credit for doing anything. I just stayed out of the way and did what I was told. Ruby, Luz and I met with the Clean Teens to talk about their involvement. They decided to organize the children into creating sidewalk artwork. They also asked for their favorite foods. Macaroni and cheese, green beans and potatoes and the special meat loaf that Sheryl's husband Andy always made.

Merry had special staff T-shirts made that said "Celebrate Hope and Joy." Everyone loved them so much, that she started a list of people who would buy them if we made more and sold them. We had over fifty orders in less than a month. So she decided to make a hundred.

Luz, Fernando and Carlos ran the door prizes and silent auction. They had all the know-how from their Guadalupe experience. They had tickets for movies and plays, coupons for meals at every restaurant in town, even coupons for groceries, clothing, shoes and toys. I don't think there was a business in the city that wasn't involved in this. And actually, why not? It was cheap advertisement and brought lots of good will.

Ruby had this great idea to put together an "absentee" support package: one meal, one T-shirt, one chance for a door prize and a one-sentence mention in our newsletter for $25. We sent them all over the country to every friend and relative anyone knew. We told them, "We know you can't attend, but could you send us a donation for what you might have spent if you had been able to come?" Checks were pouring in from coast to coast for meals we didn't have to cook, T-shirts we didn't have to buy, and door prizes we didn't give away. Some people "ordered" family packages -- and sent $25 for each of their family members!

More than two-thirds of our profit came from the absentee donations. We took a picture of a T-shirt, a plate of food, and two tickets to a local theatre, and that was sent to each donor along with a thank-you note. Franklin (who printed LaToya's poem on the sidewalk) designed the thank-you note, and the Clean Teens helped him create the same thank-you art on the sidewalk in front of the main entrance.

I love telling this story, because it makes everything sound like a Mickey Rooney and Judy Garland movie... "Hey! Let's put on a show!" and miraculously, effortlessly, it all comes into creation.

But actually, it took an entire year of planning, including six months of intensive preparation. The Festival of Hope and Joy took place on June 10, with gorgeous weather. Not too hot, not too windy. It rained two days before, and two days after, but the skies were clear on the day we needed them to cooperate. It was Thelma's birthday, and she was sure that Martin was parting the clouds just for her. Every day since that festival, we check the weather on June 10. Amazingly, it's always a beautiful day in our neighborhood.

So what made that first Festival of Hope and Joy so special?

I think creativity comes from diversity. All the ideas came from different people, from their different talents, from their different backgrounds and different points of view. Even being from different cultures made a difference. Somehow, there's a lesson to be learned from this.

The saddest part was that Sister Matilda didn't get to spend much time with us. She had become so weak. A friend of hers came to visit -- Sandra -- but she and Sister Matilda only came down for a meal and then went right back upstairs to the small apartment there.

That was the first time I remember thinking about the sisters. There is room for six sisters to live upstairs above

House of Hope and Joy, but Matilda was the only one living there now. Sometimes Sister Lucy visited, sometimes Sister Agnes visited, but for the most part, Matilda was there alone. Not the life she expected when she entered a religious community. She was getting older and had good weeks and bad weeks. I didn't know her well, but I knew her well enough to know she worried about her order, the dwindling number of sisters, and the future of House of Hope and Joy. I knew she was thrilled with this new festival idea, and Sandra said she was in high spirits all day, even though she was very tired.

Chapter 57

Dear Sister Agnes,

When did I first start thinking of the joining the order? When did I first wonder about the Friends of Clare and Francis?

I would have to say it was a beautiful June day, the birthday of one of our Clean Teens.

It was the day of the first Festival of Hope and Joy.

It seemed that Sister Matilda was old when I first met her, yet she had always had energy. Lately, she had become more tired and weak. She left much of the administrative duties to Merry. That weekend when Sandra first came to visit was the first time I really spent time thinking about what it must have been like for Sister Matilda.

Obviously, she took a vow to belong to a religious order. When she joined, there were lots of sisters in the community. They were involved in social work and ministry to the poor, all over this city and many like it. She probably thought she'd never be alone again. Who knew that so many sisters would leave the order after Vatican II and so few new young women would join?

I thought about the pride she must have felt when she saw so many people come to House of Hope and Joy to celebrate the vision of Clare and Francis. The hope and joy that comes from peaceful relationships and service to the poor.

I wondered what Sandra thought about it; Sandra, her childhood friend. They were so different. Sister Matilda's

---

mother used to be a housekeeper for Sandra's mother, and so the two children used to play together when they were young -- especially in the summer when school was out.

When I first started at HHJ, I was still involved in my teaching at St. Augustine. I never consciously thought about joining the order. I never really considered it seriously back then, but there was this first curiosity. Perhaps it was God placing the thought in my head.

Perhaps.

I am told that stranger things have happened and that God works in mysterious ways: courting us, sending us subtle love messages, and waiting for our desire to ripen. I am beginning to believe it is true.

Nell Massa

Chapter 58

Dear Kelvin,

I am trying to remember how Sandra came to have such influence at House of Hope and Joy.

Merry had pretty much been in charge since Sister Matilda had taken ill. Merry was the best "boss" there could ever be. She was beyond fair. In her eyes, every person on staff had a voice. Everyone had something to offer, and everyone had something to learn.

Maybe it's just me, but I can't imagine a bank where the woman scrubbing the toilets is allowed to give the bank president some advice.

But maybe if that's the way things worked every where, the world would be in better shape. There are certain things only floor sweepers and toilet scrubbers can know about. And bank presidents should listen to their wisdom. They should also ask them, "And how are your children?"

But that's just not done in this world.

Well, it would be done if Merry had her way.

That's one thing I really admire in her. She has respect for everyone, top and bottom, and every level in between. No one should be so high and mighty as to be above learning from someone that others might consider "down below."

Anyway, we came to learn that Sandra's brother was rather wealthy, due to superior business and investment savvy. After that first festival, Sandra took it upon herself to get us a heap of money: several million dollars. Enough to remodel and expand HHJ.

Sandra's brother, Anthony, came to visit. Merry organized meetings with staff and volunteers, even with the Clean Teens. She made sure Anthony and Sandra listened to everyone and heard all of their suggestions. He and Merry also spoke with architects, builders, and sustainability specialists; the renovation was set into motion.

The kitchen would be made larger and given more ventilation. They would install a rolling "door" to block the noise of the kitchen from the meeting room so it wasn't so noisy when people were trying to listen. A dishwasher would be put in, so House of Hope and Joy wouldn't use so much polystyrene, plastic and paper. Instead, we'd use real dishes, cups and utensils. Even paper napkins were going to be reduced, in favor of cloth ones that would be washed and reused.

The toilets were going to have "half flush" features so that full flushes were only used for solid waste. All other flushes could be half flushes to save water. Rain barrels would collect water for all flushing and solar panels would cut down on the electricity bill. This earth-friendly renovation would make St. Francis very proud. After all, he is the patron saint of ecology!

And best of all, there would be two additional "conference rooms," and one of them would be the "home turf" of the Clean Teens!

The teens asked for storage cabinets and hide-away desks, which could close up and become smaller for meetings and could open up as work space for projects.

It was Paul's idea to create a big parking lot, surrounded by a high fence, to make the place safer for staff and volunteers. He also suggested a car port and a drop-off area, to facilitate and quicken the process for when food and clothing were dropped off. Monique and Kim would each get an office, and both the clothing boutique and the food pantry would be enlarged. An entire work room was put into the basement, with tables and shelves for sorting items for holiday food and toys, and for things like the back-to-school supplies and Easter baskets.

Leah got a nicer room for meeting with guests, and of course, the lobby became larger, warmer and more welcoming.

After all the plans were made, the construction lasted from February until October. They did Easter basket distribution and back-to-school back packs and school supplies distribution at the Guadalupe Center, since HHJ was kind of a mess. Carlos was great. He found room for everything we needed.

Everyone told me he was good as gold, and I knew they were right.

The one thing I did worry about was all the dust from eight months of construction. Everything was covered with dust, and it seemed that every time I came by, everyone was coughing. We had Clean Teens meet at Guadalupe, and I only came by for short visits to see how HHJ was coming along. Every time I came by, I could only stay for an hour or two... eventually, my eyes got irritated, and I started having to clear my throat.

I don't know how everyone else managed it, but they hung in there.

We didn't do a Festival of Hope and Joy that summer, but we did "party extra hearty" at the Guadalupe fundraiser.

When all that construction was finally done, what a beautiful place it was! The secret to our success was Merry's willingness to listen to everyone. I think Sandra realized HHJ was in good hands, and that's why she worked so hard to convince her brother to take on this project as his "new favorite charity."

In return, the biggest meeting room was called the St. Anthony room after Sandra's brother and also after St. Anthony, a famous Franciscan, the patron saint of finding lost articles.

All was going well until we started moving things into the new building. Sandra was on hand to assist us, and Sister Matilda trusted her and Merry to take care of things.

Sandra insisted on decorating everything herself. She did have good taste, and so that didn't seem to be such a bad idea at first.

But eventually, our beloved House of Hope and Joy began to feel like a sterile art museum.

Nothing personal was allowed on the walls. Everything had to keep this new, professional, "polished" look. Even the Christmas decorations had to be approved.

How shall I say this? Before, the Christmas decorations were more homemade and more child-teen friendly. Cute and homey. Comfy, like your grandmother's home.

But Sandra was clear that if we expected to get additional funding, the place needed to look less mismatched and more intentional. More sleek and modern. Cleaner lines and less "clutter."

The St. Clare social committee always had an early Christmas party. This group started back when the HHJ building was part of St. Clare parish. That parish had been closed down, and the convent was converted into House of Hope and Joy years ago. But somehow, the St. Clare social committee remained. They mostly attended St. Augustine now, but they kept the name for sentimental reasons.

Anyway, they decorated HHJ on the first Sunday of Advent every year, and their decorations stayed up until the feast of the Epiphany, when they returned to take them down. It was always a nice social custom. Both the "decorating" and the "de-frocking" activities were grand events. They brought food, and HHJ staff and volunteers were always invited.

Sandra was horrified to find out that they had such old and worn out decorations. She wanted to buy all new items and have her brother pay for them.

The sweet people in the St. Clare social committee were very hurt and confused. They supported the renovation of the building and looked forward to the new space, and had been planning the decorations for quite a while. Even their new decorations were not acceptable to Sandra.

Merry described it this way: It was as if the new building had become an idol. Protecting the building from an "unprofessional" appearance had become more important than protecting the feelings of the people from insensitive policies. That was not something St. Clare or St. Francis would ever do.

Paul suggested that the St. Clare social committee decorate the Clean Teen room. It was a great idea. They -- and we -- ate our food in the St. Anthony room, but we "worked" in the Clean Teen Room. While the St. Clare committee decorated the Clean Teen room, Sandra and a few other volunteers decorated the St. Anthony room and the adult conference room.

To a stranger, I'd have to admit, the other two rooms looked "better" than the Clean Teen room. They looked like a cover of *Good Housekeeping* magazine. But I felt more comfortable in the one decorated by the St. Clare folks. Maybe because after a while, "your own" decorations seem the most comforting. (Like that song says, "the prettiest sight you'll see is the holly that will be on your own front door...")

Every year, the St. Clare folks have had their picture taken at HHJ, and they take a picture of the HHJ staff and volunteers. Once again, our new decorations posed a dilemma. Leah suggested we take two pictures of each group -- one in the Clean Teen room, and one in the St. Anthony room. Again, it was a compromise, but it worked, and it kept the peace.

Even though the St. Anthony picture was the one in the newsletter, we all kept the St. Clare picture in our homes. What a great group! What a great team! Merry our leader, and Leah, Sheryl, Monique, Kim and Paul sitting in the front row. And behind them were you, Ruby, me, Luz and Andy. I still have that picture. It's my favorite.

Thanks to Paul and Leah, we got through that little disagreement without any hard feelings.

It did make us chuckle. Paul reported to me that whenever a group asked to use a meeting room, Sheryl would reserve the adult conference room for them. Always, as they walked past the Clean Teen room and saw the old familiar decorations, they asked for a switch. As long as the Teens weren't using it, they always got it.

Once Christmas was over, I asked Merry about hanging bulletin boards in the St. Anthony room. They presented workshops to middle school students every winter and spring, and they needed to hang their posters on something.

Merry knew that Sandra wouldn't want bulletin boards on the walls of the St. Anthony room or in the other conference room. But she managed to talk Sandra into hanging bulletin boards and white boards in the Clean Teen's room.

In March, the mayor had asked to use House of Hope and Joy conference room for a meeting of local religious leaders. He was looking for a location that was not the place of worship for any one congregation. It was such an honor for us to be chosen.

Sandra went to work preparing both the St. Anthony room and the "adult" conference room. That way, either room could be used, depending on how large the crowd was.

When the mayor came in, he passed the Clean Teen room, with its bulletin boards and white board. He was brought to the adult room, with its beautiful artwork, and then the St. Anthony room, equally beautiful with paintings and wall hangings. He asked if he could use the Teen's room. "But why?" asked Sandra.

The mayor looked at her as if the answer were so obvious. "It's more practical. We can write on the white board and hang our newsprint sheets on the bulletin boards!"

Funny how certain influential people -- like the mayor -- can be heard while other "less influential people" -- such as the entire HHJ staff -- are not heard!

One week later, the adult conference room had bulletin boards and white boards hanging on one wall, with the art relocated to other walls. And brand new rolling white boards and cork boards were bought to be used in the St. Anthony room.

Yes, Paul and I still chuckle about that.

Merry was very pastoral about the whole thing. But she tried to challenge Sandra just a little bit.

"St. Clare and St. Francis were known for their hospitality, not for the beauty of the places where they offered their hospitality. St. Francis would tell you this -- and so would St. Anthony -- the way you treat guests is more important than the way you decorate your walls. We can talk the talk, but we also have to walk the walk. We don't want our walls to become more important than the needs of our guests..."

Sandra reluctantly agreed, and she stopped pushing her decoration agenda after that. Apparently, she was not willing to listen to the opinions of the Clean Teens or the HHJ staff, but she did listen to the mayor and accommodate his needs.

Months later, Merry confessed to me that she had spoken with the mayor ahead of time and set up that entire thing!

Chapter 59

Dear Kelvin,

One more story about House of Hope and Joy.

I remember when Monique's sister called HHJ. Keshia needed her fast. She wanted to get away from Tyrone, her husband, and she didn't know where to go. Keshia had been one of my students at St. Augustine.

Monique immediately got Leah, who suggested that Keshia be picked up right away. Ruby went with Monique, and they took her to Guadalupe Center, because they thought Tyrone might come to HHJ looking for her. Sure enough, he did.

You were there to talk him down and to get him to go back home.

You came over to Guadalupe, where Luz and Fernando were already talking to Keshia.

It's the first time I realized what an alcoholic personality was like. I never knew that Fernando used to work with recovering alcoholics. His parents were alcoholic. He knew exactly what Keshia's life was like. I just sat in silence, taking it all in.

I had been on a St. Augustine committee with Tyrone a long time ago. I was new and found him very hard to work with. One time someone handed him a door prize from an event he had missed. His name had been called, and so this person had kept the prize to give to him. It was a can of mixed nuts, wrapped in colorful party paper. He threw it across the room! "I'm not in the mood for presents," He yelled at her. I was shocked. At the time, I assumed he was angry at her for some other reason, but that was still no way to treat anyone. I eventually found out that she barely knew him!

There is still a mark at St. Augustine where that can of nuts hit the door frame.

He would also change his mind easily and pretend he hadn't said something he said before.

One time he was leading some subcommittee on something, and I remember asking him if he expected me to go to a particular meeting. He said, "If you knew me at all, you would know that I would not 'need' you there." Ok, I thought. I guess I somehow insulted him by implying that he couldn't get along without me. I was only trying to help.

Later, he asked me where I was that night. He had been expecting me. "I thought you said you didn't need me there," I responded. He said, "If you knew me at all, you would know that I expected you to be there."

I tried to explain that he had pretty much told me not to go, but he didn't listen to my defense. He just talked over me and said, "Yada-yada-yada, blah-blah-blah, whatever. Next time, don't be so inconsiderate."

I showed up at the next meeting. He said, "What are you doing here?" Again, I was confused. I asked, "Didn't you ask me to be here?" Same response as before, "Did you think I 'needed' you here?" That was it. I quit the committee. I never realized he was Monique's brother-in-law. I also never realized he was an alcoholic.

All that time, I felt as if I were the crazy one. Finding out he had a drinking problem made me realize that I was normal, and he was the one who was dysfunctional. He was just angry and impatient because of the drinking. I can't imagine living with someone like that.

Anyway, I heard Keshia talk about it. Whenever he made a sandwich, he made a big mess in the kitchen. If she didn't clean it up before he returned, he would yell at her for keeping such a sloppy house. He expected everything to be clean all the time. Yet, if he saw her cleaning it up, he would yell at her. "I can clean up my own messes. What do you think I am, a slob? You think I'm a slob, don't you?" and he would start poking at her. So she had to always find a way to sneak into the kitchen without him knowing it and clean up any mess before he had a chance to realize it was messy.

At night, his snoring was so loud, she couldn't sleep at all. She would sneak out of the room and sleep on the couch with the alarm clock tucked between her legs under her big bathrobe. She could shut it off in less than a second, before it made any noise he could hear, then sneak back upstairs into bed so he wouldn't know she ever left the bed. Once he found her sleeping on the couch and yelled at her. "I woke up and you weren't there! What do you think you're doing, sleeping on the couch? Who do you think you are? You are my wife, and you sleep with me!" He grabbed her and shoved her back into bed.

One time, he was driving her to work. But he started to pass by the store where she worked. He wouldn't stop the car. "I have to get out here," she said. "I'll say when you get out." A block farther, he got a red light, so she went to get out. He kept jamming on the brake, shaking the car, making it impossible for her to get out. She was being thrown back and forth in the seat. He finally pulled up so close to the car in front of them, that he had to stop the car. She got out immediately, crossed the street and started walking back. He quickly turned the car around and drove back toward her and opened the window, yelling, "Get in! Get in this car right away!" She ran in the opposite direction, even though it was away from the store, since she had to escape him. Once he was around the block, she ran back to the store. She got there safely but didn't tell anyone.

Finally, this time, she was really afraid. She came home, and he had just made a sandwich. He was cutting it with a big knife. The kitchen was a mess again, but she was more worried about the knife. He started waving it at her, saying, "What's the matter? Are you afraid of me? Are you afraid of your crazy husband? Do you think he might hurt you? You better run! Run, Keshia, run! You better get out of here fast! Your crazy husband might hurt you with this knife!"

She did run. She was afraid he would run right after her, with that knife. But he didn't. He stayed and ate his sandwich. She wondered if he would even remember the incident at all.

Fernando explained exactly what it was like living with Tyrone, because he knew completely.

Alcoholics make promises they can't keep. They lie. They make demands. They are never satisfied. They complain about things that don't make any sense. They expect you to read their minds or they get angry. They can become violent and dangerous, and they will never get better until they get sober, for good.

Keshia was convinced. She had to stay away. She was pregnant and now more afraid than ever. Ruby offered to bring her home, but Carlos thought that was a bad idea, since he might look for Keshia there. Tyrone knew everyone from the House of Peace -- Ruby, you, Monique, me and Luz.

Carlos called Carmen and Felipe. They didn't have a lot of room in their new place, but Tyrone would never think to look there. He didn't know them.

So Carlos and I brought Keshia to stay with them for a while. Once Keshia was in their living room, on their couch, she started to sob. She just sobbed and sobbed. Carmen held her and rocked her like a momma, whispering to her everything would be OK. She stopped the wailing, but the tears kept falling. I started crying, too. I couldn't help it. Carlos saw and squeezed my hand. Rosa and Raúl came out, wanting to know about the noise and what was wrong. Felipe just told them, "This is Keshia. She is very sad. Remember when we were sad, when our house burned down? And we went to live with Luz and Fernando? Keshia is going to live with us for a while."

"Did her house burn down?" Rosa asked.

"No, honey. It's just unsafe," he explained. " She can't live there or everything will fall down on top of her."

Rosa left the room and returned with her blanket and teddy bear for Keshia, the same one that Monique had given her the day after their house fire. Keshia accepted it like a child and held it and rocked back and forth. Carmen continued to hold Keshia, and Rosa climbed on the couch behind her mother and put her arms around the both of them.

What a picture. This is what ministry looks like. This is what happens when children witness love and caring... when they learn what support is all about.

I cried all the way home. Carlos and I cuddled up on my couch, and I just kept crying softly. He never asked why. He completely understood. He stayed there all night, holding me on the couch.

Chapter 60

Outline for Christian leadership course at St. Augustine

What kind of leadership works? Leadership with these five characteristics:

ONE: Same Goal, Same Direction

Everyone holds the same values sacred. For example: ministry, love, respect, hospitality, peace, ecology. When the going gets rough, everyone reflects upon their values, their calling, their mission. They make decisions based on those values.

From Scripture, the Great Commissioning: "Go, therefore, and make disciples of all nations, baptizing them in the name of the Father and of the Son and of the Holy Spirit, teaching them to observe all that I have commanded you. And behold, I am with you always, even to the end of the age." (Matt 28:19-20)

(Inspiration: The people at House of Hope and Joy and at Guadalupe Center are doing similar ministry with the same values. Each staff works well with the other to deliver services, and the two organizations cooperate with each other and share resources.)

TWO: Shared Leadership, from Top and Bottom

Everyone has something to offer; everyone has something to learn. The opinion of the bank president is heard and so is the opinion of the woman or man who scrubs toilets or sweeps the floor. The leader is not to be the "boss over others," but the servant of others.

From Scripture, the Washing of the Feet: If I, therefore, the master and teacher, have washed your feet, you ought to wash one another's feet. I have given you a model to follow, so that as I have done for you, you should also do. (John 13:14-15)

(Inspiration: Merry listened to everyone when planning the renovations for the House of Hope and Joy. Everyone had excellent ideas, and she knew even the experts would learn from the ideas of the guests, and even the teenagers. Because she insisted on everyone having a voice, the designs chosen were outstanding and efficient, meeting the needs of the guests, the volunteers and the staff.)

THREE: Creativity from Diversity

Different types of people bring different ideas, different perspectives, different ways of thinking. Different brains can solve problems better, plan projects better, and evaluate situations better. A group of different brains will always think better and learn better than a group of similar brains.

From Scripture, the Analogy of the Body: There are many parts, yet one body. The eye cannot say to the hand, "I do not need you," nor again the head to the feet, "I do not need you." (1 Corinthians 12:20-21)

(Inspiration: Everyone's different ideas for the fundraiser turned into the gigantic Festival of Hope and Joy. We had male and female, different cultures, different age groups, and different perspectives.)

FOUR: Walk the Talk Together

We need to practice what we preach. We must mean what we say and say what we mean. We must demonstrate what we believe by the way we live. If we are here to serve, we must make the needs of the ones we serve our priority. We need to have integrity, and we need to be accountable to others.

From Scripture, "Anyone who wishes to be first must be the last of all, and a servant to all." (Mark 9:35)

(Inspiration: We could not say our ministry was done in the tradition of Clare and Francis if we gave more importance to our walls than to the needs of our guests.)

FIVE: Physical and Emotional Support

We need to take care of each other. We need to notice when someone's physical or emotional well-being is in danger, or when their basic needs are not being met.

From Scripture, the Feeding of the Five Thousand: His heart was moved with pity for them for they were like sheep without a shepherd; and he began to teach them many things... Then, taking the five loaves and the two fish and looking up to heaven, he said the blessing, broke the loaves, and gave them to his disciples to set before the people; he also divided the two fish among them all. (Mark 6:34-41)

(Inspiration: The way the staff and volunteers at HHJ and GC take care of one another and their families and friends. They open their homes, share their food, and dry each other's tears. If all the world were this compassionate, there would be no violence.)

Chapter 61

Dear Syliva,

I'm so glad you were able to visit me at St. Augustine. I didn't realize you had heard about my leadership class.

The concepts aren't brand new; Jesus taught them. They are Biblical and solid. But it was my ministry at House of Hope and Joy and their excellent staff who taught me what leadership is really all about.

Once I reflected on the way they treat each other, and the way they operate as a staff, I realized these were skills I could teach teenagers. Then it evolved into a full class. We use movie clips and do simulations activities to teach the concepts. They also spend some time as interns with different businesses.

You asked how my vocational reflections are coming along.

Well, they are coming along... I have lots of questions, but as long as I keep asking them, I am sure God will provide the answers in God's good time.

I have taken your advice and am doing lots of writing on my own. It has led to some creative reflections for Sister Agnes. In the beginning, she told me I wasn't going deep enough and I wasn't tapping into my feelings. I'm certainly going deeper now.

So I guess that's an improvement.

I would love to meet with you after school next week. Thanks so much for asking.

I'll continue to keep your ministry in my prayers.

Love, Nellie

Chapter 62

Dear Kelvin,

Well, I have been writing about Carlos... about how I had absolutely fallen in love with him.

I loved everything about him. I loved the ministry we shared, and I loved being able to depend on him. He was passionate and fun and loving and delightful, funny and intelligent, deep and spiritual. He was everything I ever said I was looking for, and I wasn't even looking! And he was so clearly devoted to me. How could I want anything more?

But I guess I did. I guess I wanted to be married. I guess I wanted a family. I guess my biological clock was almost completely ticked out, but I still had hope that maybe children were in my future. And I wanted them to look like Carlos.

Then, one Friday night in the early spring, we were on our way to see a movie when we passed a church. There was a wedding taking place. I don't even remember what I said exactly, but I mentioned the wedding... and marriage in general... and something about the two of us. That's all I could remember. He didn't jump on the idea; he didn't make fun of the idea. His response was very non-committal. It was not even memorable. I didn't even pay much attention, until later.

His birthday was coming soon, and I had a great birthday present planned for him, so I decided to work on it the next day. I bought a small, unfinished book shelf, which I sanded and painted. Then I traced and painted a picture of Our Lady of Guadalupe on one side, toward the top. I worked on it all day Saturday.

I had expected to see him at church the next day, but he wasn't there. I thought that was strange, because we almost always attended church together, unless one of us had an event at another church, or I was spending the weekend with my family, or something like that.

So I worked all day Sunday on his bookshelf. I kept expecting Carlos to call. I was ready to tell him I'd meet him someplace or pick him up, to avoid him coming in and seeing his secret present. But he didn't call me. I didn't think that much of it. I expected to hear from him before the end of the day.

When the whole weekend passed without a call, I left him a message at Guadalupe early Monday morning, but he never called back. I called a few more times and was told he would get back to me. Finally, two days later, I went over to the Center to see him. I asked where he was on Sunday, and he asked, "What was Sunday?" I said I thought I'd see him in church. He said he had other things he had to do.

Other things? What other things would he have to do that would keep him from church?

I let it go and waited to see what would happen. Well, nothing happened. He never called and never came over. He didn't come to HHJ, he didn't come to my apartment. After a week of this, I went back to Guadalupe to find out what was happening.

He let me in his office and shut the door. I asked him if something was wrong. He hesitated and started to speak, but then he stopped. I asked him if I had done anything wrong. He said no.

I waited. He said nothing. I asked him if he wanted to end our relationship. He still said nothing. I was near tears and really quite surprised. I never expected this response from him. I asked him to tell me what I did so I wouldn't do it again. He said he was sure I wouldn't do it again. I said, "But you just said I didn't do anything wrong." He said, "You didn't do anything wrong." I asked him to tell me what this was all about. I asked if I had hurt him in any way, and he said he realized I didn't do anything on purpose. I asked him once more to please tell me, and he said he didn't want to play twenty questions. He asked me not to call him at home anymore, and to just limit our conversations to youth ministry.

I was in shock. To this day, I don't know what happened. It remains a mystery to me.

What could it be? What did I do by mistake -- something which was not on purpose, but still bad enough to end our relationship of several years?

It was Adam all over again. No explanation. Total mystery.

Was it my comment about the wedding? About us? About marriage? I couldn't even remember exactly what I had said! But I left his office and went home.

I completely crashed. I lost it. I cried and cried. I punched pillows. I yelled out loud. I even yelled in Spanish.

I remembered what it was like that night I ripped all the pages out of my scrap book -- the night I was supposed to marry Adam. I felt like destroying something again.

I almost took a hammer to the bookshelf, but somehow I stopped myself.

I was certain the breakup was my fault. I was furious that he wouldn't tell me what I did. But most of all, I was furious at myself.

I jumped to a terrible conclusion -- that I would always be alone because I just wasn't lovable.

That had to be it. I seem to be lovable at first, but everyone who gets close to me decides that I'm not really lovable after all. That's why they just can't keep their commitment to me. I'm not something enough: not smart enough, not dedicated enough, not "wifey" enough... What on earth was it? If someone would just tell me, then I would know. But I was certain I would always be alone, because it was always my fault. It happened again and again! Can you see why I would think that? With no other explanation, what else could I think?

I kept wondering... What was it about me that made this happen? I couldn't imagine, but I was certain it was nothing that would ever change. I called Leah. I could hardly talk. She came over. I tried to tell her the whole story, but there wasn't much to tell. She tried walking me through everything that had happened since the last time we seemed tight and right for each other. All we could come up with was the wedding and marriage thing.

But why would someone just clam up and not talk? Why after so much time? Leah called Ruby and Monique and they all came over with wine and cheese and crackers. My favorite party food. I didn't feel like partying, but I knew the wine would make me feel sleepy, and without it, I'd probably be up all night. We watched *Seinfeld* reruns, and I told them all about Ray and his weird quirks. I fell asleep on the couch, and they all crashed. I think the TV was on all night.

You called in the morning, wondering how I was doing. Ruby had told you. I said I was OK. I hadn't ripped any books or broken any furniture. You just laughed. You brought us all muffins and coffee, and I showed everyone the bookshelf. It was a consensus that I should keep the shelf myself, or bring it to House of Hope and Joy if it was too painful to see every day.

Eventually everyone went home, and I took a shower and tried to think about how I would start my new life without Carlos. I was just so sick of having to "start new lives" without someone I thought would always be by my side....

I just didn't know how to cope. I was kind of numb still, and not just from the wine.

Two days later, it was Carlos' birthday. Against everyone's advice, I put the bookshelf in my car and drove to the Guadalupe Center. Carlos was in his office, and it was full of streamers and balloons. Before he could say, "I asked you not to contact me unless it was ministry related," I started talking.

I told him I had spent an entire weekend working on a really great birthday present for him and he could refuse it if he wanted, but once he saw it, I knew he would be very happy to have it.

He agreed to accept it. I went to the car and took it out, and carried it into the center.

When he saw the painting of Our Lady of Guadalupe, he was definitely moved. He was definitely touched. He definitely lost his anger for whatever it was I did.

He said, "How can I stay upset about anything with you? Thank you so much for this beautiful and precious gift." He hugged me, for at least a minute, but he did not kiss me.

I whispered in his ear, "Is whatever I did so terrible that you really want to end everything with me?"

He whispered back, "You didn't do anything terrible."

I waited, and then asked quietly, "Then what happened?"

He held me a long time in silence. Then he just whispered, "*Nada.*"

I asked him if he would have supper with me to celebrate his birthday. He said no, but he had tears in his eyes.

I begged him, "Please tell me what happened." Again, silence.

All this time, he held me. It must have been close to five minutes in his arms. I could smell him again, hear his breathing, feel the wet of his tears on the side of my face. I wondered if this would be the last time I would ever hold him. I finally pulled away and looked at his sad face. He said nothing. We looked at each other for at least another minute. It just got to be too painful.

I said something pointless, like "See you later" and left.

This was just too much for me to take. What was next? More hitting pillows? More drinking wine and eating cheese and crackers? I had no scrapbook to tear apart, and I already gave away the bookshelf I was going to destroy. I went home and watched *M*A*S*H* reruns. At least it wasn't *Seinfeld*.

Chapter 63

Dear Adam,

If you are reading this, it means that I actually contacted your mother, got your phone number, called you, talked to you and got your commitment to work through some issues with me.

Adam, I don't know what I'm going to say to you when I get the chance, but I am determined to talk with you. You have been the center of my life ever since I can remember. And you still are! Anytime something awful happens, it's as if time stood still, and there I am again in my room, surrounded by pictures of us together, and my wedding dress, and all the wedding cards to Nellie and Adam, and I am alone, crying and looking at my scrapbooks, wondering, "What happened?"

Adam, when you left me, I fell apart. I never had any other desire except to be your wife and have your children. I never got over you. It was the worst thing to ever happen to me. I realize I have been trying to find someone just like you ever since... and that's really impossible. All I can find are some very faint copies at best. At worst, some have been real disasters.

That same "worst thing" feeling happened again to me when my husband Timothy left me. Only I realized that Timothy wasn't meant to be my soul mate. He was just someone I said yes to, because I was so lonely and so sad to have lost you.

But I have been with a wonderful man for several years. And all of a sudden, with no explanation, that relationship is over.

YOU MUST TELL ME WHAT IS SO WRONG WITH ME THAT EVERY MAN I EVER LOVED LEAVES ME WITH NO EXPLANATION! WHAT IS IT ABOUT ME? WHY DID YOU LEAVE ME?

You didn't even talk to me at my father's funeral. Do you realize how cruel that was? I can't imagine you know how painful it has been for me. You just have never been a cruel person. What happened?

You were my best friend for the first twenty years of my life. And I have spent almost that much time grieving your loss and wondering why my best friend left without a word.

I love you still, and I would marry you this minute. Well, that would be a crazy thing to do. But if I found you, and poured out my heart to you, and you were the same Adam I always remembered, and you told me it was all a big mistake, and you wanted me back, I would take you back without hesitation! I know that every relationship I've ever had has just been a substitute for you. I have tried to resolve this issue, but I just can't figure out why you would leave me and never say why. Didn't you love me for most of your early life?

Please help unlock this mystery for me. It has been ruining my life. I need you to be honest with me. I need you to tell me what it is about me that makes men want to run away from me as soon as I truly believe in them.

Please talk with me, Adam. I want to hear what happened. You really do owe me this explanation. Even if there is something horrible about me, you need to tell me. I need to know. Or I'll just keep making the same mistake over and over and over.

Please. I really need you now... more than ever.

I love you.

Nellie

Chapter 64

Dear Kelvin,

Sometimes I have very significant dreams.

I had this dream that I was back with two of our college friends, talking about Adam. We were all saying how much we liked him, how much we enjoyed this or that about him.

It was great. I felt close to him again. I was wearing a sweater he gave me when we were in college.

When I woke up, I felt very strange about the whole thing.

I hadn't done anything with my letter to him yet, but this dream made me feel more urgent about it.

Then I thought a horrible thought -- what was that dream all about? Where were we? Were we at a funeral lunch? Were we at *Adam's* funeral?

Immediately, I got up to call Adam's mother.

Before I could reach the phone, it rang. It was my mother. She had called me to tell me that Adam's father had died.

I was shocked! I didn't even tell her about my dream. It was just too weird. I asked her if she thought I could call Adam's mother, and she thought that would be a good idea.

When I called, Adam answered the phone.

I never expected that to happen.

I told him how good it was to hear his voice and that I had just had a very significant dream about him. I told him my mom had called me about his dad and how sorry I was. He agreed to meet me for lunch.

It was so good to see him. We hugged each other as if we had never parted.

I told him my dream. I told him how frightened I was when I woke up and thought perhaps it had been a dream about his funeral.

Then he told me that the two friends in my dream were the two friends he had been with the night before. They got together to talk, and they had actually talked about me last night. They said I was the first one of their group of friends to join "the club."

I asked, "What club?"

"The club of people whose fathers have died," he said. Now, he and I and both of his friends were in that club. They had been talking about this very thing last night. And then I had that dream about them.

It gave me chills.

We both cried. I told him I still missed him so much. He said he missed me, too. I told him I had just suffered a terrible heartache with someone whom I thought loved me, and it plunged me back into one of my "Adam depressions." I told him I had written a letter to him all about it. I hadn't had the nerve to mail it yet, but I had it with me, and I gave it to him.

He wanted to read it right there, in the restaurant, but I suggested we at least go sit in my car. Or his car.

We sat in my car.

We both cried and cried.

I can't even write about this now. I have to stop.

I hate that I get so emotional writing about my life. I didn't used to do this. How can I have so many tears? Don't they ever run out?

More later.

Chapter 65

Dear Adam,

Wow.

I now realize why they call these heart-to-heart talks. I guess when you really pour your heart out to someone, it physically affects your heart. Literally, my heart hurts. Like the night that was supposed to be our wedding night and I realized you weren't calling me... I thought I was going to have a heart attack and die.

Once again, I feel completely exhausted and empty. I feel as if I ripped my heart right out of my chest and put it in your hands.

After you read my letter, I told you about my sad and childless marriage to Timothy and my delightful relationship with Carlos and its mysterious ending. I cried and cried. I never expected you to listen so intently. I never expected you to cry with me and hold me.

You said your mother still hoped you and I would get back together. She was the only one who was relieved to hear that Timothy had left me.

I wanted to write down what you said, before I forgot it. You said you never stopped loving me. You said you never had a relationship with any other woman. You said leaving me was the hardest thing you ever did, and you never got over losing me, either. You said that every single night for almost twenty years, you fell asleep thinking about me.

I stared at you in disbelief. Your next two words knocked me over. And you never said them out loud to anyone before??!! All these years, and you finally told the person who has loved you like no other.

Finally, you told me. "I'm gay."

Just when I thought I was out of tears, they started flowing like never before. But it was an entirely new feeling in my heart. It was as if your courage was filling me up. And before we knew it, both of our hearts were full again. It's as if our trust in each other had cured the emptiness.

I couldn't believe you had hidden this truth all these years. It just makes you more lovable, not less.

I didn't know what to expect when you agreed to meet me for lunch. I never expected you to tell me such a secret. Not only was I surprised that you didn't tell me back then, I am still surprised you hadn't ever told anyone to this day. It's 1999! People are much more open now! It's really time you explained your life to people who love you. Make 2000 the new millennium of your new life, free and "out of the closet." At least, you should consider coming out to your family. I know they would understand and love you and support you. In fact, I bet most of your family already suspects this to be true. I bet Gemma already has a hunch.

You just need to know that day we just spent together was one of the best days in my life. Spending a whole day "remembering our relationship" was the best therapy for me -- probably for both of us. I didn't think you would have the time to come back to my apartment. What a relief to finally take the nose tape off of my box of scrapbook pages! The look on your face when you saw all the ripped pages was so pained. It was as if I had ripped you out of my life. In a way, that's what I was trying to do. But only because I had been ripped out of yours, and I thought it was my only way forward.

I'm so glad I didn't throw out all the pages. You lovingly looked at every picture. We laughed and cried all afternoon. I feel healed; I feel complete again. I feel as if I have my best friend back in my life again. I guess that's because I do.

> *"This above all -- to thine own self be true. And it must follow as the night, the day.*
>
> *Thou canst not then be false to any man."*

We found that page, where I made a red line around that quote and added, "or woman." I had forgotten that English class when you played the part of Polonius as he gave this advice to his son Laertes. What a great quote for us to find together.

What would Shakespeare think if he had realized that centuries later, a gay man and his former fiancé would be looking at *Hamlet* and seeing such deep meaning in his words. That's probably something only an English teacher would consider.

I realize now that the reason you left me without an explanation was because you didn't have an explanation. And in your own mind, what you were doing was really crazy. And perhaps you yourself indeed felt crazy! Your best friend (me) was in love with you, adored you, and wanted to have children with you. We did everything together and were inseparable ever since kindergarten! So what could be wrong?

What indeed? No wonder you ran away! No wonder you were embarrassed! How could you understand what was going on inside you? You didn't have words for it. When we were kids, no one talked about homosexuality. I didn't even know what it was until maybe college or after. And even then, it was this distant concept... it was nothing anyone I ever knew would be "involved" with, and yet look at what that ignorance did to us.

Anyway, I truly had no idea what demons you had to deal with. I did know you became depressed, but didn't know why. I secretly hoped there was some logical explanation that put the whole thing in perspective and that, eventually, you'd come running back into my arms, my hero once again!

In some ways, that's exactly what happened. It took a lot of courage for you to tell me the truth, and you are even more beautiful to me now than ever.

The Me of Us still loves the You of Us so very, very much.

Chapter 66

Dear Kelvin,

Remember that song -- "Don't you know I go to sleep and leave the lights on, hoping you'll come by and know that I'm at home, still awake?" -- you know, that song was all about me!

Lots of times, I went to sleep with my light on, hoping that Adam would come by and throw pebbles at my window. I don't know how many times I would sneak downstairs and out the back door so we could sit on the steps and talk.

I grew up with Adam. And our love grew together. In fact, our idea of what love was grew together. He never hurt me on purpose in any way.

When he walked out on our engagement, I just couldn't imagine Adam would hurt me. So it had to be my fault. And I just felt so lost and broken and ripped up and discarded.

I think I carried that shame into my marriage with Timothy, not knowing it.

It wasn't Adam's fault. I realize he wasn't able to tell me. It's just that because I didn't reflect enough, I blamed it all on myself. I assumed there was something major about me that made me unlovable. Had I gone to counseling or talked it out with someone, instead of turning inward and trying to bury my feelings, I might have learned something. I might have grown stronger. But we just didn't do that sort of thing back then. Nobody did... it wasn't done.

I wasted so much of my life living in unnecessary shame. I ended up carrying a lot of baggage with me when I married Timothy.

When Adam finally trusted me enough to tell me his biggest, darkest, most horrible secret, it became something not so horrible after all! In fact, it became something to celebrate because it took away all my shame and all his guilt. It made us best friends again!

I am so thankful that he came back into my life -- so very thankful.

I guess I started writing to you as "practice" for Sister Agnes, and now I am thinking that this writing has taken on a spirit of its own. So I decided to include letters from Adam to help me "document" my whole journey. Meeting up with Adam again really did help me turn a corner on how I see myself. I am going to keep writing, not because you need to hear how the story ends (obviously) but because I need to write it. Somehow, I really feel a need now to just keep writing it out.

Funny, the main reason I wanted to connect back with Adam was to find out what happened with Carlos. I still don't know for sure, but I know this -- it wasn't my fault. Maybe it was my mention of marriage. Maybe it was something else. But if someone isn't going to be honest with me, there is nothing I can do about it. I can cry because I love him, I can cry because I miss him, but I don't need to cry about "something unfixable that is wrong with me." I don't need to cry about "always being alone." I don't need to cry about "not being lovable."

I wish everyone could find a way to be honest. Look at the pain I suffered (and not only me, but others) because Adam, and Timothy and Carlos couldn't bear to deal with the truth. I imagine Ray and others have similar pain in their hearts. People seem to think the pain of denial is easier to bear than the pain of facing difficult truth. But once you face the truth, that pain lessens. The pain of denial never lessens. I guess that's why people keep quoting Jesus saying, "The truth shall set you free." (John 8:32)

From now on, I need to be more perceptive about the source of my pain and what is really causing it. That way I can expose my own denial and be more honest about my own issues. I can claim what's my stuff and what isn't. And when someone chooses to avoid the truth, for whatever reason, I can stay strong. That person might be afraid of honesty, but I will not allow his (or her) dysfunction to become mine.

All that being said, it was very sad that Adam didn't get to tell all this to his father. I am sure his father would have accepted him.

The funeral was very sad. Gemma and I cried in each other's arms. She's a beautiful woman now, married to Brad, with three children. She promised Ben and Mary to get together with them soon. They grew up as "playmates" and it's a shame they fell out of touch.

Adam and I knew it was confusing for so many people to see us together again, but we just didn't feel a need to explain anything. And nobody dared to ask us.

Chapter 67

Dear Kelvin,

For the first time in years, Adam's family and my family had Thanksgiving together again. And Adam and I were together again! Not together in the romantic sense, but together again as friends and closer than ever. He had a lot of catching up to do.

He had come out to his family, and then to my family. I am not sure my whole family appreciates completely what kind of pain we both had been through, but they were willing to accept him at their home because I was there, and I accepted Adam, and that's what was most important to them.

I think Ben and Mary talked with Adam and Gemma the most, but that makes sense since Gemma and Ben were such good friends growing up.

I had to give Adam a crash course ahead of time, so he could remember who was who. Then the day before, I quizzed him on all the facts. It went something like this:

"Who's the doctor?"

"Phil."

"Right. Who's the musician?"

"Trick question."

"VERY GOOD! Who are the *musicians*?"

"Phil and Charlie."

"Correct, but incomplete. There are more."

"Right! All the girls."

"Yes, and also..."

"Margaret?"

"Perfect! Who can tell you about Apollo and Zeus?"

"Ben."

"Right. Who likes dogs?"

"Connie."

"Well, 50%. That's because it was a trick question. Connie has two dogs, but Ann wants a dog, so technically they both like dogs. And actually, Beth likes dogs, too."

"OK, got it."

"Who likes horses?"

"Ann -- but is that a trick question, too?"

"Maybe. Connie might like horses, too. Not sure."

"Who's the Harry Potter fan?"

"Is that a trick question?"

"Maybe."

"OK -- all three girls."

"Well -- excellent guess. I think it's probably all three girls, plus Margaret, and maybe Beth, and maybe even Charlie."

"Oh, good to know."

"Who will beat anyone at *Trivial Pursuit*?"

"Margaret."

"Right. Who will beat you at everything?"

"Margaret."

"Right again. Who do you go to for medical advice?"

"Phil."

"Trick question."

"Oh! Right! Beth, too!"

"Ooh, you are good. Who knew my dad?"

"Trick question! It could be all your brothers and Margaret, or it could also be... Mary!"

"EXCELLENT!"

I figured Adam was ready for everyone.

Again, I know that you know all about this strange story of how Mary "met" my dad, but I thought it was important to put it in writing. I feel compelled to tell the story again, even though I wasn't there when it happened. I have tried to get Mary to talk about it on tape, but she really doesn't want to. So I'll just record it in my writings to you.

Again, nothing I will ever tell Sister Agnes, but maybe Sylvia, some day.

It had been several years ago, in December. Mary had just started dating Ben. She needed to see a doctor about an ear infection, and so Ben took her to the doctor who had been my dad's good friend. They even collaborated on some difficult cancer surgeries together. Eventually, this doctor bought my dad's old office. I was going to meet Mary that night for the first time.

I was helping my mom get things ready for Christmas: decorations, cards, sorting items into piles before I wrapped them, so I knew who received which gift. Twice that day a very strange thing happened. As I walked past the dining room, an image of my dad looked over at me from a wreath in the middle of the room. It was a familiar image -- the very same picture my brothers and I had seen many times before, because my mom has it framed in her bedroom.

After my dad died, Mom was going through his things, and she found his new camera. It had some film in it, and when the film was developed, one of the pictures was this very image -- my dad looking at the camera, with a peaceful reassuring smile. We assumed he had taken that picture of himself to test the camera. It was great to receive such a comforting image after his death.

Well, that was the image I saw in the wreath as I walked by the dining room. The second time I saw the image, it was moving, like the portraits in Hogwarts, the magical school where Harry Potter attended. Obviously, that struck me as strange. I started to go over there to take a closer look, but someone came down the steps, and I was distracted. By the time I remembered, I went over to look, and neither that image, nor any other, was sitting inside the wreath.

I thought nothing of it until that night when I met Mary. After dinner, Ben said that Mary had something to tell us. But Mary seemed a little shaken up, so she asked Ben to start off the story.

Mary had been in my dad's old office and was called in from the waiting room to one of the examining rooms. She was there alone. She looked up when she heard the door open, and in walked a doctor wearing a white coat and a stethoscope around his neck. He sat down and started taking notes. He didn't say anything, so neither did she. She waited and waited, but he still said nothing. He appeared to be busy writing something down. Then he got up and smiled and lifted up one index finger (as if to say, "Just one moment") and he left the room. She remembered he had a toothpick in his mouth.

Later, a nurse came in to take her temperature and blood pressure. She told Mary that the doctor would be in to see her soon. Mary thought that was weird, but said nothing about the doctor who had just been in there.

After seeing the doctor, who had been my dad's friend, and getting a prescription, she asked about the other doctor. "What other doctor?" he asked. "The doctor who came in before you did." He looked confused. "There is no other doctor here. That was a nurse."

Mary didn't say anything. She just returned to the waiting room to meet back up with Ben. She passed through a hallway she hadn't been in before, and right there she saw a picture of that mysterious silent doctor who had just been in the examination room with her. Underneath the picture, it said, "Joe Massa. 1930-1983."

She immediately got Ben and showed him the picture. "This doctor had just been in the examination room with me. He didn't say anything the whole time. He just wrote things down on his yellow pad, gestured to me that he'd be right back, and left."

Ben's face got white. "This is my dad. You said you just saw him?"

"Yes. I just saw him. He came in, he wrote down something, and he put up his finger as if to say, 'wait just a minute' and he left. The door opened and shut and everything. He was chewing on a toothpick."

"A toothpick!" Ben gasped. "My dad always had a toothpick in his mouth! Ever since he stopped smoking!"

The two of them tried not to get too worked up over this, but it was very freaky.

Then they decided not to tell anyone until they came back to dinner. Mary hated to tell everyone this story the very first time she met everyone, but Ben insisted.

Beth commented that now she was the only one who had never met Charlie's dad. We all laughed. We needed a funny comment like that to break the tension of the "freaky factor."

Later in the evening, I told Ben and Mary about my vision in the dining room. When I showed her the picture I thought was appearing in the wreath and coming to life, Ben said that it was the very same picture hanging in the office. In fact, when we did a time check, we discovered that it was about the same time of day this happened to both of us!

Then, that night, there was a big storm. The wind was incredible. There was a giant crash outside that woke everyone up. We all came running down the stairs. A huge branch from a tree fell down upon a bench in the backyard. Next to that bench, untouched, was the picnic table my dad had made decades ago.

I don't know what to make of all this; I never have known. Every so often, I tell someone the story, just to get their take on it. Most often, I hear that these apparitions are more common than we think. They happen often for reasons we don't understand, but always people seek to find meaning in them. One common thread is that the visions appear to people who at first don't recognize who they are. If my dad had appeared to me or one of my brothers, then it would have been easy to dismiss it. "Oh, you were just daydreaming, and your imagination took over for a moment." That was my exact feeling upon seeing what I thought was the moving image of my dad in that dining room wreath.

But when it happens to someone who couldn't have known any better, then it has more validity. Mary never met my dad and never even saw his picture until she had been in that office. She had no way of knowing that he liked chewing on toothpicks. That made it all the more real.

What does it all mean? I wish I knew. Maybe all it means is that my dad is part of the communion of saints. He is watching down on us, and his love for us is so obvious, it becomes visible from time to time.

Anyway, Adam knew my dad and remembered him chewing on toothpicks. He found that story most delightful and was glad to hear it had happened.

But he promised me he would be checking out the wreath in the dining room, come Christmastime. I was just glad that Adam had plans to be in our family's dining room again.

All in all, it was a great Thanksgiving.

Lots of stories, lots of laughter, and plenty of food. Mary's sweet potatoes have become an expected part of the meal. Adam asked for the recipe. Gemma told him she already had it and could email it to him.

We didn't talk about my dad's apparition at dinner; there were too many other things to talk about... but I was thinking the same thing Adam was thinking -- that every year at Christmastime, I look forward to checking out that wreath my mom hangs in the dining room. I haven't seen my dad there since, but I always look.

Chapter 68

Dear Agnes,

When I was in high school, I remember one year I visited a friend's family the day after Thanksgiving. She was new in school, and she left a few months later to attend another school. I can't even remember her name. But I remember her house.

They had a lot of money, and her house was beautiful. It was so beautiful, it was almost like a prison.

I was not allowed to use the "guest bathroom," since that was for "guests" (Funny, since I thought I was a guest). The furniture in the living room was off-limits, in case we got it messed up. The dining room table was off-limits because of the antique table cloth; her mom was afraid we'd spill something on it. When we ate, we did it standing up, at the counter in the kitchen, just the two of us. Even the kitchen table had a display on it we didn't want to ruin. Her parents went out to eat that night. We watched TV in this little corner room, sitting on the floor, since it was the only place that was free from expensive pieces we might knock over. It didn't feel like a home. It was more like a museum with beautiful artifacts we couldn't touch. It felt like a place where things were more important than people.

So much money, and so little comfort! I would rather be a little less rich and a little more comfortable.

Blessed are the poor... they seem to be more thankful for the things they do have, even though there is so much they don't have.

Our family was neither rich nor poor. I always felt I was rich enough to feel secure yet not so rich that I had "treasures" I had to worry about. I was so thankful for that. Even now, if I received a huge fortune, I would probably donate most of it to House of Hope and Joy... the best investment of all, a place where it would do the most good!

Here is a Thanksgiving Prayer. I know it's a little whimsical, but that's what makes it so adaptable for many different families -- those who are pious, and those who are not so pious.

We pray for harvest, for turkeys, and for pilgrims.

We are all pilgrims; the earth is just a temporary stop along our journey of faith.

> May we venture well and be considerate companions.

> May we help each other find our way back when one of us loses direction.

> May we shelter each other through the storms and celebrate when the sun shines.

> May we protect this planet and its delicate balance of life systems, as it serves us.

> **For all pilgrims:**

We pray for companionship and safety in travel.

We pray for a skilled sense of direction and favorable weather.

We have all been turkeys, at one time or another.

We have all embarrassed ourselves by unfortunate choices and less-than-holy behavior.

We have all used our power and influence in ways we are not proud of.

May we forgive ourselves and other turkeys when we do brainless things.

May we learn to respect the animals we slaughter for our own nutrition.

May we never take advantage of any of God's creatures, simply because we can.

For all of us turkeys:

We pray for compassion and understanding.

We pray for humility.

Our harvest is mostly rich. We are a wealthy and comfortable people.

Too many are becoming poorer as we become wealthier.

May we offer the poor not only our gleanings but a place at our table.

May we offer the stranger not only our tolerance but our welcome and love.

May our rich harvest reflect all the colors of our global brothers and sisters.

We recall the peace and hospitality offered by Native American "Indians" to their European guests at the first Thanksgiving.

We know God calls us to follow their example.

May we find the courage to bring radical hospitality and peace to strangers we encounter.

For **harvest**:

We pray for peace, abundance and joy.

We pray for generosity, gratitude and solidarity. Amen.

Chapter 69

Dear Kelvin,

I guess everyone's got problems.

At House of Hope and Joy, the problems of our guests and their families are so big, I don't know if anyone can solve them.

The father's in jail, but the mother needs to stay home with the baby because they have no family support and the job won't pay enough for day care...

The mother's on drugs; the father is unknown; the grandparents are raising the children. They don't have money for their medication, but if they get sick, they can't take care of the children...

The mother's brother is an alcoholic who keeps coming by every so often, yelling at everyone, throwing things, and messing up the family's life. The mother takes care of her own son, plus her brother's daughter, since her brother lost his job...

In every family, there seems to be at least one person trying to keep everything together, and that person is so tired and stressed out. Usually, that's the person who shows up at HHJ, collecting the food, signing up for the Christmas presents, asking for bus fare, choosing clothing for their kids.

People's problems are so different.

I was at the post office, waiting in line, when I heard some of the people there talking about their Christmas problems.

One woman was so stressed out because her husband gave her a Christmas pin, and then her mother gave her an heirloom Christmas pin that used to belong to her great, great grandmother. She knew her mother was trying to cause trouble by outdoing her husband, and now she didn't know which pin to wear. She was seeking advice from the next person in line, as if this were a foreign policy dilemma that could cause World War III...

Another woman was having a fight with her new husband because his tradition was to always open presents after midnight Mass as the grown-ups sipped sherry and her tradition was to open presents in the morning, after Santa came, and drink hot chocolate. They didn't have children yet, but they were arguing over how to tell "the kids" about Santa if the presents showed up after midnight Mass, and how could they take tiny children to midnight Mass anyway...

Two sisters were fighting over what to give their parents for Christmas. One wanted to give them a cruise to Alaska, and the other wanted to give them season's tickets to the dinner theater...

Our guests at HHJ show up with their number, wait in line to check in at the front desk, file past to sit in the chairs, wait for their number to be called, pick up their food, and then move into the next room to receive their big green or red colored plastic bag filled with two toys for each child in their family. They would laugh to hear the "family problems" of which pin to wear, when the not-conceived-yet children will open their presents or whether a cruise was better than dinner theater tickets. The women in line at the post office would be so embarrassed to hear about other families and their Christmas problems involving alcohol, jail, drugs, health insurance, and child care.

Or would they be embarrassed? Would it make them appreciate their blessings and stop fighting over non-issues? Maybe it would... but maybe not.

I can pictured wealthy children crying as they sat among a pile of presents because they didn't get the "one thing they wanted most of all."

I can also picture poor children crying because they miss their mommy who promised she would be there for Christmas, but who is probably too strung out on drugs to pull it together.

Poor families have poor problems. Money can solve many problems, but it doesn't guarantee happiness. Rich families can often solve their money problems, but they still manage to find family conflicts, even though they seem silly from a distance. Why can't people learn to appreciate what they have and be happy and content with their abundant blessings?

I think I'll go home for Christmas and start an argument over which place mats we should use for Christmas dinner...

Chapter 70

Dear Kelvin,

Adam decided to go back to school in the spring and take a light load. There was a week-long course on human sexuality at the local university, and he decided to take it. It's an all-day class for five days, plus a few books and papers. Adam had supper with me almost every night, and we stayed up way too late talking about sexuality and how we developed and what kinds of experiences shaped us and how and why and when we might have felt awkward or afraid or brave or ignorant...

We ended up telling each other all kinds of stories and comparing notes about our growing up and our silly notions.

I just needed to write some of this down. Again, I keep saying this, but it's nothing I would ever tell Sister Agnes. Some of it isn't new to you, but I needed to rethink it with you anyway.

Adam and I obviously talked about when we started to develop as kids in middle school. That's when Adam started to realize that he was not like other boys. He didn't thrill at the idea of girlie pictures or locker room banter. He found it all disturbing. He thought it was disrespectful and was always so surprised how universal it seemed to be. Why did so many boys want to waste their time talking about girls in that way? He couldn't imagine their fascination with it.

Maybe, he thought, because they didn't have a best friend who was a girl. Any disrespectful thing a guy said about any girl or about girls in general seemed an insult to his best friend. So he just avoided the whole scene. It never occurred to him that he wasn't "turned on" by any of this stuff because he was maturing differently. He just thought he had a different perspective about friendship and respect. That part was true.

I never really wondered why he didn't hang around with guy friends. Mostly because I didn't hang around with girl friends. Adam was my best friend, and I had all brothers. Growing up on my block, the neighborhood kids were all boys. The only girl I hung out with was really Gemma, Adam's younger sister. It was mostly Gemma, Ben, Adam and me in middle school.

In high school, our circle of friends became larger because we were in the choir, and we went to parties and movies with a larger group of kids. But no other "best friends." Everyone just knew Adam and I belonged together, so no one really questioned the lack of other guy or girl friends. I used to think it would be great to have a sister, but there was always Gemma.

Adam and I barely left a stone unturned. He told me about his first sexual dream and how surprised he was when that dream was not about me... in fact, more surprised that the dream did not include a female. It bothered him, but he didn't tell anyone. And since he loved me so much, he assumed things would be OK. The dreams continued on and off, and by high school, he realized something strange was going on inside him that he just didn't have words for. Looking back, he could say, "I was discovering my sexual orientation," but at the time, he didn't have the language or knowledge to identify himself as being gay. Since he didn't know what it was, he still thought he could will it away. He tried praying and begging God to take it from him. In college, he finally had a dream about his wedding day with me, and in the dream, he was actually happy, so he took that as a sign that he would get through this dilemma. So when he asked me to marry him, he knew I would say yes. And he assumed our deep love for each other would change him.

Naturally, I thought about having sex with Adam before we got married, but since we were such strong Catholics, it had been drilled into us for years that sex outside of the holy bond of marriage was sinful. So it was never a real option. We thought about it, but we really never seriously considered doing it. More than that, I was just not willing to take the risk of getting pregnant. I did absolutely believe that no form of birth control is 100% except for abstinence, and I could never imagine the possibility of an abortion, so I was relieved that Adam never pressed me to go too far sexually. We kissed a lot, and explored a little, so I never thought there was anything different about Adam. Only that he was far more respectful than any other boy I knew. And that was part of why I loved him so much.

Finally, the week of the wedding, it just all got to him. He was having sexual dreams every night, all of them involving male bodies, and he just couldn't keep on like that. He didn't want to ruin my life by marrying me, but he couldn't tell me why, either. So he just took off, not knowing what to do or where to go. He was stuck in a depression that lasted for years.

He even promised God he would become a priest if God would make all his feelings go away, but God never did that for him. He couldn't face me at my dad's funeral and (in his opinion) add to my burden and grief by telling me his whole horrendous, shameful story, so he just stayed away.

He must have known how hurt I was, but he couldn't bring himself to be honest. So he turned all his confusion and pain inside, came out to no one, and continued to drift along with his mental anguish and depression for all those years.

Compared to his pain, my pain seemed like nothing. That's why it was so healing for us to be together again. Forgiveness was automatic, because of our love. This new understanding made it so much easier for us to reconcile and become friends again. Actually, very close friends.

Adam also had some challenging questions for me.

He learned that one out of every three women is in some way assaulted or abused sexually. He asked me if I had any experiences like that.

For the first time in my life, I told him what happened to me at college. My very first night alone. After my parents had helped me unpack my stuff, and set up my room, they finally left and I was on my own. My roommate invited me to join her at this party, and I had no reason not to go. I found out too late that the punch they were serving was spiked, and I was already woozy. I vaguely remember dancing with a boy. I thought he was safe, since he was a resident assistant, and one of my brothers knew him. But the next thing I knew, I was on the floor in his bathroom, and he was naked, and practically sitting on my face, trying to get me to perform a sexual act.

I was alert enough to be horrified and to know I had to get out of that situation somehow, so I pinched him in a sensitive area.

I was hoping he'd think I was too drunk and clumsy, and I guess he did because he seemed to lose interest and left me alone. I was so relieved. I took off as soon as I could and somehow made it back to my room. At first, I fell right to sleep, but then, in the middle of the night, I couldn't sleep. I kept remembering what happened and then I would start shaking and sobbing. Then I'd fall asleep again, and later wake up and started shaking and sobbing again. This happened all night.

I didn't get out of bed until very late in the morning, but even when I did get up, I still felt a little drunk with a headache, and a sleepy "I'm not all here" feeling... sort of like I had the flu. My roommate never came back that first night. I don't know where she slept, and I never asked. I didn't want her to ask about my night either. She wasn't back until the early afternoon.

All I could think of was, "Welcome to college. This is what the real world is like. This is what 'normal' guys are like. Even at a Catholic college!" I imagined that if I had been at another school, perhaps I would have been raped. At least I had that to be thankful for. I was also very thankful that Adam was in my life, and that I wouldn't have to enter the dating scene with guys like that lurking at every party.

But why didn't I tell Adam that afternoon? Why didn't I ever tell him what happened? I guess I just didn't want to start trouble. I didn't want my brother getting angry, and I didn't want problems the first week of my freshman year. I figured that if I just hung out with Adam, and stuck close to him, and hoped that no one would ever bother me again, it would be OK.

That's exactly what happened: that student never bothered me again, never mentioned that night to me again. I wonder if it was because of Adam, because of my brother, or because he was too drunk to remember the incident or to even realize who I was. Not that "who I was" should matter. Guys should respect every female the same way they would respect their friend's younger sister. But apparently, that's not the way it happens in "the real world."

Anyway, hearing this story really disturbed Adam more than I had expected. He seemed as shattered as I felt that first night. I was planning to meet up with him later that evening, but never even tried to find him. Remember, we didn't have cell phones back then, and we didn't have phones in our rooms. So it was a common thing for people to look for each other and not be able to track each other down, especially if they didn't have very concrete plans. But after that, I made sure we always arranged to meet at a specific place by a specific time. I learned that lesson.

But it wasn't the last time I something creepy happened to me.

Just a year later, I had been coming out of the college theater, where I had been rehearsing for a class. My scene partner had already left, but I was still gathering my stuff together and took a bathroom break. It was dark when I began to walk down the circular stairway in the tower part of the building, and I looked toward one of the hallways and saw someone with a flashlight. It looked as if he were on his knees at one of the doors. I thought it weird, but only hesitated a moment before continuing on. I later realized he was probably trying to break into one of the offices.

He obviously saw me, because in an instant, I heard his heavy footsteps coming down the hallway toward the staircase I was on. I started going down the steps as quickly as I could, and as soon as I was by the door, I heard him enter the staircase. He threw open the door so it crashed against the wall and shouted, "Hey!"

I wasn't about to wait to see what he wanted. Dark, secluded, area; angry guy, probably very strong. Not a good combination. So I tore out of the door and started running back to my dorm room. I remember thinking, "How often am I going to have to run back to my dorm in fear of some guy? Is this normal? Is this what happens all over campuses, but nobody talks about it?"

As soon as I got to a set of steps built into the hill, he had come out of the building, so I was certain he saw me.

As soon as I reached the top of the steps, he had reached the bottom.

My dorm was within reach, but I wasn't a great runner, and I was almost out of breath. He was getting closer. My decision was this: do I try to run up to the third floor, and risk wasting time, fiddling with my key, since the girls' halls are locked? Or do I take my chances and run into the first floor hall, and hope it's filled with friendly guys who will at least intimidate this thug?

I realized I couldn't make it to the third floor. I couldn't do three more flights of stairs. So I headed right into the boys' floor, in the middle of one of their games of "throw the Frisbee into the garbage can from all the way down the hall." I ran in, and collapsed on the floor -- just on the other side of the garbage can. Not so I was in the middle of their game, but close enough so I was near a crowd, and situated so there was this big garbage can between me and the door. That door didn't open for a long time. Probably ten minutes. When it finally did open, it was someone else who lived on the floor. No one ever asked me if I was OK, or why I had come. I just sat there and watched the game. Eventually, someone from my poetry class came in, and I asked him if he would look at this poem I was working on for a paper. I didn't need his help with poetry, but I needed someone to walk me out that doorway and up the steps to my room, so I wouldn't have someone following me.

He never gave it another thought, and I was so relieved he had come by. I didn't know he lived on that floor, but I was glad he recognized me. He stayed almost half an hour, talking about the class, and about how impossible it was to guess what poets really meant by their obscure language. I couldn't agree more. But I was hardly focused on what he was saying.

Eventually, the hall phone rang, and it was Adam. He was coming over. I was so happy to hear that. I never told Adam or the poetry student. It just seemed too crazy to talk about. It was like watching a bad movie, and thinking for a moment it was real. But it couldn't have been real, right? I was too embarrassed to tell anyone about my fear, thinking that I would be ridiculed... "You must be exaggerating" or "Why would someone chase you up the steps?" or "I'm sure there's no real danger, so just forget it" And yet, the fear was still there...

Just like a bad horror movie. You can't help but feel scared, even though you know it's over and it's only a movie. But it wasn't a movie. I was still just too freaked out to tell anyone. Not even Adam. So that made two things I hadn't told him. I had begun to understand why Adam couldn't tell me his big secret; there were certain secrets I hadn't been able to tell him... or anyone.

When I think of this, it makes me think of all the secrets out there in the world -- all the rapes and assaults and domestic violence incidents, all the shouting and threats and fighting that happens. There is post traumatic stress disorder happening all over college campuses, inner city streets and domestic living rooms and bedrooms. And we are all so afraid to talk about it...

OK, I need to get some sleep. There's always more to write, but it's late, so now is a good time to stop. Good night!

Chapter 71

Dear Kelvin,

On one of our most honest nights, Carlos and I talked about past relationships.

He bluntly told me, "There are just too many men in your life."

I didn't know what he was talking about, since he had been with several women during his life as well.

I told him, "You are the only man I love now; you are the only man in my life."

Hi insisted that every relationship I ever had was still with me, that I was carrying baggage from each person who had been with me and left me and hurt me. He said I needed to unpack all that baggage so I could finally toss out what had been so heavy and dragging me down.

I realize now what he was talking about.

Every time I had a relationship that ended badly, I blamed myself. I carried that hurt with me and became even less willing to be open the next time. Over and over, that hurt grew and grew, and I was more resolved not to give away my heart. But that made me even less lovable in a way.

Think about it. I was dating Ray, a guy who was inconsistent, unpredictable and mysterious, who lied or at least kept me guessing about the truth, who wasn't open with me, who seemed to break up with me, and then popped back into my life as if nothing had happened. He was so unhealthy. Why did I settle for him? Because I knew

I didn't care about him that much, so he couldn't really hurt me. What dysfunctional criteria for a relationship!

When I met Carlos, he started to melt all that resistance away. I started to trust again. I opened myself so much, that it was really easy for him to hurt me and leave me devastated.

But his one comment stuck with me.

Until I resolved what happened <u>in</u> me -- regardless of what happened <u>to</u> me -- I would be destined to carry around all that baggage, forever, to whatever relationships I had.

I might never know what happened with Carolos, but I can stop blaming myself and realize that some things are out of our control. Some things we may never know.

Yes, it's my job to learn from my mistakes and failures. So I need to be honest, ask the hard questions, and try to be honest about what part of the failure was indeed my responsibility. But if someone chooses to leave me without explanation, that doesn't mean it's automatically my fault, that doesn't mean I'm unlovable, and that doesn't mean my life is destroyed for all time.

Wow. Why had that been such a hard lesson for me to learn?

Chapter 72

Dear Kelvin,

Adam asked me to imagine this: What if my life events were taking place in exactly the way they needed to? What if no matter what happened, God could pick you up out of that pain and make something better out of you and your situation?

Marvelous, marvelous Adam. See why I missed him so much? See why all these years I was searching for my soul mate, I was really just searching for Adam?

I think we are transformed when we become more aware of our situation -- even if it's painful -- if we go through a particular process, and I think the process is this:

- We learn from it.

- We pray and reflect on it.

- We make a decision or commitment (a plan, a new concept, a new resolution).

- We follow through with some action or service.

And then those who support us gather around us and celebrate and say, "Well done!" to certain things and "Try this instead!" to other things, and so we begin again, and this cycle starts all over again:

- Learning

- Reflection/Prayer

- Leadership

- Service/Action...

I think that's the definition of living well.

I also think the support and love of people with us is what keeps us going through all those steps... The support of a mentor (like Sylvia) as well as the support of peers (like you and Ruby, and all our teacher friends and the staff of HHJ...)

Take any one of those away, and you have an unhealthy person or a dysfunctional system.

Try living without a sense of awareness or a desire for learning. Try living without reflection, without commitment or leadership. Try living without service, without support from dear ones, loved ones. You're not really living. You certainly would not become transformed by life that way.

I think somehow this is what healthy life is all about. And maybe writing is part of it. Maybe writing is what cements our awareness in some way. It welcomes us to honesty. It holds us to accountability. It invites us out of denial. It starts the whole process going. Once we are aware, we can really start to learn and our prayer life can take off.

Well, I'm not sure what to do with this notion of transformation, but I'm going to let it simmer a bit.

Yes. Learning, reflective prayer, leadership, and service or action... held together by loving support. I do think that's the formula for transformation. That's actually the way we do ministry with the Clean Teens. It's the way I teach leadership at St. Augustine. It's even the way I teach English. It's really the way life works, isn't it?

Chapter 73

Dear Kelvin,

When St. Bernadette's held a big class reunion for all students of all classes to raise money for the high school; Adam, Gemma and I each sent a check, but none of us went to the reunion.

Why didn't any of us attend? I think I know.

None of us was proud enough of our "accomplishments" to return to our former classmates and talk about what we had done with our lives since graduation.

Adam hadn't come out to anyone yet, and he didn't know how to explain his life, period. He had drifted from job to job, and was battling this long-term depression. He wasn't willing to face our old friends and have to answer questions -- whether they were asked or not.

There was no way I was going. As I said, everyone I know had already heard that Adam had left me mysteriously, and so who knows what they were thinking about me and that whole incident... Then I married Timothy and was abandoned again. I didn't want to answer questions, either. Not only that, but what if he showed up with his new wife? That was possible! That was just something I couldn't cope with...

What surprised me the most was that Gemma had decided not to go because she felt that she hadn't accomplished anything and had nothing to brag about. She said I had this great career teaching at St. Augustine and I was volunteering at HHJ. She said that I was doing meaningful work and I was changing the world. She said I was making a difference!

Gemma had married Brad straight out of college and never had a full-time job. She worked at a Hallmark store for extra money and had three babies. She couldn't face her classmates who had all gone on to be doctors or lawyers or teachers or other worthy professions, because all she had accomplished was becoming Mrs. Somebody's Wife. She had just begun a job at a community college and wasn't even sure she would stick with it.

Gemma didn't go because she was ashamed of her "small life." She hadn't accomplished anything... She wasn't changing the world like Nellie. LIKE NELLIE!!!

Yet, she had accomplished the one thing I always wanted to do. She got married and was raising a family with a man who loved her. She was living my dream! She did what I hadn't been able to do. I didn't go because I was ashamed of my life of "rejection." I wasn't happily married with children. I didn't go because I wasn't like Gemma, and she didn't go because she wasn't like me.

Actually, both Adam and I both wanted to be Gemma, and Gemma wanted to be me. And all three of us felt ashamed because our lives had not been "good enough" to show our former classmates. So each of us stayed home that night and felt miserable, thinking about our lives of "failure."

Isn't it amazing what we human beings can do to ourselves? Thinking we aren't good enough? Not knowing that a person we think is better than we are is actually secretly wishing to be just like us?

Does this make any sense?

So much pain in the world caused by unnecessary feelings of inadequacy...

One person's "failure" is another person's "success," but we remain too isolated to understand each other, or even ourselves.

If only we could all come full circle and realize that all of us have ups and downs in our lives. All of us have seasons of plenty and seasons of want. All of us have seasons of warmth and seasons of cold, seasons of pain and seasons of joy. We all go through these cycles, and nothing lasts forever except that pattern of change...

74: Hidden Cycles

Dear Sylvia,

What a wonderful retreat you gave!

Your reflection on the four seasons really made me think.

I have always been attracted to the image of the four seasons, God's constant cycle of birth, growth, maturity, death, and then birth again...

I wanted you to have this poem I wrote. Maybe you can use it at your retreats.

And by the way, the answer is YES! I would love to have dinner with you some time to talk about where my vocational search is. I have a few interesting insights I'd like to talk about and maybe this poem can be the beginning of the conversation.

See if you can find the hidden meaning of the poem...

Nellie

Hidden Cycles

A ring is round

Autumn leaves fall

Hidden Cycles

In the name of the Father

It has no end

Winter winds blow

Here and there

The Son

Like my love

Spring buds bloom

Just look -- you'll find

The Holy Spirit

For you, my friend

Summer grasses grow

They're everywhere

Amen

PS

In case you didn't understand my poem, here's the "secret" way to see what it's all about.

Each of the verses can be separated into its four parts, and read separately.

The third line of every verse is what unlocks the meaning of the poem. There are hidden cycles everywhere. The second line of every verse gives the best example of a cycle -- the seasons. The last line of every verse tells us the source of the cycles -- and the source of everything. The first line of every verse gives the context: Love.

So once you take it apart, you get the key to the meaning (in the third line of every verse):

Hidden cycles -- here and there -- just look you'll find -- they're everywhere.

You get the example (in the second line of every verse):

Autumn leaves fall -- winter winds blow -- spring buds bloom -- summer grasses grow.

You get the source (the fourth line of every verse):

In the name of the Father -- The Son -- The Holy Spirit -- Amen.

And you get the context -- love (the first line of every verse):

A ring is round -- it has no end -- like my love -- for you, my friend.

But the cycles are all hidden. The source is hidden. Even the context is often hidden. It all needs to be discovered. Like love. That's why I "hid" the cycles within the poem!

Tell me what you think!

N.

Chapter 75

Dear Sylvia,

A while back, I wrote about Merit Jackson and his novel, *Lil Johnnie Off The Block*. We first started using stories from "Lil Johnnie" and developing materials with just two classes to see what the students thought. It was an instant hit! They really liked it! It's a terrific literacy curriculum, designed to improve reading, writing and reflection skills, as well as hope skills.

Almost immediately, these students began to participate more in class discussion. Then, they put more effort into their writing, and they just seemed to start thinking more deeply about everything. It's marvelous. We started using his materials in every freshman English class this year. What a difference it has made. I have never had students love homework so much!

Merit came to visit in the beginning of the year to meet all the students and do his "author" thing. They clearly love him. They always take to him right away, and he just eats it up.

I have been telling some of the teachers at other schools about it, and although most were skeptical at first, a few were willing to look it over. Two decided to try it with their classes. So now there are three schools using the "Lil Johnnie" literacy materials. Besides us, there is one other Catholic school and one public school. We're finally getting it into a fixed form so we can create student workbooks.

Merit started working with a friend to turn it into a play. He told me his goal was to write the play in one year and to get the play produced the very next year. When my students heard about his plans, they all jumped out of their seats, shouting that they wanted to be "Lil Johnnie," or they wanted to be this or that other character.

Unfortunately, there can only be one "Lil Johnnie." I knew there would be lots of disappointments all around from that sad but true fact. So I suggested that our classes make a video of all the different stories. That way, every story could have a different actor playing "Lil Johnnie." They loved that idea. They are planning to organize all their skits the last few weeks of the semester, once we have covered the entire curriculum and read all the stories. Merit was thrilled to see their enthusiasm.

Suddenly, teaching English became even more of an adventure. As you can see, the curriculum is very non-traditional, but it works. I can't say that I ever expected to turn a freshman English class into a collection of Shakespeare lovers, but they are more interested in poetry than I would have predicted.

Let me know what you think of the lessons I'm enclosing. I hope the principals can keep an open mind. Traditional programs don't seem to be capturing the imaginations of the typical urban student. So why not try something a little different that seems to have an instant impact? Why not try something that will make our students care about reading? If they can learn to love reading freshman year, then we can introduce more advanced topics and assignments in following years.

Chapter 76

Dear Kelvin,

Looking back, 2000 had been a great year to start things new. That's what I told Adam, and I meant it to be true for him. But I didn't realize it would be so true for me, too.

That was the spring Adam and I reconnected and revisited all of our sexual history -- what made us who we are.

That was also the spring that Merit Jackson and I first thought about creating a student workbook for the "Lil Johnnie" Literacy curriculum.

That fall, I started teaching the new leadership class as a standard offering -- no longer just an experimental class.

Most of the leadership insights have come from my volunteer work at House of Hope and Joy and watching an outstanding leadership team in action, up close and personal. The Guadalupe Center seems to operate in similar ways.

Over the years, I have learned so much from the staff and volunteers there and the Clean Teens themselves. I was in my 40s before I learned this stuff. And it was never "taught" to me; I had to pick it up by observing and imitating. I thought it made so much sense to start teaching these concepts to high school students, so they could enter their adult life already seeing themselves as leaders: being responsible, learning from mistakes, being reflective and mindful, making good decisions, setting goals, serving the world with their talents.

Well, 2000 was the year "Lil Johnnie" completely knocked the socks off the entire freshman class, and the senior class couldn't get enough of my Christian Leadership class. They were staying after school talking with me and coming up with ideas of new people to invite, projects to start and famous people they wanted to write to.

I was so energized by the students at St. Augustine.

They came up with this amazing idea.

> We invite students from all these churches and schools to House of Hope and Joy to discuss the most pressing issues related to peace and violence. We sit in mixed groups and talk about what we're most concerned about and what the best ideas we ever saw or heard about are like.

> We invite local community leaders to join us for lunch and to listen to what we've been talking about all day. We tell them what we think and how we want our city and world to be.

> We get their commitment to help us.

> Then each school and church creates its own plan of action. They design their own activity or project, and everyone shares the plans before they leave at the end of the day.

> They all work on their ideas, and then they come back at the end of the school year to see what everyone did -- what they accomplished, what they learned, how their plans worked out, and what the results were.

We decided to call it "Pebbles of Peace Outweighing Boulders of Violence."

We had talked about this idea for several classes -- the idea that violence is overwhelming like boulders: drive by shootings, rape, guns, gangs. The idea that each of us is just a tiny pebble. None of us stands a chance up against a boulder.

But if we get enough of us together, our peaceful influence can outweigh the boulders of violence.

What a splendid idea! Well, you know the rest of the story!

We did put on the Pebbles of Peace event in the fall of 2000. It went really well. We had lots of interested local leaders, and so many schools and churches wanted to participate, that we had to cut off the registrations at 150.

The TV cameras came! I never expected that!

The Clean Teens were being interviewed, and so was my Christian Leadership class who came up with the idea in the first place. Some of the former Clean Teens who were now college students came back as "community leaders" to be part of the day as well.

Thelma and LaToya talked about Martin, who was shot on his way walking home from school, and Luke and Olivia talked about Keshia, their cousin who had been caught up in the cycle of domestic abuse.

Carlos was there with some of his youth who work every summer at Guadalupe. In fact, I think almost every volunteer from both Guadalupe and HHJ came out to be with the youth and help out with all our logistic needs, like feeding 150 hungry, excited young people.

Wow! The projects being planned were great. Peace rallies, plays, videos, mentoring programs, diversity days, ministry fairs, support groups, all kinds of ways we might address issues linked to violence.

Luz and Fernando were on TV in the background, while some of the teens were interviewed. Raúl and Rosa were delighted to see them.

It was one of the best things we ever did. What a unifying event! It brought youth from all different neighborhoods, different churches, different schools, all meeting each other. All talking about violence and racism and poverty and crime and drugs and street culture and gangs and absent fathers and pregnant teenagers and fear and grief and pride and respect and hope.

We gathered again in the spring of 2001 to celebrate the leadership of young people across the whole city. All the schools and churches brought display boards and showed videos and photo albums and scrapbooks of their projects. Each group took a turn explaining its project and talked about what members did and what they learned and how they would do things differently next time.

Parents came. The mayor came. The archbishop came. The chief of police came. More TV cameras came. Representatives from every local college and university came. Younger siblings came. They all signed a large banner that said, "Pebbles of Peace Outweighing Boulders of Violence" and "Piedritas de Paz mas Fuertes que Rocas de Violencia."

Adam came. Ben and Mary came. Gemma came. My mom came. Even Sister Matilda came for a very short time -- in her wheelchair. The entire rest of the HHJ staff came.

It was spectacular. I was so proud to be part of such a tremendous idea. So proud that my leadership class thought it out and carried it through.

It was the most hopeful I had ever been about life in the central city. The most hopeful I had ever been about making a difference.

There I was in the same place as Carlos, and I was OK with that. OK with doing more ministry with him, simply because he was a good man, a gifted youth minister, and still a friend, in spite of all the pain surrounding my history with him.

There I was in the same place as Adam, and I was more than OK with that. After all we had been through, he was still my soul mate in many ways. I knew we'd be friends forever, and he'd always be a part of my life, and that brought me great joy.

There I was in the same place as my mom, and my younger brother Ben, and his wife Mary. Great for my family to see what it is I have done with my life, here in the central city, a place they often ask me to leave. ("Wouldn't it be safer and easier in a nice suburban school?") Now, they can see a glimpse of what I had been working toward.

There I was in the same place as the entire HHJ staff: Merry, who had shown me such an incredible example of leadership; Leah, who modeled pastoral care and the ministry of calm presence with every crises; Kim and

Monique, with their tireless cheer in the face of so much need and desperation that comes through the door every day; Paul, who never fails to whistle where he is working; Sheryl, everyone's mother, who delights in the pictures of the children growing up and never forgets a name or a face. And Luz, Ruby and you.

That was our shining moment, all these young people, proud of their accomplishments, hopeful they can make the world a better place, filled with hope and joy, and so many people I loved and admired there to witness what can happen in a city when young people are empowered to be leaders.

When they experience support from skilled mentors and a whole caring community; when they are taught the leadership basics; when they are caught up in the cycle of learning, prayer, leadership and service; then they become transformed!

That night, I was at my mom's, having dinner with the extended family, celebrating the day. We all watched it on TV. My nieces were the most impressed.

What a crooked journey to get to where we had arrived, but what a blessed arrival. I was so excited, you would have thought that world peace had suddenly been reached, and world hunger eliminated.

It wasn't anything that monumental. It was just my own personal peace of mind.

The transformation that Adam and I had spoken of had begun to take place. Maybe this was the beginning of something significant for our whole city. Maybe now more urban students would feel more hope and have more courage. Maybe more would consider college instead of thinking it was beyond their reach. Maybe teens would begin to be more responsible and look at consequences. Maybe... maybe... maybe...

This was the beginning of a great community organizing effort, uniting people who were previously fragmented and getting them committed to this purpose together.

I fell asleep that night so full of hope and joy.

Thinking about all of this... I was almost ready to meet with Sister Agnes and answer any question she had for me.

Almost.

Col. 3:23

Chapter 77

Dear Kelvin,

It's time I write about this.

I don't know how to write about it.

I guess I'll just start and see what happens. I'll just describe the facts as I remember them, and then if I get emotional, I'll stop and cry and see if there's anything I can learn from the lessons of the heart.

I remember the summer heat outside and the cool of the air conditioning at House of Hope and Joy.

We were having a meeting to evaluate our year.

The room was full of newsprint. I remember all the big words. "Lil Johnnie" -- Pebbles -- Clean Teens -- St. Augustine Leadership Class -- and the smaller concepts -- sidewalk art -- festival -- Transformation -- Principles of Leadership -- community projects -- future of the order -- and the rest of it was a blur of ideas, arrows, time lines and sticky dots.

Sheryl was cleaning up the kitchen. We had the most delicious meal -- fried chicken and all the sides -- and only a few of the Clean Teens were left. Most had gone home. You and Ruby and I were still at the tables, talking about how things had grown. Luz had left already. Luke and Olivia were in the kitchen helping Sheryl. Monique and Kim were getting us one more plate of cake. I don't know where Paul was.

You spotted LaToya's purse and asked Luke to go see if she was still in the front, waiting to be picked up. Olivia went along.

I remember hearing noise. Ruby went outside to check on what was happening. When she opened the door, we heard the noise get louder. Immediately you and Kim jumped up and ran. It was a hot summer night... we were situated in the city. We probably should have reminded all the teens to wait inside, behind the doors, but you know how teenagers can be...

The rest of us heard some shouting and car sounds and then we heard what sounded like guns being fired.

The rest of us jumped up and ran to the front doors.

Someone had been shot.

It was Ruby!

The rest of it was a blur.

I do remember sobbing teenagers hugging each other, ambulance and police sirens, uniforms, clipboards, endless questions, the smell of fried chicken, crowds of people watching from across the street, the smell of the hospital, the silence of the waiting room, green scrubs, red blood on green scrubs, and the look on the doctor's face, and the look on your face, when we were told that Ruby didn't make it.

I kind of remember Merry making some decisions...

Merry stayed with you, Olivia and Luke. Merry asked Leah and me to come back to HHJ to speak with the teens and parents who might still be there.

I remember my face hurting from all the crying. I remember my mouth being so dry I could hardly talk. I remember always needing to drink water. I remember not quite knowing what to say. I remember Sheryl serving coffee to everyone. I remember all the crying and sobbing...

I remember all these other people showing up. Not just teens' parents, but other adults as well. Volunteers, friends, community people.

I heard bits and pieces about Ruby's life.

Like when you and Ruby were Clean Teens yourselves... When you were the first in your families to go to college... When you came back to teach... When you got married... When Olivia was born... When Luke was born... It's what happens when people come together to comfort each other ... the stories come out in broken pieces, here and there... Who knew you when.

It's what happens when we are forced to face the most horrific reality of life -- unnecessary death. Random death caused by immaturity, reckless behavior, hopelessness, a senseless need for bravado, anger, and the availability of weapons that make killing all too easy.

Leah was amazing. She had such a way with the people there. She knew when to let them talk, when to let them cry and struggle with their words, when to finally go over and hug them, and lead them back to their chairs, and when to say something and when to say nothing at all.

Me -- I was pretty much useless. I was numb. I couldn't imagine Luke and Olivia without Ruby. You without Ruby. Us without Ruby. It didn't seem real yet.

It was after midnight when the last group of people left. Leah and I were exhausted. Sheryl had cleaned up the kitchen twice, and it sparkled, as always. Monique and Kim had already gone over to your place. So Leah and I wiped up the tables and put away the extra chairs. We looked at the floor. It really was dirty. But neither of us had the energy or the will to clean it. So we decided we could get away with doing it in the morning.

We got our stuff and were turning off lights, ready to lock up, when we noticed the light was back on in the St. Anthony room. It was Paul. We thought he had already gone, but there he was, with that yellow bucket on wheels, filled with sudsy water, mopping the floor. "I just couldn't leave it like this," he said.

Just when I think I have enough to contemplate, and my mind is completely spent, something like this comes along. I wonder if God does these things on purpose.

Paul had such pride in House of Hope and Joy that he needed to finish the job. He really taught me a lesson that night. Yes, we have all these "higher" things to think about: life and death, peace and violence -- and yet, the floor was dirty, and guests would be coming in first thing in the morning. He reminded me what leaders do. They keep an eye on excellence, even when they are tired and it would be just as easy to settle for "almost good enough."

Every time I am tempted to get away with "almost good enough," I remember Paul and remember the importance of excellence and pride in my work.

What an honor to serve on the staff with people like Paul.

I don't know how you can cry from intense sadness and hopelessness, when your friend gets shot for no reason, and at the same time, cry from gratitude and pride because you work with the best people you have ever known, but I did. I couldn't tell if I was thankful or angry because I was both, and either one was enough to bring on the weeping. But I had both and didn't know what to feel. It was just too overwhelming.

That moment has stuck with me, even until today.

People think I'm strange because I can get teary-eyed when I see a floor being mopped with one of those yellow buckets. It always reminds me of Paul...

and Ruby.

Chapter 78

Dear Kelvin,

I can hardly remember that week.

I know that Leah and I spent half our time at your house, and half at HHJ. I remember sleeping on your couch more than once... several late nights talking with Olivia and Luke... and talking with you. I remember one night, Monique and Kim and I helped all of you put together the collage of pictures for the funeral.

I remember one morning slowly waking up in my own bed and feeling a little disoriented. I almost said to myself, "What's wrong? I know I'm sad. Why am I sad?" and then I remembered about Ruby. I was probably so sleep-deprived that even when I got some sleep, I wasn't really rested. I wasn't refreshed. I was still groggy enough to momentarily forget why I was sad. How strange is that?

I remember Sheryl cooking up a storm. And always making coffee. The pot was always full. I wasn't sure whether she was doing all that cooking because it was her way of coping or because she knew that people were going to keep coming and keep wanting to talk. And some of them wanted to just stay there all day and talk. Having food gave them something to do, and somehow comfort food feeds the soul. I guess she had that wisdom inside her. I guess when you feed the body with love, and you sit and listen, and the soul gets fed, too.

I can't even tell you who came when, but I know there were lots of people.

It's all a blur because that's how grief is in the beginning... there is nothing but shock and disbelief... and the only way to cope is to deal with the everyday things that must be done.

People have to eat. Arrangements need to be made. The floor needs to be mopped. Somehow, it's only these silly little necessities that keep us focused enough to get through the day. Because all you really want to do is lie on your bed and cry. You just want to cry until you wake up from the nightmare and it's all over, and you get your loved one back. But it's a nightmare you can never wake up from, because it's real. Grief is how the completely unreal becomes real. It's a long, long process, and I don't remember the beginning, because it's so overwhelming and impossible to grasp and cope with.

I was like that when my dad died, too. I hardly remember the week of his funeral.

When I think back, so much of that first week without Ruby is also a blur...

I do remember moments from the funeral. I remember you speaking. I remember marveling that you could actually do that... speak in front of all those people about Ruby, without breaking down and crying. Seeing you do that brought comfort to us all. Yet, I was thinking it was our job to bring you comfort and there you were, a pillar of strength.

When my dad died, none of us from the immediate family spoke in front of anyone. None of us could have handled that, especially not my mom. All we could do is sit in the pews and cry. Your composure was amazing to me. You were so articulate and strong. So full of faith. So full of hope. How did you do it? I just don't know...

I remember none of us wanted to be alone. As soon as I went home alone, I would find myself crying on the couch or the bed, thinking, "My God, my God, why have you forsaken us?" How could you let city violence take away one of your biggest champions for justice, for hope, for building up the urban young people everyone else forgets? They look right past our teens and see nothing. We see the future. Ruby saw a hopeful future, a successful future. And how do you reward her? By letting some thugs take her life.

Those were the thoughts sucking the life out of me when I was alone. I couldn't handle it. So I'd come over to your house, or I'd hang out at HHJ until someone warmed my heart (which never took too long).

In some ways, I think we were all walking around in that grief-induced twilight zone. It doesn't go away after the funeral... it lingers for weeks, months, and sometimes a year or two or more. It depends on how much love is in your life and how much other grief you have already experienced. As I have said before, every time there is a hurt, all the previous unresolved hurts come crashing down around you, until your face is in the dirt and you cannot breathe...

But this one was different. This one threatened to change everything in our lives. This one made my family start begging me all over again to move out of the city and come live near them, in the safe suburbs. This one tempted me to leave city ministry behind completely. To forget about the world of St. Augustine and House of Hope and Joy, where we think we are making a difference. To abandon completely the world of false successes like "Lil Johnnie" and Pebbles of Peace because they can never outweigh the enormous boulders of violence that come crashing through the night and kill innocent children and women who are treasures of our community. The only way is to escape.

But where do we go? The more of us who leave, the more desperate are those who stay. What would it say to my students, to the Clean Teens, if I moved to the suburbs? And how can they escape?

I had to stay. I just wish my family could understand that. I know you understood it. I know Sister Matilda could understand it. I really don't know what kept her alive. Every time I saw her, she looked frailer than the time before. So many times I looked at her and thought she was on her deathbed. "Today would be her last day," I'd say to myself. But somehow, she kept hanging on.

I thought she'd die after Ruby was shot. I thought she'd have a heart attack before the funeral. But she hung on. Another amazing miracle.

Just weeks later, I remember sitting next to you at the diocesan "Welcome Back" day for teachers. I remember thinking that you always sat between me and Ruby. You noticed the picture slid inside the clear panel in the front of my binder... it was that Christmas picture of all of us in the Teen room -- Ruby and you smiling with the rest of us. For some reason, I had to carry that picture with me wherever I went. You didn't say anything. You just tapped it twice with your finger and nodded your head. You never seemed to lose your composure. It made me tear up -- just that gesture of tapping and nodding.

Again, when they did that slide show memorial for Ruby, I was weeping all over again. And you just hugged everyone afterward, saying over and over, "Thank you" and "Ruby would have loved that" and "You know Ruby loved you" and there you were again, comforting the people who should have been comforting you.

I didn't now how to comfort you. There is no comfort for this. There is no easy hope to be found in this. I remember thinking, "How do we start our year off, talking about Pebbles and 'Lil Johnnie,' when we know that at any time, a stray bullet can kill one of us again?"

I guess, that's when a whole lot of us peaceful pebbles gather together, and we surround each other, and that's when we first notice that maybe we do outweigh those boulders of violence, even when we can't get rid of them. They can't take away our spirit, because there's more to us than that. Maybe that's the lesson here. That we can cry from sadness and gratitude at the same time. That we can be overwhelmed with grief over our loss and pride for our community at the same time. That we can be devastated and joyful at the same time. Maybe that's what keeps hope and joy in our hearts, in the midst of senseless killing.

This was all just too much for me... I wasn't really sure I could be an effective teacher like this. But you had faith in me. You told me to just keep doing what I was doing. That my being there was more of a sign of hope than anything. That I didn't give up on the city, that I was still there, believing in the young people, believing in the goodness of the city and the joy of the ministry.

I didn't know how to tell you that I didn't feel any of those feelings. I didn't really "still believe" in anything. I was just going through the motions. That's what we do when we are steeped in grief. We just keep going through the motions, hoping that eventually we would feel the confidence that we were pretending to have.

I think later you confessed to me that was all you were doing, too... going through the motions. But after a while, you get so good at those motions, you can go through them pretty smoothly. And eventually, you even fake yourself out and start believing in hope and joy again... it happens so gradually, and it takes such a long time, but eventually it does happen.

So that was how we began the school year in 2001.

Chapter 79

Dear Adam,

I just needed to write this down for you.

My brother Ben was in Japan, at a conference. I guess there are people all over the world who study Greek and Latin and are still trying to unlock the secrets of mythology.

He told me he had come back from a workshop and flipped on the TV. There was a movie, but it didn't have subtitles so he couldn't understand what was happening. But the movie had really great special effects. He was amazed at how clear and lifelike everything looked.

As best he could tell, it was this disaster movie about some evil syndicate attacking the US. There were planes flying into the World Trade Center -- first one tower, and then the next.

They kept showing the scene over and over. And it was shocking -- the picture of the clear blue sky, the bright orange and yellow flames, the black smoke pouring from the towers where the planes had crashed into the metal and steel of the buildings, even people jumping out of the windows.

He started thinking that the movie was getting a little boring, since they kept showing that same scene over and over and over.

Then he had this terrifying thought... that perhaps it wasn't a movie... perhaps it was the news... *perhaps this really had happened.*

He was certain it couldn't be real, but at the same time, something in the bottom of his gut made him think it might be, and he had to find out right away, so he bolted from his room, looking for a colleague who spoke both English and Japanese. But as soon as he spotted anyone who knew him -- and therefore knew he was American -- he knew it was real. He didn't have to ask. The look in their eyes told him.

That's how Ben found out about the events of September 11.

Chapter 80

Dear Kelvin,

That autumn, we were already so wrapped up in the grief of Ruby's senseless killing, the destruction and loss of life from four plane crashes didn't even seem to make things worse. It just made them bigger. They just confirmed our fears. We had already felt as if the world were ending.

I remember talking with Merry about it... that was actually her insight.

Those of us in the heart of city violence were already in shock and pain. White Americans, feeling safer in the suburbs, never expect outrageous violence to touch their lives in such as sudden way. It seems we city folk were already used to hearing about unexpected violence, if in fact, you can ever get used to something "unexpected."

In a way, Merry was right. As if the rest of America were catching up to the everyday feelings of the inner city -- the fear of violence that could break out at any time, for no reason. The feeling that you were never really safe. We have known that feeling for a long time, and we chose to keep living here anyway... to keep finding ways to be peaceful pebbles. But now it was like a slow panic sweeping the rest of the country.

You might even say that it was a feeling so many people already felt around the world. But most people in America thought it was a foreign thing -- that here in the US, we were protected by our wealth, our safe society, and two oceans separating us. As long as we were in the suburbs, away from the violence of the city, we could stay away from random violence.

However, those planes were not an example of random violence. The only thing random about it were the innocent bystanders: those who happened to be on the planes, and who happened to be in the buildings at the time. The plane crashes were the result of a very detailed planning process.

The violence that ended Ruby's life was different. That was random. The actual act was completely unplanned. But it's very possible to look back and see all the events and situations that led to the likelihood that such events happen and keep happening.

We were shocked when we learned that Ruby's killer was the brother of one of my former St. Augustine students. I remember LaQuondra. Years earlier, she told me she didn't have much hope for the world. She said she wished there were some adult males in her family. All the aunts were single mothers; all the men were in prison or someplace working the streets.

No healthy male role models. I remember first learning that 98% of the people in prison grew up in homes with no father present. How long can we ignore statistics like this?

Well, we had to visit LaQuondra's mother. What a tearful meeting that was. This is what you told me: "You don't know sorrow until you meet with the mother of the young man who just killed your wife." I don't know who was sadder; I don't know which was more tragic.

Vera told us LaQuondra was living with a cousin in another city; she did not return when her brother Dirk was arrested. She didn't want to see him. She couldn't deal with a member of her family being a murderer. She couldn't face us, knowing her family killed someone from House of Hope and Joy. She felt as if she had committed the act herself.

Her mother knew she would have been welcomed. She knew that we would have held her in our arms and loved her even more, if that's ever possible. We asked Vera to please tell her to come home and visit us, so we can help her grieve.

Behind every senseless act of violence is another story that will break your heart. What is it like to know that you bore that child, you nursed that child, you held that child in your arms and sang to him and prayed for him, you raised that child, you sat that child on your knee and read him stories, you taught that child the difference between right and wrong, and he still grew up, took to the streets, and killed someone who had been instrumental in helping people just like your son and daughter?

We knew Vera felt responsible...

You were amazing, again comforting her. I knew you helped her forgive herself, even though she was not guilty. She had done her best. It wasn't her failure that led Dirk to the streets. It was the whole community's fault. It was a situation that was started centuries before.

When I think about the history of slavery in our country, and the situation of prejudice based on skin color, it's easy for me to feel overwhelmed as well.

Let's think about it... what did our country do so long ago? They kidnapped a whole population, forced them into slavery, separated the families, filled them with fear and intimidation and anger, made it impossible for them to develop any kind of healthy family structure, then freed them without giving them any resources. They made it impossible for people with dark skin to get a good education, prevented them from earning fair wages for work, forced them to have separate bathrooms and water fountains, made them sit in the back of every bus or assembly hall, and pretty much prevented them from any expression of dignity or respect...

What is the effect of this oppression and generational poverty? What is the effect when no one in an entire family has any memory of ever seeing a male cousin, uncle, father or grandfather marry the mother of their child, live at home, go to work, and model what a normal relationship looks like? How do the boys grow up and know how to act? How do the women know how to raise such boys? If every man they ever knew is hustling the streets or in jail or prison for getting caught hustling the streets, what's their image of adult life going to be?

It's easy to see the obstacles we face. What kind of low-wage jobs can keep you content when you see pimps and drug lords in fancy clothes driving fancy cars? What would keep you in school, thinking of the future, imagining a career, when no one in your family has ever done such a thing? When almost all the men die in their 20s? If you think you'll be dead before 30, there's not much motivation to plan ahead. You just hope you look good at your funeral and all the girls will cry for you.

It's not just the poverty and the lack of resources. It's the lack of imagination and the lack of hope.

So many courageous, persistent members of the African American community refuse to be victims, and they accomplish amazing things. But it's so difficult, and the path is filled with setbacks and disappointments and heartache...

It's clear there is a misunderstanding of generational racism when White America asks Black America, "Why can't you just get your act together like my family did? When we came to America, we were poor, and we didn't speak the language, and now our grandchildren are teachers and doctors and lawyers... "

The huge difference is the "mark" that never fades... because of racism, it's the skin color that keeps you down, that keeps people second-guessing, that makes people lock their doors or cross the street to avoid you, no matter what you have accomplished in life. White immigrants whose families learn English without an accent no longer have such a "mark" to warn others, "Beware!"

And I think that's where all the fear and suspicion and personal prejudice and systemic racism comes from. It creates such a circular effect that it keeps reinforcing itself, even when there are so many examples of progress.

Such a tragic, ugly, mess.

Anyway, we knew we would eventually visit Dirk. I never met him, but you did. When he was a child, their family had come to HHJ, in need of food and clothing from time to time. He and LaQuondra never joined the Clean Teens. I wonder... how might things have been different if they had been more involved with positive members of their community?

Chapter 81

Dear Kelvin,

You remember this story, because you were there. But I wanted to write it down anyway.

We were having our fall retreat with the Clean Teens. It was still a difficult time for everyone, and I knew the retreat would be a good experience for us.

Sister Matilda had been moved back to the mother house, and the entire upstairs was empty. We decided the girls could sleep upstairs, and the boys could sleep downstairs. No one had moved their stuff any place yet; it was still in the lobby. In fact, I had only been upstairs a few times myself, and wasn't all that familiar with it.

I went upstairs the week before the retreat, to see how many actual beds and couches there were, and how many bathrooms. I remember seeing a series of old portraits on the wall -- sisters who had held leadership positions in the order over the years. There were doilies over the backs and arms of all the chairs and couches. It was such an old-fashioned way to decorate, but charming. I tried to imagine all these sisters crocheting their doilies to make their simple living space look welcoming and cozy.

One of the sisters was there, looking through Sister Matilda's things and trying to locate a few items for her. I had met this sister before but couldn't remember her name. She introduced herself, "I'm Sister Brigid," and then I remembered meeting her at the festival. She told me that Sr. Matilda was enjoying the social life of the mother house. "There's always a TV on, there's always someone to talk with, there's always hot cocoa or tea, and there's never a need to worry or feel lonely." I was relieved to hear that.

When the weekend for the retreat arrived, there was the usual banter about how it's not fair that the girls get to sleep upstairs on beds and the guys have to sleep on air mats. Yet it also wasn't fair that the girls had to wake up earlier to take their showers and come downstairs, so the guys could go upstairs to take their showers... Yes, yes, life is unfair all around.

At one point, I had to go upstairs to get my sweater. I was getting chilly, and I had left it with my stuff up there. I turned on the bedroom light, grabbed it, turned off the light, and faced the hallway. I thought I heard a noise but had assumed I was alone upstairs, so I said out loud, "Hello?" and heard no response.

I stepped out into the hallway. It was dimly lit, but I could see well enough to get to the stairway and switch on the other light for going down the steps. I passed Sister Matilda's room and thought I saw Sr. Brigid. I wondered what she was looking for this late at night. When the woman came out, I realized it was a sister, but not Brigid. "Can I help you?" I asked. She just nodded and smiled at me and went into the next room. I followed her and flicked on the lights. The room was completely empty. There was no one there at all. I opened the closet. I went back into the hallway and turned on the light. I went into all six bedrooms. No one. I kept saying, "Hello? Sister? Can I help you?" but found no one at all. I stood still for a moment, trying to take this in. Was I dreaming? Then I refocused and decided to go back downstairs. I passed that group of portraits and immediately saw the face of the sister who had smiled at me. Without thinking, I said, "OH MY GOD!" in quite a loud voice.

Luz came flying up the stairs. "Are you OK?" she asked. "Yes, I'm fine, I'm fine," I answered, although my heart was pounding. "Let's go." I got my sweater.

"I thought I heard you talking to someone," she said.

"I thought I was, but I ended up talking to myself... I think."

We got back to the group in the St. Anthony room, and you came up to me and immediately said, "Nellie! Are you OK? You look like you just..."

"What?" I asked. "Saw a ghost? Is that what you were going to say?"

"Yes." you admitted reluctantly.

I quietly told you and Luz what had happened upstairs. Luz got a little creeped out, but you didn't. You asked, "Who was she?" I really didn't know. I didn't notice the name, since the names didn't have much meaning for me... I was not familiar with the history of the order, and I didn't even pay attention. But I didn't want to go back to look yet. I was still shaken up. Luz insisted. The teens were on a break, playing music and dancing, and Kim and Monique could take care of them for another few minutes. So the three of us went back upstairs.

I think Luz was more shaken than I was. We had all the lights on, and I pointed to the picture. You read, "Sister Mary Booker." You looked at me. I asked, "Who's Sister Mary Booker?" You said, "Hmm... she's the woman who founded this convent in this building, before it was House of Hope and Joy."

Luz almost fainted.

You asked me again, "What did you say to her?" All I said was "Can I help you?" and she nodded, as if to say yes, and she smiled, and so I followed her into the next room. But it was dark and I couldn't see her, so I put on the light, and she was gone.

You repeated, "So you asked. 'Can I help you?' and she nodded yes. Yes, you could help her. And she led you into that bedroom. Let's take a look." It looked like every other bedroom, except it had a bookcase along the wall with all the books from the old convent -- Bibles and hymnals, and history books and Bible study books and catechisms and things like that. It was probably the convent's library. But nothing stood out as a particular task we were supposed to accomplish.

Luz spoke up. "I think she wants you to take care of the history of the order. Make sure House of Hope and Joy keeps doing the work of Clare and Francis, keeps on doing the things we are doing."

I wondered if the sisters who used to live there are sad that there are no more sisters living there anymore. Matilda was the last one, and now a bunch of teenager girls are going to stay up half the night, giggling and talking about boys and who knows what in the very beds where the sisters used to fall asleep fingering their rosary beads...

We decided not to tell anyone, not even Kim and Monique. The teenagers would be so spooked, they would not be able to fall asleep. We'd wait until the retreat was over, and we'd have the time to process it more.

The next morning, we waited until the last of the teens had gone before telling everyone. The adults were a little fazed, but Luz most of all. Monique was kind of mad at us. "You let me sleep up there without telling me it was haunted! How could you do that to me?"

Luz jumped right in. "We're the ones who slept in that library bedroom! That's why we swapped rooms with you! We didn't want you sleeping in that room in case the ghost came back."

Fernando asked, "Why didn't you call me if you were so afraid? I would have come over."

"What if you suddenly showed up? What would we tell the teens? 'Fernando misses me?' You would have been sleeping with the boys downstairs anyway. So that would not have helped."

Sheryl was really glad she hadn't been there last night; she was not sure she ever wanted to go up there again. Andy was teasing her... "Come on, let's go visit that library bedroom right now!" She threatened to hit him on the head with a frying pan.

Monique wanted to tell Sr. Matilda and find out what she thought. Merry and Leah weren't sure if that was a good idea... Merry said maybe she'd ask Sr. Brigid's advice on that one. We didn't want any shock to cause too much stress on her heart.

Funny thing, I was the one who saw the ghost, but I wasn't really all that afraid to go back to the library bedroom. I was more intrigued by the whole thing. What was I being called to do? Was Sister Mary Booker just expressing confidence in what we were doing? Was I supposed to have a more responsible role? I just didn't know for sure.

I just kept all that tucked in the back of my mind for later meditation.

Chapter 82

Dear Kelvin,

2001 had been the year of our first Pebbles of Peace projects. It was also the year of Ruby's death and Sister Mary Booker's appearance. It had been the year of September 11, and we were very happy to move ahead to a new year and a better world.

But I can't say any of us were in a festive mood on New Year's Eve. There had been too much sadness, and we were just doing the best we could, going through he motions.

We had set up some good things that could start that forward motion for us...

At school, we had Merit Jackson visiting occasionally and the "Lil Johnnie" Literacy program, which was becoming a well-known success. We also had my leadership class and the annual Pebbles project.

At HHJ, we had the Clean Teens and the Thanksgiving and Christmas distribution programs. There were things we always did. We just did them on automatic pilot, and every so often something would happen like the appearance of Sister Mary Booker, and we would feel alive again for a short time.

Most of the time, we were in this slightly depressed state... just going through the motions. I keep saying it only because that's exactly how it felt.

We'd decorate the Christmas tree, and almost call out to Ruby, "Want some egg nog?" and then remember, oh, right, Ruby's not here. I'll hear something on the radio and say to myself, "I have to tell that one to Ruby." And then catch myself again.

But New Year's Eve that year did give us some joy. Olivia and Luke were home from college, and Olivia's boyfriend Marquis was visiting. They announced that they were engaged. It was actually delightful to have something happy to celebrate, even though we were sad that Ruby wasn't there to be part of it.

Olivia and Marquis would be our ticket out of the personal funk we found ourselves in… that was a wonderful gift! When the clock struck midnight, it was the most joyful I had felt in a long time. Since that night we spent in the hospital waiting room, there just hadn't been much celebrating of anything.

Chapter 83

Dear Kelvin,

I can't say that Olivia and Marquis made "everything better" for 2002, but it sure helped to have something positive to focus on.

The whole country was like us, still going through the motions, still in shock from what happened on September 11. That was just not going to go away. How could it?

Certain neighborhoods in our city had been going through the motions in many ways for quite a while, as we discovered like a slap in the face. A few programs like "Lil Johnnie" and Pebbles of Peace were not ever going to change that....

And more than ever, at House of Hope and Joy, you and I were really still just numb ...

Probably the thing that moved us out of our collective trance was the outreach we decided to do with Dirk and his family.

We met with Vera a few times. We took her out to supper, and we had her over for a few HHJ events. I thought it was important for us to show her that she was going to be embraced and not rejected. We discovered that Dirk had a child, and so we also met him and his mother. We wanted this act of violence to end with forgiveness and reconciliation instead of retaliation, shame and isolation on the part of all the family members involved.

Vera was quite worried about her grandson Ezekiel and his mother Deborah. Young single mothers are almost always destined for a life of poverty. Vera was willing to let Deborah and Zeke live with her, because Deborah's mother had issues of her own and was unable to offer much assistance. We invited Vera, Deb and Zeke to meet with us for supper at the Guadalupe Center one evening. We also invited Jaquez and his grandmother Alberta. We thought the grandmothers could use the support, and Jaquez was ready to babysit Zeke when Deb needed a break.

I was hoping that Jaquez could become like an "older brother" for Zeke for the rest of their lives. This could be just what both of them needed. Jaquez, already determined to live a successful life, could be a positive role model for Zeke, and Zeke would grow up with the example of an adult male who went to college, got started out of a career, and never went to jail.

It was your idea to invite Keshia and her daughter Sammy. Single women raising children need each other's support as well as the nurturing wisdom of grandparent figures. Keshia was divorced by then. We had all been hoping that Tyrone could change and stop drinking, but we knew not to put too much energy into that wish. Monique came along with Keshia.

It was good for all of us to meet away from HHJ at the start, since that was an emotional place for everyone.

Vera and Alberta took to each other like magic. We knew if that could happen, the rest of this networking would be easy. Alberta knew the heartache of raising a grandchild with "a daddy in jail and a momma who's messed up," and she saw the hope in Deb's eyes. Supporting Deb was important; she knew that girl needed to find a way to finish school and find a career so she could support herself and her son. She needed to have resources available so she could make wise decisions about her life and Zeke's life without being so desperate that she needed to turn to drugs or prostitution to put bread on the table.

Vera was also worried about LaQuondra, Dirk's sister. It was comforting to Vera to see Keshia... and to remember she had been friends with LaQuondra in school. Keshia gave Vera the hope that maybe her daughter might come back and live in the area and accept what her brother had done, and realize that she would be loved -- and not rejected -- by a community ready to reach out to her.

Monique was very protective of her sister Keshia. I really noticed it that evening. Not that she hovered or ever interrupted or spoke for Keshia. Never, not once. She always let Keshia be her own independent person. But Monique watched. I could see it in her eyes. I could see her concern at times; I could see her relief at other times. She had that look when it appeared that perhaps Keshia wasn't watching Sammy as closely as she should, but she always hesitated and sure enough, Keshia would notice what Monique had noticed, and Monique would register that look of relief.

You noticed that, too. That's really the way you operated as well. You did that a lot. You brought people together, and let them start to care about each other, and establish relationships and trust. You didn't hover, but you stood by in case there was a problem. Mostly, you trusted things would work out. Most often they did. But you were always there, just in case.

That's what we saw happening at the dinner... the relationships between Keshia and Sammy, Alberta and Vera, Jaquez and Zeke, between Deb and Keshia, and so on.

I just remember admiring you for the way you dealt with all of this. Determined that Ruby would not have died in vain, determined to find a way to bring love and hope out of her senseless murder, you just kept looking for ways to find reconciliation.

I still admire you. I don't know many people who would ever make such an effort.

The Guadalupe Center had an extensive ministry to the families of the incarcerated. Carlos had "Angel Tree" parties every December to gather gifts for the children whose parents were in jail or prison, and there were events and retreats throughout the year. Three times a year, rides were arranged for families who had no transportation to visit relatives in faraway facilities. Most of all, they worked with area churches to be sure that every person coming out of prison had a mentor to walk the journey back to a healthy, well-adjusted life. This transition time was crucial. A person coming back to life on the outside has lots of temptations and little experience for "normalcy" in employment, recreation and relationships. New friends are needed in order to avoid old friends, old hang-outs and old bad habits. The mentoring often begins while the person is still behind bars so trust can be established and a relationship can be built.

I remember the story you told me about Jaquez when he was younger. He asked you when you had been in jail, probably because he was looking for information about his dad. You told him you had never gone to jail, and he didn't believe you. He said, "Come on! Just tell me! Everyone goes to jail!" Now he can be part of creating the opposite assumption for another little boy.

Imagine believing that jail was a common part of everyone's life. No wonder these things happen with generational poverty.

The first time I went with you to meet Dirk, I was really nervous. A prison is a very intimidating place. I had done no crime and was not being punished, yet I felt punished for being there. Turning over all of my items to be put into a locker, going through a metal detector, getting patted down, hearing the loud slam of so many iron doors, seeing all the guards with their visible weapons -- all of this made my heart race. How do mothers and grandmothers go through this alone?

When I came face-to-face with Dirk, he did not look like a vicious killer. He looked like a scared child. How easy it is to forgive someone who seems so frightened and sad and sorry. He seemed so small, even though he was taller than I was. I wanted to rock him and give him a teddy bear. I wanted to tell him everything was going to be all right. He would get through this and come out and be embraced by a community ready to support him and make sure he gets everything he needs so nothing like this ever happens again. I guess that's what Ruby would have done. I felt her spirit with us.

He broke down and sobbed in your arms, and I knew he was going to be all right. There's nothing as powerful as being forgiven for the biggest mistake of your life. Like so many teen killers, he had no idea of the consequences of his actions.

These ridiculous fights break out all the time between rival gangs... over turf, over some girl, over some type of "disrespecting" behavior, and the first thing they think of is to show their superiority by shooting off their guns, never thinking that they would be the one to kill an innocent child or woman or community leader.

One of our teacher friends, Ronald Stevenson, agreed to be Dirk's mentor.

Sometimes pebbles of peace do outweigh boulders of violence. It just takes lots and lots of loving, peaceful pebbles.

Chapter 84

Dear Sister Agnes,

Helping families learn how to support each other reminded me of what Mary and Elizabeth might have talked about when they got together. What kinds of things did their children do when they played together? What observations did their mothers make? What did they think about?

That inspired this reflection.

> *Mary, raising kids is tough!*
> *Some days I think I'm not enough!*
> *Not fast enough to stay in sight,*
> *not smart enough to raise him right.*
>
> *Honestly! Some days John clings*
> *and won't let go of my apron strings.*
> *Other days, he sulks and shrugs...*
> *He's off to play with bees and bugs!*
>
> *Mary, how can I enjoy*
> *the task of raising such a boy?*

Liz -- I know -- young boys are wild!
Like a man and like a child!

Some days, Jesus wants a cake
and promises to help me bake.
Then all at once he's out the door
and isn't hungry anymore!
He's down the hill and by the lake,
then tuckered out, he takes a break.
Runs back home in half an hour,
looking for my yeast and flour!

Liz, some days I shake my head!
I feel like going back to bed!
Then I think, "What lies ahead?"

Mary, I'm so glad our boys
get along so well and share their toys.
Tossing balls and molding clay --
so busy with their active play.

My John -- he wants the world to be
a better place. It seems to me
He tries to fix things -- people, too --
and they don't like what he tries to do.

Your Jesus always has been mild,
since he was a little child.
But John is stubborn and wants his way.
He'll make someone mad some day!
He's making all my hair turn gray!

Liz, it's true. I sometimes worry...
But they'll grow up! There is no hurry!
Right now, Jesus seems so gentle,
I fear he's over-sentimental.
Sometimes, when he's criticized,
he won't look anyone in the eyes.
He just sits down, with stick in hand,
and doodles in the dirt and sand.
He finally thinks of what to say;
by then his friends have walked away!

But there is time. And they will learn.
That fire in their hearts will burn.
They'll do great things. I know they will.
They'll move beyond our little hill.

God will take them by the hand
and walk them to their Promised Land.
Once they're men -- all strong and tall --
we'll wish for the days our boys were small.

Chapter 85

Dear Sylvia,

I would like to invite you to join us at a luncheon next week -- on Wednesday. Enclosed is the information card. Several people are being given awards for their work in the community, and Merit Jackson will be receiving an award for his work creating the "Lil Johnnie" Literacy Project.

We finally finished the "Lil Johnnie Student Workbook" and are thrilled with the results we've been seeing at St. Augustine.

Merit will be at our table, along with Kelvin, Sister Brigid, Merry, Leah and me -- so far. I invited Sister Agnes, but she has a previous commitment.

I hope you can celebrate with us. I know you are busy, but I hope you find this free spot on your calendar.

Nellie

Chapter 86

Dear Kelvin,

When Sister Agnes started me with all this spiritual direction and Sylvia suggested I just write on my own, I thought I'd start at the very beginning. I have tried to keep the major events in order, but I have found that certain events trigger insights from other events, and I realize that I'm not really writing things in perfect order.

I remember we had spent a fun Saturday afternoon at your place, with Luke and with Olivia and Marquis, talking about college graduation plans and wedding plans, and I was just so impressed with this young couple and their desire to be teachers like you, to work in the central city area, and to model a simple and joyful life, with a simple wedding. You and Ruby did an amazing job raising your two children, and Olivia knew how to recognize a young man who would fit right in with your family's values and priorities.

After we had cleaned up from supper, the three of them had plans and took off rather abruptly. We were watching something on TV when you said so casually, "Would you like to go to a movie?" I said, "Really?"

You were surprised by that response. You probably didn't fully realize what went through my head. "Really?" wasn't reacting to the idea of seeing a movie with you, since we had seen movies before…

It was reacting to the idea that you were perhaps seeing me as more than a friend… and I was reacting to that new perception… as in, "Do you really see me as more than a friend?" As in, "Do you mean a DATE?"

Naturally, we didn't clarify all that deeper meaning at the time. You simply said, "Yes, really!" and off we went.

What's really funny is that I have no idea what movie we saw, and you couldn't remember either, because later we had talked about this. But I do remember the movie had kissing in it, and when the kissing started in the movie, I started to feel hot inside. I was suddenly aware of how we were sitting, and that my right hand was resting on my right leg, and your left hand was resting on your left leg, and that meant our pinkie fingers were only about an inch away from each other. Then you shifted your weight, and your knee was touching my knee, and our fingers were even closer. I didn't know if you had done that on purpose, but once you did, I shifted my weight, so our pinkies did touch. Immediately, you took my hand, and I was overjoyed.

What's even funnier about this is our conversation months later about that night. You said it was your memory that I took *your* hand -- that I initiated that hand holding. I insisted it was *you* who had initiated the hand holding. And neither of us could sway the other.

After this funny disagreement, later on that same evening, I purposely brushed my pinky against your pinky. You automatically took my hand. I said to you, "Who decided to hold hands right there?" You told me, "You did."

"Aha!" I replied. "See -- this is what happened that first night at the movies! I did NOT take your hand! I just touched you in the slightest manner... and you sensed that openness, and responded by wrapping your hand around mine. But you are the one who started the hand holding!" Of course you protested! You insisted that the process of hand holding begins with the initiating event, which was my "brushing my pinky against your pinky."

I think the point here is clear -- when two people are ready for affection, then the slightest indication on one person's part is perceived as an invitation -- as the "initiating event."

But what if that first initiating event was not intentional? Who initiated that first hand holding at the movies? Was it you -- because you shifted your weight and your knee was then touching my knee? Was that intentional or unintentional? You would never admit that to me either way.

Or was it me, because I sensed your movement (intentional or not) and wanted to respond?

Well, at any rate, this was a funny story for months, because I insisted I would never just grab your hand in the movies, and yet it was your memory I had done exactly that!

I think this is how children in the backseat fight... "Stop touching me or I'll hit you." (Later, there is an unintentional touch, followed by an intentional hitting.) "He hit me for no reason!" ... "You touched me!" ... "I did not!" ... And "You hit me on purpose!" followed by parents' intervention.

But it's the same principle. When two people are ready to fight, the slightest indication (even if it's unintentional) is perceived as a threat, and the other person feels justified in making a "return" strike, even if the "first strike" was completely unintentional.

I would love for gangs to have this conversation. They might see how circular this is. Each side just waiting for the other to give them a reason to retaliate...

So who really "starts" it -- the first one to do something intentional? What if someone pretends it's unintentional, and the other one is certain they are pretending?

See why this argument of ours was never solved?

What was discovered that night was this: Not only did I love holding your warm, strong hand, but later I had the first joy of kissing your lovely mouth... your soft lips brushing and embracing my lips... and I just melted inside at how gentle you were. There was something so loving about the way you approached me... so delightful. It was as if every touch and kiss was hesitant at first, waiting for me to respond with a welcoming gesture. Once I seemed to invite you to kiss more, to touch more, you came back toward me with more confidence and more love. Amazing that this tender exploration could be so articulate without any words. But we understood perfectly. "Can I do... this?" ... "I would absolutely love you to do this..." ... "Can I do... this, too?" ... "It is delightful for you to do that..." ... and so on.

The last thing I ever imagined was that I would fall in love with you, Kelvin, but you made it so easy.

I fell in love with you so gradually, I hardly saw it coming. But by the time we were alone at your home, and the kids had left, and it was just the two of us, it seemed as if we were becoming "new best friends." And what's easier than falling in love with your new best friend?

Chapter 87

Dear Kelvin,

Carlos called me.

It was Tyrone. He had started coming by Guadalupe Center, asking for small amounts of cash. Five dollars, eight dollars.

Carlos had talked with Fernando about this. Luz was worried that Tyrone would start looking for Keshia again. They wanted to keep him away from her and Sammy.

Tyrone kept saying that he wasn't drinking anymore. But alcoholics always say that. They need to lie. Their whole way of living is a lie. Until they are safely ensconced in a recovery program and have been completely sober for at least six months, they are not to be trusted.

The fact that he kept coming by asking for money was troubling to Carlos.

He never gave Tyrone any cash. He'd say, "I need money for gas," and Carlos would give him a gas card, good for $5.00. He'd say, "I need money for food," and Carlos would give him a food card for a grocery store nearby, one that did not sell any alcohol products.

Carlos said he wanted us at HHJ not to be fooled by whatever Tyrone said if he came by.

Luz and Fernando had already warned us of that. We were never to let him in, never to talk to him. We were told to always refer him to the Guadalupe Center. This was nothing new. I hadn't had to turn him away, but Merry and Leah did. I wondered what the other guests

---

thought when they saw us refuse someone on purpose, without giving any details.

Then Carlos asked me, "So how are you doing?"

I wondered about this... was the Tyrone story just an excuse for him to follow up with me and find out what I had been doing with my life? I told him I was just fine.

I was happy with my teaching, I was happy with my ministry at House of Hope and Joy, and I was happy with the Clean Teens and all we were doing. I told him it was good that the Guadalupe Center continued to stay involved with Pebbles. He said it was a great program.

I was very careful not to give him any openings. He was careful not to say too much, but I wondered if he was trying to give me every opportunity to give him an opening. Kind of like the pinky finger thing with us. But every time he moved his pinky, I did not respond at all.

Funny. For the first time I can remember, I looked back at the years I spent with Carlos in what I thought was a very loving and healthy relationship, and I said to myself, "What a shame for him. He really missed out on a good thing."

Prior to this, I would look back and say to myself, "What a shame. I really lost a good thing."

See the difference? I felt sorry for Carlos because he left me for no good reason. He hurt me terribly, and I still don't know why. But instead of blaming myself, as I did in the past, and instead of focusing on what I lost, as I did A LOT in the past, I chose to see myself as valuable and precious. He was in a relationship with a woman who loved him and cared for him and admired him and was a partner to him in everything he did. And like a fool, he just dumped it all. He is the one who really lost.

That was a big change in me... I had never seen myself that way before. If it took me so long to see myself as a precious human being that someone else should respect, imagine how long it takes someone like Keshia to recover? Someone who was beaten up, emotionally, and shoved physically, someone who started to see herself as deserving of all that abuse, someone with very few resources and a really steep road ahead?

How does such a person ever recover and trust again? How does such a person learn to only trust a person who is really trustworthy and safe?

I felt myself feeling very protective of Keshia, and of Deborah, and of Sammy and Zeke, and even LaQuondra who ran away from everything. I wondered how they would be able to establish healthy relationships and see themselves as precious human beings that deserve respect?

This is yet another consequence of generational poverty. If unhealthy relationships can happen to someone like me, who grew up in a happy family with two successful and nurturing parents who were crazy in love with each other, just imagine what happens when there is no adult wisdom figure to help a young girl (or boy) see what an unhealthy relationship is.

This was something we'd have to spend more time with. It wasn't something we really discussed directly with the Clean Teens. It was just beginning to dawn on me because of my own personal journey, and my writing about it.

Chapter 88

Dear Adam,

I know you know this story, but I want to write it down, because that way I have it on paper. I have been discovering that as I write things down, I reflect on them, and it spills into my prayer life, and I find myself making decisions based on my new insights, and I just end up serving the world better.

In fact, that's my new way of describing transformation.

Anyway, here's the story.

I remember you telling me that you wanted me to meet your friend Simon. He was going to come over for dinner with us on a Saturday night: me, Kelvin, Sheryl, Andy, Kim, Monique, you and Simon.

I was excited about having another opportunity for everyone to get to know you, and I knew you wanted me to meet Simon.

I was nervous about cooking for Sheryl and Andy, since they were the major chefs at HHJ. Monique suggested that everyone bring something, and I thought that was great. Kim brought egg rolls and "his famous jello," Sheryl and Andy brought chicken wings, but I don't even remember what everyone else brought. I remember I made "St. Louis" salad from a recipe that a dear friend had given me years earlier... I knew Sheryl was from St. Louis, and I had never made this salad for her, so I thought that was a good choice.

You got along with everyone. They had all met you before, but this was the first time we were in such a small group setting, and so they kept pumping you for stories about us growing up together. Kelvin and Kim and Andy were the worst -- they kept pressing you for more and more details. Sheryl kept telling Andy to stop, but when Andy stopped, she would ask you for the details! I think she wanted to get the scoop on me as much as Andy did!

Time went by, and although we were having fun, we were worried about Simon. He was often late for things, but when an hour had passed, you were worried. You called his cell phone -- no answer. You called his home phone -- no answer.

Sheryl and Andy told us the story about how they met. Andy started off talking about how they met at church, but Sheryl just started laughing too hard for him to continue. Then he admitted, "OK, we met in a bar." Actually, there was some ruckus, and Andy ended up protecting Sheryl and getting her safely out of the crowd and back into her car. They knew a good thing when they saw it. They started dating right after that... and going to church... I think.

Kim told us the first time he met Andy was when Andy pretended to be a HHJ guest, looking for clothing. It was in the middle of the summer, and he was asking for an overcoat, and a warm sweater, and a hat and gloves. Sheryl had told Andy how polite Kim was, so he was just messing with Kim, trying to see what this polite young man would do.

Kim would say, "Sir, we don't have any overcoats right now, because it's summer. We put the winter clothing in storage during the summer months."

Andy would seem to understand. "Oh. No winter coats now?"

"No, sir. I'm sorry."

"OK. I understand. So, you got winter hats?"

"No sir, our hats are with the winter clothing. It's summer now. It's hot outside. People don't usually ask for winter clothing during the summer."

"OK. No hats. I understand."

"Thank you, sir."

"OK, you got any woolen sweaters?"

And on and on...

Apparently, Kim never lost his temper. He stayed positively polite until Andy ran out of ridiculous things to ask for. He started to laugh and finally admitted, "I'm jus' messin' with you, man. I'm Sheryl's husband. She told me how polite you were, and I wanted to see if I could get you to yell at me or throw me out! You passed the test, man! You are the most polite person I ever met"

We were all laughing about this when your cell phone rang. It was Simon's sister Ashley. Simon was in the hospital. He had been stabbed. You jumped up, said good-bye and rushed out the door. Kim decided to go with you. I was glad he did.

You called us to let us know that he would be OK -- his arm and his face were all cut up, but no injuries to any organs and no broken bones. We were relieved it wasn't worse, but still concerned.

Kim stayed all night at the hospital with you and Simon and Ashley.

Later, we heard what had happened... he was attacked coming out of a coffee shop known as a "gay hang-out." It seemed that there was a car with a few guys who had been drinking, who decided it would be fun to just wait in the parking lot and stab whoever the first guy was to walk out of the place. Unfortunately, it was Simon. He had bought some pastries for our dinner party. They jumped him and sliced him up, yelled some nasty insults, and drove off.

He was OK, still shaken by the whole thing, but extremely grateful he had survived and didn't have worse injuries.

When I finally met Simon, I could see why you liked him so much. He was sweet, gentle, unassuming, and filled with joy. Even in the hospital, with his left arm in a sling and his face patched up, he seemed so positive, so delighted we visited, so affirming of you, so excited to meet your friends, so complimentary to his sister. Yet when we spoke about the incident, I could see him tremble.

Kim and I kept wondering what we could do for him... we felt kind of helpless and wanted to find a way to calm his fears. Later, we were talking with Monique, who hadn't met him, but who gave us an idea.

She simply said, "What can I do? I am a complete stranger to him." That was the key phrase for us. She was a *complete stranger!* The people who mugged him were complete strangers! We needed to restore his faith in "complete strangers!" We could show him that even though there were three complete strangers who had no reason to hate him, but chose to hurt him... there were also lots and lots of other complete strangers who had no reason to love him but chose to care about him.

So, the next time the Clean Teens met with the Clean Kids, we told them a little bit of Simon's story. We told them that this nice man bought some pastries at a coffee shop and was beaten up by some strangers who just wanted to be nasty. Since teddy bears had become a symbol of compassion for Monique, we got a teddy bear and tied a bandage around his left arm. We also put some band-aids on his face. We showed the teddy bear to the Clean Kids, and we asked them to draw some pictures to help Simon feel better. The Clean Teens helped the younger ones stay focused on the task and write their names clearly.

The next time we visited Simon, we took their artwork. Kim and Monique presented him with the bandaged-up teddy bear and 17 original drawings by children and 13 cards made by teenagers -- all perfect strangers who cared about him. I think it was just what Simon needed.

I think we should never underestimate the power of a loving gesture. We should never underestimate a person's need for support and reassurance.

Basically, we should never underestimate our own power.

We can always ask ourselves, "What can I do? I am a complete stranger..." and we can always look for a creative and loving answer to that question.

It's the only way for peaceful pebbles to outweigh violent boulders...

Chapter 89

Dear Kelvin,

I remember this most famous story about St. Teresa of Avila. She had travelled all night, carrying her basic needs in a wheelbarrow, to get to a new convent, so she could get things set up to welcome the new women who would be joining her in the order... and then the wheelbarrow got stuck in the mud. She prayed to God for assistance, and then it overturned and she fell down into the mud herself. More than miffed by this turn of events, she shouted up to God, "If this is the way you treat your friends, no wonder you have so few of them!"

Yes, that's how I feel sometimes... that's exactly how I feel.

I have always loved my teaching at St. Augustine. I started out as an English teacher, and then I developed a leadership class. The leadership class grew to be so popular, we started a second leadership class.

Then we started The "Lil Johnnie" Literacy Program with one freshman English class, and later it grew to be part of all the English classes. They loved the program, and Merit Jackson came by almost every month to do some activity with the students.

You started "Lil Johnnie" over at Blessed Savior, and you got some of the student council members to come to Pebbles every year. The stuff from St. Augustine was spilling out to other schools as well. I think we had at least five schools doing "Lil Johnnie" and over a dozen doing Pebbles.

Once Pebbles and "Lil Johnnie" took off, we had all these new student-designed projects, since Pebbles, "Lil Johnnie," and the leadership class all applied our model of transformation.

That meant the students were spending more and more time planning projects, organizing the efforts, gathering supplies, implementing their plans, and evaluating their success.

I thought these projects were great -- they gave the students meaningful ways to use their skills in real-life situations. They were using problem solving, planning, and forecasting skills to design projects to meet the needs of the community. They used math skills to compute the budgets for projects, timelines for raising funds and paying bills, and to analyze the stats they collected from pre- and post-tests as well as evaluation assessments to demonstrate the impact of their projects. They used advanced reading, writing and presentation skills to do the research needed to identify needs, write proposals, write reports and give presentations. They used advanced computer skills to create Power Points presentations, update their website, embed video and audio files, and do email blasts.

St. Augustine, much to its credit, asked me to be the director of youth leadership for the school. That way, it could be my full-time job to direct the projects and interface with the community's resources and the leaders of churches, organizations, and other schools involved with Pebbles and the "Lil Johnnie" projects.

It seemed like a dream come true until the "sexual abuse crisis" of the Catholic Church created a huge hole in the collective purse of the diocese. Legal fees and compensation to past victims of sexual abuse resulted in this enormous hemorrhage of funds.

Consequently, the position of director of youth leadership had to be cut. So I was let go by the school. I found myself out of a job and feeling a bit like a failure, even though I knew it was not my fault.

If I hadn't been such a "success," then I would still be an English teacher. The English teacher's position wasn't cut.

God, if this is the way you treat your friends, no wonder you have so few of them!

So I went to Merry's office, and cried and cried, and told her my whole story.

Merry has always had incredible insight. She is truly a wise woman. She encouraged me and comforted me. She reminded me that whenever God closes one door, another door is opened. Or at least a window.

She asked me to consider a position at House of Hope and Joy -- of joining them as a full-time staff member. She warned me that they didn't have much money, and if they took me on, I couldn't make as much money as I did at St. Augustine. I would need to assist them with raising funds to pay for the programming for the Clean Teens and all the other youth leadership projects I would be doing.

I thought I could do that. If I weren't teaching at St. Augustine, I would have more time to write grants, to visit foundations, and to meet with donors who might be interested in supporting the ministry. I made a lot of contacts through Pebbles and "Lil Johnnie." Perhaps this new idea could work.

Merry was so optimistic. She assured me that I was involved in God's work, and sometimes we have to be patient and wait for God's time. She promised to help me find ways to fund the program. She was so full of hope, it just spilled over into my soul.

She really believed in me... she had faith in me. It could have been the saddest time for me, but instead, I couldn't deny the joy in my heart.

Why should this white suburban girl have even a modicum of success in an urban Black and Latino setting with teenagers whose life experiences were worlds apart from mine?

How did I ever get here?

Well, it's all just been a mystery to me. But I guess God is all about mystery and miracles.

And perhaps this is what Sister Mary Booker had in mind all along, when she nodded yes to my question, "Can I help you?"

I asked Merry if I could convert the library bedroom into my office. She thought it was an excellent idea. I could use all the help I could get from Sister Mary Booker. I wanted her to be proud of what we were trying to accomplish at House of Hope and Joy.

Chapter 90

Dear Sister Agnes,

Thank you for your compassionate letter regarding the sudden need for St. Augustine to eliminate the position of director of youth leadership from the school due to the recent decrease in diocesan funding.

I appreciate your suggestion to look for schools in other dioceses and the list of contacts you provided to me.

Thank you for calling several of the principals in advance to recommend me as an English teacher. I was surprised at all the contacts you have in other states. You are obviously a well-known educator with a nationwide reputation for excellence.

It is clear that you want to support me in the search for a school that can afford to employ me. I am lucky to have such an ally at this difficult time.

You will be happy to know that I have accepted a full-time position at House of Hope and Joy. I will be the director of youth leadership at that site, in order to continue the ministry of Pebbles and "Lil Johnnie" projects.

Nell Massa

Chapter 91

Dear Kelvin,

We didn't waste any time. Merry gave me the names of twenty-one foundations, and I spent two weeks writing grant proposals. I asked for different amounts of money, depending on how big each foundation was and what they typically handed out. Added together, I was asking for a total of $200,000. I never expected to get even half of it, but all we really needed was $50,000 to cover the most bare basics, to be in good shape for the near future.

When the packets were all in envelopes, ready to be mailed, the whole staff gathered together.

We stood in a circle: Merry, Leah, Sheryl, Monique, Paul, Kim and me. We each held three grants with our left hand and three with our right hand. We made this strange kind of circle... sort of holding hands with envelopes; we each had three envelopes between each pair of hands.

Merry prayed:

"Loving God, we just praise you and thank you for Nellie's dedication to the Clean Teens and House of Hope and Joy...

"Loving God, Thank you for her gifts...

"We just ask you, loving God, to bless these grant proposals for $200,000 and to touch the hearts of the foundations who receive them...

"Loving God, please look down on our ministry and know that we are doing works of service in your name, to bring you glory and to bring comfort to all your people...

"Loving God, please bring us at least $100,000 to pay for Nellie's salary and health insurance and the program needs of the Clean Teens and Pebbles and "Lil Johnnie" projects...

"Loving God, we don't mean to be greedy, but we need this money desperately. We ask you for $100,000, but we'll settle for $50,000."

(At this point, we really struggled to choke back the snickers and giggles as she continued...)

"So in conclusion, loving God, we ask you to bless us with this much-needed money, somewhere between $50,000 and $100,000, for your youth leadership ministry. Amen."

We all repeated "AMEN" before dropping all the envelopes on the floor and dissolving into uncontrollable laughter.

Chapter 92

Dear Kelvin,

I will always remember our "chocolate chip pancake" date. You asked me to breakfast on this snowy February morning. The restaurant had chocolate chip pancakes as a special that morning, and I decided that sounded great!

We started to talk and talk and talk...

I asked you what you thought about Carlos -- and what happened between us.

I still laugh at your response.

You said, "Maybe it was just a cultural thing we won't ever be able to understand!"

Now that just cracked me up. Here's the Black urban dude telling the White suburban girl that "we" (you and I) won't be able to understand that other "foreign" culture! (Especially since Puerto Rico is part of the USA! So "they" are part of "us"!)

We laughed and laughed over that one...

I told you how much I admired you. I told you what it meant to me that you and Ruby had been with me through so many things... the teaching, the ministry, everything leading up to Ruby's death...

We talked about how you reached out to Dirk's family and brought in Alberta with her grandson Jaquez to meet Vera and Deb and Zeke...

I told you that I was so impressed with your wisdom, and how well you can read people, and how even tempered you are, and what an amazing dad you have been to Luke and Olivia... and of course, how much I had loved Ruby.

You told me your conversation with Ruby after first meeting me. How surprised you were with this white-bread girl who left the safe suburbs to care about inner-city youth. What was up with that? -- You said, "I told Ruby, 'We need to keep an eye on her.'"

I remember I blushed at that.

We stayed so late, we ordered supper and told them to pack it "to go," and you followed me back to my place. By then the snow was deeper and I was nervous. But they kept plowing the roads, so it wasn't too bad. You still wanted to see me safely to my parking garage.

Then you came in, and we kept talking. For some reason, we decided to watch *Mr. Holland's Opus* on TV, and we fell asleep together on the couch.

It was so comfortable together... the first of many such naps.

I loved to have your head on my lap. I loved the way you smelled and the way you snuggled up to me in your sleep. I loved to hold you -- I especially liked touching your jaw line and the smooth skin of your temples.

That night was the first time I told you I thought your lips were like soft, moist pillows that hugged my lips... and you about fell off the couch laughing at me. That's when I knew I would never make my living writing romantic poetry... Especially because I really thought that was a good description!

But I knew I had found a warm, comfortable, natural romance -- and that made my whole life feel like poetry...

Chapter 93

Dear Kelvin,

Olivia and Marquis had a marvelous wedding at House of Hope and Joy.

What a joyful occasion, even though all of us were very aware of Ruby's absence. We knew she would have loved the wedding. Most of all, Olivia would have enjoyed planning it and sharing all those memories with her.

Again, a simple wedding -- two witnesses -- Olivia's brother Luke and Marquis's sister Sequoia.

No long train that needed an army of women to reposition with every move. The focus was not on the glamour of the couple, but the faith of the couple and their proclamation of love to each other.

You were bursting with joy as you saw your children. You really came to see Marquis as a son, and celebrating with his parents was delightful. Vanessa and Seth had so much praise for Olivia. They claimed that she was the one who set Marquis straight, giving him motivation to finish college and take his studies more seriously. We were just pleased with the finished product -- Marquis was a gentleman in every way.

Sheryl and Andy outdid themselves creating a wedding feast, and everyone was licking their fingers, even though it was a formal occasion.

I remember having a conversation with Sheryl and Andy about the cooking. Didn't they want to sit back and enjoy a meal instead of worrying about preparing it? Didn't they just want to be a wedding guest instead of being the ones to prepare the feast? They both had the same response -- they wanted Olivia and Marquis to have the very best, and they knew that only they could provide that meal. To make their point, they asked me a direct question: "Who's gonna cook the best meal in town?" My immediate answer: YOU! And Andy's follow up question was rhetorical, "So don't you want the very best?" How could anyone disagree?

Olivia took Marquis to visit Sister Matilda at the mother-house, in her wedding dress. She wanted Sister Matilda to see them on their wedding day. What a tribute to the woman who prayed for her before she was born. You told me that she gave a baby blessing on Ruby's stomach for Olivia, and that the following year, Ruby asked for it when she was pregnant with Luke. Olivia and Luke had heard that story countless times. Since they practically grew up at HHJ, Sister Matilda would always have a special place in their hearts.

Chapter 94

Dear Sylvia,

I'm so glad you asked about the "Four G's of Teaching."

I have been using this with my St. Augustine students for years, as well as the Clean Teens at HHJ.

Sister Brigid recently asked me about it, too, because Sister Matilda had told her about it but couldn't remember the details.

It's my way of explaining the learning cycle to young people -- it helps them give better presentations.

1. Grab my attention

This is the fun part. We come up with an ice-breaker, a puzzle, a puzzling question, a scenario or skit, something to spark curiosity, something to create an interest in what we will be teaching.

2. Give me something new

This is the part most people think of as the actual teaching: "Give me that new information. Teach me something I don't know." But it can't be a long lecture. It has to be more engaging. Short lectures are OK -- but no more than maybe 5 minutes. Maybe 10 minutes if there is some video clip or visual or activity that's part of the actual lesson.

3. Get something out of me

This is when you get the participants or students to apply what they learned. So we ask them a few questions to make sure they get the concept, or if we just taught them a skill, we give them a role-play so they can practice the skill. If it's a group of children, we might ask them to draw a picture of what we just talked about. Or we divide the group into subgroups and ask each one to do a skit, make a poster, explore a related issue or do a short presentation. This is when we get the learners involved so they really internalize the concept.

4. Go make a difference

In school, this would be the creative homework or the long-term projects. With my leadership students and the Clean Teens, I would ask them, "How can this new knowledge help you make the world a better place?" or "What can we do to serve the world, now that we know this and have this new information or skill?" And we let them design something that combines their interests, their skill set, and the issues of their neighborhoods and families.

I have been teaching our concept of transformation to some of the community leaders that work with Pebbles. I think the Four G's are related to the movements of transformation. I see it this way: just as the Four G's apply to one finite lesson, I think the movements of transformation are more like a continuous cycle.

Action or Service	---	Grabs my attention
Learning	---	Gives me something new
Reflection/Prayer	---	Gets something out of me
Leadership	---	Planning on how to "Go make a difference"
Action/Service	---	Doing it, trying it out, which brings about more awareness

Learning	---	More new information you didn't get before
Reflection/Prayer	---	Which brings on more clarity, more unity of purpose
Leadership	---	Which creates a better plan, a stronger commitment, improvement
Action/Service	---	and so on! We just keep transforming!

Remember -- none of this happens without the support from a skilled, caring mentor and positive peers.

In a school setting, the mentor is the teacher or the activity director. The positive peers are the study group or the club or the class. In a community center, the mentors could be parents, coaches, youth workers, even supervisors. The peers could be other students, club members, team members, or colleagues.

Let me know if you think this makes sense. Wish you lived closer.

Call me next time you are in town.

Love, Nellie

Chapter 95

Dear Kelvin,

House of Hope and Joy had become a second home to me, and a second family. You and I hadn't said anything about our growing relationship, but it's possible that our subtle affection was beginning to show. Nobody asked any questions, and yet I couldn't help but think that everyone was watching us closely, looking for a sign.

Well, that sign came quite unexpectedly -- in a way we hadn't intended. You and I took to kissing hello and good-bye, as long as we were not in a public place. We did plenty of kissing and cuddling; we were just very private about it.

Olivia and Luke had gotten used to seeing me at your home a lot. The weeks after Ruby died, one of us -- either Monique, Kim or I – had spent the night there on the couch. Every single night, one of us was there, and that went on until Luke and Olivia were back at college. But when they came back for holiday breaks, it was definitely more of me, and less Monique and Kim hanging out over at your place.

But here's how everyone found us out...

Merit Jackson had come by with some really exciting news. He had just sold "Lil Johnnie" workbooks to a school system in a nearby city that wanted to equip several high schools with enough books to teach 2,000 students -- at $20 a book -- that was going to bring in $40,000! House of Hope and Joy was going to get 25% of that sale -- $10,000! What terrific news! That meant the word would spread and more books would be sold in the future.

After sharing the good news, everyone was yipping and yapping and jumping up and down and screaming with excitement! Before he left, Merit gave me a big, long hug, followed by a kiss -- on the lips.

During the hug, he was whispering in my ear that he knew we would make it big some day with this project, and he was so honored to have accomplished this with his wonderful business partner, meaning me.

Immediately, Monique slapped the seat of a chair, indicating to me that she wanted me to sit down. "Tell me about this!" she said with an almost naughty look on her face. "About what?" I asked, a little puzzled. "Tell me about you and that Mr. Jackson!"

Oh! It was that kiss! I told her, "No -- really -- we are just friends! He's just excited about our work together. We've been working on this project for years, and we had hoped that some day, it would bring in some money to support this ministry, and we are just so jazzed right now!"

It was Kim who said, "Nellie's not after Merit -- I think she's sweet on someone else!" And darn it, we white women can really blush deep red! "Who???" demanded Monique. I didn't say a word, but Kim said, "Monique, can't you guess? Who's always hanging out here? Who's Nellie always hanging around with? Who's her new best friend?"

"KELVIN???" She shrieked. My face gave me away. I never was a good liar. I just can't pull it off! Secrets about other people I can keep, but if someone guesses the truth about me, I just can't play with a poker face. It's all over. My face gives me away. That's how everyone knew.

So when you showed up that day after school, everyone just watched you walk in and walk toward my office with silly grins. You knew something was up, but you were afraid to ask.

So I told you what happened with Merit. You thought that was hilarious. "Oh, you enjoyed that, didn't you? You liked it that they suddenly thought you were so cool."

"Wait -- what?" I didn't even realize what you were saying at first, but then it suddenly dawned on me. "You're saying that Monique thought I was cool because a cool guy kissed me! That she was SURPRISED that such a cool guy would kiss me?"

I gasped at the realization. "So you are saying that I am SO very un-cool and THAT'S what surprised Monique so much! That some COOL guy like Merit would be interested in me!

Your skin doesn't change much when you blush, but I was certain I saw a slight cherry tint to your gorgeous chocolate color at that moment...

I wouldn't let you off the hook. "No! Say it! I'm not cool. Just say it! Say that you think I am not cool!"

"Hey, I'm not afraid to say it -- I just thought you knew -- it's common knowledge!"

"Wait -- WHAT?"

I didn't think you'd crumble so easily. In fact, it wasn't even a crumble. It was just... plain fact! Like you were saying, "So this is news to you?" or "Where have you been?" or "On what planet do you think people find YOU to be cool?"

OK, I had to admit it... you were right. Even my brothers will affectionately refer to me as a "doofus" from time to time. I even refer to myself that way. As in, "What's a white girl 'doofus' like me going out with a cool black dude like you?"

But I guess I thought since I hung around with you and Merit and folks like Monique and Kim... I just assumed that your cool rubbed off on me... a little... but I soon saw the error in that logic!

So I guess all of you liked me not because I became a bit more cool... but IN SPITE OF THE FACT that I had not become any more cool?

Hmm... So does that make you more cool for not caring that I am so un-cool?

OK... analyzing this whole dynamic made my head hurt....

But I should have known this "lack of cool" was never going to change...

There was that one time we were watching TV together, and on this one show a really hot chick was making fun of this geeky guy. He insisted he had a girlfriend, but the hot chick just laughed. "What kind of girlfriend could YOU have? One with big glasses and a flannel skirt? And knee socks?"

At this point, both of us busted out laughing! There I was sitting on the couch, wearing my big glasses, my flannel skirt and my knee socks!

OK. You win. I am NOT cool, and I will NEVER BE cool. And that's apparently always been OK with you.

Anyway, back to HHJ...

At some point, Kim and Monique had snuck up the stairs and were sticking their heads in the doorway.

"What?" you asked, still unaware of the total picture.

Kim just grinned and made his index finger go back and forth, pointing to the two of us, and then clapped his hands with glee. Monique teased, "Kelvin, it's all over! We know Nellie is sweet on you! It's time to come clean!"

So you put your arm around me and pulled me over to you, kissed me on the cheek, and just grinned back at them.

Monique was not having it. "Listen, brother, I just saw Merit Jackson give her a better kiss than that!"

And yes, you planted a big one on me -- jus' showin' off!

Chapter 96

Dear Kelvin,

As we suspected, Olivia and Marquis did not even think our "news" was news. They had already figured us out months ago.

But they brought us some wonderful news just a few months after their wedding. Olivia was pregnant! That was the biggest thrill ever.

You loved knowing that you were going to become a grandfather.

Especially since Olivia and Marquis were both teaching at Blessed Savior, and all the teachers would be teasing you and calling you Grandpa.

You didn't tell me you had twins in your family until Olivia found out she was having triplets! What first came as good news next became news of concern. Olivia was not a large woman to begin with, and this was going to be very demanding of her body. After six months, she had to go into the hospital to avoid pre-eclampsia -- the high blood pressure that could shut down her major organs. They tried to keep her from going into labor, but after three and a half more weeks, it was hard to stop those babies -- they wanted out, and we all rushed to the hospital.

Leah came with us. There we were, sitting in the hospital waiting room. I remembered a horrible August night in that same waiting room, when we were waiting to hear about Ruby... and here we were again, waiting and praying for Ruby's daughter and grandchildren.

Finally, the doctor came out to tell us that three tiny babies -- two boys and a girl -- were rushed to incubators, and they were just trying to keep Olivia stable. She said Marquis was a trooper, too. When we finally saw him, he looked horrible. I could only imagine how Olivia looked. He was there just long enough to tell us their names -- Michael, Raphael, and Gabriella. I burst into simultaneous tears and laughter. Of course -- it was September 29 -- the feast of the archangels -- Michael, Raphael and Gabriel! Whatever made them think of that? It must have been their Catholic school education.

We couldn't see Olivia until the next day, and we could only see the babies through the window. They looked so helpless, dwarfed by the tubes coming out of their noses, mouths, and hands. There was more bandage than skin for us to see. We could only pray that they would make it.

Leah kept reminding us that Ruby had a lot more influence now, and if there was anything she could do about it, those children would survive this ordeal and come home healthy and happy.

Ultimately, Leah was right. Olivia came home first, and Marquis was doing a constant shuttle between home and hospital every day. Then after another two weeks, the boys came home. With Olivia still weak, Luz had set up a full schedule of assistants -- cooks, cleaners, and baby helpers -- coming to their house around the clock to keep these babies fed, burped, held and cleaned, and to make sure Marquis and Olivia had nothing else to do except recover from their ordeal and bond with their babies. Finally, one full month after her brothers, Gabbie came home to join Mickey and Rafe.

The full-time help continued for months.

It was probably a year before we breathed a collective sigh of relief. They had the biggest "first birthday party" I have ever seen, in the St. Anthony room, of course. I remember hearing Keshia and Deb talk about how much work it was to take care of their babies when they were first born, but Marquis spoke with the greatest authority on this. "I don't EVER want to hear ANYONE complain about how tired they are from taking care of ONE baby. If you have only one child, and that child is healthy, and you do not have a spouse who is recovering from surgery, then SHUT UP! You are a wimp! You will get NO sympathy from me!" Naturally, he said all this with a smile.

Olivia only agreed to the big party at HHJ under the following conditions:

1.   There would be no presents for the children. They had already received a year of presents and presence -- everyone on staff at HHJ and the Guadalupe Center had showered them with gifts and spent the night at their home countless times.

2.   All the baby helpers and home assistants who had been helping them through the past year were to be invited.

3.   Sheryl and Andy had the option of just being guests and not cooking any food (They thanked Olivia, but politely declined and prepared a birthday feast.)

4.   Every guest of the party received a framed picture of the triplets in their matching custom-made onesies (embroidered with the words, "Bundle of Hope and Joy"). The frame said, "It takes a village to raise a child." and

"Thank-You!" (It was your idea! You took the pictures and got the frames, and we spent an evening putting them together before the party.)

At your grandchildren's birthday party, with Luke and Olivia present, and all of our extended community from the Guadalupe Center and House of Hope and Joy, you announced our engagement to great whoops and cheers.

Chapter 97

Dear Kelvin,

We were married on Nov. 2, just a month or so after the triplets turned one. Nov. 2 is the traditional feast of all soul's day, the last day of the "Autumn trilogy" -- Halloween (or All Hallo's eve), All Saints Day (or day of the dead) and All Soul's Day.

It was the traditional day for people to visit the graves of their loved ones, and we thought it was a great way to include Ruby's memory.

Another simple wedding at House of Hope and Joy. Sheryl and Andy were our witnesses, and the triplets stole the show. That's OK; we didn't need the spotlight! Basically, we are fairly shy people after all...

We followed Olivia's lead and told everyone they could only attend if they brought no gifts. We wanted PRESENCE, not PRESENTS. They reluctantly agreed.

We also followed Olivia's lead and told Sheryl and Andy NOT TO COOK, and they also agreed... very reluctantly. We really didn't want them to be working for our wedding supper, since they were the entire wedding party.

We made it a pot luck -- very Franciscan, very informal. Just the way I liked it.

It was great to have our families there. There was a lot of old fashioned visiting. My nieces really took to the triplets and they asked Olivia and Marquis lots of questions.

My brother Ben decided to get up and give everyone a lesson in ancient Greek. He had little cards printed up.

They were placed all over the tables. On the one side showing, they said, "Congratulations, Nellie and Kelvin."

He pronounced a sentence in ancient Greek and asked everyone to repeat it after him. They just stared at him. It was clear that they couldn't possibly repeat what he had just said.

"What?" he asked. "You can't pronounce that? Would it help if you saw it written down?"

"Oh, yes" everyone agreed. Of course, seeing it written down would help.

So he instructed everyone to pick up the "Congratulations Nellie and Kelvin" cards and flip them over so they could read the sentence. On the other side of the card, they saw this:

$$\text{Τισ ανωεθαι ταυτα γενεστι}$$

He got a big laugh with that. Then he asked his "helpers," (Rose, Ann and Connie) to hold up the giant poster boards. They had this pronunciation key on them:

Tis On – away – thay   **Tau – tah Gah – nes – tie**

He actually had everyone saying this phrase. He made them repeat it several times. Then he had them repeat it in a call-and-response format.

He would say, "Tis On–away–thay" and they would reply, "Tau–tah Gah–nes–tie."

What does it mean?

He taught us that it means "Who would have thought this could have happened?"

He instructed everyone to memorize this phrase and to teach it to others. It would always be a fun thing to say when something unexpected comes up.

So everyone said it back and forth at the tables, a few times, until they either learned it or dissolved into laughter and gave up trying.

He added that he had actually taught this phrase to Ruby the day he met her at our first Pebbles celebration several years ago. She laughed and thought it was a great phrase to say. So if we kept saying it, we would be holding her in our memory as well.

Ben asked you if Ruby had ever mentioned it to him.

Embarrassed, but rising to the occasion, you replied that she had actually tried to teach it to you, but you never got it right, and you had since forgotten all about it. You said you had no idea that it was Nellie's brother she learned it from. All you could remember was something like, "Kiss on a wafer, Papa gesundheit." And that didn't seem to ever be an appropriate thing to say to anyone!

Lots of laughs...

I knew our families would get along.

Chapter 98

Dear Kelvin,

My older brother Phil had this great idea. He had written a song and played it for me on the piano when we were visiting, last Thanksgiving weekend. He said, "Can you write words for this song?" Not thinking, I said, "Sure." Then he said, "By Christmas? So it can be a Christmas carol? As a present for Mom?"

I wanted to say, "By Christmas? Are you nuts?" But instead, I just said, "Sure!"

So I got right to work on it and created the first draft. I emailed it to Ben, and he and I discussed rhythm and cadence, and dangling participles, and alliteration and parallelism and first person singular and anachronisms and all of those things writers talk about when they are alone and there is no fear of boring the non-writers in the room because there aren't any.

And we sent what we thought was the "almost final draft" to Phil and Charlie.

Then the real editing began! Every day there would be four emails about this or that choice of words, or this phrase or that term, and we had to invert several lines and move around stanzas and change the words to better match the tune because of musical principles Ben and I couldn't spell and never heard of.

And after the most intense work and the most creative fun I've ever had with my brothers, we ended up with a final product. Phi's music, Charlie's arrangement, my original words, Ben's editing, and then everyone else's "finishing touches" that went on and on, during Advent...

It was great. The plan was for my three nieces to perform it at a Christmas party at my mom's house. Rose played the piano, Ann sang, and Connie sang two stanzas, played the flute during an instrumental interlude, and then sang the last stanza with Ann. Everyone applauded, my mother cried, I cried, Olivia cried. The triplets had already been crying most of the evening!

Then the big surprise was when we went to church together at St. Dominic. THE CHOIR SANG IT!

My brothers had gotten them together to teach them the song and practice it with them. In fact, my nieces were part of the choir. What a treat! What a surprise! What a delight! All of us cried all over again, except the triplets -- luckily, they slept all through the Mass.

This writing thing... it's really neat. I like writing little poems and reflections -- like the ones I have been writing for Sister Agnes, in order to avoid writing about the really personal matters. Somewhere along the way, I think I realized that my vocation was all about reflecting and finding meaning and writing, and then helping others learn and reflect and find meaning from their writing, too.

But the experience of hearing my/our words sung to music by a whole choir, at Mass, as an offering to God... wow... I hardly have words for that feeling... I'm kind of like Joseph, at Christmas, surprised to find myself in the middle of a miracle I still don't quite understand...

Chapter 99

Dear Sister Agnes,

Here is a reflection on Christmas from Joseph's point of view. It was a family effort; a present to my mother. If you'd like to hear it set to music, let me know.

The choir of St. Dominic sang it Christmas eve.

Nell Massa

Joseph's Noel

I

Nazareth seems so far away
To strangers here with no place to stay

My wife with child, my sandals are thin
Do you have room for us to come in?

Wear faces, dusty roads,
Travelers and donkeys carrying loads

Many miles we have trod
No one knows we are walking with God

II

Cave with cattle, goats and sheep
A place for Mary to lie down and sleep

Sounds of the village, smell of the hay
A baby is born as animals play

Mother and child, I watch you rest
Praising God for a moment so blest

Bethlehem, you are so small
To welcome the greatest King of all

III

Comfort comes from the clouds in the sky
A choir of angels, a soft lullaby

Shepherds gather to witness the sight
Music so holy and halos so bright

Angels, shepherds, cattle and I
Peaceful mother, a prayer and a sigh

Newborn babe, the Prince of Light
Our gift of faith through the darkness of night

Chapter 100

Dear Kelvin,

You know I'm not really good with romantic poetry, so I won't try to describe your lips like warm, moist pillows anymore. But I really did want to write down something about sexuality.

Once we were married, I learned something important, and I think other people should learn about it, but I really don't know how to teach this thing to anyone. Nobody that needs to learn about it would ever listen to me anyway. But if I've learned anything in the last few years, it's the importance of reflection. And I think as human beings we were made to write. We were made to reflect. We were made to be mindful. That's what feeds our souls. So I'm going to attempt to say this in as articulate a way as possible.

I learned that many men do not know how to treat women. And women, who are not treated well, may not understand what it's like to be treated well. They can't imagine it because they haven't seen it or experienced it.

On one level, this means honest communication, and doing your best to be sure (1) your partner receives the actual message you are trying to send and (2) you receive the actual message your partner is trying to send.

Many men get fed up with this because it takes time and practice. They would rather just expect their women to read their minds. They assume that because they know what they mean, and they have expressed themselves, it should be up to their woman to figure this out.

I'm not saying there aren't women who are poor communicators married to men who are excellent communicators -- this happens as well. I'm just saying in the grand scheme of things, I have met far more men who need practice with communicating than women.

How many times have your heard a woman say, "What do you mean?" and the man say, "You heard me." And then he refuses to clarify what he's trying to say. Either he likes to keep her guessing, or he likes seeing her work hard to please him. It's not good communication. It's not honest or loving. It's actually a way for him to manipulate her. If she gets it right, he can stand justified. If she gets it wrong, he can criticize her.

You never did that.

When it comes to sexual communication, I think the same thing applies. Often, men think they know what a woman wants, so they rush to deliver it, and then women don't know how to respond to their disappointment. Just because men know what buttons to push doesn't mean they know how to be sensitive lovers. It's not a race to push the buttons. Lovemaking is all about finding the most loving and sensitive ways to make contact with those buttons.

Timothy just pushed buttons. It was like a business transaction. But I didn't feel loved and cherished. I felt like someone whose buttons were being pushed so we could get to the finish line and declare the race over.

Some of us might believe that's all there is to lovemaking.

Certainly, that's all you need to know in order to make babies. And it's quite possible that for some men, their need to feel manly and satisfied is completely met by just pushing the buttons.

But everything isn't a race. The main purpose isn't to just get to the finish line.

What you did with your lips and fingertips the night we first went to the movies was what you always did with your whole body. You always moved so hesitantly at first, as if to ask the question, "This?" and I would respond with my body as if to answer, "Yes, this!"

It's like a gentle dance... and it accomplishes a lot.

First of all, it's a delightful reminder for us to slow down and enjoy each other. Sometimes, we think we know where we're going, so why ask for directions? But when we always rush to the destination, we often miss the scenery along the way. Sometimes the scenery is the best part. Sometimes the best part of loving is being reminded that your partner is crazy about your scenery.

Second, the gentle dance gives each of us a chance to say these things without using words: "You are so beautiful. It is such a privilege to be with you. I am so honored to touch you in this way. I am so thrilled to behold this part of you. I am so lucky to be with you." When two people communicate this adoring message to each other on a regular basis, their trust and appreciation for each other deepens and minor misunderstandings are easily forgiven and forgotten... because the purest message of love is being communicated with great consistency.

This attitude is so different from what many men seem to be saying with their behavior: "You are mine, and I am doing this because I have the right to do this. And it's your job to enjoy it and thank me for it." This arrogant attitude is the opposite of love. It's manipulative and controlling, but if it's the only attitude a woman has experienced, then she might begin to think that this is the only way things are or could be... and that it's her fault if her partner isn't happier because it's her job to make him happy.

See where this is going? These are the unhealthy patterns that hurt and confuse women who are with those men who do not understand the gentle dance of lovemaking.

Third, the gentle dance gives both people a chance to steer the direction of what will happen. You may think you know exactly what I like, but my mood tonight might be different from what my mood was last time. (Your mood could change, too.) I might welcome more of this and less of that. And sometimes I am ready to go faster to the destination, but it's never good idea to assume that. So it's best to always assume the direction could change and to always assume the journey would be long and full of gorgeous scenery. And by doing the gentle dance of "This?" ... "Yes, This!" we are open to the possibility of "This?" ... "No, This!"

Never once did Timothy do the gentle dance. He was not aware of it. He took what was his and was sometimes more rough than he needed to be. I wondered why everyone else seemed so crazy about the process, since it seemed kind of harsh to me. If someone wants harsh, they can steer things to become harder and stronger, but assuming someone wants gentle is always the best way to begin.

I didn't know enough to explain all of this to Timothy. I imagine most lovers on the wrong side of "harsh" can't imagine how to explain it. You can't do the gentle dance without being gentle.

Funny... Adam always did the gentle dance. With his lips and his fingertips... on my face, and on my hands, and sometimes my shoulders and back. And always with his lips and tongue. He was a gay boy with a straight girl, and I never knew it. Probably because he did love me and still does. He still finds me beautiful, and I still find him beautiful. We won't express ourselves with romantic kisses now, but when we were in high school and college, we certainly did. His lips and fingertips made me feel absolutely gorgeous, completely loved and cherished, totally appreciated. I felt so lucky to have a wonderful boy so crazy in love with me. If you don't have that feeling at the end of the race, then it was not worth running, even if you do cross the finish line with confidence and vigor.

I didn't realize it, but Adam set me up to search for something amazing. That's why I was so sad to have lost him and so happy to have re-found him. No one else seemed as wonderful as Adam.

And then, eventually, you held my hand, and my whole world changed.

I just wish there was a way to tell this to young men... how to explain the power of the gentle dance... a way to teach them to be gentle lovers...

I think most women instinctively communicate in a similar way with their babies. They need to say, "I love you more than my own life" without using words. Watch a mother with her newborn. She constantly kisses him or rubs her nose in her skin. She fingers his arms and legs, or kisses her tummy. She sings, she rocks, she prays, she giggles. She does everything possible to say, "You are so beautiful. I am so lucky to be with you. I will protect you and love you and give you all the best."

She does it all gently, and she watches to see what the baby enjoys.

There are many men who instinctively know this as well.

But for the men who do not know it... I simply don't know how to tell them.

And I don't know how to tell women to look for it and to recognize it in the small things so they can expect it in all things. I'm not talking about abusive men. Timothy was never abusive, he was just clueless... and I was clueless. I missed Adam and the loving, respectful ways he had with me. I missed feeling loved and cherished. Adam brought me that feeling in ways Timothy never even tried to do. And I didn't know how to communicate that to Timothy because I hadn't yet understood it myself.

Anyway, I loved the way you loved me. I loved the way you did the gentle dance...

I wish there was some way to explain to men all over the world that it's the gentle dance that women love. Stronger passion can always come later, but if the man never learns how to do the gentle dance with a woman, then that deeper passion never really comes at all... it's just a race with a finish line.

101: Dear Kelvin,

I wrote this for your birthday, January 17. This is the extent of my romantic poetry!

I love your nose
I love your toes.
I love the way your chin hair grows.

I love your hands.
I love your fingers.
I love the way your soft touch lingers.

I love your hair.
I love you bare.
I love you out of underwear.

I love your face.
I love your place.
You can make my heartbeat race.

Every single
Way we mingle
Makes my happy body tingle.

Your hair is bushy
Your hug is cushy
And boy I really love your tushy!

Birthday boy,
You're just so cute,
Especially in your birthday suit!

It's our fate
Today's the date
So now's the time to celebrate!

Happy Birthday! I love you!

102: Dear Kelvin,

Leo Tolstoy said "All happy families are alike; each unhappy family is unhappy in its own way."

It's from *Anna Karenina*. I know that is quoted a lot, and I always sort of understood it. But I think it's even more profound than most people realize.

I think it's true of relationships, and families, and even workplaces.

When I think of relationships, I think of all the unhealthy situations I had been in -- each of them was different. Each relationship was unhealthy, and therefore "unhappy," for a different reason. Either someone wasn't honest, or we weren't looking for the same things, or we didn't have the same interests, and yet we were trying so hard to make it work, and it was like trying to fit together two pieces of a jigsaw puzzle that weren't made to fit together. We can push all we want, and maybe we can even force it together and pretend that it's OK, but the truth is that those two pieces just weren't made to be together.

Look at our family. It's so far from "traditional" that I have to laugh. You're Black, raised in the city with an absent father and single mother. I'm White, raised in the suburbs with an affectionate father and mother. Yet we came together, you as a widower from your childhood sweetheart (the only woman you ever really dated), me as someone who was left almost at the altar, later divorced, and a fine example of SEVERAL unhealthy relationships. And yet, together, we formed a happy marriage. Whenever

---

we gather together with our new family, it reminds me of my parents' marriage.

True, "my" grandchildren are really Ruby's grandchildren, and our family had to make a few adjustments (and that first Christmas was kind of awkward as we figured out how to balance and marry our two families' traditions), but deep down, our family is happy the same way other families are happy -- with lots of laughter, lots of affection, arguments that end in hugs and apologies, support and shared tears during the difficult times, and celebration and gratitude for the lucky times.

In fact, when I think about it, the staff at House of Hope and Joy is even similar to Blessed Savior School -- not at all in what we do, the type of meetings we have, or even the way the positions are structured. But they both follow those same five leadership principles I learned at HHJ. And I think happy families do, too. I might write a paper or an article about this some day. I want to test out my thoughts...

Same Goal, Same Direction.

In happy and healthy families, everyone holds the same values sacred. Because family members love each other, they are always making each other's needs a priority. They value the discovery and encouragement of individual talents and styles, and they also value each person's journey toward fulfillment and "life work." They value family togetherness, family traditions, laughter and doing things together whenever possible. Honesty, respect, hospitality, faith, care, commitment -- that's what love is, and that's what family is all about. In happy and healthy families, everyone seems to understand this because it is modeled from they time they are in the womb.

They never learn this in unhealthy and unhappy families, because one or both of the parents had never learned it. So everyone in the family grows up trying to pull the family in a different direction, and no one completely understands why the whole thing keeps unraveling.

And family traditions! You know it's a tradition when there is protest from the children. "Aren't we going to do this like we always do?" Perhaps you only did it once or twice, but once it's perceived as a "tradition," it's part of your family culture, and it's an outward demonstration of the whole family going in the same direction.

Family traditions are different in every family. Yet "having traditions" is universal. For example, at first, I didn't understand your family's tradition of eating pizza on the floor while watching TV or DVDs. But that used to be a treat for your family when Olivia and Luke were little. Ruby spread out towels on the living room floor -- like an indoor picnic -- so they could watch TV and eat pizza and get messy. You couldn't see the TV from the kitchen counter in your apartment back then.

But even after you moved to a bigger place, and you ate at a table that was in full view of the living room and TV, you still chose to eat on the floor because it was your tradition. We did it the week after Ruby died -- and it was somehow comforting to all of you. I sensed that, even though Monique and I were surprised that young adults would still want to sit on the floor and eat on towels, when there was a perfectly good table and comfortable chairs so close by. Luke and Olivia insisted that we all sit on the floor, so we did. And that's what happens with family traditions.

We also learned that when you sat at the table, the TV was never on. Meal times were for conversation. It was only on "movie night" that the TV would be on during the meal. And that meant pizza, popcorn, and towels on the floor!

Leadership Shared, From Top and Bottom

Everyone has something to offer, everyone has something to learn. The feelings and thoughts of the children are important, and so they feel valued and proud to speak up to give their opinion on family matters. Parents foster this early on, by laying out several acceptable choices, and letting the children choose. They choose what to wear to school from three outfits parents lay out. They can choose what supper from three options Mom or Dad offer.

That doesn't mean that children get everything they want. Children always push their limits, because that's their job. And parents will always need to rein them in, because that's their job. The parents still make the final decisions, but the feelings and opinions of children are never ignored or dismissed. They are named and they are validated, but at times they need to be set aside for other reasons that the children can't always appreciate. That's what healthy parenting looks like. You can recognize it in every healthy family. It certainly becomes more challenging when teens enter middle school and are mature enough to know how to argue well and manipulate situations and play off their parents' weaknesses, but not mature enough to make good decisions in general. Then it's most challenging.

But if parents have always modeled this "be firm about appropriate limits, but continue to listen to children's opinions and validate children's feelings" method, then the transition from childhood to young adulthood is a little less traumatic.

When we were kids, our family had "family meetings" on all kinds of things: What to do on a particular Sunday after church, which relatives to visit, what movie to see, which toppings on pizza, which of several charitable organizations our family would send money to. All of these things made me feel like an important, contributing member of the family. The older we got, the more influence we had, and the more we could contribute.

If parents model this from the beginning, than it isn't such a huge problem when the children start learning things and becoming more expert than the parents in some areas. I've seen that happen in families. As soon as children start realizing that their parents don't know everything, they start challenging the parents on everything. But if parents have listened to their children all along, then they still listen. And when children point out mistakes or show adults how to do certain things (especially electronic things), then adults don't feel threatened and start major fights to avoid loosing their "authority and identity." They can begin to accept that sometimes their children will know more about certain areas... and it doesn't become a "contest" for the child to prove that the adult is wrong about something and for the adult to prove that adults still know more than children. Many unhappy families fight that impossible endless war for years!

The older the children become, the more often that will happen until, eventually, it will seem as if the children know more than the parents do about most things. That's when the elderly parents become wisdom figures, with timeless learning that applies in all ages and all situations, even when they don't know which button to press on the computer, iPod, iPhone, iPad, or whatever the latest iGadget is...

The parents who age with grace are the ones who understand this principle.

Creativity From Diversity

Different types of people bring different ideas, different perspectives, different ways of thinking. A group of different brains will always think better and learn better than a group of similar brains. This is essential to remember in a family. When children have different ideas from parents, it can sometimes seem threatening. Children don't always want to do things the same way the adults have always done it. As I have just written, sometimes children have not only different ideas from the parents, but also better ideas. It is a wise parent who understands this, and is willing to entertain all possible options before choosing well.

It also means that families welcome all kinds of friends. Back when our parents were growing up, this was very rare. How often did white families come to visit black families in their homes in the 1940s, when it was illegal for them to sit together on the bus or use the same restrooms? I shudder to think of that! And yet now, racial intermarriage is common. How times have changed!

Here's another example. Adam stayed "underground" for years, trying to deny his emerging homosexuality, until he finally had to run away and deal with it apart from his family. But both his family and our relationship became healthier when we could accept the way he different from us and still show him how much we loved him. That's another case of family accepting diversity and becoming more creative in their (our) thinking.

Think of all the little ways that families learn from each other -- from cooking recipes to child discipline, to home health remedies. Every time there is a marriage, there is a coming together of two different ways of doing things, and the sharing of two sets of great ideas for celebrating holidays, for organizing the home, for communication, for all expectations in general. In healthy families, that diversity brings new creativity. In unhealthy families, either one family dominates, or one family is resentful, or one of the couple feels dismissed or ignored while the other one controls. There are lots of ways families can become unhealthy by resisting diversity and rejecting any new creativity that might come from learning new ways of living.

Look at the way we have blended our Christmas traditions. My family always left candy in the children's bedroom slippers on Dec 6, the feast of Saint Nick. Your family never did. But now Olivia has started that with the triplets. It's a great way to blend the Santa stuff they see at the mall with the Advent stuff they see at church. It helps remind us that Saint Nick is a real saint with a real holy day.

Our family always opens tiny presents at the Christmas morning breakfast table. Now you and I do that when we share Christmas morning with our children and grandchildren. They like it, too. It calms the children down, so it's not such a race to the pile under the tree.

Your family always gave personal presents on Christmas Eve, after coming home from Mass, saving Christmas morning for the "Santa presents." I thought that was a great idea. My brothers started doing that with their children, even after they were too old to "believe" that Santa literally came down their chimney (despite a fire in the fireplace) to leave the gifts.

Most touching of all was that your family always came up with gifts to give away on Jan. 6, the feast of the Epiphany. It became your tradition that Luke and Olivia would play with their presents for the 12 days of Christmas, and then they each had to give one away to House of Hope and Joy, to share with children who didn't have as many toys. You and Ruby would each give away something as well. What a touching tradition that is, and what a great way to teach generosity to children. It became a tradition my brothers began with their families as well. And their daughters didn't even object!

So much diversity and creativity, even though that first year was a series of "You do WHAT every year?" and "What's the point of THAT?" Our shared values and vision (teaching generosity, wanting fair limits, seeking practical ways for our traditions to model our faith), helped us become more creative because of the diversity of our families and our personal histories.

Walk the Talk Together

We have to practice what we preach. We have to mean what we say. We have to demonstrate what we believe by the way we live. This is nothing less than integrity.

And when one of us falls short, then we expect our loved ones to come forward and set us straight. This can sometimes be the most difficult one of all. But if a family is not good at apologizing and reconciling, then the children might never learn the real meaning of forgiveness. In fact, they might never really understand what God is all about.

Show me a family with parents who can never admit they were wrong and can never apologize to each other -- or to their children -- and I will show you another family that is unhappy and unhealthy. To me, forgiveness is the best part of family. It's the best part of marriage. It's the best part of life. Everyone is rooting for you to become the "best you" possible. So when people help you see how you messed up, it doesn't mean you are being rejected. It means you are loved so much, that someone cares that you continue being your best and doing your best. And if you want to be and do your best (that's what healthy people care about), then you get over the initial embarrassment and accept the gentle correction, and apologize and get forgiven and realize you are so lucky to be surrounded by such unconditional love.

And what happens when that "correction" is not so "gentle"? Well, then there's a bigger argument, lots of misunderstanding, sometimes things are said that aren't meant, and there's a cooling off period before the apologies come. And then apologies are needed from both sides, and sometimes by then, the whole family has become involved and everyone needs to apologize for one thing or another.

But after all the apologies, the family feels closer, the family is stronger, and everyone has learned something about humility and human nature, and they will do a better job the next time there is an argument or misunderstanding -- whether it is within their own family, or at school, with friends, or even at the workplace. That's the healthy and happy version.

I remember when you and Luke had some misunderstanding at some HHJ event. Luke remained angry, but you didn't hold onto it. During a break you went up to him and whispered something to him. I never knew what you were saying, but first I saw Luke roll his eyes. Then I saw him look sort of sheepish and guilty. Then I saw him perk up and look more confident. Then he laughed. Then finally he looked up at you, into your eyes, and the two of you hugged. You were in the corner of the room, but lots of other teenagers were watching the interaction. Even without the soundtrack, we learned what it looks like when two men admit their mistakes, apologize and reconcile.

Of course some families never learn how to "fight" fairly, how to apologize and how to forgive. It's a very important skill to develop. If the parents don't know how, the children never can learn, and they have problems all the way growing up. If the father is absent, the boys especially never see how a man can resolve conflicts, talk calmly, articulate feelings and personal points of view, apologize, and finally forgive and be forgiven. That's the unhealthy and unhappy version.

It's no coincidence that 98% of males in prison grew up with absent fathers.

With women who are raising their children as single parents, it is SO IMPORTANT for them to have stable male friends or other family members who can demonstrate this type of love and expression so the boys can learn how to settle conflicts "like a man" and not like some adolescent male trying to project a powerful presence. That's not manly. It's just immature bravado. Real men -- meaning adult, mature males -- aren't so easily threatened. They don't need to flaunt because they are secure enough to understand that real power, real influence, comes from knowing how to negotiate well and influence well within a healthy and respectful context.

That's not usually something most boys will see much in the movies, unless they enjoy watching "chick flicks," and usually, that's not the case. But that is why women like dragging their men to see those types of films. They often model gentle, respectful, tender manhood. If there's no one in your family to show you how it's done, then "chick flick" movies can actually be a good option. But it takes an adult mature man to convince a boy that going to such movies can actually help him become more successful not only with girls, but with families, friends, and all of life.

Physical and Emotional Support

In families, we take care of each other. We need to notice when someone's physical or emotional well-being is in danger, or their basic needs are not being met.

This is really what defines us as family. We love each other. Your needs become my priority. My needs are your priority. We help each other out when we are down. We care.

The best part of being married is that I don't live my life alone and unnoticed. Someone is there to witness everything I do. What I say and do has extra meaning because someone is watching and loving and caring -- and growing -- with me. Helping me become a better me. Knowing that my presence and my love is also helping you become a better you.

Studies show that married men live longer. That people involved in church and faith communities are healthier and live longer. There's something healthy about being around people who care and give your life meaning.

That's why little Rosa offered her teddy bear to Keshia. She learned compassion from her family and from the people who love her family. Someone did it for her; she knows to do it for others.

That's why we drop everything when there is a crisis to attend to those in need. Because we care, and their needs become our priority. We couldn't keep doing it if people didn't drop everything and attend to us when we were in crisis as well. That's the way we learn how.

But I do wish there weren't so many crisis moments in life...

God created us to be free, to make free choices, and unfortunately, many people make poor choices. And the result of poor choices is often pain -- not only for those involved -- but sometimes for innocent bystanders.

Sometimes people ask, "How could God allow evil in the world if God is so almighty and all-powerful?"

I counter with the obvious question, "If you could remove freedom from your child, would you do it? Would you allow a surgeon to implant something in your children's brain that would prevent them from ever disobeying you?" Of course not! You'd want your own child to have the freedom to make choices, and even make mistakes, so he or she could learn from them, grow into maturity, and do the right things for the world. The same is true with God. Freedom is a requirement for love. No one can be forced to love. Love is the greatest thing in the universe. No one would want to deprive children from the freedom to love and be loved.

Same with God. God would never want to take away our freedom to love. In fact, God is Love.

Now that I have had the experience of living with you in a marriage with this kind of freedom, this kind of love, and all these other things I have been trying to describe, I realized the type of joy that can only be described as God. No matter what happens for the rest of my life, I will always have that with me.

I saw it in my parents. And I saw it with Adam. But I didn't see it with all these other relationships that somehow were steered wrong. I couldn't understand why at the time, but I understand it now. We weren't operating with those five essential components -- we didn't have shared values and vision for family and marriage. We didn't have shared "leadership" for the relationship. We didn't embrace diversity the same way, and we weren't creative together. We didn't have the trust and intimacy to walk the talk together and experience forgiveness together, and, therefore, we were ill-equipped to provide emotional support. That's it in a nutshell.

I didn't see it then; I only knew things weren't the way they were with Adam. I thought I was looking for Adam literally -- the person Adam. But what I was looking for was the type of love I knew I had with Adam. I didn't know that type of love could exist for me with anyone else, but once I was reconnected with Adam, I realized a lot more about myself.

Anyway, I do believe that these happy family methods are essential. If they are modeled, then the children grow up knowing them, even if they can't be articulated. And if not, then "each unhappy family is unhappy in its own way."

Leo Tolstoy would understand this.

And every happy family would recognize it, once it was articulated. They would recognize themselves in the story.

That's probably all God wants us to do: to recognize God in all of our loving relationships, and to bring that Love -- that God -- to everyone in our lives.

How simple.

How challenging.

How impossible!

Unless you have profound faith in God, for with God (Love), all things are possible.

Chapter 103

Dear Kelvin,

As we get older, not only do we realize we're not as cool as we used to be (OK, I was never cool to begin with; we've already established that!), but we realize that we're not as agile, or energetic, as we used to be. We don't bounce back from anything as easily.

I look at some of the pictures of my parents together, and I realize I am older now than my mother was when those pictures were taken. That's hard to believe.

My father died very suddenly, when he was 53. Adam's dad left us just as suddenly. Both had heart attacks.

My mother is probably going to die more gradually. She had gone through an episode with breast cancer many years ago, when I was a young adult just out of college. More recently, it had metastasized in her bones.

In the beginning, she told me without hesitation that she was not going through chemotherapy. She had done radiation, and that was bad enough. But chemo was out of the question. She was just going to die sooner rather than have a longer life with less mobility and less independence.

I respected her decision. I could completely understand that. I was just thinking that I would probably make that same decision, if I were to be faced with the same situation.

Then all of sudden, my brother told me she was starting chemo. I was amazed. Her doctors convinced her to give it a try. So she did.

The family members who live closer to her are usually the ones who go with her for the treatments, but when I can get away and visit, I go with her as well.

It's not entirely unpleasant -- she sits on a comfy chair for the whole process. She can recline if she wants. The TV is on. She often brings a book. She often falls asleep. Sometimes I have read from a book while she sleeps; sometimes we talk. The room has several brown leather-look recliner chairs for the patients receiving chemo and several regular chairs sprinkled around for visitors. There are various beeps and tones that indicate to nurses when it's time to check something or when something needs to be changed. It's fairly quiet. When people talk, they talk quietly. The TV is on, but it is not so loud that people can't sleep if they want.

Her hair came out in clumps. She and Margaret went to get a few wigs.

She wears the wigs when she goes out, or when we have visitors.

Otherwise, she wears one of the soft hats Ben and Mary found for her.

She's been losing weight, she's more tired, she forgets things more often. But she still laughs easily and loves a good joke.

She wants to start giving things away while she is still alive, so she can better enjoy the giving and receiving. I told her I'd help her start to sort her things out.

Dying quickly, as my dad did, was really hard on us. But it was easy for him. He went fast and painlessly. He always said that's what he hoped for. He didn't want to get old and sick and become a bother to everyone. He got his wish.

But dying more slowing, as my mom is, will be harder on her. It's frustrating and painful to suffer through the gradual loss of this or that function. It's difficult to give up control and not always understand what is happening.

As we get older, we should logically understand that our parents will die, sooner rather than later. But we never outgrow the need for our parents and the desire to be with them.

Chapter 104

Dear Kelvin,

As you know, the economy took a nose dive, and that sort of thing always hurts low income people the most.

It's crazy that no one wanted to use the "recession" word, but those of us in the real world have known for quite a while that things had not been good.

At HHJ, we noticed that more and more people came by for food and that our shelves were starting to look emptier, more often.

Rosa and Felipe started coming by for food, since Felipe's hours had been cut. A short time later, he was laid off from the store and only had the painting/landscaping job. True, people still need snow removed every winter and grass cut every summer, but when times are tight, they let services like that stretch a little.

Keshia and Sammy had moved in with Monique.

Carlos had to take a cut in salary, and the whole staff at Guadalupe decided to take salary cuts, rather than have to let anyone go.

We were having the same conversation at House of Hope and Joy.

When the economy slows down, people donate less, because they have less "extra income." When investments go down, foundations have smaller endowments, because their value has been reduced. They can't give as many grants as before.

Businesses like shoe repair do very well, because people would rather fix old shoes than buy new ones. Businesses like discount outlets do very well, because people will drive out of their way to find a "good deal."

But services to the poor? Even though the need goes up, our resources go down, because we rely on grants and donations.

We didn't want to let anyone go at HHJ. So Merry was ready for suggestions for cutting corners and finding other sources for funding.

I fully realize that of all the services we provide, youth leadership ministry was the least urgent. When stomachs are empty and bones are shaking in the wind, people come to HHJ because they want food and clothing. They need help finding jobs.

They aren't banging on our doors, begging, "Please teach our children leadership skills!"

So I agreed to take a big salary cut -- $10,000. I figured my family could help me out.

And we agreed to spend the next few days thinking of ways we could spend less or bring in more.

I had this dream that first night:

Merry and I and Leah were having a meeting about finances. We had out our note pads and our calculators and we were sitting on brown recliners. I looked over to my left, and there I saw my mother, hooked up to the machine giving her chemo.

Then I looked back to Merry and Leah and noticed that I was also hooked up, getting chemo.

I woke up with a start, and realized my fear that the entire youth leadership ministry of HHJ was on life support... it was in danger of completely dying.

Chapter 105

Dear Sister Agnes,

I guess the students at St. Augustine haven't forgotten me. They asked Sister Brigid to send me a few poems they worked on, as part of their "Lil Johnnie" homework. Here are some of them:

Newspaper Headlines

"If it bleeds, it leads."
Forget those violent scenes!
Write about HHJ
And all the Clean Teens!

No Hope in the City

Lost my job
Just fed up
Staring into
My coffee cup
What's the use
To get ahead
A few more years
And I'll be dead

Bad Economy

Your pocket's empty
Your purse is bare
Can't ride the bus
Without the fare
Your stomach growls
There's no enjoyment
When you're laid off
From your employment

Undocumented Immigrant

I love America
But what can I do?
I was brought to this country
Before I was two.

I'm a straight-A student
With excellent grounding.
But I can't attend college.
No federal funding.

I can't tell my secret
And betray mi padre.
He must remain hidden
With me and mi madre.

Help is coming!
Hunger, violence, crime!
The worth of US dollars!
Who is going to save the world?
The "Lil Johnnie" scholars!

Chapter 106

Dear Kelvin,

Another dream about my father...

I found him in a crowd. Usually, I have to go after him and follow him all over before he will give me a few words of wisdom.

This time, when I saw him, it was clear he was looking for me.

He spoke with such urgency in his voice.

He put both his hands on my shoulders, leaned in and looked deep into my eyes.

He told me, "There's not much time left. Remember, I had only 53 years. Take care of the things you need to take care of."

When I had this dream, I was 51.

Was he telling me that I only had 2 years to live?

Chapter 107

Dear Sylvia,

My brilliant Clean Teens were talking with me about an upcoming workshop about the Four Gs of Teaching.

And when we were looking at our posters, a few of the teens started to talk about the five essentials of Transformation.

We made this observation:

4 Gs of Teaching	Transformation	Leadership Essentials
Grab my attention	Action/Service	Walk the Talk Together
Give me something new	Learning	Diversity Brings Creativity
Get something out of me	Prayer/Reflection	Same Goal, Same Direction
Go make a difference	Leadership	Shared Leadership, Top and Bottom
(Taught by the teacher, learned with other students)	(with support of mentors and positive peers)	Emotional and Physical Support

In other words, the five essentials of Leadership I have been teaching match up with the four movements of transformation (plus the need for support) and also match up with the steps of the four Gs of Teaching!

Isn't that great? I say we are on to something here!

Chapter 108

Dear Kelvin,

I wish more couples could have what we had.

We started out as friends because we both taught school -- you and Ruby at Blessed Savior, me at St. Augustine.

We had shared a calling to urban ministry, in a school setting as well as in the community center setting at House of Hope and Joy.

I realized I had to break a few traditional rules in order to be more effective. You and Ruby believed in me long before I had the chance to prove anything to you. I don't know why you trusted me as you did, but I will be ever grateful for your confidence in my abilities. You had more confidence in me than I did!

I learned to give my students more autonomy in choosing how our class could better operate. The requirements of the English curriculum would not help us meet our goals without learning what it was like to be a teenager living in the city. They had to help me see their needs before we could be successful together. They had to take a leadership role in their education, too.

They taught me to be humble. They told me -- right away -- and often not so gently -- when my methods showed my lack of experience in the urban world. I was so naive at first. Good thing I was an eager learner, or I would have been a complete failure my first year at St. Augustine.

So much wisdom came from the young people at House of Hope and Joy as well. I think if more adults listened to teenagers and gave them respect, they would find that there is nothing to fear from most of them.

Yes, there are some frightening teenagers out there and many frightening adults as well.

What I learned from all of you was how to form a community of support.

I paid attention to how Merry, Leah, Paul, Sheryl, Kim and Monique were doing their ministry HHJ. What I learned from them started an entire leadership theory.

I empowered the young people in my leadership class, and they came up with the idea for Pebbles of Peace.

I listened to Merit Jackson after he spent time in prison, and together we came up with the "Lil Johnnie" Literacy Program.

We worked together to meet the needs of so many guests at HHJ who were less fortunate than we were and found it was they who gave us our best understanding of God.

We struggled with Carmen and Felipe when their apartment burned down and with Keshia when she had to get away from Tyrone. We struggled together with Thelma's family when Martin was shot. And we struggled together when Ruby was shot. It hardly felt like a struggle.

You and I became such good friends, and we learned so much from each other, that by the time we realized we had fallen in love, Olivia and Luke were wondering why it took us so long to figure it out.

I admired you from the moment I met you. You were always so insightful, so articulate, so gentle, and so strong. You listened to me. You believed in me. You challenged me. You wanted me to succeed. You wanted me to find happiness. You and Ruby were crushed when Carlos mysteriously left me. You welcomed me into your family and your home, quite completely when Ruby died. Your whole family loved me and accepted me. You told me I was beautiful. You told me I was brilliant. And you really believed it to be true. You made me want to be the best "me" possible. And in return, I tried to give you everything possible to help you feel supported, loved, and cherished.

We "fought well" and didn't hold grudges. We apologized, forgave, and experienced the deep joy of forgiveness and reconciliation. Others shared our joy when Olivia and Marquis had their three tiny babies and the whole community saw their crisis as "our crisis" and came forward to provide all our family needed. Who could ask for anything more?

If I could ask for anything more, it would be to ask for a few more precious years with you. I used to worry that perhaps you'd die the way Ruby died -- as an innocent victim in a drive by -- or maybe at the hands of an angry teenager with a weapon in his hand. I never thought you would die so young, so peacefully, so suddenly, so beautiful, in my arms, in bed, without a single whimper or gasp...

I remember waking up in the middle of the night for no reason -- because I am such a light sleeper, I would wake up often through the night. Usually, I would reposition myself and in your sleep, you would automatically move closer to me.

I used to find that so comforting. Whenever I'd roll over, you'd roll over and put your arms around me. Whenever I shifted position, you would find a way to cuddle without ever waking up. You'd never remember it in the morning, but I could always describe it to you. You'd smile. Our bodies were so comfortable together.

That night I rolled over, and you didn't follow me. I rolled back and put your arm around me, and it seemed heavy and unresponsive. I whispered in your ear and you didn't pull me closer to snuggle. You had no reaction at all. I put my arm around you and didn't feel you breathing. Then I sat up and listened hard and still didn't hear you breathing. I tried to wake you up, and you didn't open your eyes. I turned on the light and screamed at you to wake up, and you just... didn't.

I called 911 and the ambulance came right away. I had tried to start CPR, but could tell it wasn't working. I later remembered not even being embarrassed or noticing that my robe didn't always completely cover me up. We slept in the nude, and I started CPR without grabbing any clothes. I called Luke and kept doing CPR while shouting into the phone for him to come over. I didn't take time to grab my robe until EMS was at the door, with Luke right behind them.

They took over. I prayed for them to bring back your breath and your heartbeat.

But they couldn't.

I started to grab my keys and slippers to follow them to the hospital when Luke said, "Maybe you should get dressed first. You might be at the hospital for a while."

Good advice from a wise young man.

We went together, once I put some clothes on. I wish we had been there when you arrived, but they said they knew right away that you were not going to come back. Luke and I just sobbed in each other's arms.

Heart attack. High cholesterol. High blood pressure. These silent killers claim many lives suddenly. They overcame you at an early age -- 53 -- same age as my dad -- and yet you seemed so healthy. You were not overweight, and you did physical things -- walking, basketball, yard work -- without any trouble. You did indulge in salty and fatty foods -- but not all the time. Just "in moderation," as they always say.

As expected, the community rallied around our family once again. I never saw so many casseroles. So many people came to visit, I thought the house would cave in. I never had to cook or clean a thing. The help poured in. People not only brought food, they even brought their own cleaning supplies. They not only cleaned the kitchen each night, but the bathrooms! What a considerate group.

I remember being numb from the shock, but so grateful for the love surrounding our family. Most of all, I hated that Olivia and Luke would have to grow up without their father, in a world with so few African American male role models, it was even more tragic to lose another good man. Everyone knew that. I would have gladly died young in your place, so you could have continued to be an active presence in our community, but of course, we are never given that choice...

Before we got married, you and I talked about how there might be some animosity in general because there are so few eligible Black men for Black women to marry... it does seem unfair for a White woman to steal away one of the best. I completely understood that. I still do. But you and I just couldn't help ourselves. We really loved each other. Respected each other. Cared about each other. We had been friends for so long, and we had supported each other and understood each other.

I guess in a way I still felt like apologizing to the Black women of the neighborhood. I know it still seems a shame to many of them. I think -- I hope -- I have received forgiveness from most of them. I hope I have earned my place in the community because of my years of service there.

During our entire marriage, I never heard anyone say anything to suggest I did wrong by marrying you, and no one said any such thing at the funeral. I guess I always wondered if something like that would happen, but it never did.

You and Ruby were both such heroes to us. It was so devastating for your family, and the whole community, to lose you both so young.

Mickey and Gabbie and Rafe would never know their amazing grandparents. We would have to be great story tellers in order to pass on the wisdom and love and family identity you provided for Luke and Olivia.

I remember talking to Leah the day you died. She spent the night with me. My heart ached so much once again,

I thought I'd have that heart attack myself. Leah told me that was our reward for having been so much in love.

She said that some women have been so hurt in the past, that they just stop loving so much. They'll always stay guarded, they'll always hold back, they'll always stop themselves from caring and putting their hearts on the line. She said men do that all the time to protect themselves from pain. As long as a person stays closed up and protected, they can't be hurt. It's like walking around with your hand in a fist. No one can put a knife through your hand if it's tightly closed and protecting itself. But if you walk around all the time like a closed up fist, she said, you can't really live either. You can't wave or tickle someone or play the piano or do anything fun with a closed up fist, because you always look threatening and cold. Not inviting. Not welcoming. But you won't get hurt that way. So some of us keep our fists tight so that every gesture we do makes us appear to be tough. It protects us.

But once we really love someone, we open ourselves up to them, and then we're vulnerable. Once that tight fist is open again, we can tickle and wave and play the piano and do all kinds of things. But we're vulnerable to pain, and that's the consequence of loving so much.

Wow. What insight. Leah was right. Only those who love deeply can be so sad. I guess I'd rather be the type of person who loves deeply, even if that makes me vulnerable to such deep pain. Somehow that really helped me. It gave meaning to all that suffering. Why do we suffer? Because we love so much. And those of us who are lucky enough to love that way... well, the pain we suffer is the price we pay for the chance to love and be loved so deeply. Is the price high? Very high. Is it worth it? You bet.

Leah stayed all night that first night after you died. Every night that week, someone different spent the night at our place. Monique, Leah, Merry, Sheryl. They all took their turn. No one wanted me to be left alone. What love, what support. What did I ever do to earn such love and affection?

That's the joy if it all -- we don't do anything to earn it. We just give it and receive it because it's God, remember? God is Love. Whenever we feel that kind of joy and support, it's God's love coming through to remind us that there is always hope. There is no need for despair. Together, we can get through anything... even the most painful separation that death brings us.

I slept with your T-shirts, especially your favorite soft green one. I dug them all out of the hamper and wrapped the green one around my face. I used the others as pillow cases and slept hugging the pillows. I knew I would keep that up until your scent was no longer in them.

Marquis' family was wonderful. His dad Seth recorded everything said at the wake and the funeral. His mom Vanessa wrote it up so we could have it in print. His sister Sequoia helped Sheryl, Andy and Luke put together a whole DVD of family pictures, starting when you and Ruby were Clean Teens. We showed the pictures all during the funeral lunch.

I wish we had thought to do that at Ruby's funeral.

My mom and brothers said the same thing about my dad's funeral.

Adam stayed over on the night of the funeral. He stayed for the whole week after that. What a blessing. Once again, I don't know how it's possible to feel both devastated and grateful at the same time, but I did -- for weeks and weeks and weeks.

In fact, every time I think of you now, I feel profound joy and profound sadness That's not so strange, is it? Deep joy that I had the privilege to share marriage with you for almost four years and deep sadness that it wasn't forty years or longer...

Kelvin, my love, with your gorgeous full lips and your gentle dance...

With your delicious scent -- especially at your collarbone -- and your sweet whispers that would tickle my ear.

With all the delight you brought to my body... and the peace you brought to my soul...

With the example of integrity and moral living you gave your family and your community...

How I miss you.

Even now, I can smell you in your green T-shirt. I'm not sure if your scent is really still there, or if my imagination just comes alive when I bury my face in it every night. But really, does it matter? It brings me comfort and helps me feel close to you.

So does this journal.

How blessed I was to have had you in my life -- in such an intimate and loving way.

Good night, Sweetheart. I still miss you. Especially at night. There's this Kelvin-sized space in the bed that never gets filled up. The mattress still seems so big...

I reach out and hate that you are not there beside me...

Thanks for always listening to me. Or reading these words. Or whatever it is you do in heaven.

Chapter 109

Dear Sister Agnes,

This is my reflection for Holy Week... imagining Mary Magdalene on Holy Saturday.

Holy Saturday

The men who didn't see it

Will never understand

The soldiers and the passersby

The spectacle was grand

The mocking and the insults, the humiliation and the shame

The agonizing torture

The desperate cries of pain

The blood and water dripping

Like dirty, wounded rain

How can God let such a beautiful man suffer like this?

Not even the apostles

Could understand my loss

All day long I watched him die

While hanging on that cross

Every breath struggled, sharp and jagged, every movement excruciating

His other friends just left him

They hid or ran away

Just a few sad women left

We knew we had to stay

Why did they abandon him? Was it fear? Was it guilt? Was it the pain of watching?

His eyes were fixed on mine all day

As mine welled up with tears

I tried to love him with my eyes

This man I knew three years

His feet were all I could reach to touch -- his swollen, bloody feet

The hands that healed and comforted

Were held by spikes in place

Those fingers gashed and clawed

One time caressed my hair and face

His playful fingertips... I long for their tenderness again

He spoke to John and Mary

He sipped that wine and died

They took his body off the cross

The women watched and cried

Joseph and Nicodemus never said a word, just silently laid him in the tomb

The women cried, the women sobbed

And we are weeping still

I do not understand how this

Can be the Father's will

But whatever Jesus told me, I try to believe

So now it is the Sabbath

A day of rest and sorrow

I cannot go anoint his skin

Til Sunday. Til tomorrow.

The last time I will ever get to see and touch his body. How will I live without him?

A strange and haunting Saturday

It's lingered much too long

My memories are sharp and clear

My grief is dark and strong

I review every conversation we ever had, over and over

I'm waiting for tomorrow

An endless wait it seems

Jesus fills my every thought

He visits me in dreams

But tomorrow, when I go to his tomb, who will roll back the stone for me?

Chapter 110

Dear Kelvin,

One thing I have realized over the years... you just never know how things are going to turn out.

Life is full of surprises you can never expect or even imagine.

When the economy goes bad, many nonprofits have to shut down... This is old news by now.

But same as always, I have tried to stay positive. The money has trickled in. We received much less, but we spent less too.

It's been raining on the outside, but not raining on the inside!

Recently, the Clean Teens decided to do a program about goals and vision. They wanted to invite celebrities, but they knew that celebrities get famous by being seen in important places with important people. They don't usually come to the inner city and talk at community centers. They speak to rich audiences who can afford to pay for tickets.

So their creativity led them to the next best thing. They decided to become the celebrities they wanted to invite. This led to a marvelous discussion about their heroes. They talked about famous sports heroes and rock stars and movie stars and TV stars, but they also talked about Martin Luther King and Cesar Chavez and Rosa Parks.

They decided to choose heroes -- alive or deceased -- and dress up like them, and deliver short original speeches, saying the kinds of things they might say to urban teenagers. What a great idea that was! If you can't get celebrities to come see you, then just become the celebrities you want to meet.

Naturally, many teens wanted to be Barak and Michele Obama. We had to have a drawing to decide who would deliver those speeches. And several wanted to be MLK and Rosa Parks as well. Two wanted Coretta Scott King. But there were a few teens who wanted someone different. Then they asked me whom I would choose to be.

Good Question -- who have been my heroes?

I wrote a paper once about the three heroes represented by three stuffed animals hanging in my living room -- Snoopy (for Charles Schulz), The Cat in the Hat (for Theodore Geisel, better known as Dr. Seuss) and Kermit the Frog (for Jim Henson). Charles Schulz transformed comic strips and found a way to combine humor and simple drawings of children to get some very profound results from adults. Theo Geisel transformed the way children learn to read by writing fun, silly, entertaining books with a very small set of words. In fact, Bennett Cerf, another children's author, bet Dr. Seuss that he couldn't write a book with just 50 words. He did it -- with *Green Eggs and Ham*. Finally, Jim Henson transformed TV and imagination with his Muppets on Sesame Street, a show designed from the start to show people of different races caring for each other, working together, and enjoying deep friendships.

Everyone knew these three famous people and agreed that they made a huge impact on life in America, but nobody chose them. I think they thought it would seem too immature for an audience of teenagers. I could see their point.

I had one more idea: Roger Staubach. I told them my stories of how I first wrote to football players in middle school and kept writing to Roger throughout high school, college, and part of my adult life.

I even showed them the picture of us when I met him.

Here's what was so funny. I was thinking the Clean Teens would say something like, "Wow! I can't believe you met the Super Bowl champion when you were in college!"

Instead, they all said something like, "Wow! I can't believe that's you in that picture! You look so different. You look so young. You don't look like that now."

OK, so we all get old! That picture was taken over 30 years ago, twice as many years as most of them have lived.

One young man -- Lyle -- couldn't believe that I would keep writing to a football player. He said most girls he knew hated football. He decided to accept the challenge. He wanted to be Roger Staubach for a day. I thought, "GREAT!" I told him I'd bring him a few letters and trinkets and tell him a few stories. He said he'd collect some facts from the Internet.

Well... I never would have imagined that in an audience of mostly African American and Latino youth, the Black guy pretending to be a White quarterback-turned-successful-business-leader would make the biggest impact, but he did. He wore a business suit, and brought up a Dallas Cowboy football helmet (the kind that you turn upside down and use for chips during a super bowl party) and placed it on the table near the podium.

This is my favorite part of what Lyle said:

> What's most important in life is not how fast you can run or how hard you can throw a football. What's most important in life is the person you become. Do you love your family? Do they love you? Are you a role model for others? Do you make good choices for honorable reasons? Do you have integrity? Are you on the path toward God? Do you avoid the kinds of things that would take you away from God?
>
> Because being a famous athlete is just the icing on the cake. Without the cake, too much icing is ... well... just kind of sickening. Some people like it, but it really doesn't do them any good.
>
> You can become a famous athlete and still make lots of poor choices. You can embarrass your family, maybe even push them away. You can get into all kinds of illegal activities and become a terrible role model. What good are your physical skills if your character and your life are negative? How does that serve the world?
>
> Being famous doesn't make us terrific or important people. It just makes us more visible. So whatever we do is on display for the whole country to see. Very often, being famous makes us worse people; it doesn't improve us. Fame can make some of us think that we're better than everyone else. After all, photographers and reporters follow us around,

hoping to take a photo, catch a sound byte. It's tempting...

But if you don't keep that positive, important stuff in your life -- love, family, integrity, character, faith, service -- then being a famous athlete is nothing... nothing at all. Worshipping superstar athletes is crazy... they can throw, run and jump. So what?

Talk to me about the way you serve your community, talk to me about what you are doing to make the world a better place, talk to me about the way your family and friends see you as a positive role model for others... then we'll talk about what makes someone a real superstar.

Take away my Super Bowl rings, take away my Heisman Trophy... and it's no big deal. But if you take away my family's love... if you take away my integrity, my character, my sense of justice, my faith in following God's call to serve my neighbors and love my enemies, then my life is in ruins.

What an outstanding message! Lyle was fantastic. And the Clean Teens really listened. So did Mr. Andrew Stephen Josiah, a man I had never met or heard of before.

Mr. Josiah came because a friend of his was on the HHJ board of directors.

He brought his son, Andrew Stephen Josiah, Jr, a boy who had been a contender for the Heisman Trophy his sophomore year of college. He had to drop off the football team because he had developed leukemia.

From what I understand, Andy was a great kid, super kid. Did all the right things, dearly loved by his family and friends. Great role model. Active in his church. And he could throw the football and dodge like Roger "The Dodger" Staubach!

If anyone needed to hear that message, it was Andrew Jr. and Andrew Sr. "Take away my *Heisman Trophy*... it's no big deal" Those were the words that did it. I thought I had heard a gasp in the audience, but had no idea of the story behind that gasp... that double gasp.

I learned the whole story the day after the talk. Both Andys returned to HHJ to tell me what it meant to hear the "Roger Staubach actor" speak about his life. They both talked to Lyle afterward and told him about Andy's diagnosis and the successful football career he had to walk away from. Lyle didn't know what to say, but Lyle's mother put her arms around Andy Jr., and Lyle realized he really didn't have to say anything.

I was completely unaware as that drama unfolded in the same room where I sat, just a few yards away from me. I was so glad they came back to tell me about it.

I started to explain the Clean Teens to Mr. Josiah, but they told me they learned about them from our website. I didn't know they had already become experts on HHJ programming. I also didn't know that Mr. Josiah Senior was a very wealthy man.

He was so impressed with all the leadership activities we provided for teenagers, that he wanted to become a major funder. MAJOR funder!

He gave me a check for $50,000 and promised to continue to donate this amount *every year!*

I wanted to scream and jump up and down and hug and kiss him, but I was afraid I might scare him and then he'd take his check back, so I just sat there with my mouth open for a few seconds, struggling to find something to say. I was so embarrassed that not a single word came out. What did come out were a few tears...

I just couldn't imagine such generosity... I was amazed... I just froze... I thought I must have heard him incorrectly... I must be reading the check incorrectly... I tried to count the zeros again through my watering eyes.

Andy Jr. said he wanted to volunteer with me. He didn't know what his life would be like or how long it would last, but he wanted to spend his time showing people that the real heroes were not the ones who could just jump, run and throw. The real heroes weren't the ones who spent their lives showing off. The real heroes were the ones who knew what was important and the ones who gave back to their community and who struggled together to make the world a better and safer place. He said he wanted to be a real hero for a change.

He planned to continue college, but was free evenings, weekends, and summers, the same time that the Clean Teens were free. And he would do whatever I needed help with.

"Thank you... Thank you... Thank you..." I kept repeating ... almost in a whisper...

And Andy -- such a sweet, humble kid -- he just kept saying, "No, no... you are the blessing to me. You have no idea how much I needed this."

So, I guess you just never know how things are going to turn out. You never know what life is going to bring you. You can't ever know the ways God can weave in blessings among the tragedies of life.

I have always known House of Hope and Joy had a Spirit, something you can't quantify. I felt it when I first walked through the doors. Kelvin, you know just what I'm talking about.

All I can say is... we have been blessed... so blessed... so very blessed...

Chapter 111

Dear Kelvin,

While writing all these "letters" to you, I have tried to do a good job with reflecting.

The only thing that has bothered me was that I was unwilling to share anything with Agnes. At times, I saw that as childish rebellion to this notion that she was the "mother superior."

(So what would that make me, the "daughter inferior"?)

Anyway, I didn't really trust her. Was that because I had issues with authority? Or because she didn't seem worthy of my trust?

I had wanted to bring this up to Sylvia for the longest time. But every time I tried, I got all tongue-tied. I couldn't find a way to say it.

Finally, Sylvia and I had a heart-to-heart talk. I simply told her I didn't want to meet with Agnes anymore. She told me she was ready to come to me herself, because Agnes had put her in an impossible situation. Sylvia's task was to get me to trust her so she could betray me to Agnes! Sylvia simply wasn't willing to do that, she said she disagreed with Agnes's assessment of me, and she kept finding ways to put off Agnes as long as she could before having a confrontation.

The way I perceived Agnes was not my imagination. It's a good thing I didn't trust her. But eventually, I realized that Agnes didn't even matter anymore. It wasn't really about her. This writing was all about me.

Sylvia gave me copies of the memos she received from Agnes. I have tried to arrange them in chronological order, along with my own notes to Agnes and Sylvia, and notes to Adam, and even a letter from Carlos. I have integrated all of those papers into my notebook of letters to you, trying to find the best spots to place them all. I guess I have come full circle. I have told the most significant parts of the story of my life -- leading up to the week of your death.

I know I will need to succinctly summarize the rest, but I'll just make some comments here. I will be meeting with Sylvia soon -- my new spiritual director -- to continue the process that I started with Agnes. I think with Sylvia, it really might be beneficial. For now, here's how I see different parts of my life.

#1~ My professional life -- this is really easy to summarize.

Pebbles of Peace became a model for several nearby cities. We still do it every year here as well.

The "Lil Johnnie" Literacy Program really took off and is taught in several cities around the country. The money from the books is helping to support the ministry at House of Hope and Joy. That is a real blessing.

I named our leadership theory "Transformational Teaching" and have taught it in several Catholic schools and churches, not only in our diocese, but in several other states. The money I earned with these speaking engagements also helps to support the HHJ ministry. Another blessing.

Sister Bridget encouraged me to do this, starting with the community centers run by the Friends of Clare and Francis.

I remember when Merry asked me if I had ever thought of joining the sisters. That's what led to my meeting with Agnes and exploring my possible vocation. That's what led to all this writing, which I originally thought was so pointless....

Although the economy is still in trouble, we are hoping for and expecting things to turn around and improve. A few key donations made all the difference for House of Hope and Joy. We are just so blessed and lucky. It's hard to understand our good fortune in that area. Maybe it's you and Ruby looking over us. This really is a success story with many contributing team players.

#2~ My family life -- also kind of easy to summarize.

Mickey, Rafe and Gabbie are in kindergarten. They are my supreme delight! Marquis and Olivia are incredible parents. They obviously had excellent role models growing up. You and Ruby would have loved playing with the triplets and telling them stories.

Luke is engaged to Sequoia. I guess all that working together on your funeral pictures and the community's story telling brought out some common interests and mutual affection. They will become the new coordinators of "Urban Naturally," a city center for ecology education, staffed by a local environmental liberal arts college.

Rose and Connie will be starting college; Ann is in high school. My brothers and sisters (in law) are very proud of their bright children, wanting to make a difference, still trying to figure out how. Ann is interested in working with animals and volunteers at a local animal shelter. Rose will study art history, literature and languages -- Greek, Latin, and maybe Italian. She might end up being a graphic artist or a teacher. Connie will study music and physics. How wonderful that so many opportunities are available to girls! My mother would say, "I remember when the only options available to women were teaching, nursing, and being a secretary."

#3~ My emotional life

This is the most interesting part.

I started out being made to write. I hated being forced to put things on paper and give them to someone I didn't trust. As it turns out, that feeling was there for a good reason. Agnes wasn't trustworthy. She didn't have my best interests at heart. She thought I was a poor candidate for the order, and she tried to get Sylvia on her side. Sylvia started out as a "double spy," appearing to dig up dirt on me, while finding ways to help me succeed.

I thought Sister Agnes had finally begun to appreciate me when she suggested that St. Augustine "promote" me to be the director of youth leadership. But as it turned out, it was her plan all along to eventually cut the position, hoping to find me another job in another diocese, far away from the ministry at HHJ. She never imagined Merry might hire me.

Sylvia was impressed with my leadership class and our "Lil Johnnie" Literacy Program, as well as the ministry at HHJ. And she even enjoyed my prayers and creative musings. That's something I never would have even attempted on my own. Sylvia was the one who encouraged me to choose someone I loved and trusted. That turned out to be you.

So eventually, I discovered a great joy in writing. I got my students to write. The "Lil Johnnie" program is full of writing assignments -- letters, essays, poetry, drama, story boards, dialogs and monologs. The Clean Teens wrote "This I Believe" essays and poetry on sidewalks.

And I kept getting more daring with my own writing. Sylvia eventually asked me to submit some of my poems and reflections to St. Francis Messenger Press, and they began to publish some in their monthly magazine. I might start my own column, with regular reflections for Lent and Easter, Advent and Christmas, and the "Ordinary Time" that takes place during the summer and fall.

So many opportunities! And new sources of income for House of Hope and Joy!

I realized that maybe all of us are made to write. Maybe that's what separates us from animals. We reflect upon things and write them and share them with others, and sometimes even publish them so many more of us can read them and reflect upon such things with us.

In a way, I'm almost embarrassed about the whole thing. I'm an English teacher! I have always known the power of writing. So I should have known all along that all of us were made to write -- and that the power of writing is the power that comes from honest reflection in a situation of trust.

I think writing and reflecting is what helped turn my students into leaders. It focused them on their own personal development, as well as the ongoing development of their community.

Sylvia became convinced of the benefit of "Transformational Teaching." She finally challenged Agnes, who backed down. Eventually, Agnes visited one of my workshops and was actually impressed herself. It surprised her. She even apologized for initially not being open to my nontraditional methods. By then, I had already talked with Sylvia and knew the whole story, but it was really good that Agnes finally became honest with me.

#4~ My spiritual and vocational life

So here I am, still trying to explore a possible vocation with the Friends of Clare and Francis, still trying to figure out what God has in mind for me. Still trying to unfold this new knowledge that all of us are made to write, made to reflect and share our reflections.

Sometimes I wonder if the reason I couldn't trust Agnes was because she couldn't trust me. I was never really honest with her either. Perhaps she thought I wasn't really taking my vocational search seriously. Perhaps I wasn't.

I feel more ready now, and I think maybe that feeling came from a recent visit with my family.

I took some time off to spend a few days with my mom for Mothers Day.

My brothers were so inspired by the words and pictures that Marquis and his family put together for your funeral, that they went ahead and gathered all the pictures they could find from my parents' life -- from the time my dad and mom met.

They put them together as a present for my mom, but it was also a present to me, their wives and children. All weekend, we could hardly take our eyes off the monitor as these pictures flashed by.... And Mom would tell us stories about what was happening. Mary knows short hand, so she kept jotting down what Mom said, and we're going to put the stories together with the pictures, so we have a complete family record.

Just watching all those pictures was amazing... I never sat for two days straight and focused that intently on anything. The stories kept pouring out, not only from Mom, from but all of us, as we remembered bits and pieces of what had happened over the years...

For example, when I was first born, there were no infant carriers. My dad made a carrier for me that they lined with blankets, and he called it the "Nellie Mobile." Before that, babies were carried in their mother's arms, or put into laundry baskets in the car, I guess... So every time a picture of me or Ben came up, everyone said, "The Nellie Mobile!" Funny, they never said the "Ben Mobile" -- instead they said, "Ben in the Nellie Mobile!"

They set the pictures on "random," so old, old photos would come up right after fairly recent photos, and the like. We were all mesmerized.

So many baptisms, weddings, graduations, first communions and confirmations...

So many Christmas trees with a great abundance of presents beneath them...

So many smiles!

We also noticed babies crying... people missing from the pictures... the impact of divorce...

Not all of life is pretty.

I was painfully reminded of my failed attempts at forming healthy relationships... the pictures reminded me of everything, even though my brothers had been very discreet in the pictures they chose to include (Adam, for example) and those they chose to eliminate (Timothy, for example).

I was painfully reminded that three different times, I looked at a man with love in my eyes, and agreed to marry him, convinced we would share our lives, our beds, our families, and that we would always be together. Each time, I had complete and total trust that I had met my soul mate and partner for life.

Twice I was obviously wrong, but once I was deliciously correct. (Thank God you came into in my life!)

All the pictures and family stories made it such an emotional time.

I watched my mother react to her image at my age, and younger, and wondered what she thought when she looked upon her children and prayed for them...

We saw lots of pictures of my dad, and some with a toothpick in his mouth.

We saw pictures of my three nieces when they were toddlers... sometimes it made me think, "I wish I could get that little girl back" just so I could sing silly songs with her again.

But time has a way of moving forward, somehow more quickly the older we get.

We each find our own way to make our mark on the world.

After two days of watching pictures and reflecting on the meaning of family, it was time to get up and get back to life.

Because of that two day photo-retreat experience, I know we have a greater sense of family identity, a bit more pride, a bit more understanding of who we are as human beings, a better perspective of life. I even think that we were each transformed just a bit.

Now, we are ready to launch back into life as better people.

After writing over a hundred chapters on my life and its meaning, I'm also eager to see what comes next.

What will I do? I'm not sure. Maybe I'll join the order. Maybe I'll write a book. Maybe I'll fall in love again. Maybe I'll do all of it.

Whatever I do, I know I am surrounded by family and extended family who love me and bring me great hope and joy.

I am ready to continue my discernment and find the best way to serve God during this stage of my life.

Perhaps I'll write a sequel; perhaps Luke or Olivia or one of my nieces or one of the triplets will write it for me.

Somehow I have a feeling the story will continue... since all of us have been made to write.

Back notes regarding three poems previously published:

1. The poem about Integrity found in chapter 40:

2. The comic Strip prayer found in chapters 43:

3. Versions of "As for Me and My House," found in chapters 47 and 48: